well, this is awkward

Also by Esther Walker

The Bad Mother
The Bad Cook

well, this is awkward

ESTHER WALKER

First published in the UK in 2025 by Bedford Square Publishers Ltd, London, UK

bedfordsquarepublishers.co.uk
@bedsqpublishers

© Esther Walker, 2025

The right of Esther Walker to be identified as the author of this work has been asserted in accordance with the Copyright, Designs and Patents Act 1988. All rights reserved. No part of this book may be reproduced, stored in or introduced into a retrieval system, or transmitted, in any form or by any means (electronic, mechanical, photocopying, recording or otherwise) without the written permission of the publishers.

Any person who does any unauthorised act in relation to this publication may be liable to criminal prosecution and civil claims for damages.
A CIP catalogue record for this book is available from the British Library.

This is a work of fiction. Names, characters, places, and incidents either are the product of the author's imagination or are used fictitiously, and any resemblance to actual persons, living or dead, businesses, companies, events or locales is entirely coincidental.

ISBN
978-1-83501-255-0 (Hardback)
978-1-83501-256-7 (eBook)

2 4 6 8 10 9 7 5 3 1

The manufacturer's authorised representative in the EU for product safety is Easy Access System Europe, Mustamäe tee 50, 10621 Tallinn, Estonia
gpsr.requests@easproject.com

Printed in Great Britain by CPI Group (UK) Ltd, Croydon CR0 4YY

For my parents, Annie and Angus

ONE

'So, *Mairéad*,' said Richard. He shrugged off his coat, a thigh-length navy Barbour jacket, and hung it on the back of the bar stool. 'That's an Irish name, isn't it? Are you Irish?'

Wait. Stop. Interesting. He'd got her name right. 'Muh-RAID'. Not 'Mare-aid', not 'Merry-ad' but a confident 'Muh-raid'. Was she Irish, though?

Mairéad was so surprised Richard had pronounced her name right first time that she almost told him the truth, which was this: 'No. My mother is a career activist. Anti-apartheid, CND, Greenham Common, Stop the War. I'm sure you know the type. My sister and I were born during the Troubles. Nowhere near Ireland, because that would make too much sense. But Mum was fanatic about it all. So I'm named after Mairéad Farrell. You won't have heard of her, but she was a big deal in all that. Mum's pin-up. Get this, my full name is Mairéad Mandela Boudicca Alexander. My sister is called Dolours Joan Cudjoe Alexander. She calls herself Lenny, but that's a different story.'

She didn't say any of this. She knew from experience that this was too much for a first date; there was a danger of eyes glazing over, or widening, or cutting left and right. Instead she said what she always did, which was, 'No. I think my mother just thought it was a pretty name.'

'Some of those Irish names,' said Richard. 'Phew. With all the flourishes and the crazy spellings, you know?'

'Yes,' she said. 'Yes, I do.'

For this date, Richard had chosen a chic bar in town. It had flattering low lighting, pretty chandeliers and a sophisticated cocktail list: not just margaritas, but spicy margaritas and fresh herb garnishes on everything. While Mairéad had waited for Richard to arrive, she'd caught her own eye in the antique mirror behind the bottles of spirits. Since turning forty, she found that what would come back from mirrors and photographs was a bit unpredictable: sometimes it was Florence Pugh's older sister and sometimes it was Miss Trunchbull. This evening it was the Pugh sister, with very expensive blonde highlights. She took a sip of her drink and batted her eyelashes at herself, but then missed the bar with her elbow and splashed some spicy margarita in her eye.

So Richard knew how to pick a venue. Yet in he walked in this flapping Barbour, like he had just come in from getting a sheep out of a ditch up the lane. The pockets looked heavy with things. And it was June. Yes, it was a cool night, but it was June. Who wears a very large Barbour in June?

She was bothered by the Barbour. She was also bothered when Richard said, 'And how about you – no bambinos?' *Bambinos!* What a stupid question. Richard must know, because this date is a set-up, that she has no *bambinos*. She knew before agreeing to meet him that he has two bambinos – not on him, although he could probably fit a bambino in each vast Barbour pocket, in amongst all the other *things* – but they live in Hampshire with their mother.

Perhaps, before the divorce (which she also knows about), when he was living in Hampshire, Richard really did have to get sheep out of ditches up the lane while wearing his huge Barbour. Yes, he must know that she has no bambinos because Cass, who has set up this blind date, will have told him. But, of course, he will be curious as to *why*. No one ever wants to know why people have children, only why they don't. Mairéad used to rage passionately about this injustice, but now she regards it with the blank, don't-care face of a bored horse.

'No bambinos for me,' she said. She was two sips into her second margarita and it was delicious. 'I had other things to do.' Like her pat answer to 'Are you Irish?', her answer to 'Why no children?' had been honed and refined over the years until it was distilled into a droplet of fierce efficiency. Through trial and error, she'd found that 'I had other things to do' was the response most likely to make people shut up about it. But was that what had happened? *Had* it been 'other things'? She wasn't even sure of the exact truth anymore. She closed one eye and looked at the ceiling. She was a bit drunk, now, and her thoughts slithered about.

The Barbour jacket was terrible and 'bambinos' was a nightmare, but Richard was actually rather seductive. He was forty-eight, with salt-and-pepper hair, very straight teeth and a confident walk. But it was his eyes that were the thing. He really looked at you. Not over your shoulder, or off to the side. He looked at you, *in* you. It was borderline indecent.

He was a surgeon, a liver specialist. A Mister. All the looking will be part of the training, she supposed. It will be the what-do-you-call-it, the bedside manner. Do they learn it? Perhaps medical students gather in a room and a professor stands at the front and says, 'Listen, chaps, we all know that patients are nothing more than malfunctioning bags of organs and fluid but still, you need to *look into their eyes*.'

Mairéad tuned back in to Richard. He was talking about how much serious alcoholics drink. You know, the major ones. Not the part-timers.

'These middle-class people,' he said grandly. 'They get their knickers in a twist that a few glasses of wine a night are going to be a problem. I had a fellow in my clinic last week who had been drinking a bottle of vodka a day for ten years. The cheap stuff. Rocket fuel. His liver was only just starting to properly pack up.'

'The liver. What an extraordinary organ,' she said, leaning forwards. She rattled the fashionably large ice cube about in her glass, enjoying lolling about in Richard's lascivious eye-bath. 'Considering all that, shall we have another?'

'I'd say so,' he said. He turned on his bar stool and lifted his hand. She saw the barman return Richard's smile.

But thirty minutes later, she was saying goodbye from her taxi window – 'Night!' – and setting off home. From the kerb, Richard waved despondently. She then saw him rummage in his vast pockets for a particular thing amongst all the other things. He leaned first one way, and then the other, frowning.

The shiny black car slid along the streets, past closed boutiques and June flowers blooming in tubs. Mairéad had not finished her third drink. Richard had put her right off it, by resting his chin in his hand and saying, 'Do you ever get lonely?'

She could cope with the Barbour and the bambinos. She could cope with the fact that Richard probably saw her as nothing more than a potentially malfunctioning bag of organs and fluid. She was willing to be seduced by the eyes. But that question crossed a line. What a buzzkill. She replied, lightly, 'Not really.' Then she looked at her third margarita and decided, in that moment, to drink half of it – then say it was time for her to go home.

In the taxi, she drew her phone out of her pocket. She felt the need to communicate something to someone about this experience. She opened up her previous conversation with Cass but her fingers paused over the screen. Cass had been excited at the prospect of this date and Mairéad couldn't bear to text her with Richard's shortcomings so immediately. It felt ungrateful.

Well, This Is Awkward

And so her fingers took a walk to her chat with Dodie, instead. Mairéad had learned in her twenties that it was just fine to have different friends for different things: different activities, different problems. Different moods, even. Cass was for positivity and action. Dodie's gift, on the other hand, was her limitless capacity for soaking up other people's feelings and information. 'Mmm,' she would say. 'Mmm, yes, go on.' Also, Dodie never pushed back. You could have killed someone and she would just say, 'Quite right. Deserved it.'

Dodie – real name, Josephine – would be in bed, but awake, propped up by about fourteen pillows, wearing her black-rimmed glasses and reading a very long Victorian novel. Dodie had always preferred to be lying down and went back to bed whenever possible. When her third and final child had been born seven years earlier, she'd silently decided to more or less live in bed.

'In can back from a date,' wrote Mairéad. 'Just thinking about how many less men I'd have slept with had there always been Uber. You know that thing where you think, "I could get the night bus… or pray for a taxi… or go home with this person".' She re-read the message and edited 'can' to 'cab'.

She watched as the little grey ticks next to the message went blue. Less than a minute later, Dodie started typing.

'It's FEWER men, not less,' she wrote. And then, 'Yes. Uber is the fourth emergency service.'

'It's actually the fifth,' replied Mairéad.

She looked out of the cab window for a bit. Then she scrunched up her nose and said in a quiet, simpering voice, 'Do you ever get lonely?' and blew a tiny raspberry.

Back in her building, she walked up the carpeted stairway to the third floor and let herself into her neighbour's flat.

'Mrs Nibs!' she called.

There was a jingle of a cat-collar bell and Mrs Nibs appeared from the bedroom.

'Mneeeow,' said Mrs Nibs, showing a set of sharp, white teeth.

'Hi Nibsy!' crooned Mairéad. Mrs Nibs had the softest blue-grey fur and bright yellow eyes. She followed Mairéad to the kitchen, purring and circling her ankles. Mairéad cleaned and dried the dirty food bowl and emptied in a new sachet, then rinsed the packet and placed it with the others on the side, ready to be sent off to the specialist recycling centre. Her neighbour Jason was at great pains to point out that he paid a premium for this service so that the pouches didn't end up 'in landfill'. She took a nice picture of Mrs Nibs and then sent it to Jason, who was away for a night.

She checked the water bowl, then stood looking at the cat for a while.

'I am *not* lonely!' she said. Mrs Nibs looked up, licked her chops, then went back to her turkey-flavoured Gourmet Perle Chef's Collection dinner.

Back at her own flat, across the hall, Mairéad double-cleansed in her pristine pink marble bathroom and applied high-strength retinol. Next to the sink there was a posy of flowers in a small art deco glass vase. She turned it slightly so that she had a better view of the tiny blushing roses. She no longer even felt tipsy, the lonely comment had sobered her up that much. She took two milk thistle tablets and an ibuprofen anyway and went to bed.

Her phone lit up with a message – from Richard. 'Wonderful to meet you. Let's do it again soon, I don't feel like my liver was challenged enough.' She regarded the message and blew some air through her lips in an exhausted way. Had she been too harsh? Her fingers poised over the screen, uncertain.

Then she played a tape forwards in her head, the one where they went on a second date and a third. And all the extra bad things about this Richard person emerged – drip, drip, drip – until she was ankle-deep in red, pink and beige flags. And

Well, This Is Awkward

then the final, terrible Deal Breaker would appear, looming in her mind's eye like a ransom note constructed from snipped-up newspaper headlines. And it would say 'ChEWs LouDLY' or 'MaMA's BoY' or 'sTinGY'. She would ignore this for six months, while the font got bigger and bigger, before finally admitting that this, whatever it was, was not working. It was exhausting to contemplate. She could save herself so much future stress and heartache if she neatly stunt-rolled out of the situation right now.

She was distracted by Dodie.

'It's *actually* the ninth emergency service,' she wrote. 'Police, Ambulance, Fire Service, Coastguard, Mountain Rescue, Lowland Rescue, Cave Rescue, Moorland Rescue.'

'And Uber.'

'Accidental Sex Rescue.'

'Walk of Shame Rescue.'

'Cystitis Rescue.'

'Do you think the Lowland Rescue team get annoyed when they hear people saying that there are only three emergency services?'

They carried on like this for a bit. Dodie agreed that wearing a giant Barbour in June was barbaric and that Mairéad had done exactly the right thing. Then Mairéad put her phone away, having forgotten to reply to Richard at all. She looked at the two books on her bedside table. She ought to press on with *Americanah*. But her hand passed over it and she felt a guilty pinch. The book she actually pulled towards her was called *The English Cottage*, which was a coffee table book filled with pictures of idyllic English cottages. She turned the pages contentedly until she felt sleepy, then she switched off the light.

TWO

Mairéad walked into the IGS offices the next morning feeling good. She had dealt with that non-starter date brilliantly, actually. Once upon a time she might have sat there, stuck it out. Even gone on another date, who knows? But experience, and a series of those Deal Breaker ransom notes, had taught her she was wasting her time. And she really liked her outfit that morning. It had felt powerful and right when she'd chosen it and she felt confident and modern on the way to work. This was important, because when she didn't like her outfit, it affected her mood for the entire day.

Clothes *mattered* – just look at what a turn-off that Barbour had been. Who knows, if Richard hadn't worn it, he might not have made such a terrible first impression. So the people who said that clothes didn't matter were just wrong. She felt this even more keenly working, as she did, with young people who seemed to have very little to think about other than what they were wearing.

They browsed charity shops and scrolled Vinted and were young and dazzling and looked fabulous in everything, from an old *A-Team* T-shirt to vintage Pleats Please. She often felt wrong-footed by what they wore. She sometimes wondered if working in influencer marketing had driven her a bit mad about clothes. Her clients, who poured their heart and soul into their OOTD and GRWM posts, immersed Mairéad in a world where undue importance – even by her standards – was given to outfits. She liked getting dressed, but not *that* much. It did sometimes strike her as preposterous, the hysteria of indecision over trainer or pyjama brands. But she set that aside, because working with passionate people was a blessing. And don't all lives contain compromise?

From the office kitchen there came the luxurious smell of toast. Her stomach growled. She really wanted some toast, but she was doing 16:8 and wasn't allowed to eat until 11 a.m. This was extra hard when it had been a two and a half margarita night. But she really had to go into the kitchen in order to make herself a very necessary cup of tea. PG Tips, hot, nice and strong, a tiny touch of sugar. In the kitchen was Biba, her assistant.

'Hey gorgeous!' said Mairéad as she entered the kitchen. This was not quite her real self, this cheery boss self she had, but she had learned that it was the only self that worked in the office.

'Oh, I'll get that for you!' said Biba. She was wearing high-waisted, baggy, sand-coloured chinos, a black racerback vest and about a billion necklaces. She paused with a knife in her hand as Mairéad reached for a tea bag and a mug. On a plate in front of Biba was a thick slice of toasted sourdough, piled high with peanut butter.

'No, no,' said Mairéad, pressing the Zip tap. 'I got it, babe.' She clamped her nose shut against the smell. Breathed through her mouth. She had a vision of her pupils dilating hideously, shark-like, at the scent of the carbohydrate, the oozing peanut butter. She had to get out quickly or she might snatch Biba's toast with both hands and stuff it into her mouth.

She escaped the temptations of the kitchen and went to sit at her desk. She whacked the space bar to wake her desktop computer up, then battered in her password 'thisismyPassword88!!' and checked her email, which she strictly never did outside office hours, because it was so manic, such a swirling headache of demands and alerts and questions. The Americans could not compute this attitude. She had spent the last eighteen months training Gretchen from New York HQ out of expecting instant replies to emails that arrived at 11 p.m. GMT. A little whiney voice buzzed every now and again in her head: *You're not cut out for this. You do not have corporate American energy. You have one-man-band energy. Perhaps plucky start-up energy. Not Gretchen energy.*

Today, her inbox bristled with confirmations for upcoming mini-breaks, theatre trips to hot shows she felt a pressing need to have an opinion about and parties. An email from her mother, containing an appeal for Yemen. A confirmation from Andrew of Bombardiers Costume Hire Shop of her Harley Quinn outfit for Cass's costume party. Gretchen had sent every employee an extremely long interview with a transcendental meditation guru, with no accompanying instruction or explanation.

A WhatsApp slid sideways onto the screen. From Cass. 'You have bewitched Richard.' Mairéad quickly replied, 'He's nice. Thanks for the set-up. There were some red flags.'

She moved on, recoiling at one email, subject line: 'Amazing news!', which she knew would be a birth announcement. From Eliza! Of course. Third child. Who bothers sending a birth announcement for a third? (Answer: Eliza. When she's not 'busy making memories', of course.) Scrolling down, an email from Dodie, with links to three garish Rixo dresses, sent at 1 a.m. 'Which one shall I buy? QUICKLY.'

Cass again, on WhatsApp. 'Don't say he wore the Barbour'.

Mairéad sent back a winking emoji. She sent emojis to Cass as often as she could, ever since Cass had told her that 'only old people' send emojis.

Well, This Is Awkward

Biba came into her office. 'Do you wanna go through what's up today?' She pushed a speck of peanut butter into her mouth with the crook of her finger and then brushed her elegantly tattooed hands together in front of her. Her fingernails were painted a milky, creamy colour.

'Oh, not now,' said Mairéad dismissively. Then she snapped on a smile. 'I mean, yes! Thank you *so* much. But finish your breakfast first. No hurry!'

'Okay, but right up I need to remind you we've got an onboarding today. Gabriel, he's the new tech guy.'

'Tech guy, Gabriel. Got it. Onboarding,' she said, patting around her tidy desk for something, though she wasn't sure what.

'He's actually here right now,' said Biba.

Mairéad looked sharply up at her assistant, who was baring her teeth in apology.

'Sure!' she said, as if it was a delightful treat to onboard the new tech guy right now, this minute. Where was Andreas? Andreas had hired Gabriel, not her. She had wanted a few minutes to gather her thoughts and read her emails, but they would have to wait.

'Yes, yes, send him in. Brilliant. Where is Andreas?'

'Paris?' said Biba.

'Oh, okay. Fine.'

A calendar notification popped up on her computer, reminding her that it was godchild number one's fifth birthday next week.

Cass started sending a string of WhatsApps about Richard and his Barbour. They stacked up on the screen, a spluttering pyramid, shrieking What Is It With This Man and Do I Need To Dress Him For Dates Now? Mairéad decided that all her screens were behaving badly and needed to be disciplined. She switched off her monitor and flipped over her phone, silencing Cass and Dodie and the tide of emails.

She had thought that Gabriel, the new tech guy, was a tall, thin dark man of about her age with a French accent. But what walked into her office, ready to be onboarded, was a slight young man. He had a puff of peroxide blond hair sticking out of the front of his rolled-up beanie, which was perched on the tippy-top of his head. He had a nose piercing and picked-at black nail varnish.

'Gabriel,' she gushed, leaping up and rushing over to envelop his hand in both of hers. 'Please come and sit down. We are just so, so completely delighted to welcome you to IGS.'

'Thanks,' whispered Gabriel. He pressed his hands together in front of himself in a prayer position.

'Knock knock!' Jenna was at the door. 'May I join?' She was wearing wide, white jeans, big clunky black sandals and a tight black T-shirt. Her tiny dachshund, Margot, was tucked under her arm. Jenna's lustrous brunette hair was tastefully lowlighted and curled around her shoulders. Margot the dachshund, herself a very glossy brunette, looked around with little beady eyes and cocked ears. At times, it looked like Jenna was carrying around an extra head under her arm.

'Morning, babe!' said Mairéad. Jenna was twenty-eight, breezy and confident, and had declared at her interview six months earlier that she would only come to work at IGS if she was allowed to bring Margot in every day. She had been a hire from Google. Jenna mentioned this frequently.

'Hey you,' said Jenna. 'Ugh, great outfit. You are so done with fashion today, right? Like, you are just N-O-T interested.'

Mairéad double-blinked. What? She was wearing pale blue kick-flare jeans, a white vest and a gold necklace – real gold, thanks very much. Was Jenna saying her outfit showed a total lack of care? She had been so pleased with it. She caught sight of her reflection in the surface of her computer monitor. Her face looked surprised and slightly fearful. She recovered and reached for something polite to say.

Well, This Is Awkward

'Exactly, right? I know!'

'Are you okay with dogs, sweetie?' said Jenna. Gabriel tucked his hands inside the sleeves of his tan work-jacket. He sat on the edge of his chair, hunched practically down to his knees.

'Umm, yeah,' he said in a tiny voice.

'Do you want to pet her? She's so super gentle.'

Gabriel reached out a trembling hand and stroked Margot's satin, unperturbed head with one nicotine-stained finger.

Mairéad watched the scene with a glazed smile on her face.

'So, I'm head agent,' said Jenna to Gabriel in her most patronising voice. 'I look after some of our really big stars like Molly BB, Hysteriana and That Divorced Girl. And Mairéad is our super big boss. I will intro you online to our other agent, Barrie – he's in Scotland right now – and that's really all there is to know! But as head of tech, you are of course the most important person here!'

'We're so, super sorry that there's no handover with the previous head of tech,' said Mairéad.

'But we hear you're just a whizz,' said Jenna, quickly. The previous head of tech, Frankie, had left after a huge row with Andreas, which was best not dwelt on.

Gabriel smiled shyly and said, 'Yeah, kinda.'

'We're a small, friendly company,' said Jenna. 'I actually came from Google and it's such a change, you wouldn't believe. You'll get used to Mairéad and her weird old-lady big-boss stuff. Mind out for all the emojis! I'm only kidding, she's the *most* fun. In just a minute I'll get you all set up with passwords and everything. Show you round the kitchen. Do you have any allergies, babe?'

'Um, uh-huh,' said Gabriel. 'Sesame, dairy and wheat. But I'm pretty good at, like, working round it.'

'That is so considerate of you,' said Jenna, beaming and shaking her head beatifically at Gabriel's bravery at being in the same building as those food items.

'Well, like I said, just so pleased to have you with us,' said Mairéad. She was thrown by the apparent 'old-lady' stuff she did, along with her lazy, no-fashion outfit. Her emojis were *ironic*. Some days she wanted to smack Jenna smartly in the face with her keyboard. But she never did or said anything, obviously.

'Okay, LOL, you guys,' said Jenna. 'Come with me, Gabriel, my lovely. Yes, Margot! Yes, yes we're going to show Gabriel his new desk, aren't we? Lovely girl, lovely, lovely…'

The next appointment was with Susie Twill, who ran a small Instagram account, rather unimaginatively called @susietwillceramics. Susie was early, fidgety and looked incredibly uncomfortable in her outfit of a blue shiny swishy pleated skirt, high-top white Converse, leopard-print top and bright orange lipstick.

'Okay, so we've taken a look at your account,' said Jenna. 'Love it, love your work. It's so funny, it's got such humour.'

Jenna hit a button on a remote control and Susie's Instagram grid appeared on a screen on the wall of the meeting room.

'Ooh, wow! That's clever,' said Susie.

Mairéad looked at Jenna, who was smiling at Susie. 'Isn't tech incredible?' Jenna used a tone of voice that Susie no doubt took as light-hearted, but Mairéad understood to be withering. She was briefly distracted by a WhatsApp from Andreas, which said, 'How is Gabriel settling in?' She ignored it.

Susie had created a series of ceramics featuring a scribbled drawing of a frazzled woman with haystack hair and dowdy clothes. The woman appeared across the bottom of mugs, lying flat on her back, with the scrawled caption 'Why do I bother?' in faux-naif handwriting. The same woman appeared cross-legged in the middle of plates saying, 'No food, too tired'. In another she was drawn curled up in a ball, one extended hand holding a wine glass, with the caption 'Rock bottom'.

Well, This Is Awkward

Mairéad loved the work and was touched by the cluelessness of Susie. Her account was something of a mess, filled with caption-less pictures of food, children and beaches, as well as her ceramics. All she needed was a little nudge in the right direction and she would do very well. She would never be a huge star, she just didn't have the sociopathic persistence of someone like Pottery Mama, but she could do fine. Or at least, better.

'At thirteen thousand followers, your account definitely needs some work,' said Jenna. Susie's face fell. 'Yes, I know it's not very many,' she said.

'Oh! Oh no, not at all!' said Jenna. She splatted a hand against her chest. 'Oh gosh, sorry – that came out completely wrong.'

'Numbers are just numbers,' said Mairéad. 'Don't fall into the trap of assigning your sense of self-worth to them.'

Susie nodded and looked scared.

'But, just to be clear, you do also need better numbers,' said Jenna. 'I'm going to run through a weekly plan with you that will boost your numbers significantly but authentically. It's about posting daily, at around the same time, on a different theme each day with no more than five hashtags.'

Mairéad watched Jenna explain these basic how-tos of Instagram to Susie, who looked increasingly daunted with each passing second at the work she had ahead of her.

'...and we'd like to see your sweet face!' said Jenna. 'Pictures of human faces do so well.'

'Oh,' said Susie. 'I feel a bit awkward about doing that.'

'Of course,' said Jenna. 'But we've got an amazing workshop to help. It's just about finding the right angles, the tricks and, you know, the *look* that works for you. That's authentically you. A bit like Pottery Mama, you know? She wears all those very loud blouses. I don't mean wear very loud blouses – that's *her* thing, obv, I mean find a look that's yours, that's truly Susie.'

'But that's the problem,' said Susie. 'I'm not sure who I even am. These clothes – I don't normally dress like this. It's just what I thought I ought to wear.'

'Totally understand. We'll help you discover the real you,' said Jenna.

'Uhh…' Susie laughed nervously, 'is that the authentic way of going about it?'

'Ha, you're so cute,' said Jenna. 'Yes, it is.'

Mairéad's heart sank as she listened to Jenna. Bloody Pottery Mama. Who flogged mugs that said '…And breathe' in swirly writing on them. This hadn't been her dream when she'd set up her business. She wanted to help creative people, who perhaps didn't quite have the business smarts (and why should they?) to find a way to pay for their creativity. She got angrier and angrier as the meeting went on, and decided that she'd had enough of bloody Jenna.

She resolved that, once Susie had left, she was going to give Jenna a talking-to. She was going to explain that they were not a factory, churning out identikit influencers who all said and did and wore the same things. You could leave that to those evil cash-grab robots over at ShowTime. She had a more holistic, caring vision. It's why she had been voted Social Media Visionary of the Year, 2019! It's why That Divorced Girl was still with them and specifically not with ShowTime, even though Mairéad knew full well that they had tried to poach her several times. If Susie didn't want to put on a jazzy blouse and gurn at the camera, she didn't have to. Jenna could cope with it. Jenna was tough. Jenna needed to know this.

'So, Jenna,' she said with a smile, once they were alone. 'I totally respect your commercial approach with Susie. But, you know, when I set up this company it was really important to me to have a sort of holistic—'

'Sorry, can I stop you there,' said Jenna. She was even holding her hand up, in a 'Stop' gesture. 'Totally dig that. And that might have been fine, like, before. But when you sell to a company like IGS, things change. It's not playtime anymore.'

'Playtime!'

Please don't say, 'When I was at Google...'

'When I was at Google,' said Jenna, 'I got a real sense of how Americans work. And when you interviewed me you did say that you were looking for someone with experience of that US work culture. Trust me, the New York office wants to see results and only results. We're not a charity.'

Jenna put her head on one side. She reached a hand across the table but didn't quite touch Mairéad. 'I know you have trouble maintaining critical distance from clients and that you have your passion projects,' she said, with a sympathetic squidge of her lips, 'but that should maybe be, like, on your own time?'

Then she cheerfully sashayed out of the meeting room and left Mairéad alone. Mairéad sat for a moment and let her hands slide off the table into her lap. She fantasised about keeling sideways out of her chair and onto the floor.

She remembered the WhatsApp from Andreas. She replied, telling him that Gabriel had arrived and seemed fine. 'That's great,' replied Andreas. 'He did amazing work in Paris on a project I was involved in. I love his style.'

This struck her as odd. Andreas's style was the opposite of Gabriel's. He wore crisp white T-shirts, pristine trainers and cashmere half-zip sweaters that probably cost a thousand pounds. Andreas was also confident and bullish, with an accent that could have been American, German, Israeli or even, at times, Australian.

She wasn't even sure that Andreas was his real name. When they'd first met, he had said, 'You can call me Andreas,' and it was such a strange thing to say. As in, *you* can call me 'Andreas', because my real name is on an Interpol wanted list or spoken in an alien language. Andreas said things like, 'Cut the crap,' and pronounced all foreign words in the local style. Muslim was always 'Muss-lim', moussaka was 'moo-SAKA', Gandhi was 'Gahhhn-thi'. Dollars were never 'dollars', they were 'bucks'.

She hadn't hired Andreas. Until eighteen months ago, the office she sat in hadn't even been called IGS, it had been called Vision: her own small, independent influencer agency. Then IGS approached her with an offer and she took it. IGS stood for 'Integrated Group Systems'. It was a shell company Gretchen had bought while she was still at Harvard Business School, and it now gobbled up small companies like a blob monster in a computer game. Gretchen seemed to know a lot about influencer agencies but in an offhand, detached way. Mairéad had also heard her talking about courier systems and 'food tech' in a similarly flawless, cold manner

Mairéad had known from the business podcasts she listened to that this transaction would not be without risk: she would become a subsidiary of her own agency and be expected to conform to someone else's work culture. But she'd been tired and it had been a significant sum of money, which had allowed her to buy her flat outright, fill up her pension and purchase an ISA. So the upside was the money and also a new perk of excellent health insurance. The downside was the interference.

Andreas had been just that sort of interference. Gretchen had sent him as 'Operation Support' a few months after the deal had been done. 'You'll love him,' she'd ordered during a Zoom call. 'He's so much fun.' Mairéad had immediately assumed that Andreas had been sent to fire everyone, but he'd been based in the London office for three months and everyone still had their job. Except for Frankie, of course.

From the little she knew of Andreas, Gabriel seemed like the kind of shivering Zoomer that wound him right up. Gabriel as a hire made no sense. But still, Gabriel was very stylish in his way. Perhaps Andreas knew something she didn't.

THREE

Dodie answered Mairéad's FaceTime the next morning.

'I bought all three of those Rixo dresses, just to annoy you,' she said. She was sitting in bed, wearing her heavy-framed, thick spectacles and an elaborate linen nightgown with ruffles at the neckline. She was propped up by pillows covered in a dark green and white, wide-stripe fabric, edged with more ruffles.

'Why would you even ask me, on email, at one in the morning, which revolting Rixo dress you ought to buy?' said Mairéad.

'I was having a panic attack,' said Dodie, calmly. 'Olly had earache and was moaning on all night and I suddenly felt this choking panic clawing at me.' Dodie scrabbled her fingers at her throat to demonstrate. 'Like, I'm never going to be anything other than a slave to my children and I needed to buy inappropriate dresses.'

'Where will you even wear them? You never leave your bed.'

'I do! I go to Waitrose!' shrieked Dodie. She sat up, her face suddenly close to the camera and enormous. 'I'll wear them on the school run! I don't care!' She pushed her glasses up her nose. 'Anyway. What's going on with you?'

An incoming call appeared across the top of Mairéad's phone screen.

'Sorry, sorry, I've got to go,' she said. 'Crazy Andreas is calling me.'

'Hot Andreas,' said Dodie. 'Whenever you describe him he sounds hot.'

'You think Patrick Bateman is hot.'

'PATRICK BATEMAN *IS* HOT!' bellowed Dodie.

'I'll call you back, bye,' she said. Dodie disappeared and Andreas's disembodied head, with its slicked-back hairdo, appeared on the screen, looking annoyed.

'Andreas,' she said, feeling like Mark Zuckerberg, because she had switched calls without cutting anyone off.

'Okay, we have an issue,' said Andreas, and sipped from a teeny espresso cup.

'What is it?'

'You have hired the wrong guy.'

'What do you mean?'

'The wrong Gabriel. That is not the Gabriel I meant to hire. For director of tech – yes? You know what I am talking about?'

'Yes, yes, I know what you're talking about. Has he done something wrong, or—'

'No, he's the wrong Gabriel! There were two Gabriels. The Gabriel I meant to hire was French! Tall! Dark! You know – French! This guy is a ...I don't know what even he is with this hat and this face that he has. I remember interviewing him, he was the last one I interviewed. I thought he was an asshole!'

'Okay, I see. I did think that he was an unusual choice from you.'

'Then why didn't you check with me?' shrieked Andreas. 'Tch, this really serves me right for going away.'

'Are you still in Paris?'

'I am now in Budapest,' said Andreas.

'Shit,' said Mairéad, grasping what this all meant. 'What are we going to do?'

'What do you mean "we"? *You* have to fire him.'

'Me? Why me? I had nothing to do with hiring Gabriel.'

'Because you are the London president of IGS!' barked Andreas. 'The buck stops with you! Listen to me,' he continued. 'I am confiding in you big time, here. Do you know why New York sent me to London?'

'Operation Support?' she guessed.

'Operation what? Support? No, this is just some bullshit Gretchen told you. It's because they're thinking they want you to set up a new IGS office – but they wanted me to check you out first.'

'A new IGS office? Where?'

LA, she thought. Her heart took up a staccato beat, but she wasn't sure if it was excitement or fear. Both? She told herself it was excitement. Being relocated to LA was the dream. Wasn't it?

'They are considering options. From what I have seen so far I think you are a really great person, but I wonder if you have the killer instinct. It's not your fault, the English are just all the same. You are so nice and all, like, "Sure, you got cramps? Go home, babe!" Americans, they don't mess around. I was once there when Kevin was looking at CVs for internships, okay? You know Kevin, right? And he picks up half the stack of CVs and tosses them and says, "I can't work with anyone who isn't lucky."

'I mean I kind of know where he is coming from, but do you see what I mean? They are real assholes. If I am going to say, "Yes, this Mairéad is an assassin," I need to know that you are. So, prove to me you are a killer, okay? Kill Gabriel.'

'You want me to *kill* Gabriel?' Her voice hit a confused, shrill note.

'No, I don't want you to kill him! I want you to fire him. But I want you to fire him *today*, yes? Being the boss is not a nice, lovely job for nice, cosy people. You need to find out where your teeth are if you are going to do this.'

'Okay, I'll get to the bottom of how this happened,' she said.

She would, but later. First, she had to go for a smear test. And she wasn't about to tell Andreas that.

An hour later she pressed the buzzer at number 153 Harley Street and heard the loud click of the door release. She pushed against the heavy, glossy blackness of it and found herself inside a narrow hallway with a checked black and white floor.

'Dr Childs?' she said to the receptionist. The receptionist gestured, unsmilingly, towards a luxurious waiting room decked out in gold, yellow and cream. Large blue and white chinoiserie lamps with sickly yellow shades rested on dark wood sideboards.

She waited on a hard, velour-covered sofa and stared at a stack of *Country Life* magazines.

After about five minutes, a blonde lady in a striped shirt dress appeared at the doorway of the waiting room. 'May-reed Alexander?' she said.

'It's Muh-raid. Yes,' said Mairéad.

The blonde lady showed her up a flight of stairs into a spacious office and invited her to have a seat. Presently, she heard loud talking, then laughing. The door banged back open and a woman of about fifty barged in.

She wore a white coat that flapped around her. Underneath that was a tight black wiggle skirt with a slit up the thigh, red calf-length boots with a pointy toe, and a turquoise cardigan, which was unbuttoned a rather scandalous amount. She had curly chestnut hair styled into a neat, short haircut, with a kiss curl dangling in front of her forehead.

'Righty-ho,' she said, sitting down heavily on a squashy black swivel chair. 'Mare-ad? Maya-read? How do you say it?'

'Muh-raid,' said Mairéad.

'What sort of name is that?'

'Irish.'

'Oh, are you Irish?'

'No,' said Mairéad.

'But you *are* forty...' Dr Childs put on her glasses as she started to read off her notes. 'Wait, forty-four years old. Four... *four*...' continued Dr Childs, looking at her file.

'Yes, that's right,' said Mairéad, getting annoyed. 'Forty-four,' she confirmed loudly.

'Okay. Dum de dummm, looks from this like it's all reproductively normal... regular periods... no suspected endometriosis... no clotting... just a bit on the geriatric side! Now!' Dr Childs plucked off her glasses and dropped them. They fell forwards and then jerked back and dangled, suspended, round Dr Childs' neck by a gold chain.

'How can I help?'

'I'm just here for a smear test,' said Mairéad. *Geriatric!*

'Oh, right,' said Dr Childs. 'Why haven't I seen you before?'

'I only just got health insurance through work, last year.'

'I see. Well I'm sure you know the drill. Bottoms off, towel over your, you know.'

'Right.'

Mairéad moved over to the hospital bed in the corner of the room. Dr Childs swooshed a blue curtain around her, and she shuffled off her sandals, jeans and underwear.

Dr Childs bellowed, 'MIRIAM!', making her jump.

She heard the door open.

'I'll have that salmon thing for lunch, please,' said Dr Childs.

'Sure,' said Miriam, and left.

'Ready?' called Dr Childs.

'Yes.' She draped a towel over her bottom half, which felt

terribly exposed and vulnerable, then lowered her head uncertainly onto the rustling paper cover of the bed.

Dr Childs clanked about, snapping on gloves and rummaging in amongst utensils.

'So no kids then, eh?'

'No.'

'Me neither. Never saw the point. Ankles together, knees floppity-flop to the side. That's it.'

Mairéad's phone started ringing.

'Oh shit, sorry,' she said.

'Well, do you wanna get it?' said Dr Childs. She stood with her hip cocked, a speculum aloft.

'Well no, but it'll just ring for ages if I don't,' said Mairéad. 'Bit off-putting.' She snapped her knees shut and pulled the towel down.

'Okay, hang on,' said Dr Childs. She put down the speculum with a clatter and located Mairéad's bag. She rummaged in it for the ringing phone.

'No, sorry, it's in my trousers back pocket,' she said, raising her head from the bed and pointing.

Dr Childs eventually tracked down the ringing phone and held it out to Mairéad. In the fumbled exchange, she accidentally hit 'Answer'.

'Oh!' she said. 'Damn.' She automatically put the phone to her ear.

'Hello?' she said.

'Is that Mairéad... Alexander?'

'Yes, speaking.' She mouthed, 'Sorry,' at Dr Childs.

Dr Childs raised her eyebrows and blinked a little.

'Oh hi there, this is Bronwyn, I'm calling from [unintelligible] hospital.'

'Okay, I'm actually at my appointment.'

'What?'

'I said, I'm here, I'm with Dr Childs now.'

'Sorry,' said Bronwyn, 'I think we've got some crossed wires. I'm calling about your sister.'

Mairéad paused, deeply confused. 'Lenny? What?'

'Your sister, Dolours,' said Bronwyn patiently, 'is in hospital, with us. At Castell Cerys. In Wales.'

'Oh my god,' said Mairéad, finally understanding. 'What happened?'

'She had an accident; there's some damage to her leg and head. She's okay, she'll be fine, but she has to stay with us for a while for assessment.'

'Okay. Woah. Poor Lenny. Can I talk to her?'

'She's under quite heavy sedation,' said Bronwyn. 'So not just now. I'm actually calling about her daughter.'

'Sunshine?'

'Yes. Your sister told us to call you,' said Bronwyn.

'Really?' said Mairéad, very surprised.

'Yes,' said Bronwyn firmly. 'Sunshine will need somewhere to stay.'

'Well, I… can I actually call you back? I'm sort of in the middle of something. I've got your number on my phone. Can I reach you on that?'

'Yes, any time,' said Bronwyn. If Mairéad would come and get Sunshine, she added, they would bend the rules and keep the girl in Lenny's room for another few days. But after that, if there was no family to help, they would have to contact social services.

Mairéad ended the call, switched off the ringer and handed the phone to Dr Childs.

'Sorry,' she said.

'No, no,' said Dr Childs in a chilly voice. 'I'm at your service. Right, let's get on with it, shall we?'

Mairéad pinched the bridge of her nose, closed her eyes and willed the process to be over. She tried to recall whether or not Dr Childs had changed her gloves after rummaging in

Mairéad's bag and through her pockets. She braced herself for the invasive moment, the ominous screwing-open sound and the brief scrabble with a collection device.

'All done!' barked Dr Childs.

'That was quick.'

'Not my first rodeo,' said Dr Childs, snapping off her gloves, stamping on a bio-waste bin lever and tossing them in.

She heard the doctor sit heavily back down in her chair. She got dressed and sat back down, too.

Dr Childs was scribbling something in a folder of notes. Mairéad looked at the certificates in frames on the wall. She, too, was an award-winner. Women's Health Practitioner of the Year, 2001.

'Oh wait,' said Dr Childs, flicking through the notes and then flipping the page to look at the front of the folder. 'Hang on, hang on... Oh no, phew. Sorry, for a minute there I thought I'd got the wrong notes.'

Mairéad wanted to shriek, 'What happened to you! Where has the Women's Health Practitioner of the Year, 2001 gone?'

'What contraception are you using?' Dr Childs asked. 'Married? Partner?'

'Condoms. And no.'

'Condoms!'

'What's wrong with condoms?'

'It's a bit nineties, isn't it?'

'Is it?'

'Yes! Get yourself a nice coil.'

'I've never fancied the sound of that.'

'Oh, it's great. Brilliant for the peri-menopause.' Dr Childs pointed her pen angrily. 'Do not listen to any of that crap on Mumsnet about it. It's life-changing. I mean, unless you want to have a baby any time soon.'

'I don't.'

'Yes, best not to,' said Dr Childs. 'I mean, not at *forty-four*.

It's not impossible but, you know… Anyway, you've got the right idea. You can be light on your feet, swift. If you're like us, it's all about the three Ps. Property, pension and… uhhh… there was one other one.' She clicked her fingers. 'You know. I want to say "savings" but it needs to start with a "P".'

'ISA?' Mairéad was starting to feel faint.

'No!' snapped Dr Childs. 'I said it had to start with a "P"! Otherwise it's not the three Ps, is it?' She tutted.

Mairéad left Dr Childs' office feeling like she had jumped from a speeding train. *If you're like us.* She didn't want to be anything like Dr Childs. She set off in the direction of the tube station, then suddenly remembered: Lenny! She phoned Castell Cerys Hospital.

'So,' said Bronwyn. 'Can I tell Sunshine you'll be coming to get her?'

'Yes, I'll be there. Of course. When's the latest I can come? I just need to get some things ready – this is all a bit unexpected.'

'She needs to be collected by Saturday afternoon,' said Bronwyn.

'Saturday. As in, today is Wednesday and I have to be there by Saturday?'

'That's right,' said Bronwyn calmly. 'Saturday.'

Saturday. Fine. Feeling a little dizzy, Mairéad headed back to the office.

It quickly turned out that the mix-up with the Gabriels was Biba's fault. Biba had been tasked with handling and sorting the applicants for the job. No one had told her, and it hadn't occurred to her, to attach pictures to the applications. So when Andreas had said, 'We're going with Gabriel,' over his shoulder, as he ran to catch a flight to Paris, Biba had assumed he meant the Gabriel that he had interviewed that day. French Gabriel had been seen a week previously. This might as well have been a year previously for all that Biba could remember him.

'Don't worry, don't worry,' said Mairéad, patting Biba on her shoulder. Biba was sitting in Mairéad's office, with her elbows on the desk and her hands tented over her face. 'Uuuuhmmygud,' she said through her hands. 'Uuuhmygud I'm so sorry.'

'The good news,' said Jenna, 'is that he hasn't signed his contract yet. There was a delay getting the papers through from the lawyers. You know, we had a similar issue at Google, once.'

'Okay,' said Mairéad. 'Fine. So he can't sue us. But we still have to tell him.'

They all three turned to look through the plate-glass window at Gabriel. He was sitting hunched at his desk, wearing huge headphones and a red, black and green patterned sweater, even though it was a balmy 21°C day.

'Did you know he suffers from brachi-cardio something something-iasis?' said Biba.

'What's that?' Mairéad asked.

'I don't know,' whispered Biba. 'But I think it's something to do with his heart.'

She shot Mairéad a terrified look.

'Okay, you guys,' she said. 'Leave this with me. I'll think of something.'

She sat at her desk for an hour and could see no way of firing Gabriel that would not result in him having a heart attack or hating her, personally, forever. Or, worse, suing IGS for distress. Her guts twisted at the potential reputational damage to IGS, which was, naturally, a very online company.

She got nothing done. She stood up and looked out of the window. Across the street was a red-brick disused warehouse, identical to the one she stood in. It also now housed modern companies and start-ups just like hers. She gazed at the man in the office opposite, who was wearing his customary blue open-necked shirt. He was pacing about, gesturing with his hands. She wondered if he was having a good day or a bad day. A WhatsApp came through from Andreas: 'Is it done?'

She frowned with frustration and dislike and did not respond. She went to the bathroom for a change of scene, pushing open the heavy wooden door that made a terrible sucking, tearing noise as it opened. She was hit by the scent of warm toilet, cleaning product and air freshener. She heard sniffing coming from a cubicle, a nose being blown and then a cistern flushing. She washed her hands for something to do, just to kill time, while she was thinking about what came next. Biba emerged from the cubicle, red-eyed. They looked at each other for a moment, then Biba tented her hands over her nose again, her oval nails painted that fleshy-pink colour, and once more dissolved into tears.

'Oh dear!' Mairéad gave her a hug. 'You've really taken this hard.'

Biba's shoulders shook. 'I'm such an idiot,' she said, gratefully leaning into the hug. She smelled of coconut and something else — was it green tea? 'I'm so useless and stupid. I've ruined everything and now you've got to clear up my mess.'

'Honestly, this is my job,' said Mairéad, and meant it. 'Really. It's not much fun being in charge, because you have to do stuff like this — clear up messes that you didn't make.' As soon as she said it, she realised it was true. Being the boss wasn't very much fun — it *was* an awful lot of clearing up messes that other people had made.

'When I was twenty-three, I made so many mistakes,' she continued. 'That's why you don't run companies when you're twenty-three.'

'You're so nice.' Biba sniffed. 'Don't take this the wrong

way, but you're like this really caring mummy and we all… we all really love you…'

In shock, Mairéad stopped patting Biba.

'Sorry, I didn't mean like you're old,' said Biba, sensing her surprise. 'You're just very maternal.'

'Am I?' She gave a bark of laughter. 'Well, I suppose that's a good thing.'

'Yeah, I mean you should hear what other bosses are like, the people who my friends have to work for. They're like…' Biba flicked her eyes left and right and then whispered, 'They're all like Andreas, but worse. They're *bullies*.'

Mairéad didn't know what to say, so she said nothing. She didn't want to say something that sounded like, 'In my day…' because it made her feel a hundred and fifty years old, but she did know that in her day it had been much worse. So she just stood in companionable silence.

Maternal.

'Okay, well. You take as long as you need in here,' she said eventually. 'I'll see you out there.'

She returned to her desk and was just about to call Andreas and tell him that, tough luck, Gabriel was just going to have to stay, when she received a Slack message from Gabriel.

The wrong Gabriel.

'Hi, there's something I need to discuss with you.'
'Sure. Do you want to pop into my office?'
'I'd actually rather do this over IM if you don't mind. I'm actually not great with intense eye contact.'
'I understand. What's up?'
'Unfortunately I have been made aware of some really upsetting activity by your colleague Andreas Pinto.'
'I see. Can you say more?'

Well, This Is Awkward

She felt a tickle of panic in her stomach. In her head she heard slithery violin noises of the sort you get at tense moments in horror movies.

'In 2018 he liked a tweet from the charity Zen, which is for displaced peoples.'

'I'm afraid I'm not familiar with Zen – you might have to explain more.'

'In 2017 Zen invited the journalist Charles Hofmann as their keynote speaker to talk on child poverty and I'm afraid Charles Hofmann's views on immigration as he often talks about in his newspaper are absolutely unacceptable.'

'Oh dear,' she typed. Her prick of anxiety burst suddenly into hope, a way out of her awkward situation. 'Gabriel, I can see this is very distressing for you.'

'VERY DISTRESSING,' typed Gabriel. 'I cannot comfortably work for a company that does not align with my views and principles. I would never have accepted the job in the first place had I known this, but this information has only recently been made available to me.'

'I can absolutely see your problem,' she said. 'I will not insult your principles by arguing with you. If you feel your position is untenable we would be happy to offer you one month's severance pay?' There was a pause. Gabriel was clearly thinking about this.

She started to feel herself sweat. Had she made the offer too quickly? She had. It was too quick. It looked too eager. She pinched the side of her bottom lip with a thumb and forefinger.

'That would be acceptable,' he finally wrote. She breathed out.

'I would also ask that you tell anyone who asks that I have resigned for health reasons as I do not want any repercussions from this on social media,' he said.

'I totally understand,' she typed, barely able to believe her luck. 'That would work for us, too, if you could be discreet about this.'

She sat back in her chair, blew out a big breath, picked up her phone and typed to Andreas, 'It's done.' She looked at Gabriel through the glass wall of her office, with his stupid hat and his gross, picked-at nail varnish. What a jerk. *Maternal*. She shook her head and blinked rapidly a few times to signal to herself, because sometimes she felt like she was the only person who was truly on her side, that this was all a bit crazy.

She flicked through her diary to see when she could visit her mother to talk to her about this whole Lenny business. Maternal or not, there was no way in hell that she could take in Sunshine.

FOUR

Everyone at IGS was surprised that the party for That Divorced Girl's first book: *Get Divorced! (with That Divorced Girl)* turned out to be a hot ticket. The book was the first of a three-book deal IGS had brokered with Carbon, the publishing arm of the newspaper and TV company MediaCorp, who'd offered a six-figure deal for what was, in effect, just a re-hash of That Divorced Girl's Instagram content. That Divorced Girl (real name Ashley) had been worried about the content of the other two books.

'We thought fiction,' said one of the editors at Carbon, airily. 'You know, something about a divorced woman living happily ever after. With a twist. We'll think of something. A lot of appetite for that.'

'I've never written a novel, though,' said Ashley, turning pale underneath her Tan Luxe sunless tanner face drops. 'I didn't even do English A level.'

'We've got a team you can work with,' said the editor. 'The most important thing is that you've got an amazing platform and brilliant brand recognition.'

Tonight, the first floor of a restaurant in a fashionable part of town had been decked out in That Divorced Girl's trademark colours of purple and blue. A balloon arch soared over the entrance, the waiters were in blue and purple T-shirts and there were pots of purple and blue flowers everywhere. The effect was hideous but undeniably on-brand. Clearly Jenna's work.

Mairéad arrived and realised that, quite coincidentally, she was wearing a T-shirt in That Divorced Girl blue.

'Mairéad,' said Jenna, clutching her elbow.

'Oh hi. How's it all going?'

'Amazing, really good,' said Jenna, who was wearing a bright orange bodycon dress with a peep-hole cut-out over her cleavage and huge bovver boots. It was strange to see her without Margot's head poking out from under her armpit.

'Ha ha! Love the T-shirt. You *are* the job. You know people are going to confuse you for a waitress all night, right?'

Jenna caught sight of someone and waved. 'Dre!' she said.

Andreas arrived, holding a glass of champagne, looking very suave in a dark blue suit and a light blue shirt, open at the neck.

'A suit!' said Mairéad. 'You look like the Wolf of Wall Street.'

'Are you helping with drinks?' said Andreas. 'Why are you wearing the wait-staff shirt?'

'Just showing my support.'

'That's great. Great thinking. Hey, this party is amazing,' said Andreas, taking a sip of champagne. 'Usually a book party is so pathetic and sad with some tray of crap from a supermarket. Even Carbon don't usually throw this kind of party. I still cannot get over that deal.' He clicked his fingers and said, 'Damn, we are so good.'

'Stone & Stone lawyers actually paid for all this,' said Jenna, sweeping her arm around in an arc. 'Turns out divorce lawyers are absolutely crazy for publicity and god, they've got money.'

'That's more great thinking,' said Andreas. 'What a great team. Great job.'

'Someone's got to take the initiative around here,' said Jenna.

Well, This Is Awkward

'Am I right?' She elbowed Mairéad, making her drink spill a little.

'Ooh, there's Min Cohen, I just want to go and say hi quickly.' Jenna beetled over to the grumpy fashion photographer Min, who Jenna had been trying to sign up to IGS since the day she'd arrived. Min was in even larger bovver boots than Jenna's.

'And well done to you with that Gabriel,' said Andreas. 'I was having flashbacks to Frankie. Jesus.' He shuddered dramatically. 'Thank god for NDAs.'

'Thanks. Does this mean I'm a killer?' She made a gun out of her fingers and pointed it at Andreas.

'Maybe,' he said. 'It's looking positive. Make sure your passport is up to date, okay?'

LA. It was definitely LA. Wow. Actual Los Angeles.

She took a sip of her drink and looked over at Jenna, nose to nose with the stern Min Cohen, but Min was actually smiling. She bet Jenna didn't accuse Min of not being bothered with fashion, or lacking initiative, or being a weird, old, passion-project freak. Min was cool. She was on the verge of being very big, and everyone knew it.

'But it's not settled as to where the new office is?' she said.

'Oh my god!' said Andreas, waving his champagne glass around. 'If someone says they have a space on a rocket ship, you don't ask where the rocket ship is going!'

'I'm not sure that's what Sheryl Sandberg actually said.'

'Whatever,' said Andreas. 'You need to loosen up.' He took another sip of his drink. 'You know what I think it is?'

'What?'

'You're scared that it's something you can't control. You are a very controlling person.'

'I'm really not.' She blinked in outrage.

'Ha,' said Andreas. 'Okay. You are not a controlling person. I think it would be very good for you, this leap into the

unknown. Just try to relax and have fun. Not always be so…'
He gripped a fist in front of his face and started gnawing on a knuckle, his eyes open very wide.

'That is a very annoying thing to say,' she said. I am relaxed, I am fun, she thought crossly.

'You will thank me later. This is a good deal.'

She looked across the room at Jenna, who had neatly dispatched Min Cohen and was now talking to the editorial director of Carbon, an icy blonde woman called KC. Jenna said something and KC touched her arm and laughed.

She heard the off-stage horror-movie violin noises again and suddenly got a feeling like she was being tipped out of a long, slippery container. Was she really going to LA? The not knowing was unsettling. Not because she was unrelaxed or controlling! What kind of person is okay with having no clue where they're going to be living and working by the same time next year? She glared at Jenna again. Probably Jenna. She would be fine with it. She'd pack a Hunza G bikini and a vintage sundress, toss Margot into the nearest dog shelter and split.

'Now,' said Andreas, 'we must go and find Ashley and tell her she is a great and wonderful superstar. She will love that shirt.'

Mairéad felt uneasy.

'Okay,' she said. 'Okay, let's do that.'

She stayed at the party for another forty-five minutes. It was gratifying to see Ashley so happy, but she couldn't think of a single thing to say to Min Cohen, who had a stern face, like an American border agent. In a terrible moment, which Mairéad was relieved no one had witnessed, KC said, 'Sorry, can I give you this?' and held out a drained wine glass. Mairéad had smiled broadly and taken the glass, saying, 'Of course.' Once she had left the glass with an actual waiter, she slunk off to meet Cass at The Hare, a high-ceilinged pub equidistant between their homes, for something to eat.

Cass really was Irish. And when they'd first met, the fact that Mairéad was called Mairéad, without being Irish, was the funniest thing that Cass had ever heard.

'And also, it's like…' she bent over with laughter, 'Mairéad is like what your friend's auntie is called. Not even your own auntie. It's like the name Beryl or Mavis or something. You have all the Irish names to choose from and you choose… Mairéad? Have you siblings, then? I can't wait to hear what they're called.'

When she told her that Lenny's real name was Dolours, after Dolours Price, Cass stopped laughing. 'That's less funny, really. But look at the pair of us. On paper, which one is Irish?' Cass was a small, blonde voiceover artist of thirty-five. She was one of those people everyone knew, but no one was sure how. As Mairéad's friends and acquaintances of the same age trickled away into the steel clutches of family life, the people she spent time with started to skew younger. Cass was resolutely single and hyperactive. She was always up to something. She didn't own a handbag and wore her door key on a chain around her neck. She had the vivacious energy of a bright teenage boy.

When Mairéad arrived at The Hare, Cass was at the bar talking to three men Mairéad didn't recognise. Cass was gesturing in the air with one hand.

'Hi,' said Mairéad.

'Oh here she is, now,' said Cass. 'This is Leonard, Bernie and Stu. Would you know it, they're in a band! They're playing at the Boston Arms later.'

Mairéad gave the three men a weak wave. They were all bald and overweight and wore leather waistcoats and faded Grateful Dead and Janis Joplin T-shirts. They politely raised a hand back. This was typical of Cass, to fall to amiably chatting with whoever else was at the bar, even three old blokes.

'Come on, come on,' said Cass, picking up her translucent, fizzing drink from the bar. She gestured with her chin. 'Get the wine, there, that's yours. It's usually a chardonnay, isn't it? Over here.' She inclined with her head again towards a corner table. She sat down and said, 'Ahh... Right. Now. I need to know everything that happened with Richard.'

'Oh, he was great!' Why had her voice come out so high-pitched?

'But the Barbour,' said Cass.

'Yes, but I don't want to sound ungrateful. It was good meeting him, really. But I just...' She paused and looked blankly over Cass's shoulder. She considered telling her about the 'Do you ever get lonely?' faux pas, but rejected the idea. She didn't want to give it the oxygen of publicity.

'It's just these days I don't see the point of settling. I've looked past red flags before and it never ends well. I know too much.'

'No, no, I see, I see. You don't have to worry about explaining yourself,' said Cass, waving her hand. 'I don't mind what you do. When you swore off the apps and said only real-life meets from now on I wanted to help, but there's a load of buck eejits out there. Richard is the only guy I thought was suitable for you. I thought you'd connect on, like, a cellular level.'

'I love the fact that I told you I'd sworn off apps a year ago and you're still working that playbook,' said Mairéad. 'But that cellular level thing, that's a myth,' she added.

'Oh, go on,' said Cass. 'That's the most uptight thing I've ever heard anyone say. You don't believe in an instant connection?'

'Yes I do, but I don't think it necessarily translates to long-term love.'

'Okay, okay.'

'How do you know Richard, again?'

'He's the boss of my mate Kathleen. You know, the doctor?'

She gave Cass a blank look. Kathleen could be any one of Cass's thousands of friends.

'You know! She's yer one at Carnival that time. She's the one with all the…' Cass made a twirling motion in the air with both hands to denote all of the whatever it was that Kathleen had. She stopped and regarded Mairéad's blank face. 'Oh, forget it. Anyway, he's some big deal in her department and I met him at a party on a boat. Wait, was it a boat? Yes, it was. And he's just a laugh, you know? A total gas. They love him to bits at the hospital. Something terrible happened with the wife,' Cass added darkly. 'Don't know what, but it wasn't his fault, I'm sure. Anyway, he's a little older, sophisticated, charming. Recently we were all somewhere – where was it, now? It was something with food, outside. And he was chatting away like the loveliest dad you've ever met and it struck me, it did. It struck me like a beam of light. Mairéad, I thought. You are perfect for Mairéad.'

Mairéad paused and raised her eyebrows at Cass. 'Because he's a lovely old dad?'

'Don't be so sensitive! Be realistic. How old are you? Ninety?'

She narrowed her eyes. 'But you knew about the Barbour,' she said.

'Yes. I knew about the blessed Barbour. And I know the man, but not really well enough yet to say, "Hey, pal, leave the wax jacket at home." Honestly I thought it was obvious not to wear such a tragic item.' Cass took a sip of her drink and looked mournful. 'So you won't be seeing him again?'

Mairéad made a hesitant and then an apologetic face.

'Ah, forget it,' said Cass. 'What else is new with you, then?'

'It's all a bit mad, actually. I got this call about my sister and she's in hospital.'

'Oh dear,' said Cass. 'That'll be Lenny, I'm guessing. What's the matter?'

Mairéad realised that she hadn't been curious enough to

ask for details and felt a prick of guilt. 'I'm not totally sure what happened, I'll find out when I go down. But the point is my niece, Sunshine. She can't stay in the hospital and it doesn't sound like Lenny's got anyone else, so I've got to work out what to do with her.'

'*Sunshine*,' said Cass. 'What the hell is wrong with you people you can't have a child and just give it a normal name?'

'I know,' said Mairéad. She held up her hands and closed her eyes. 'Lenny's a, she's… I don't know. Hippy is the wrong word – she's not a hippy, but she's definitely hippy-adjacent.'

Lenny lived in Wales, in a remote, off-grid wooden cabin, with her daughter and two Tamworth pigs called Dennis and Minnie. The pigs were rented out as natural land-clearing machines, and Lenny travelled the country, with the pigs rattling along behind in a trailer, to clear abandoned spaces of nettles, brambles and anything else that could be uprooted – no petrol-powered machinery or weed-killer necessary.

'Oh she's a kind of a back-to-the-earth person or whatever. I know the type. How old is the kid, then?' said Cass.

Mairéad thought for a moment. 'Eleven? I think.'

'Poor little mite. Don't look so gloomy – children are funny,' said Cass. 'And they're a great excuse to get out of all sorts of shite you don't want to do. Especially if the child isn't yours. If it's yours, people are like, "Well that's your own stupid fault for having one", but imagine the sympathy you'll get!'

Mairéad blew a puff of air through her lips. 'I suppose, but then there's all this drama at work. I think I might be going away. I mean, relocating full-time, not just going on a trip.'

'Where?'

'Possibly LA.'

Cass did a dramatic intake of breath.

'Stop the lights! Why aren't you doing cartwheels?'

'I don't know. I've just got a spooky feeling about it. Like someone's trying to get me out of the way.' She said this without even knowing that it was what she thought. But it was absolutely what she thought.

Cass was dismissive. 'You've just been in that cloak-and-dagger business world for too long. Catch yourself on. You're paranoid! You literally are. That's what paranoia is, thinking people are plotting against you.'

'It's not paranoia if they are actually plotting against you.'

'Okay, Woody Allen. My advice is take this at face value. It's a sign. Maybe not to you, but to me. You've got to just make it be LA. Manifest it! Do you do that? I'll send you this thing that tells you all about it. Take me with you. We'll be flatmates! I'll go and do the animation pilot season. They'll want me to be a little leprechaun in something. That kind of thing ought to make me angry but I'll admit I'm actually up for it.' Cass drummed her fingers on the table and stared dreamily into the middle distance.

'LA, hey? That's the big time, isn't it,' she continued. 'That's the dream. The palm trees and all the sun and so on. Those big cars they have. We could go camping in the desert!'

'Have you ever been?'

'No, never made it there. You?'

'Yes. For work. The beaches aren't as nice as you think they're going to be. And, I don't know. It's all just so uncertain. What kind of person is cool with not knowing where they're going to be living and working a year from now?'

'Me! I'd be fine about it. Tch. You're a terrible fusspot,' said Cass. 'That's what my ma would say about you.'

As they didn't have much else on, they decided to go from The Hare to Leonard, Bernie and Stu's gig at the Boston Arms. They were an old-fashioned English folk band and actually pretty good. Mairéad had to dig Cass out of a corner at 10.30 p.m., where she was swaying and hiccupping in a corner, typing away furiously on WhatsApp with one thumb.

'You don't have to go home,' said an Australian barman as he stacked up empties. 'But you can't stay here.'

Later, as she was washing her face, Mairéad tried to remember Sunshine, who must have been about two when she'd last seen her, at their mother's house. Lenny had brought Sunshine to town in order to have grommets fitted in her ears.

The meeting had been tense. Their father, Gavin, had been dead only two years. His death, the nature of it, the circumstances, were still not discussed openly. And, without him, the structure of the family sagged, threatening to collapse completely.

Sunshine had been wearing baggy, dirty leggings with the flap of a button-up bodysuit dangling outside the waistband. Her hair was wild and she had a thick green rope of snot running from one nostril down to her mouth. Mairéad recalled that she'd been a quiet but busy presence. Lenny had put out some coloured wooden blocks in front of Sunshine, who she always called 'Sunny'. Sunny diligently lined the blocks up in rows, from smallest to largest. She went down her row of blocks, touching each one caringly with her forefinger as she went. Lenny looked exhausted. She didn't smile.

FIVE

Mairéad's childhood home was a Victorian detached townhouse with the words 'Cable House' chiselled into a block of stone above the porch. The house was very slightly grander than the ones around it, being on a corner and double-fronted, while all the neighbouring houses were terraced. But Mairéad's mother, Helen, had taken this up-step in status rather seriously.

Helen always referred to her home as 'Cable House'. Never 'home' or 'our house'. Mairéad and Lenny referred to their childhood home in this way, too. At first, it was in order to make fun of their mother's obsession with it, but in later years calling their home 'Cable House' became a habit.

Mairéad took the tube from her flat six stops north. Then she got out and walked ten minutes through the suburban streets. It was a short journey in distance, but felt, to her, like going back in time.

As she reached the front door, it opened. Two young people, looking not more than about twenty, stepped out.

'Mairéad,' she said clearly, pointing to herself. 'Helen's daughter.' The Cable House lodgers had been utterly entwined in her life when she was younger. She no longer knew any of them, but still recognised them instantly for who they were.

The two young people made an 'ah' expression, clearly only really understanding the word 'Helen'. But this was the shibboleth. She smiled widely at the pair and they smiled widely back, then she walked past and through the still-open front door. The window next to the front door had a fresh appeal poster for Yemen taped to the inside, alongside yellowing and faded posters for End Apartheid Now, Free Palestine and some so faded by the sun that they were unreadable.

'Mother!' she called through the house.

She heard Helen's voice and followed the sound to her usual seat by the kitchen window. Helen referred to it as 'mission control'. She sat in a grand armchair with the telephone point next to it. On a side table sat Helen's laptop, a newish MacBook Air: the centre of Helen's world.

Helen was talking on the phone and showed no sign of ending the call in order to talk to her daughter. '. . . oh really, how awful!' she said into the receiver. 'But you must have been... well of course! My goodness, can't anyone *do* anything about it?'

Then she said: 'Hang on,' and put her hand over the mouthpiece of the telephone, 'one sec!'

Mairéad nodded, put her bag down and wandered off through the house to the garden. Nothing about the house had changed since she'd moved out twenty-three years earlier. The living room was still painted an unattractive, muddy green. Helen had done it herself one day, on a whim. The curtains, made from a chintzy Laura Ashley fabric, were thinning, sun-stained and sagged off their rings. She marvelled at how exactly the same everything was: the same ratty books on the shelves, the same rug, the same throw over the same sofa. The French doors with their peeling paint and worn-out handles led out to the garden, which was dominated by an enormous cherry tree. Gavin had battled for years to redecorate the house and get the cherry tree taken down, but Helen powerfully resisted change of any sort that was not her idea and it rarely occurred to her to change anything.

For want of anything else to do, Mairéad wandered down to the end of the garden towards her father's shed. When her father had been in charge, the garden had been rather nice: unfussy, with a regularly mown lawn, edged by what gardeners might call mature borders, full of blowsy roses, red-hot pokers, foxgloves, ox-eye daisies and lady's mantle. It had been a peaceful garden, not too neat.

Now weeds reigned and a bramble in one corner looked like it was considering a hostile takeover. The grass was inexpertly cut, probably by one of the lodgers in lieu of rent, and grew in ragged chunks, turning to a mulchy yellow close to the roots. Gavin's roses were still in full bloom, pink, red and orange petals bursting out and fighting valiantly for their place in the garden amongst swarming nettles and long grasses.

She reached the shed and pulled open the door. Then she stopped, wondering if she could really go in, if she could face the avalanche of memories and emotions it would bring. Then she pushed onwards. The shed smelled of something, she wasn't sure what. Perhaps it was linseed. Or instant coffee, or paint or varnish. Or perhaps a mixture of all these things. It was a most particular and individual smell that she had never smelled anywhere else. The shed was reasonably big, with shelves down one side, a work bench across the back and a wall filled with pegs holding various hacksaws, wrenches, screwdrivers, gardening forks and spades.

In one corner was a brown corduroy armchair and a table. In another was a small fridge, disconnected, with its flex and plug draped over the open door. On top of the fridge was a kettle and a battered tin. Next to the armchair was an old-fashioned bar heater, switched off and cold. She looked around the shed. It was tidy, spotless in fact, just the way her father liked it. She had made sure it was left this way.

'Mairéad?!' Helen called through the house, now off the phone.

'Here!' She stepped out of the shed and into the garden.

'I was just talking to *Simone*,' said Helen, emerging from the French doors, a hand up to her eyes, shielding them from the sun. 'She's got this just wonderful sweet Filipina living with her and, god! The terrible life she's had. Her husband was just vile to her and she's over here cleaning houses and living in fear of the Home Office finding her.' Helen looked wistfully into the air.

'Well I hope Simone has got a good lawyer!' said Mairéad brightly and not for the first time. 'The maximum prison sentence for harbouring an illegal immigrant is fourteen years.' She felt perfectly compassionate about desperate undocumented immigrants, but her mother's habit of ranking them in importance above her children infuriated her.

'Mmmm,' said Helen.

'Full house?' In later life, lodgers had become Helen's passion. They had always been a presence in Cable House, with their new and strange smells, unfamiliar cooking and halting English. Once Lenny had left home, at twenty-one, there had been room for more. Two years younger, at nineteen, Mairéad felt like a turkey close to Christmas. She felt that Helen was desperate to get rid of her, so that she might have more lodgers.

'Nearly,' said Helen. 'You must have seen the Greek twins leaving just now. They're super, so hard-working. They've had a terrible time trying to get here – they're lucky they found me. And I am just so, so proud of Roxana, you know. She has just completed her accountancy exams with top marks, such a wonderful hard-working girl. And such a terrible start in life! I mean she really is an inspiration.'

There was a muted 'bloop' sound from the voluminous pocket of Helen's loose linen dress. She took out her phone, popped her reading glasses on, and delicately tapped around on the screen. A gust of warm summer air passed across her, pushing the wisps of hair escaping her messy top-knot and her brown linen dress all to one side.

It had never occurred to Helen that ignoring the people she was with in favour of her phone was rude. A reluctance to leave the house had always stalked her, but since the death of her husband it had closed its grip on her. This desire was simultaneously alleviated and enabled by the internet. Without ever leaving the house, Helen could live what felt to her like a full and independent life. She could buy groceries and gadgets online, she could Skype her GP and order her angina medicine to be delivered. She could watch films, talk to people, find new lodgers and read about humanitarian atrocities across the globe.

Her smartphone allowed her to keep in constant touch with all her lodgers. They were meticulously added and removed from her WhatsApp group entitled 'Cable House' as they bodily moved in and moved out of the actual house. She now had no reason to leave her home. Her symbiotic relationship with the tech, which allowed her to self-imprison in Cable House, had become increasingly one-sided. Just as Helen's lodgers had once superseded her children in importance, now the internet came before absolutely everything. A power cut would finish her. Mairéad had once been horrified at how many notifications Helen had on her phone, which constantly lit up like an arcade game. 'You know, most people have their notifications turned off,' she said. 'I can show you how to do it.'

'Oh, but then,' countered Helen, 'I don't know what's going on.'

The most baffling thing was how Helen pretended that she did, in fact, leave the house. She often wandered around in a coat, looking like she was just about to go out. She sometimes declared that she was going to the theatre and would talk for days about how she was going to go, only to inevitably 'change her mind' at the last minute. She would claim a headache or declare it was too windy, or that her friend had cancelled.

Mairéad had never noticed any sort of pattern to this until she was in her late twenties, when Lenny had dismissively referred to Helen as a recluse.

'What?' Mairéad had said.

'She never leaves the house,' said Lenny.

'She does, she...' started Mairéad. But then she thought for a moment and realised that, no, Helen never left the house.

Helen was now typing away on her phone, totally oblivious.

'I need to talk to you about something,' said Mairéad.

'Oh yes, why *are* you here?' said Helen, still looking at her phone.

'It's Lenny. Mum!' said Mairéad sharply. 'Can you concentrate, please?'

'What *is* it?' Helen said, irritably.

'Lenny has had an accident.'

'What?'

'She's broken her leg or something, not sure totally. But it doesn't sound great; she's going to be in hospital for a while. The main problem is Sunshine – she's got nowhere else to go.'

'Oh!' said Helen. 'Oh poor Lenny.' She looked into the distance and blinked a bit. 'She'll hate that, being in hospital.' Then Helen went back to her phone and said as she typed, 'Have you spoken to her?'

Mairéad said nothing, just looked at Helen. She did this sometimes, when Helen was only half listening because she was typing on her phone. She hated Helen's habit of asking a question and then turning to her phone while the question was being answered, so she resolved not to talk to Helen unless she was looking at her. Helen ignored Mairéad for a while and then looked up expectantly. 'Have you spoken to her?' she repeated.

'The hospital wouldn't let me, they said she was too out of it. I'm sure she'll be fine, you know how tough Lenny is.'

'I certainly do,' scoffed Helen. 'Amazed she hasn't punched her way out of there already.'

'It's more Sunshine we need to worry about,' said Mairéad. 'We've got to take her in or she'll go into foster care.'

'Oh, no, Misha will have to take her in.'

'Misha! God knows where he is! Last time I think Lenny said he was in Poland?'

'Yes but he's her father,' said Helen, her eyes sucked back to her phone again. 'About time he took some responsibility for her.'

'Sunshine can't suddenly go and live in Poland.'

'Oh you're being silly,' said Helen. 'She's been before, a while ago. I remember the fuss Lenny made about getting her a passport. And you're also being very prejudiced. There are many wonderful places to live in Poland and the Polish are a marvellous, stoic people. Lenny chose to go and live in Wales and have her baby on her own and never come and see us, not even at Christmas. Honestly, I've been quite sad enough about it in my life, I don't intend to suddenly scrabble about doing things for Lenny now that she's decided she needs us.'

'I wouldn't even know where to start looking for Misha, though,' said Mairéad. 'And anyway, didn't he go and live in a monastery? Or become a hermit or something?'

Helen frowned. 'Oh yes, that does ring a bell. Well, I suppose she can come here. Maybe. If I've got a room.'

Mairéad sat back, relieved. That's what she had wanted Helen to say. Lenny had instructed the hospital to ring her, and not Helen, but she'd made the wrong call. She didn't want to sound to Bronwyn at the hospital like she didn't want to help, but she didn't.

She had no idea how to look after a child and wasn't interested in learning. Then, she needed to be present at IGS to make sure she wasn't relocated if she didn't want to be, while also making sure that Jenna didn't eat her lunch. Last of all, she didn't exactly feel like she owed Lenny any sort of favour. And this was a big one.

Cable House was a chaotic dump, sure, but Helen's lodgers would also make great companions for Sunshine. Mairéad set aside her own memories of living at Cable House, her needs and wants constantly coming second to the lodgers and Helen's activist groups. She reckoned that Lenny and Sunshine lived in a sort of commune situation anyway, with hippy types coming and going, so Sunshine would be used to that atmosphere.

'So *do* you have a room?'

Helen drew a martyred breath in through her nose and then out through her mouth. 'I suppose so,' she said. 'I think the music room will be empty for the summer.' Then, 'Don't *you* have a spare room?' she added suspiciously.

'No,' Mairéad lied. Her flat absolutely did have a spare room, but Helen had never seen her flat and almost certainly never would, so she could safely say anything she liked about it.

Her spare room was, in fact, lovely. She had decorated it as if she herself were coming to stay, with a charming iron bedstead, piles of antique blankets, a proper wardrobe, a desk and a lovely mirror she had found in a market, which had a little wooden bird perched at the top. She had decided that the mirror was so twee as to be fabulous. A small chest of drawers doubled as a bedside table. She'd decorated the room in her fantasy of a country bedroom, egged on by *The English Cottage*, with sprigged wallpaper, flounced blinds and dainty oil paintings on the wall of pretty maids tending to cows next to ponds. The woodwork was picked out in apple green and creamy yellow. The effect was charming and homely, if a bit incongruous with the rest of the flat, which was fresh and modern.

Well, This Is Awkward

'I'll help you get the music room set up and sorted out,' she said.

'And how is Sunshine going to get here?' said Helen. 'I can't drive to Wales and back.'

'I'll get her. Happily.' It would be a small price to pay, she thought, for not having to look after an entire child.

Why Cable House had a room that was called 'the music room' was a mystery. It had just always been 'the music room', even though no one in the family played so much as a tin whistle. These days, Mairéad could see that it was part of the same pretension that drove Helen to call their home 'Cable House'.

She left Helen typing at her laptop and climbed the shallow, wide stairs through the house and turned right down a corridor that led to the music room at the end. She passed a door standing open to what had been Lenny's room, her posters and black-painted walls now replaced by white and beige things. It was a chic and spotless bedroom, at odds with the rest of the crumbling Cable House. It smelled zingy, with linen curtains at the window and plants positioned in corners to hide the cracks in the paint. The bed was neatly made and there was the same style of flat-weave geometric-patterned rug on the floor as in Mairéad's house.

The next door along was to the music room. She knocked – you always needed to knock on doors at Cable House as you never knew who or what was going to be behind them – and when there was no answer she turned the handle.

The comparison with the bedroom she'd just seen was stark, like this was some sort of dream house where each room led into a separate world. There was junk everywhere, and dust. The sagging bed was piled with bulging black bin liners and there were boxes here and there, some opened, some not. An exercise bike that Mairéad had never seen before had abandoned clothes draped over the handlebars. On the floor there was a small printer, also very dusty, with a piece of paper, stuck at an angle, coming out of it. One half of a pair of curtains at the window was hanging off. It smelled strongly of cheap men's deodorant.

It was so typical of Cable House to have a disgusting junk room like this. Opposite the bedroom was a small bathroom that Sunshine would have to share with the adult lodgers.

'Okay,' said Mairéad, coming down the stairs. 'The music room will be fine, but it needs a really good clear-out.' She looked at her mother, who was typing away on her laptop.

'Mum? MUM!'

'Yes? What is it?' said Helen.

'The music room, it needs a clear-out.'

'Yes, yes. Not up to your standards, I'm sure.'

'What?' challenged Mairéad.

'Nothing!' said Helen, typing away. 'Oh, did you get my email about Yemen?'

Mairéad folded her arms and thought for a moment. 'Yes I did. Look, Sunshine can sleep on my sofa for a few days after she arrives, while we sort the room out. And when I say "we", I obviously mean "I".'

'Okay.' Helen shrugged.

There was the sound of a key turning in a door and some muted voices. Two people arrived in the room, bringing with them a strong smell of weed.

'Jethro! Maggie!' said Helen, her face lighting up. 'How was your trip?'

'Really great, thanks,' said Maggie. She wore striped baggy trousers tied with a tattered long red piece of fabric, and had a piercing in each nostril. Her matted hair had more fabric wound in it.

'Hey Helen, yeah, great to see you. Great trip. We were, like, wondering if it was cool to have some people round?'

said Jethro, who had an ear tunnel and was holding a bong. 'Kind of a gathering to celebrate being back?'

'Excellent! Of course!' said Helen, beaming. 'Wonderful, take whatever you need. Use the garden! It's a lovely evening.'

'That's amazing,' said Maggie dreamily. 'Thanks, H.' Maggie and Jethro wandered out, bumping into each other slightly.

Mairéad turned to her mother in disbelief. 'You're going to let them have a party, here? With a load of strangers?'

'They're not strangers. They're their friends. They're perfectly nice, leave them alone. Wonderful artists. And it's my house, can I remind you?' spluttered Helen. 'I don't come round to your flat and tell you what to do.'

Mairéad noticed that next to Helen's mission-control armchair there was a single photo: a picture of a pretty blonde woman in a graduation gown, holding a scroll. Mairéad knew without asking that this must be Roxana.

She held both hands up in defeat. 'Quite right,' she said.

It was a beautiful summer evening; robins were singing their heads off in the trees and pigeons cooed drunkenly into the balmy air. On a whim, Mairéad took a detour on her journey home to visit her father's grave, which was in a lovely old shambling graveyard tucked away next to the small church behind a playing field. She arrived at the same time as a whole load of Brownies who were meeting in the church hall, twittering away amongst themselves like a flock of little birds, holding bits of paper covered in scribbles. She wondered how old they were. Eleven, Sunshine's age?

She passed the church hall and then the church itself and walked around to the back. Gavin Alexander's gravestone was a rough granite thing, not shiny or bright white like the others. She hadn't even asked Helen or Lenny about the headstone. After the way they'd behaved while he was dying, she'd decided that neither of them got a say in it. She'd chosen the stone and the inscription: 'Gavin Alexander, 1942–2011'. And that was it. Dog daisies waved in a light breeze next to the headstone. On the other side bloomed a small foxglove. The effect was really rather lovely. She suddenly felt a stab of shame at not visiting more often. It was just so much easier not to.

A wren sang piercingly loudly from a hedge. She sat down next to the headstone, which wasn't something that she had ever done before. She was pleased that she was wearing her khaki trousers as the grass would surely have stained the seat of her white jeans. She heard the chatter and laughter of the Brownies' voices dancing through the evening light from the church hall to where she was sitting.

It had been a sunny evening, just like this, when Lenny had met Misha. Mairéad had spent the summer after her A levels working for a waitressing agency, with Dodie, saving money for a holiday. One evening, they'd done a job at a party in a museum – a big party, requiring almost all the barmen and waitresses at the agency.

Nathan had been one of the barmen: tall, loose and handsome with curly brown hair. He'd flirted with Dodie all night (or so Dodie claimed), and Dodie had nagged Mairéad to come back to his house after the event was over.

'I bet he's an amazing kisser,' Dodie whispered hotly. 'He looks like he is.' Dodie was obsessed with the quality of kissing back then. Quality kissing and being able to drive: those were her lines in the sand.

Nathan lived nearby and others from the agency were going. They met outside the museum, a gaggle of them, and Nathan led the way, a duffel bag slung over his shoulder and an earring – taken out for work – back in his ear.

His house was huge, grand and deserted, with wide, bare wooden boards on the floor and tall sash windows. His parents were away. One room was completely empty except for a huge African grey parrot on a stand. It said, 'Oh, fuck off,' when anyone opened the door.

They drank beers and listened to music, went out into the garden for cigarettes, crept closer and closer to the parrot. 'He bites,' said Nathan.

Around 2 a.m., Mairéad was tired and wanted to go. She called a cab and while she waited for it to arrive she tugged at Dodie to come with her, who refused.

In the morning, she wondered if she had completely imagined the parrot. She checked in with Dodie, who was back home and in a rage. After an evening of flirting and writhing about, Dodie had been put firmly in Nathan's sister's bed and left there, completely alone, for the rest of the night.

'My work shoes are at his house,' said Mairéad. 'In a grey bag in the kitchen. I need them, but I don't know how I'm going to get them back.'

'Oh, that's perfect,' said Dodie. 'Gives me an excuse to text him. Leave it with me.'

But boneheaded Nathan still didn't get it. Or he did get it, but he wasn't interested. All that happened was that two days later when Mairéad got home she found Nathan sitting in the garden with Lenny and a boy she didn't recognise. She paused at the French doors for a moment. Golden sunlight illuminated the three of them, and a bumblebee lumbered from flower to flower near where they were seated.

They were all three smoking, but Nathan looked bored, his head on his hand. The boy Mairéad didn't know was rangy, bone pale, with jet-black hair. He wore a faded black T-shirt that said 'True Earth' on it and camouflage combat trousers. He looked as though he might be wearing eyeliner and had nicotine-stained fingers. He and Lenny were talking expressively to each other and ignoring Nathan.

Nathan looked up and saw Mairéad. A great relief spread across his face.

'Hey,' he said. 'These are yours.' He picked up a grey bag containing the ugly black work shoes.

'Oh, that's so kind of you to bring them over. You didn't have to.'

'Yeah, no worries,' said Nathan. He jerked his head in the direction of the stranger boy. 'We love a mission, me and Misha.'

Lenny turned and shaded her eyes with her hand. 'It's actually "Misha and I",' she said. Misha laughed.

Mairéad was starting to feel uncomfortable where she was sitting, leaning against the cold, hard granite headstone. Soon it would be time to leave. She got up after allowing herself another few minutes to watch the golden summer light filter through the yew and birch trees dotted around the graveyard.

'Good to see you, Dad,' she said, and then felt stupid about talking to a gravestone. She added, in her head, 'You've found a great spot here.' She knew that he would be happy to be amongst all the flowers, within earshot of the Brownies' lively chatter. It really was a rather magical sound.

SIX

Mairéad got up early on Saturday morning, wanting to beat the weekend traffic out of town. Just before 8 a.m. saw her hitting the button on her black convertible BMW to send the roof trundling backwards. She was wearing a casual outfit of jeans and a T-shirt, accessorised with her second-best sunglasses and a low-key bag. She didn't want to arrive at the hospital looking too absurdly 'London'.

As she drove, London faded away, jagged concrete monoliths giving way to low green vistas, and she was soon out in the open countryside, pounding up the M1 towards Northampton. She stopped to put the roof of the car back up, as the roaring wind on the motorway was starting to give her a headache, and for petrol. She passed a mother with two children, a girl and a boy, coming out of WHSmith. Each child held a magazine in both hands, gazing adoringly at the front.

A gift. That's what a nice aunt would do, bring Sunshine a gift. She walked up and down the aisles, regarding the garish plush toys, books and comics aimed at children. What would she have been excited by when she was eleven? She gazed, unseeing, at a Polly Pocket magazine.

There had been a tiny red cosmetics compact from her own aunt, one Christmas. That had been an infinitely treasured item, mostly because it had annoyed Helen so much: Helen, who didn't so much as shave her armpits and ranted about deodorant causing breast cancer. The compact had two tiny eyeshadows, a blusher and, most excitingly, two little lipsticks in a drawer that pulled out underneath, complete with a doll-sized brush. The tang of the lipstick wax was intoxicating. Both she and Lenny had received a compact and Lenny had tossed hers aside, unimpressed, but Mairéad had loved hers. If she tried hard, she could still faintly conjure in her mind the crayon scent of it.

She reached for a packet of felt-tip pens, an exercise book and a packet of puffy stickers featuring suns, moons and rainbows. What child wasn't excited by a brand-new pack of felt-tip pens? Then she got back on the road, chewing up the miles to Rugby, then onto the M6 towards Coventry.

The weather was stunning, the white-hot sun beat down hour after hour. The motorway central reservations gleamed with grasses, poppies and daisies. The sidings were bursting with hawthorn trees and buddleias and she drove past wide-open fields with their crops waving in the breeze. How long had it been since she'd been in the countryside? A year, perhaps.

She'd last gone with an ex, Josh. They'd met on Hinge, with Josh conforming to every single one of Mairéad's stipulated preferences. They both, in theory, liked Nature, Reading Books, Cooking and Movies. The kissing was fine. After three months of dating, she suggested to him that they make a long weekend of a wedding she had been invited to, in Rye. She spent hours choosing a rental cottage and dreaming up romantic activities for them either side of the main event. She was trying to mollify him; at first he'd been impressed by how busy and sociable Mairéad was, but he soon grew tired of it. He was only three years younger than her but she slipped into a power role and he, in turn, grew childish and sullen.

Well, This Is Awkward

Even though she had fussed over the details of the weekend specifically in order to amuse Josh, he had taken no interest in the plans, other than saying, 'Sounds good,' every now and again. He kept asking her for the dates of the weekend until she finally snapped and said, 'Can you please make a note of them? I've told you six times now.'

As the Rye weekend drew closer, she had been frantic to cancel the whole thing, but it would have looked so dramatic and rather cussed.

So, grimly, she stuck to the plans. They ground through the weekend, Josh glued to his phone and wanting to laze about in bed reading the papers and complaining about the coffee machine rather than do any of the wholesome countryside activities (Nature!) Mairéad had researched, planned and organised. At the wedding, Mairéad was overly bright and forced, in order to make up for Josh's uninterested, slack energy. Throughout the entire unhappy two days, she felt as though she were heaving a bag filled with heavy, misshapen objects up a hill. It was all just no good. The Deal Breaker ransom note loomed and it said 'sTRoppY aNd Sulks'. And on top of everything, he was a bit sneery about the time and effort she had put into the refurbishment of her flat. He often put the glasses away on the mug shelf and vice versa in a way that she was convinced was on purpose, to make a mockery of it all.

Josh had left her life as seamlessly as he'd entered it. It had been remarkably easy to get rid of him; she had simply not replied to his last message. As the gap between the present moment and their last communication became ever longer, she'd begun to think about how she had woven, on her own, her entire relationship with Josh. Without her frantically spinning her spinning wheel, the whole thing had unravelled easily, silently, quickly.

She'd declared to Cass that she would no longer be using

dating apps. The interests and preferences were arbitrary and stupid, and no more guaranteed a 'good match' than a wild stab in the dark, which was what most Hinge dates made Mairéad want to do by 9 p.m.

Before Josh there had been Eddie, who had turned out to be a pathological liar. Before Eddie, Adam – lovely, sweet Adam who had been so great but was just too desperate to turn Mairéad into some sort of pony-loving Sloane, even though he himself was from a down-to-earth Northern family. 'sOciaL CLimBER!' screamed the Deal Breaker ransom note. He eventually got married to a very blonde girl who literally did do something with racehorses, and Mairéad genuinely hoped that they were both very happy.

This was the thing about children, as it appeared to Mairéad: everyone knows about 'the window' when it comes to children, but it's not the window you think it is. It's not about 'meeting Mr Right', or fertility, or any of that. It's about the point at which you suddenly know far too much about parenthood. When you're twenty-seven or twenty-nine you've got no clue about what children are really like. You're still broadly a child yourself. But if you haven't had children by then and start seeing other people you know having children and glimpse the crushing toll it takes on all aspects of their lives, then, well. That's a different matter. The idea of 'Mr Right' is neither here nor there once you've seen several friends' 'Mr Rights' turn into Mr Wrong as soon as there's a nappy to change or a toddler to get dressed.

All men, once they had children, seemed to turn into the same man. The same half-blind, deaf, chaotic, irritable, snoring, lazy man. Even Dodie's husband, Miles, who seemed to Mairéad like a charming, long-suffering gent, was the perpetrator (according to Dodie) of unforgivable marital crimes. 'The most important thing to have if you want to stay married,' Dodie said, 'is a bad memory.'

Well, This Is Awkward

In order to have children, thought Mairéad, you have to tell yourself a story that you will be different. Your husband will be different. It will all be different. But when you see everyone around you go into the children tunnel and emerge the other side with the same story, the same problems, the same woes and gripes, you realise that it's not different for anyone. No one gets away with it.

She fell into such a reverie about all this that she didn't even notice that she was now on smaller, more winding roads. At about noon she pulled into a little lane by a gate and got out of the car. She stretched and felt the warm breeze ruffle her crumpled clothes, then hung over a five-bar gate, gazing at a lush green field full of cows. Looking at her satnav, she found that she was only forty-five minutes away from Castell Cerys Hospital. A lurch of nervous apprehension sucked at her stomach.

She spent the last part of the journey practising greeting Lenny in her head – and Sunshine. 'Hey, you must be Sunshine, hi. I'm your Auntie Mairéad.' The name Sunshine conjured up images of a neat little blonde girl, wearing a lot of yellow, but she was pretty sure that the toddler she'd met had had the resolute dark brown curly hair of all the Alexanders.

She wound through villages and little towns with buildings painted pink, yellow and green, sometimes with bunting stretched either side of high streets, fluttering merrily. Castell Cerys Memorial Hospital did not look like any London hospital she had ever seen; it resembled a charming old Welsh stone house with a modern extension tacked onto the back.

The reception area was very quiet, with only an elderly lady in a voluminous flowery dress with a walking stick, slowly making her way across the floor. A nurse in a blue uniform with a watch on the lapel and shiny brown hair sat behind a desk.

'Hello?'

'Hi, love, how can I help?' said the lady in a strong Welsh accent.

'Are you Bronwyn, by any chance?'

'I'm Bethan – it's Bronnie's day off,' said Bethan.

'Oh, right. I'm Mairéad. I'm here to collect Sunshine Alexander. I'm Lenny Alexander's sister.'

'Oh o'course,' said Bethan. 'Follow me.'

Their shoes squeaked along the floor as they went past a humming vending machine, down a corridor and past a lift that had an out of order sign on it. Mairéad started feeling really quite ill with nerves at the prospect of seeing Lenny and Sunshine for the first time in so many years.

'Has my sister been behaving herself? No rants about antibiotics?'

'Nothing like that,' said Bethan. 'Or not that I know of, anyway.'

'How long do you think she'll be here for?'

'It depends how she gets on,' said Bethan. 'She's broken her leg just below the knee and she has a fractured cheekbone. We're not totally sure about the damage to her head so we're keeping her in just to be sure. We'd hope to see her up and about in a fortnight? But we'll have to see.'

Bethan knocked and pushed open the door. Lenny was lying on a bed with her leg bandaged and balanced on a pillow. A messy camp bed with sheets and a mauve hospital-issue blanket in disarray was next to it. The head end of the hospital bed was tilted up and Lenny's mass of dark curly hair fell about her shoulders. She turned and tilted up one corner of her mouth. The right side of her face was bandaged, leaving only her eye clear, but purple bruises leaked across her face from under the material. Her right arm was also covered in bandages. Mairéad stopped herself from putting a hand to her mouth in horror.

'I can only smile on this side,' said Lenny. 'Hurts too much the other side.'

Well, This Is Awkward

'What *happened*?'

Bethan brought a chair over and Mairéad collapsed into it.

'The pig trailer fell on me,' said Lenny, a little sloppily. A drip snaked into the back of her left hand. 'We had a thunderstorm and it was late and dark. Very wet and slippery. I'd just got the pigs away and I fell and somehow pulled the trailer over and it landed on me.'

Mairéad followed Lenny's gaze over her shoulder and into a corner. She turned to see a small figure she had not noticed before. It was curled up in an armchair with a fuzzy royal blue cover, reading a thick paperback and sucking its thumb.

Sunshine. She didn't look up. She was wearing a striped hoodie with the hood up and baggy jogging bottoms. Curly dark hair escaped from underneath the hood, the shade and type that Mairéad's own hair would be if it wasn't chemically straightened every six weeks and dyed a carefully nonchalant blonde. Sunshine's feet were bare and dirty. A pair of squashed and filthy trainers lay discarded on the floor beside the chair, along with a pair of odd socks.

'Sunny? Sunny?' Lenny called Sunny's name a few times.

Sunny looked up and pulled her thumb out of her mouth.

'Wuh?' she said.

'This is your Auntie Mairéad,' said Lenny.

'Okay,' said Sunny vaguely and went back to her book. She slipped her thumb back into her mouth.

'I'll leave you all to chat, then,' said Bethan. 'Mairéad, there's just some paperwork you need to fill in before you leave.'

'Thank you for taking her,' said Lenny, reaching out and grabbing Mairéad's hand. Sudden physical contact was so out of character for Lenny that Mairéad knew instantly that whatever was coming through that drip was making her high as a kite. 'She's no trouble. She just wants to read.' Lenny squeezed her eyes shut and then opened just one, looking like she was trying to focus on something out of the window. 'I think maybe there's something in what they're giving me,' she confirmed, conspiratorially. She wiggled her hand with the drip in it. 'Can't think straight. Need to get out of here.'

Mairéad turned again to look at Sunny. Slender, hunched and pale. The resemblance to the entire Alexander family was clear. Mairéad could see even from where she was sitting that Sunny had inherited her grandfather's long feet, although it was doubtful that Gavin Alexander's feet had ever been that dirty. Sunny turned a page in her book using a long forefinger topped with a jagged, dirty nail.

'I wish, I just wish we had the kind of mother who might be able to look after her own grandchild,' Lenny continued. 'But of course she can't. Doesn't have a clue. There's nowhere else for her. Misha – absolutely not. The local farmer is a nice guy but he's a single bloke. No way he can look after a kid for long. I know that you're angry with me about… about…' Lenny trailed off. 'It's only for a bit. I'll get out of here as quick as I can.'

'I'll take care of Sunny,' said Mairéad, brushing aside whatever it was that Lenny wanted to say, not wanting to address the topic she was hinting at. She hoped her voice was soothing yet confident. 'I promise.'

'I'll get myself out of here,' said Lenny. 'I won't let them poison me with their shit.'

'Okay, yes. No poisoning. It'll be all right. All right?'

Sunny had no belongings with her, so Lenny gave Mairéad directions to the cabin, where they would be able to pick up a few things.

'Sunny…' said Lenny in that quiet, patient tone again.

'Yeah?' said Sunny, finally.

'You're going with Auntie Mairéad now.'

'Who?' said Sunny.

'Auntie Mairéad, this is Auntie Mairéad,' said Lenny. 'Remember? You're going to go with her to the cabin and

Well, This Is Awkward

then to London. She'll look after you for a bit and then you'll come back to me, okay? Evan is going to look after Dennis and Minnie. I've got my phone now, so you can call me.' Lenny patted around on a table for a battered and scratched Nokia.

'Is it still the same number?' said Mairéad, checking the contacts on her phone. 'Ending five nine five?'

'Yeah, same as always,' said Lenny.

Sunny nodded. 'Okay, Mum,' she said, then got up and started walking to the door, barefoot.

'Shall we get your shoes on?' Mairéad asked.

'Oh yeah.' Sunny walked back to the disgusting shoes and jammed her feet into them.

'How about the socks?'

Sunny turned and looked at the socks, lying on the floor. Mairéad looked at the socks, too. Sunny looked from Mairéad to her mother to the socks and back again.

'Oh, well. I'll just…' Mairéad picked up the socks and put them in her pocket.

Sunny went to give her mother an awkward hug and then stood by the door, waiting, her book tucked under her arm.

It was strange to walk around Lenny's cabin. So this was where she had been all this time. The view was beautiful, of undulating land rolling to the sea, which was about 5 miles away. It was just visible in the far distance, the tips of the waves crested with white. The day had grown uncomfortably warm but a brisk breeze whisked through and around the cabin, setting the daisies and wildflowers growing around the porch dipping and dancing.

The pigsty was about 50 metres away from the cabin, built from stone, with a wooden roof covered in creosote. Next to it was a strip of allotment, a riot of thick green tangled vegetable plants and vibrant nasturtium flowers growing up a tepee of bamboo canes. Sunny collected the key, which was hanging in a cupboard cut into the wooden planks that made up the walls of the cabin – when closed, it was invisible save for a small hole that served as a handle.

A sign to the left of the door said, 'Llechwedd'.

Mairéad attempted to pronounce it. 'Leckwed,' she said.

'Hhlechweth,' said Sunny, expertly.

'Does that mean something?'

'Hillside,' Sunny said.

'Oh, do you speak Welsh?'

'No.'

The cabin smelled of freshly chopped wood and woodsmoke and was lit by large, thick picture windows. Considering Sunny's wild appearance, Mairéad had rather dreaded what she would find in the home, but it was only well used and a little shabby. The main living area had a large broken-looking sofa covered in blankets and throws, an armchair and a log burner. There was a wooden desk in the corner with a chair pushed in and Lenny's laptop resting on top.

'Okay, just thinking about what you'll need.' Mairéad looked around for a bag and found a khaki army rucksack hanging on the back of the desk chair. There was nothing inside except, at the bottom, a scrunch of black woollen material. She pulled it out and then stretched it this way and that to work out what it was: a black balaclava. She looked at it, horrified. Then she folded it and placed it on the desk.

Sunny stood in the middle of the cabin and looked at Mairéad blankly.

'Where do you keep your clothes?'

'Umm...' Sunshine frowned. 'I don't know. Mum just gives them to me.'

'Okay. Well, let's just have a look around, then. I'm sure Mum won't mind.'

She found some small underwear on a drying line and a T-shirt she concluded must be Sunny's. Outside, at a deep

Well, This Is Awkward

stone basin, there was a toothbrush and some paste. What else did an eleven-year-old need?

'Is there anything else you want to take?' said Mairéad.

Sunny held up a bunch of pink and white flowery material that had a distinctly greyish tinge. 'My blanket,' she said.

'Oh yes, good. Don't forget your blanket.'

'I like it because it's so soft. Feel.'

Sunny held out the blanket and Mairéad plucked a bit of it between her fingers. 'Very soft,' she agreed.

She wandered around the cabin, listening to the tread of her footsteps on the floorboards in the quiet, feeling faintly dazed. She rummaged about in Lenny's desk and in a drawer came across Sunny's passport, which was together with Lenny's. Mairéad put it in the bag. Then she slipped the balaclava off the surface of the desk and into the drawer.

She checked around the rest of the cabin, not really knowing what she was looking for, finding herself just wanting to snoop but feeling self-conscious because Sunny was standing there. She went into the bedroom. There were two single, unmade beds in wooden frames and another log burner. She found some musty-smelling pyjamas scrumpled up on a bed but left them where they were.

She stopped looking, concluding that she wasn't finding very much to take with them simply because Lenny and Sunny didn't have very much.

'Right,' she said, finally.

Sunny took her thumb out of her mouth and said, 'Do you want to see the pigs?'

'Sure!'

Mairéad followed Sunny out of the back door of the cabin, past a covered outdoor kitchen. A few pieces of enamel crockery and a huge black kettle sat on a ledge. She looked back and saw Lenny's outdoor terrace. It had been fitted with flagstones and was shaded by a lush green plant that was climbing up a wooden pergola. Under the pergola was a wooden table and some chairs, and to the side there was a fire pit with a grill rack resting on top.

Sunny walked rather quickly with her head bowed. As they approached the sty, Mairéad heard grunting and rustling. She was surprised at how dainty the pigs were. Knee-high to an adult, the two Tamworth pigs were clearly excited to see Sunny and one heaved itself up on the side of the sty. Sunny stuck her thumb in her mouth and gazed at the pig, petting its head as it grunted and closed its eyes. Mairéad recoiled as she thought about Sunny petting the pig with her hand and then putting her thumb directly into her mouth.

Mairéad looked around, wondering where the accident had happened. She saw what must be Lenny's car – a very muddy and dented SUV – and the pig trailer hooked to the back of it. But where had it fallen? Having seen the balaclava, she was now suspicious. She imagined the night. Dark, wild and rainy – a summer-night thunderstorm. Lenny struggling with the trailer, a critical loss of grip of the wheels on the grass and then a terrible, inexorable keeling-over of metal and rubber. But was that what had happened?

'Where did the accident happen?'
'What accident?' said Sunny.
'With Mummy – the trailer.'
'I don't know.'
'What's down there?'
'Evan. The farmer,' said Sunny.
'Do you see Evan much?'
'Sometimes he comes for dinner with us.' Sunny talked around the thumb in her mouth, and addressed the pig. 'He's nice. He can juggle.'

They stood for a while longer, looking at the pigs, Sunny occasionally crooning to the animals and stroking their hairy ears.

Well, This Is Awkward

'Will Evan look after Dennis and Minnie while you're away?' Mairéad didn't know why she was asking this when she already knew the answer.

Sunny nodded her head, her thumb still in her mouth.

Mairéad looked about herself, at the trailer, at the pigsty.

'I'm just going back inside for a minute.'

Sunny didn't reply.

Lenny answered her mobile after many rings.

'What really happened? I know a trailer didn't fall on you,' said Mairéad.

'This line isn't secure,' said Lenny.

The horror violins were back, but now they were being plucked at *pizzicato*, the kind of sound effect you get in a film when the star is about to be attacked by spiders.

'Does Sunny know?'

'No,' said Lenny. 'Don't tell her. It wasn't meant to go wrong.'

'It's never *meant* to go wrong.'

She left the cabin, locked up and went to find Sunny.

'We'd better make a move. Quite a long drive back. Let's go, babe.'

Sunny turned and screwed up her face in disgust. 'Babe,' she said. 'Why did you call me that?'

'Oh, I... Nothing. I mean, it's what I call the young people at work,' Mairéad finished, lamely.

Sunny said nothing, but stopped petting the pig, put her hand into her hoodie's joey pocket and turned back towards the cabin. Mairéad cleared her throat in embarrassment and started patting around her, making sure she had everything that she needed for the journey home.

She got in the car and felt angry. Angry that Lenny was so selfish and reckless. Angry that she was so dumb as to think that she could carry on like she was nineteen, when she was in fact a fully adult woman and had a child to look after. But by the second hour of the drive back to London, Mairéad was fantasising about one thing only and that was getting Sunny into a nice, hot, scented bath. Or perhaps a shower. Hell, a good blast with a garden hose would do. She also fantasised as she drove about tossing Sunny's clothes into the nearest incinerator. In the open air it hadn't been obvious quite how smelly Sunny was, but in the confines of a car it turned out that she was very smelly indeed. It was a combination of body odour, acrid smoke and some other indefinable thing; a sort of terrible barnyardy smell, which must be from the pigs.

Mairéad turned the air conditioning up, in order to combat the stench. Sunny said nothing but pulled her hoodie around her and scrunched up tighter as she read her book in silent protest. Whenever the car came to a stop at lights or in a tailback, Mairéad opened all the windows wide, saying, 'I do love a bit of fresh air from time to time.'

When they stopped at a service station for a snack, Sunny looked at the array of packets and said, 'I don't know what any of this is.'

Back in the car Sunny said, 'You shouldn't use plastic bottles,' staring at a bottle of water in the footwell.

Mairéad opened her mouth to say something but she couldn't think what.

'You're right,' she said eventually.

At one point, Sunny nodded off. Mairéad only noticed because her book fell out of her hand and landed with a rippling thud in the footwell. As they entered the outskirts of London, and the concrete monoliths crowded back into the sky and people filled the streets on this warm and sunny early evening, she felt a mounting dread of the task ahead of her.

As they neared home, however, she found she was able to be genuinely excited about getting Sunny in the bath – like bringing a found object home and being curious to clean it up and examine its true potential. Entering the flat, she felt as if she had been gone for days, when in fact it was only

8 p.m. on the day she'd left. She felt slightly dizzy and motorway-drunk from the sheer amount of driving. She went gratefully to the kettle. Tea, tea, tea. Please some tea.

'Would you like a cup of tea?' she said to Sunny, who lurked in the doorway, her hoodie firmly pulled up. Sunny gave her head a small, frenzied, insistent shake.

'Okay, come in. Please. This is your home too now. At least for a bit. Try to relax.'

Sunny stuck her thumb in her mouth and shuffled in with her head slightly bowed.

'This is your room,' said Mairéad, pushing open the door to the spare room proudly. Comparing it with the practical and honest simplicity of Lenny's cabin, with its magnificent views of the sea and priceless aspect onto glorious countryside, Mairéad was surprised to find that the spare room of which she had been so proud appeared to her now, starkly, like the most hideous pastiche. A grotesque, ersatz copy with its dead air. It was like comparing a mural of an Italian palazzo painted on the wall of a suburban spa pool with the real thing. Her smile briefly faded but she pasted it back on.

Sunny sat down on the edge of the cosy bed, her army green rucksack still on her shoulders. She shucked off her trainers.

'I got you these,' said Mairéad, setting the book, pens and stickers down on the chest of drawers.

Sunny didn't look up, but sat with her head bent, and after a few seconds Mairéad noticed a tear dripping onto her trousers.

'Oh dear,' she said, alarmed. She crouched down next to her and patted Sunny's knee. 'It must be very upsetting,' she said.

Sunny said nothing, just wiped her face.

Mairéad sat down next to her on the bed and put her arm round Sunny, who stiffened and then gradually slid out of Mairéad's embrace.

Embarrassed, Mairéad got up and lingered in the doorway awkwardly.

'Don't worry. We'll have you back to Mum in no time. Let's send her a message, shall we? Let's say we've arrived and you're fine. Do you want to send it? No? Okay, I'll do it.' Mairéad got out her phone and spoke as she typed.

'Arrived safely exclamation mark hope you are well love Sunny and Mairéad ex ex. There.'

Sunny still said nothing.

'How about a friend. Do you have a friend we can text, just to say hi?'

Sunny shrugged.

'You know what always cheers me up?'

'What?' said Sunny.

'A nice hot bath.'

'We have showers.'

'Well, I've got a shower here too, but a bath is nicer. It's like going for a nice warm swim. There's something really great about a bath. Why don't you just come and have a look at it? If you don't like the look of it, you can have a shower instead.'

'I don't really feel like it,' said Sunny.

She didn't understand. At no point at any moment did Mairéad not quite fancy a bath. And how could Sunny not badly *want* a bath? How could she stand being so profoundly filthy and smelly? Now Mairéad was close to her, she could see how incredibly grimy Sunny was, the black dirt under her fingernails, her greyish face.

'Just come and have a *look* at the bath. It's completely private – you'll be able to shut the door and even lock it if you like.'

There was a long pause.

'Okay then,' said Sunny.

She showed Sunny the bathroom, with its claw-foot bath, its expanse of marble, pinks, greens and golds, huge rainfall

Well, This Is Awkward

shower and pristine ceramic bottles of product. It was the jewel in the crown of her refurbishment of the flat.

Mairéad waited for Sunny to say, 'Wow!' but she didn't.

'So,' she said, crushed at Sunny's lack of appreciation for her interior decorating skills, 'this is the bath, and look – I've even got some bubble bath.'

Sunny gave another little insistent shake of her head. 'Soap is really bad for you,' she said. 'It gives you eczema.'

'Oh, okay,' said Mairéad, her hopes of getting Sunny really clean and watching muddy bubbles drain down the plughole dashed. 'No bubbles then. But you're okay with the bath?'

Sunny shrugged, which she took as a yes.

'Pop back to your room and take off the bag and your hoodie, and I'll run the bath for you.'

Mairéad bustled around, running the bath and fetching a nail brush and some nail clippers. She was going to get those awful witch nails off Sunny if it was the last thing she did. She waited for a while but there was no Sunny. She sat on a charming little wooden stool that she'd found in an antiques market and waited a bit more. After a good five minutes, which is quite a long time when you're just sitting on a charming wooden stool not doing anything else, she went back to the guest room to investigate and found Sunny sitting on her bed, reading her book and sucking her thumb.

She felt a small prick of irritation. What was up with this kid? She was reading *Watership Down*, so she couldn't be stupid. Why was she so vague and forgetful?

'Hey, Sunny,' she said brightly. 'How about getting that stuff off and coming for a bath?'

'Oh yeah.' Sunny finally shrugged off the rucksack.

'Great. And the hoodie. Brill. Right, off to the bathroom now.' She stopped herself from adding a brisk, 'Chop-chop.'

Sunny was a pitiful figure. She was tall, only a few inches shorter than Mairéad, slender and pale, and her hopelessly dirty clothes looked even more shabby in the smart flat. She wore a faded olive green T-shirt, which was on the small side, and her navy joggers were stained. She stooped, her shoulders rounded. Mairéad and Sunny stood in the steamy bathroom as the bath filled. Mairéad held up the nail brush. 'This is for your fingernails, okay? And toenails – give them a good old scrub. This flannel is for your face and under your arms. Get your hair under the water and give it a good rinse?'

'Okay,' said Sunny.

Mairéad left the bathroom with little confidence that Sunny would be able to follow any of her instructions. Talking to her felt like whispering into a howling gale. She went to the guest room and picked up Sunny's discarded hoodie and trainers with a thumb and forefinger. She placed the foul trainers outside on her balcony and put the hoodie in the washing machine.

She was about to set off to find a pair of her pyjamas that might fit Sunny when she had another thought. She turned on her heel, headed smartly to the kitchen and made herself a single-measure gin and tonic. She took a long, deep, reverential sip.

'How are you getting on in there?' she said through the bathroom door after another long five minutes.

'Don't come in!' barked Sunny.

'Wouldn't dream of it. Are you using the nail brush to get your hands and feet clean?'

'Yeah,' said Sunny after a pause. There was some splashing about.

'And give your hair a good rinse. And wash your face with the flannel.'

''Kay,' said Sunny.

Mairéad took another huge slug of her gin and tonic and then went to find the pyjamas. She rootled out a slim-fitting pair that were also childishly covered in moons and stars – some whimsical Anthropologie purchase, no doubt. She

Well, This Is Awkward

left them on Sunny's bed. She picked up the green army rucksack and left that out on the balcony, too, then she removed the meagre underthings and put them in the washing machine along with the hoodie. She put the passport with her own, in her desk, looking briefly at it before tucking it away: Sunny must have been about five or six when the picture was taken and her surname was listed as 'Alexander'.

Sunny said something inaudible from the bathroom.

'What?'

'I said, "Can I come out now?"'

'Yes, sure. There are towels on the rail there. I've put some PJs on your bed. Leave your clothes on the floor.'

She heard Sunny come out of the bath and rummage for a towel. She went to the kitchen and started looking about for what they might have for dinner. Out of the corner of her eye, she saw Sunny, wrapped in a towel, dart from the bathroom to her bedroom and shut the door. Mairéad hurried back to the bathroom and goggled at the brown water that Sunny had left behind. Grimacing, she plucked at the bathplug chain to release the fouled water, waited for it to drain and then blasted the bath with the hand-held shower on full and very hot to rinse out the grit that Sunny had left behind. She frowned as she found that even hot, blasting water would not remove a ring of grime from where the waterline had been. She rummaged in a cupboard for a cloth and cleaner and scrubbed at the dirt. Hot, sweaty and annoyed, she gave the bath a final rinse.

Then, feeling wasteful, she ran another bath for herself, adding a few drops of her most expensive bath oil, a luscious zingy mixture of eucalyptus and lime. She picked up Sunny's soiled clothes and added them to the washing machine. Then she added washing powder and then, with another prick of guilt, set the machine to 90°C when she usually washed everything at 30°C, like a good citizen. She went back to the kitchen and had another slug of the gin and tonic. The gin was starting to work, now, and she was feeling like things might be okay.

She kept looking through her cupboards for something that they could both eat, and alighted on pasta with a bottled sauce that she didn't remember buying. Then she found some bread and cheese and considered cheese on toast. She had not eaten cheese on toast for probably fourteen years. She began to understand how totally unprepared she was for this whole situation.

She called from the kitchen, 'How are those PJs?'

'Um, fine I think,' said Sunny. 'Can I have my hoodie back?'

'Oh, it's just in the wash. I'll get you another.'

She went to her cupboards and pulled out a navy hoodie that said 'NYC' on it. She went to knock on Sunny's door. Sunny opened it a crack and then stuck a skinny arm through and groped for the hoodie, then closed the door again.

'I didn't know what you like eating so I thought we could have some pasta? Or perhaps cheese on toast?'

Sunny opened the door. Her hair was still soaking wet, dripping directly onto the shoulders of the hoodie, and she hadn't done a totally thorough job of cleaning her face, with a tidemark of grime still evident on her neck and near her hairline.

'Oh…'

'What?' said Sunny defensively.

'No, nothing. Let's just dry your hair a little, otherwise it will make your hoodie wet and that won't be nice, will it? Wearing a wet sweater.'

She picked up the towel from where it had been dropped on the floor and approached Sunny, who shied away like a horse.

'What are you doing?' she barked, holding up two hands.

'Just drying your hair a bit. It won't hurt. Just get a bit of the water out.'

'Okay,' said Sunny warily.

Mairéad patted at Sunny's shiny wet curls. Very gently, she thought, but Sunny shrieked and jerked this way and that. 'Ow!' she shouted. 'Stop it!' She aimed a very hard smack at Mairéad's arm. She did not hold back any of her strength in the smack and it hurt.

'Ow!' exclaimed Mairéad. 'Bloody hell. Woah. What was that for?'

'You pulled my hair,' snapped Sunny. 'Just don't *touch* me.'

She stood square, scowling. There was no sound in the flat except for the thundering of the bathwater into the tub. They glared at each other for a bit. Then Sunny sniffed the air and her expression changed completely.

'What's that smell?' she said.

Mairéad inhaled thoughtfully. 'Oh, that's just my bath oil.'

'It's *amazing*,' breathed Sunny intensely. 'I've got to smell it.' She barged past and made for the bathroom. Mairéad arrived at the doorway of the bathroom to find Sunny with her hands resting on the side of the tub, breathing in the scented air.

'Next time I have a bath, can it smell like this?'

'Yes, of course. And it's an oil, not even soap. So no risk of eczema,' she said, like a cheery salesperson, feeling faintly cowed at ingratiating herself with the violent Sunny, but seeing no other way to be. Sunny didn't reply, she just sniffed deeply at the steam rising off the bath.

Once Mairéad had bathed and got dressed again in some pale pink sweatpants and a white T-shirt, she placed a plate of cheese on toast and a glass of water in front of Sunny and sat down opposite her at the kitchen table with her own slice.

Sunny regarded the toast with a glum face, then bent close to it and sniffed it. She picked it up gingerly – Mairéad noted with huge satisfaction that Sunny's fingernails were almost entirely clean, if not yet trimmed – sniffed it a bit more and then delicately nibbled one corner of it and rolled the morsel around her mouth, smacking her lips together and narrowing her eyes. She dibbled her lips and tongue together for a while, looking up and away to the left, as if trying to identify a mysterious flavour.

'Does Mum give you cheese on toast?'

'Sometimes, but the bread is different.'

'Is the toast… okay?' said Mairéad, like a sickly praise junkie, but also genuinely desperate to know if the toast *was* okay.

'It's fine. I'm very hungry, though, so my standards are possibly lower.'

Mairéad let out a little huff of laughter at this bald statement. Sunny gave her an odd look. She ate her toast painfully slowly, silently getting up in the middle of eating to fetch her book and returning, equally silently, to her toast. She held the book open against the table with one hand and ate her toast with the other, ignoring Mairéad entirely. Mairéad didn't know what to make of this, so she just ate and thought about how much she wanted to dunk Sunny back in the bath and really get those remaining rings of grime off her neck, really properly wash her hair, get some deodorant on her, clip all her nails. It was almost a physical itch. But after the hair-drying freak-out, she was reluctant to get too close.

'What time do you go to bed?'

There was no reply; Sunny just kept on reading.

'Sunny?'

'Sunny?'

'Wuh?'

'Did you not hear what I said?'

'What did you say?'

'I said, "What time do you go to bed?"'

'Oh, right. I dunno. Whenever we've finished for the day. I go to bed same time Mum does.'

'And how do you go to bed? Do you have a...' Mairéad wondered what she was trying to ask. 'Do you have a routine?'

Sunny shrugged. 'I read until I feel sleepy.'

'All right, then. Well, let's get your teeth brushed and tuck you in. It's pretty late and it's been a long day. It must have been hard to sleep in the hospital, too.'

'Not really,' said Sunny.

Mairéad went to fetch Sunny's toothbrush and paste. The toothbrush was a bamboo thing with hopelessly soft, splayed bristles.

Mairéad mentally added 'toothbrush' to the list of things she wanted to buy for Sunny.

'Are you going to watch me brush my teeth?' said Sunny, standing at the sink and looking at Mairéad sideways.

'No, no, of course not.'

Afterwards, Sunny got into bed and Mairéad concealed a shudder at her gnarly toenails as she pushed her legs down into the sweet-smelling linen sheets.

'I don't think you need this,' she said, taking off the quilted, squashy eiderdown. 'Bit hot for it.'

Sunny sank into the clean, crisp pillows and held her book against her chest, a finger marking her place. She had her blanket tucked under her arm.

'Your house is nice,' said Sunny, sombrely. 'It smells nice.'

'Oh, good,' said Mairéad, sitting on the side of the bed. A yellowish beam of light bloomed in her chest at the compliment. 'It's more a flat than a house, but whatever. Thanks. I'm glad to hear that.' In films, she knew, tucking-in time was the moment that tender words were spoken between grown-ups and children. She seized her chance.

'I'm sorry you're away from Mum. This must all be really new and confusing. But like I said, we'll have you back to her in no time.'

Sunny regarded her for a few seconds. 'Sure,' she said, raising her book to her face.

Mairéad blinked. 'Well. Night, then,' she said.

'Yup,' said Sunny.

Mairéad walked to her bedroom, although it felt like she was crawling on her hands and knees. She had never, not even wildly hungover or after a three-day wedding, felt so physically exhausted and mentally wrung out. Was it the long day? The driving? The gin? All that cheese she had eaten, which was probably now sitting in a plasticised lump in her gut? Was it the mental stress of having to ESP the wants and needs of a strange child? How did parents do it? How?

She reached her bed and allowed herself to rigidly face-plant onto it. At least it was the end of the day. They were both bathed, fed, teeth-brushed and ready for bed. She only had to pull back the covers and insert herself between the sheets. She didn't even want to think what time it was, even though it was probably only about 10 p.m.

Just as she considered all this, she heard the washing machine's insistent 'I'm finished!' bleep.

'What's that noise?' cried Sunny.

'Nothing!' called Mairéad, slithering off the bed and onto the floor, crawling a few paces before standing up. 'Just the washing machine, turning it off now, coming…'

She turned off the washing machine and opened its round porthole door, then hauled out Sunny's things and dropped them into a laundry basket. Then she took them to the airing cupboard and stood by it. She flapped out the striped hoodie, the joggers and the underwear to straighten them before hanging them up neatly to dry in the natty little space-saving pullout drying space she had designed herself. The energy-gobbling tumble drier was for emergencies only.

As she made her way back to her bedroom, she heard footsteps coming from Sunny's room. Thump, thump, thump, thump. Thump, thump, thump, thump. Mairéad pressed the pads of her fingers against her aching eyes and went to Sunny's room to find her walking in tight circles around the charming small Turkish rug that was from the same antiques market as the charming wooden bathroom stool.

'What are you doing?'

Sunny pulled her thumb out of her mouth. 'I'm pacing.'

'Why?'

'Errr,' said Sunny, 'because it's what I do?'

'Just round and round in circles like that?'

Sunny stood in the middle of the room with her arms folded. 'Yes. Round and round.'

'Don't you get dizzy?'

'Dizzy?'

'From all the spinning round?'

'Maybe,' said Sunny. 'Maybe that's why it's fun.'

'All right. Well, I'm going to bed now. Can I trust you to get into bed and turn out the light?'

'Oh yeah. Fine,' said Sunny.

'You won't just pace in circles until 1 a.m. or anything?'

Sunny gave the small frenzied head-shake again.

'All right then. Night.'

Sunny said nothing, just slipped her thumb back into her mouth and set off again on her tiny circular journey.

SEVEN

Mairéad slept extremely soundly and when she woke up, even though she had designed the flat specifically so it would remain dark even on the brightest summer morning, she knew instinctively that it was late. She lunged for her phone and saw that it was 8.30 a.m. There was no noise in the flat. She threw back the covers in a panic and hurried to Sunny's room. She didn't know why, but her heart was racing and she felt sure, just so incredibly sure, that Sunny would not be in her bed. That she had somehow vanished, or that the whole of yesterday had been conjured up by her imagination. She pushed open the door carefully and quietly – the new door on its oiled brass hinges moving without a crack or a squeak – and saw Sunny's dark head on the pillow.

She put a hand on her chest in both disappointment and relief. Feeling a little dizzy at her sudden fit of energy so soon after waking up, she went back to bed and pulled the covers up to her neck. She breathed deeply through her nose and then out through her mouth. Then she squeezed the skin between her thumb and forefinger, because she'd once read in a magazine that this was an effective self-soothing measure.

Sunny arrived in the kitchen at about 9.15 a.m., while

Mairéad was having her second cup of tea. Not as life-giving as the first, but welcome nonetheless.

She appeared silently in the doorway, wearing the NYC hoodie over her pyjamas and carrying her blanket, which she fussed about with and turned in her hands.

'Morning,' said Mairéad.

'Hi,' said Sunny.

'Hungry?'

'I'm always hungry,' said Sunny matter-of-factly.

'What sort of thing do you have for breakfast?'

'Whatever,' said Sunny. 'Sometimes muesli.'

'Muesli it is.'

They established that Sunny and Lenny did not drink cow's milk, but oat milk, but that, said Sunny, was more to do with the fact that they didn't own a fridge and milk has a tendency to go off. 'I can drink cow's milk,' she clarified. 'I just don't usually.'

'Where do you keep your food?'

'On the side,' said Sunny mysteriously. She nibbled at her muesli. 'Do you have any coffee?'

'Coffee? You drink coffee?'

'Yes,' said Sunny. 'Like Pippi Longstocking, I drink coffee.'

'Okay, let me find some,' said Mairéad, who did not drink coffee.

Once Sunny had her muesli and her coffee, which she drank black, Mairéad returned again to the list that she was making. She was going to CEO the hell out of this situation. And that meant lists.

'I'm just making a...' she started, but found that she was talking to thin air. Sunny had vanished without a word. She reappeared with her book, then sat down and started reading. Mairéad frowned at the top of Sunny's head, baffled. She returned to her list. It read:

- sort out music room
- toenails and fingernails
- deodorant
- CLOTHES
- SHOES
- activities
- the movies?
- books
- food??

'Pumpkin seeds,' said Sunny.
'What?'
'Are you making a list of things to buy?'
'Yes. Do you like pumpkin seeds?'
Sunny shrugged. 'They're all right, but I need them.'
'Why?'
'Because I've got worms.' Sunny squirmed about in her chair to illustrate.
'*Worms?*' said Mairéad, feeling a little panicky. 'Worms in your... ?'
'Bum?' said Sunny.
'And the pumpkin seeds... ?'
'. . . get rid of them... ?' said Sunny slowly, like she was talking to someone very stupid.
'But surely some sort of... some sort of medicine is what you need?'
'Medicine is poison,' said Sunny, calmly. 'Pumpkin seeds work fine,' she added, turning back to her book.
'Oh-kay. I'll be back in a moment,' said Mairéad. But Sunny didn't hear her, or didn't care. Either way, she didn't reply.
Mairéad knew that Dodie would never answer the phone at 9.30 a.m. on a Sunday but she rang anyway, to communicate urgency. When the call went unanswered she opened WhatsApp to send a message. Her fingers paused over the

keys. How could she even begin to explain what was going on? She simply typed out, 'Call me! Nothing bad x'.

She returned from her bedroom to the kitchen, and in the living room she found Sunny standing by a bookcase, holding a Farrow & Ball paint colour card in her hands. The card was in a concertina shape and unfolded to reveal its sludgy rainbow of colours. It was stretched between Sunny's hands and she was silently examining the little patches of colour.

'That's from a paint company,' explained Mairéad. 'So you can see what all the different paints look like.'

'It's really nice,' said Sunny. Then she let out a laugh, the first Mairéad had heard from her. It was a girlish, rising giggle. 'Pigeon!' she said. Then, 'Look! This one is called Dead Salmon!' Sunny's shoulders were juddering up and down as she read the outlandish names of the paints. 'Sulking Room Pink!' she exclaimed. 'Why would you call a paint "Bone"?' She nearly collapsed when she got to 'Bamboozle' and 'Mizzle'.

'That company is famous for calling their paints all sorts of mad names.'

'Yeah,' said Sunny absently. 'Can I keep this?' she asked.

'Of course.'

The Marks & Spencer on the high street opened at 11 a.m. Mairéad was surprised at this, having rarely ventured out of her flat before lunchtime on Sundays. Sunny was reluctant to come with her, declaring that Lenny often left her alone in their cabin and she was fine. But Mairéad insisted and went out onto the balcony to retrieve Sunny's smelly, squashed trainers, arranging her face in a purposefully placid way so as not to show how gross she thought they were.

Sunny jammed her feet into the trainers, sockless, without taking her eyes off her book. The Farrow & Ball paint card was tucked under her arm.

'I think we might leave the book behind for this?'

'Okay,' said Sunny, still reading.

Mairéad went and fetched her bag and checked she had her phone, wallet and keys and then said, 'Let's go,' to Sunny, who was still reading.

'Let me just get to the end of this,' said Sunny.

'The end of the page? The chapter? The book?'

Sunny looked up and squinted. 'The chapter.'

'Well, how many pages is that?'

Sunny flipped the pages. 'Four.'

'Can't you come back to it later?'

Sunny looked around the flat. 'Are we in a hurry?' she said.

There was no answer to this. No, they were not in a hurry, but Mairéad was ready now, was the point.

'No, I suppose not a massive hurry.'

'Well... so can I just finish reading this, then?'

'Sure.' Mairéad put down all her things and went to stand on the balcony for a bit. She came back in a few times to find Sunny still reading.

'You haven't started a new chapter, have you?'

'No,' said Sunny flatly, not taking her eyes off the page.

Mairéad scrolled through her phone a bit.

'Done!' called Sunny.

'Right!' said Mairéad.

Sunny stood in the middle of the living room with her arms folded, not moving.

'What is it *now*?'

'I need the loo,' said Sunny.

Mairéad clenched her teeth and closed her eyes.

It took thirty-five minutes to leave the flat.

'I don't want to go in,' said Sunny as they both stood at the entrance to Marks & Spencer. She had agreed to leave the book behind, but still had the paint card and turned it over in her hands, anxiously, fretfully, the same way she'd turned over her blanket in her fingers.

Well, This Is Awkward

'Why not?' Just as with having a bath, Mairéad was always delighted to walk into a Marks & Spencer. Or any shop, really. Why would Sunny not want to go in?

'It looks noisy,' said Sunny, her arms now crossed behind her back, each hand clutching the opposite upper arm.

'I don't think it will be noisy. And if it is, we can leave, okay? Promise.'

'Okay,' said Sunny after a pause.

Mairéad took a basket. Sunny trailed behind her.

'So, what's the best thing that Mum makes for you for dinner?'

'Lentils,' said Sunny. 'They're spicy.'

'Okay, lentils. Spicy…'

'Fruit!' said Sunny, stopping in front of a humming fridge full of a range of berries, apples and peaches.

'Fruit? You like fruit? What kinds? You choose. Pick anything!'

Sunny picked out some apples, grapes and nectarines. 'What are these?' she said, pointing to some flat peaches. 'Did someone sit on these peaches?'

'No, I don't know how they make them like that. Let's get some.'

'Steak.'

'Steak? I thought you were a vegetarian.'

'Why? Who told you I was a vegetarian?' said Sunny.

Mairéad realised this had been a total assumption on her part.

'Oh, I must have misheard your mum, then.'

Mairéad tossed into her basket some steak and some more pasta, some lentils – although she had no idea what to do with them – some potatoes and more cheese. Sunny pointed out any food that she recognised, which included sausages and burgers. They bought two packets of pumpkin seeds.

'See, it's not too noisy in here.'

'It's okay,' said Sunny.

They were on such a roll that Mairéad had to swap her basket for a trolley. Sunny stopped short in front of a greetings-card rack and could not be budged. She picked up and read inside every single one, holding the cards up close to her face, as she did with her book. Mairéad left her there and turned into the bakery aisle and picked out some bagels and pitta. She paused in front of a pair of cupcakes, a twin-pack. They were absurdly elaborate, with a pastel-coloured whip of butter-cream icing decorated with edible stars and a lot of glitter. With a trolley-full of Sunny-approved food and feeling briefly positive, Mairéad took the packet of cupcakes off the shelf as a treat.

Everything about the shopping trip was fine, in fact, until they had to queue to pay. Sunny became agitated, hanging her hands by her sides and flopping her head back on her neck. 'Ungh, I'm really uncomfortable,' she fretted rather loudly, flapping her paint card around. 'It's hot, my feet hurt, I wanna go. I wanna GO!'

The man in front of them in the queue turned his head slightly.

'Just a bit longer, not much more,' said Mairéad, worried that Sunny was going to make a scene. 'Look, we're next, look. Why don't you help me put stuff on the belt?'

This used to be one of Mairéad's favourite jobs as a child, helping her mother to load things onto the supermarket conveyor belt, but Sunny treated it as a dreadful chore, refusing to take her thumb out of her mouth while she tossed items carelessly onto the belt. Mairéad rescued the cupcakes before Sunny's brute handling ruined their Mr Whippy crowns.

'Careful!'

'Can I wait outside?'

Mairéad paused. Sunny's agitation was making her feel very tense and agitated, too, and she thought that going to wait by the exit was a brilliant idea – but didn't children get kidnapped if you left them alone on London streets? Although whoever kidnapped Sunny, Mairéad thought meanly, would get a pretty nasty shock.

'Okay, then. Don't wander off. Don't speak to anyone. Wait by the exit.'

Sunny walked off with her thumb in her mouth, her arms crossed defensively, the paint card held limply in one hand.

Mairéad packed up her shopping, feeling now far less buoyant and a little moody. She left the shop and found Sunny sitting on the dirty pavement, sucking her thumb and staring at her paint colour chart with her head on one side.

'Don't sit there!' said Mairéad. 'It's filthy.'

Sunny got up, putting her hand directly down on a stain on the pavement that Mairéad would have put money on being dog urine.

Back at the flat, Mairéad said, 'Don't touch anything!' then stood over Sunny as she washed her hands with soap and water, even though Sunny complained about the smell, colour and feel of the handwash.

This ordeal over, Sunny sat on the sofa with *Watership Down*, her paint card, her blanket and a bowlful of pumpkin seeds. Mairéad had handed her a pumpkin seed packet and gone back to unloading and putting away the rest of the shopping. Sunny plucked and pulled and hassled the pumpkin seed packet and it eventually burst open, scattering seeds all over the freshly waxed parquet. Sunny held the empty packet by her side and just stared and stared at the mess.

'For god's sake!' said Mairéad. Then she checked herself. 'Good thing we've got another packet.' The next packet she opened herself, and decanted it into a bowl. Then she swept up the spilled pumpkin seeds and put all the shopping away. Her phone rang; it was Dodie. 'Hi, hang on a sec.' She sidled out onto her balcony to take the call, even though she was pretty confident that Sunny wouldn't register a word of the conversation even if she had it sitting right next to her.

'I mean you said it's nothing bad,' said Dodie, 'but that immediately made me think it's something extra bad. What's the emergency? Have you been kidnapped?'

Mairéad explained as best she could about Lenny's accident and Sunny.

'It's... I mean...' said Dodie, briefly stumped. 'A whole eleven-year-old. It feels a bit too much too soon.'

'I don't know what to do with her. I don't know what to feed her or what she ought to be doing or anything. She just wants to read.'

'But that's great, surely?' said Dodie. 'Isn't that the dream? A child that reads? Mine are still mostly eating books, and Olly's seven.'

'Yes but it's all she wants to do. I'm a bit worried about what will happen when she finishes her book.'

'What book is it?'

'*Watership Down*. It looks pretty long,' added Mairéad hopefully.

'Start her on *War and Peace* next.'

'Ha,' said Mairéad drily.

'Look, come to Devon to see us. We're there from when school breaks up. It's kid heaven, seriously. Loads of other kids to run about with, the seaside, crabbing, ice cream. You won't have to stay with me and my vile children,' said Dodie. 'Miles's aunt's got a cottage and I think she's going to be away for a few weeks – you can stay there. I mean, I say "aunt"; she might actually be a cousin.'

'No, Sunny will be long gone by then. I hope. Oh, and she's got worms.'

'Who, Sunny?'

'Yeah.'

'That's pretty normal,' said Dodie. 'I mean, revolting but

normal. At least for toddlers and tiny ones. Not sure about older ones. You can get medicine for it – it's called Ovex. You might want to check her for headlice, though. They sort of go hand in hand.'

Mairéad heard Dodie talking to someone, away from the phone. 'Yeah, take him. His lead's hanging up by the door.' There was another question. 'Yes, it's in the fridge.'

Mairéad went to fill up a watering can as Dodie talked to whoever it was in the background. The balcony was filled with lush parlour palms, fiddle-leaf figs, yuccas in tasteful woven baskets and string-of-hearts cascading from macramé hanging baskets. The tubs secured to the balcony edge foamed with herbs and ferns. The idea was that the plants lived outside on the balcony in the summer and then came inside in the winter. She knew full well that she was something of a cliché with all her glossy plants, but she didn't care. Sometimes she thought that of all the wonderful things about her flat, these were the best.

'A lead? Have you got a puppy?'

'Not quite a puppy – a young dog. He's called Digger and if you think that's a stupid name you should have heard the other suggestions. But yeah. Jesus. I finally got ground down. I have nothing to do with him, let me just be clear. I told Miles if he wants a bloody dog he has to look after it. Children love him, though. If you come and see us in Devon you'll meet him. Come with or without Sunny. Oh and also there's Dibs, he's a character.'

'Who is Dibs?'

'Local scallywag. Artful Dodger meets Just William,' she added. 'I'm sure we're related somehow, too, but not sure of exact details. He'll be there with his family in a few weeks' time.'

'You're related to half of that place. All sounds very idyllic,' said Mairéad, enviously. She suddenly felt more alone than she ever had in her life.

'The village is called Blorcombe but spelled B-L-O-X-C-O-M-B-E. I'll text it to you. I'll find you a place to stay, the aunt's cottage or somewhere else. I'll send you some dates.'

'That sounds nice.' But Mairéad had no intention of hanging out with dogs and children. Once Sunny was gone, she was going to take herself to the most bougie, adults-only spot in the Mediterranean she could find.

'Anyway, I'd better get back to Little Miss Wormery,' she said, with a lightness that she didn't feel.

At teatime, Sunny appeared in the kitchen with the alert and responsive look on her face that Mairéad had quickly learned meant that she was searching for a snack. She remembered the elaborate cupcakes and presented one to Sunny with a flourish.

'What is this?' said Sunny, looking at it from all angles. 'Is it soap?'

'It's a cake.'

'Why is it all these different colours?'

Mairéad was lost for words. 'I think maybe the shop thinks it looks pretty,' she said at last.

'It's got glitter on it,' said Sunny.

'Yes, but you can eat it.'

Sunny poked the icing with a finger and then tasted it. 'Woah!' she said, blinking. 'That is really sweet.' She looked up and then back at the table. 'Why aren't you having one?'

'Oh, far too much sugar for me.'

'Why are you giving it to me, then? If it's too much sugar for you?'

There was no answer to this.

That night, Mairéad spent an hour composing an email to the entire London office explaining that she would be bringing Sunny into the office until she found a childcare solution.

Well, This Is Awkward

Then she sent an email to her mother saying that she would be round in a few days, although she had no idea when exactly she would have the time.

On Monday morning, Mairéad made Sunny a coffee and they set off together. There was a meeting that day with Ashley – aka That Divorced Girl – that she did not want to miss.

EIGHT

Sunny slunk into the office behind Mairéad, who felt like she was dragging a corpse around.

'Hello!' said Biba. She was wearing a pink tulle skirt, Converse high-tops and a camo-print tank top that said 'LA Lakers' on it.

Sunny stared at her.

'Say hello,' nudged Mairéad.

'Hello,' said Sunny.

'She's... she's...' said Mairéad, searching for some sort of simple explanation.

'She'd rather be anywhere else!' said Biba. 'Don't worry, I get it. I've got younger cousins. Do you want to come over here with me and do some drawing?' she asked.

'No,' said Sunny.

'Oh,' said Biba, looking hurt. 'Okay.'

'She's fine, she's got her book.'

Mairéad steered Sunny to her office, with a hand on her shoulder. Sunny shrugged it off. Mairéad tutted.

'Chill on that sofa, okay?' she said. 'Read your book.'

Sunny sat down on the coral-pink sofa and looked around.

'Where are we?'

Well, This Is Awkward

'My office,' said Mairéad, staring at her computer.

'It's very bright.'

'Yup.'

'Knock knock!' said Jenna. She was wearing a loose bronze dress with a skinny tan belt and brown gladiator sandals. Margot was back under her arm.

'This must be the famous Sunny!' she exclaimed.

Sunny squinted at Jenna. 'Is that a dog?'

'Yes, this is Margot,' said Jenna. 'Do you want to pet her? She is so super gentle.'

'It looks like a rat,' said Sunny.

'Sunny!' exclaimed Mairéad. But Sunny was already leaning back on the sofa, reading *Watership Down* and entirely unresponsive.

'Sorry,' apologised Mairéad. 'She's my sister's daughter. They're a bit... It's a bit of a wild situation.'

'No, no, that's fine,' said Jenna. It was clearly not fine. She looked at Mairéad with accusing eyes. 'What's that awful smell? Can you smell it?'

Sunny's trainers. Mairéad had completely forgotten about them. Had she got used to the smell so quickly?

'Don't know. Are you in the Ashley meeting later?' said Mairéad, dearly wanting to change the subject.

'Yes, I'll be there,' said Jenna curtly. She stalked out of the office. Mairéad got up and closed the door.

'Sunny,' she snapped.

'Yeah?' said Sunny, not looking up from her book.

'Can you not be so rude, please?'

'When?'

'To... about... everything! About the dog – you can't say that someone's dog looks like a rat! On this planet, we try not to insult each other.'

'Rats are sweet,' said Sunny. She shuffled off her shoes and wiggled her toes. Mairéad looked at the shoes. She couldn't really smell them anymore. It was called 'nose blindness'. She'd read about it.

Mairéad spent another half an hour on her emails and then heard the now-familiar rippling thud of a book being cast aside.

'Finished,' said Sunny. She sat up and put her hands on her knees. 'What do I do now?'

It was 10.15 a.m.

'Well, can you… can you maybe go and do some drawing with Biba?'

Sunny didn't reply, she just stuck her thumb in her mouth.

'Do you want to play with my phone?' said Mairéad desperately.

'No,' said Sunny, scrunching up her face. 'I should have brought my blanket,' she declared and then lay down on the sofa with an arm flung over her face.

Biba came into the office. 'Just to let you know, Andreas is in Stockholm.' She stopped and sniffed the air. 'Gosh, have we got a drains problem? What's that smell? Smells like something dead. Maybe a dead rat. Oh my god, have we got rats?'

'That lady has got a dog that looks like a rat,' called out Sunny.

'Sunny!' shrieked Mairéad, slapping her palms on her desk. She glared at Sunny, who still had her arm over her eyes and didn't notice.

Mairéad googled 'bookshops near me'.

Five minutes later she was leaving the office, with Sunny slouching along behind her. 'Back in a minute,' she said to Biba.

'Where are we going?' said Sunny.

'Waterstones.'

The shop was about ten minutes away and they walked in silence. Mairéad felt deeply irritated and knew that she

Well, This Is Awkward

shouldn't, that she ought to be nice to Sunny, but she just felt annoyed and resentful. And enraged with Lenny for being so sloppy and neglectful that she couldn't bring up a child with even basic manners.

They arrived at the sweeping black façade of the bookshop.

'Wow,' said Sunny. 'Wow,' she repeated, stepping inside. 'Oooh,' she said. 'Smell.' She breathed in the bookshop aroma.

'I think the children's books are at the back,' said Mairéad. But Sunny wasn't listening; she had stalled at the first book-covered table. She gazed at the cover of each one, the blurb on the back and the first page.

'At the back, the kids' books are at the back. Sunny… *Sunny*.'

Mairéad looked at her watch. The meeting with Ashley was starting in half an hour. She left Sunny reading the back of *The Poisonwood Bible*, feeling a real and acute fear that Sunny was capable of staying in the bookshop until she had read the back of every single book, and quickly went to check that there were copies of *Get Divorced! (with That Divorced Girl)* in 'New Non-Fiction'.

Ashley had been Mairéad's first client. They'd struck up a friendship on Instagram when Mairéad had messaged her to say she loved her account. Ashley had been young, only twenty-four, and already divorced with two children. Her ex was a medium-level football player and had been unpleasant and unkind. Ashley had paid no attention at school and was financially incompetent, but helped her followers navigate both divorce and personal finance. She screenshotted bizarre bits of legal and finance terminology and wrote 'Wot is this crap?' next to it, followed by a translation into plain English. Mairéad described her account content as 'blithely jaded'. She steered Ashley towards lucrative partnerships with independent financial advisors, then with stationery supply companies, cleaning products and clothing stores. Within five years, Ashley was clearing six figures from advertising.

Mairéad worried at least once a month that Ashley was going to leave IGS and move to another, bigger agency – the nightmare being ShowTime. The book deal had signified a significant step up in Ashley's visibility and ShowTime would be wooing her like crazy. Mairéad did not want this catch-up meeting to happen without her. A hysterical catastrophe-loop of Jenna snatching Ashley and streaking away to ShowTime started playing in her head.

She looked up to see Sunny wandering about, holding two books.

'How long can we check these out for?'

'Check them out?'

'Yeah, how long can we borrow them for?'

'No, this isn't a library. You buy them and keep them.'

'Oh, right,' said Sunny. 'But then how do other people read them?'

'They make loads of copies, enough so everyone can have one?'

'Can I have these, then?'

'Sure. Have as many as you like. But hurry up, okay?'

They bought so many books that they were entitled to a free canvas tote bag. She hustled Sunny out of the shop and onto the street.

'Can we get a snack?'

Mairéad looked at her watch. Ten minutes to the start of the meeting. 'Sure, yes,' she said. 'In here, in here.' They walked into a corner shop.

Sunny looked at the array of things in packets. 'I don't know what any of this is.'

'Oh yes, of course. Okay, let's try somewhere else.' They took a minute-chewing detour to Whole Foods, where Sunny bought two peaches and a packet of nuts. Despite the fact that it was only 10.50 a.m., Mairéad bought herself a pastry and angrily devoured it on the walk back to the office.

Well, This Is Awkward

They arrived five minutes late for the meeting.

'Sorry, sorry,' said Mairéad, dizzy from the sudden and unexpected carb-intake and panting a bit. She peered at the meeting room, brushing some icing sugar off her dark blue linen trousers. 'Where is everyone?'

'Jenna moved the meeting – didn't you get the note?' said Biba. 'She changed it on the calendar. She needed to be the other side of town for a different meeting afterwards, so she called in on Ashley at home.'

'*What?*' Mairéad pored over her phone and, sure enough, there was the meeting change on the calendar. But she must have done it as soon as Mairéad had stepped out of the office. She heard the horror violins, both slithery and *pizzicato*. And loud.

'Are you all right?' said Biba. 'Mairéad? Are you okay?'

That night, Mairéad spent another hour composing an email to the entire London office explaining that she needed to take a few days working from home until she could find some suitable childcare for Sunny. Something had to give.

She then rang Ashley, who did not pick up the phone. She spent a further hour composing a ticking-off email to Jenna, but ended up staring at it helplessly: Jenna would either ignore it or rebut her with some sort of cruel insult that would send her reeling to her fashionable art deco drinks trolley. She deleted the whole thing and then got up to go and put Sunny's trainers in the washing machine.

NINE

The next day, Tuesday, Mairéad took Sunny to Cable House.

She rang the doorbell and it took Helen a while to answer. As she waited, Mairéad glared at the Bob Marley quote in the window that read, 'If you live for others, you live again.'

After a while Helen answered, looking surprised, 'Hello?!' she said.

'You will have forgotten, but Sunny is here.'

'Of course!' said Helen. 'I hadn't forgotten. Hello, Sunny,' she said grandly. 'I am your grandmother.'

Sunny didn't reply and Mairéad didn't bother prompting her. 'Have you taken everything out of the music room that you want to keep?'

'Yes, yes,' said Helen. Mairéad knew that Helen almost definitely hadn't even set foot in the music room since she'd last seen her. As they walked into the kitchen, the doorbell rang again, and Mairéad returned down the hallway and opened the door to find two unsmiling, burly men wearing rubber work gloves and heavy boots. If she hadn't known that they were workmen that she'd hired in order to clear out the junk from the spare room, she would have supposed that they were a pair of contract killers.

'Oh hi. This way.'

Well, This Is Awkward

The men removed bags and bags of junk from the music room, while Mairéad encouraged Sunny to sit on a sofa and got one of her new books out of her rucksack for her to read. 'Touch anything you like,' she said. 'Break stuff, I don't care.' Sunny looked at her and the corner of her mouth twitched in a small gesture of amusement.

'Okay,' she said. She stuck her thumb in her mouth and carried on reading.

Mairéad went to the music room and opened dusty box after dusty box to make sure that nothing precious had been dumped in there and forgotten. It was mostly junk: broken things, sheafs of paper that didn't seem to pertain to anything and old clothes, balled up and forgotten, smelling of dust and skin. One of the boxes contained her old A-level notes and she paused, looking at them, considering the extremely neat handwriting, honed from years of writing essays. It was always so difficult, confronted like this, to harden your heart and throw this sort of thing away. But she reasoned that she hadn't thought about these notes even once since she'd finished her exams, so they couldn't possibly have been that meaningful to her. Did they spark joy? No way. Out they went.

She opened another box and stopped. In it, amongst other detritus, was her unnamed ginger teddy bear, which she had not seen or thought about for ten years. Unbidden, as if she was a water-balloon pricked by a very fine needle, tears formed in her eyes. She put a bunched fist under her nose and reached for the bear. He had been bought for her by her grandmother, Helen's mother, and had never had a name. She remembered attempting to call him 'Biscuit' when she was about five, but one of the lodgers, a Spanish dental assistant in her mid-thirties called Paola, laughed and said, 'Biscuit? Maybe I will eat him,' and pretended to nibble a corner of his ear. Lenny had joined in. 'Yeah, what a dumb name for a teddy,' she had said.

This drove Mairéad wild: that she was being made fun of;

that her bear was being fake-eaten; that there was this strange woman in her house, who had not been invited in by her, who was now disrespecting the choice of name for her possession, pretending to nibble its ear and riling up Lenny. She felt an almost uncontrollable desire to weep but instead just coughed hard, then closed her eyes and breathed in deeply through her nostrils. She tucked the teddy under her arm.

She tipped the men, now red and sweaty, with the £20 in cash she had brought along especially for this task. She waved them off as they trundled down the suburban street with a roomful of rubbish on the back of their van, then went back inside to continue tidying. Helen walked into the music room to find Mairéad stripping the bed.

'What are you doing?' she said.

'This place is filthy.' Mairéad felt her desire to weep metabolise into something closer to rage. 'I'm going to wash these sheets. I'm going to *boil* them and then put them back on the bed. Where's your vacuum?'

'In the hallway cupboard, where it always is.'

She went to fetch the vacuum, noting a strong and unpleasant smell of frying fish mingled with marijuana smoke coming from the kitchen. She came back with the old, heavy machine. Helen was sitting on the edge of the sagging bed with her glasses on, peering down at her phone, poking it every now and again.

'It's Roxana,' she murmured, only half aware that she was even talking.

Mairéad wanted to scream *I don't give a fuck if it's Roxana!* but did not and started barging across the room towards the plug socket. She plugged in the vacuum and smacked her palm at the on-switch. The vacuum started up, wheezily and feebly.

'Why aren't you downstairs bonding with Sunny?'

Well, This Is Awkward

'I tried! She totally ignored me,' said Helen. 'She's her mother's daughter all right.'

'She was on a mission, you know. A True Earth thing. That night, that's what the accident was.'

Helen looked up. 'I thought she gave all that up,' she said. 'When she came back.'

'So did I.'

Lenny had always been contrary. When Mairéad was little – five or so – and people asked her what she wanted to be, she said, 'A ballerina,' despite never having had a single ballet lesson. Lenny's answer was, 'The man who drives the truck with the big ball on it that smashes into buildings.' She had changed her own name to Lenny, after Lenny Henry. She and Mairéad watched *The Lenny Henry Show* together, dancing along to the opening title music and crooning, 'The Lenny Henry shoooooww'. One night Lenny decided that she loved *The Lenny Henry Show* so much that she was going to call herself Lenny. And it stuck. It suited her.

In her desire to be at the helm of a demolition ball, Lenny had found a soulmate in Misha. He was a member of True Earth, which, on the surface, was an off-grid, survivalist community near Alberta in Canada. But as well as being an off-grid, survivalist community, True Earth was also a loose global community of anti-capitalist, anti-fossil fuel, pro-planet trouble-makers. Unlike Extinction Rebellion or Just Stop Oil, True Earth weren't looking for publicity. They were looking to destroy things. They didn't care about fur or meat or animal testing. They sabotaged oil pipelines, mining sites and ring-road construction. Usually at night, usually while wearing head-to-toe black. They adored balaclavas. They were often an un-cited reason any airport, anywhere, didn't add an extra runway.

Misha talked about the True Earth headquarters in Canada in a credulous and starry way. Then Lenny started talking about the True Earth headquarters in Canada in a credulous and starry way. Mairéad, Helen and Gavin only became aware of True Earth's true purpose when, six months after meeting Misha, Lenny was arrested and charged with criminal damage on land owned by BP. She argued in court that she was simply lost on a 3 a.m. hike in the countryside, and that the bolt-cutters in her rucksack were related to farmhand work, and she had used them to free herself from some barbed wire she had stumbled up against. The balaclava? It was cold!

At the time, Mairéad had felt terrible guilt at being the one who had introduced Lenny to Misha, even if it had been completely inadvertent. Later, from a distance, she saw that Lenny had been waiting for Misha to happen and, if it hadn't been him, it would have been someone else.

Before Helen had retreated from the world, what she most loved to do at the weekend was demonstrations. Anywhere, about anything. Mairéad hated the demos — they were noisy and tiring and occasionally scary. She preferred to dreamily browse Boots and Topshop with Dodie or rearrange her bedroom for the third time that month. She and Dodie were obsessed with beautiful things; they could spend three hours in a stationery department.

Up until the age of about twelve, Lenny had also not been keen on demonstrations. Less obsessed with stationery and shopping, Lenny had spent her free time riding her bike or conducting various pitched battles against the Cooper boys round the corner. So before they were teenagers, Mairéad had had an ally and a witness to the weirdness of Helen.

Their father was no help. He travelled with his work as a civil engineer, bringing back stories of bridges he had built in Kuala Lumpur and road networks in Oman. At the time this had all seemed normal and just what parents did, but as an adult Mairéad wondered if Gavin took the foreign jobs and built the shed in order to get away from Helen.

Mairéad and Lenny used to sit on the stairs, smelling the patchouli oil and strong rolled-cigarette smoke of the meetings, giving Helen's activist friends nicknames: 'Shaggy', 'Dracula', 'Poufy-Head'. Then one day Poufy-Head – a woman with tinted aviators and a lot of frizzy hair cut into a mullet – struck up a conversation with Lenny in the hallway. Mairéad, hidden, listened to Poufy-Head heap praise on Lenny. 'I can see that you're a really thoughtful kid,' she said, and 'I bet no one else at school thinks cool things like that.' Mairéad found Lenny later. 'You actually spoke to Poufy-Head,' she said, excitedly.

'Yeah,' replied Lenny, rather airily. 'She was nice.' The following year, Lenny returned to her first demonstration.

At first Helen was delighted with Lenny's activism, declaring loudly and often that she was so relieved some young people were determined to keep doing What Was Right, despite the onslaught of consumerism and multi-channel TV from America. Mairéad learned that, when Helen got that tone of voice out, she needed to get up from where she was sitting and take her *Just Seventeen* and Diet Coke to her bedroom.

But then one evening, following a PETA rally, Helen and Lenny had argued.

'You can't just smash things up!' Helen had cried. 'That window, I don't know what you were thinking. You could have been caught on a security camera!'

'Direct action is the only way to get real attention,' Lenny countered.

'No, it isn't! And then people just start calling you a criminal, rather than listening to your cause.'

'Coming from you!' scoffed Lenny. 'Who was more direct action than the IR bloody A?'

'I never offered blanket support to the IRA,' said Helen, hotly. 'And it became a very divisive issue, it was complicated. You wouldn't understand!'

Later, Lenny stamped up to her bedroom. Mairéad knocked

on the door and pushed it open. Lenny was standing next to her bedroom window. The lights were still off and she was illuminated only by the streetlight.

'Did you smash a window, then?' said Mairéad, laughing a little.

'Yeah, big one,' said Lenny. She turned and Mairéad saw an electric look on her face. 'It was fucking *amazing*.'

Lenny was fined for the minor damage to the BP fence but escaped a criminal record, which visibly disappointed her. She then explained abruptly and rudely that in fact, the lack of criminal record was a sign. While it would have been a badge of honour, it would make travelling difficult, so she was going to make the most of her freedom by leaving for Europe with Misha. They would connect up with proper off-grid communities who lived with *honour* and *purpose*.

Their ultimate goal was to be offered a place at the True Earth headquarters, the mothership, ground zero. But you had to apply to join and then be recognised as a *true* True Earther in order to receive an invitation. They didn't want whiners who couldn't deal with the real hardships of off-grid living. Applicants had to prove themselves. So Misha and Lenny trekked from off-grid community to off-grid community, from Belgium to Germany to Poland, in order to wait for their summons.

For years Mairéad expected to one day get a postcard from Alberta, Canada, with a note from Lenny saying something like 'Made it!' But, after years of living in Europe with Misha, biology intervened. Lenny's set course to Canada deviated suddenly and finally.

It was a hard-line policy: you were not allowed to bring children to True Earth who hadn't been born there. Lenny departed immediately for Wales, to stay with a lapsed True Earth comrade who had succumbed to the siren call of indoor plumbing. From there came the cabin. Mairéad had assumed that with the arrival of Sunny, Lenny had calmed down, left all the midnight wrecking-ball stuff in the past and was happy doing good work with the pigs. But now it seemed that she had not left it behind. She had brought it all right with her.

'God, there's something *wrong* with this,' snapped Mairéad at the vacuum. She turned off the machine and started trying to find a way in, to check the bag. She took the lid off and there was a horrible puff of lint and dust.

'This bag is rammed!' she said accusingly to Helen. 'When was it last changed?'

'Oh gosh,' said Helen vaguely. 'I don't know. Long time ago, probably.'

'Okay. Fine, do you have another bag?'

'Maybe in the basement,' said Helen, standing up. 'I've got to answer this email on my laptop. Tell me if you can't find them there.'

Mairéad went down to the basement but there were no replacement bags there, then she checked under the sink and in the odds-and-ends drawer in the kitchen. Finally she looked under the sink in Helen's own bathroom and found a dusty packet of bags, which looked like they had been purchased at some point in the eighties. On the cover was a stylised picture of a slim woman wearing a floral apron, pushing an upright vacuum. Her face, eyeless, was turned to the viewer, dainty eyebrows lifted in surprise.

She put in a new bag and flipped the top of the vacuum cleaner shut. With her teddy absent-mindedly tucked under one arm, she ran the now-functional vacuum around the music room, stopping only briefly to open the windows wide. She wrinkled her nose at the smell of the marijuana and frying fish as she vacuumed. When she'd finished cleaning the carpet, she looked around the room. There.

Absolutely fine space for a child to spend a few weeks in. Perhaps even less time than that. Bethan had said she wasn't even sure how long Lenny would be in hospital, and her sister would surely hate to be stuck there, in the belly of the poison beast, for any longer than she had to. Sunny could walk around in circles and suck her thumb and read her book in this room and be in clover and Mairéad would be able to get back to her life. She wound the electrical cord of the vacuum around the cleat on the handle. There was a small 'snap' noise and one half of a pair of curtains crumpled to the floor.

Mairéad left the bedroom, pretending she hadn't seen the curtains. She looked at the bathroom door opposite. She decided that she didn't want to know what was in there. She could hear a drip and she could smell the stale, grey smell of Old Bathroom. Not your problem, she thought to herself. It's just a bathroom.

Sunny appeared at the doorway of the living room with her finger stuck in her book as a place marker. She stood there silently until Mairéad looked up.

'What is it?'

'There's a very bad smell,' said Sunny.

'Is there?' said Mairéad, innocently. 'Well, I'm sure it will go away soon.'

She was exhausted, grimy and sweaty. She wanted a cold drink of water and a refreshing shower in her tasteful flat. She wanted to get the hell away from Cable House. There was the sound of voices chatting in the kitchen and the gentle patter of bongos. The doorbell rang and Mairéad went to answer it. On the doorstep were about five young people all dressed in a variety of mulchy clothes, sporting dreadlocks and holding assorted wooden instruments.

'Wait. Are we in the right place?' said one of them to another, closing one eye and looking a bit dizzy. 'Are Maggie and Jethro here?'

Mairéad smiled and stepped aside. She held out her arm to indicate they must go to the kitchen. She glanced up and saw Sunny looking at her, then at the kitchen and then back.

'Are you going to leave me here?' she said, her eyes wide.

Mairéad paused. Sunny was shoeless and picking absently and anxiously at her thumb cuticle with her third finger.

Yes. Yes, I am. Just do it, Mairéad. Just leave her, she'll be fine.

'Well,' she fudged. 'It's nice here, isn't it? Big garden, lots of stuff going on? My flat's a bit boring.'

Sunny looked around. A burst of laughter came from the kitchen and some loud flutey noises started to accompany the bongos.

She gave the little head-shake again. 'No, it's not nice here. I thought your flat was nice. It had nice smells. It was quiet.'

Mairéad looked at Sunny, at her dark curls and her frightened face and her long feet.

'No,' she said, flapping her hand. 'Of course I'm not going to leave you here. I just had a few things to do. Come on, let's get our stuff together.'

She went into the living room where she had left her backpack, put Sunny's books inside and then, without saying goodbye to Helen, left, closing the front door firmly behind her and Sunny.

'Let's walk for a bit. It's a nice day.'

'All right,' said Sunny.

They walked down the hill towards town. It was about lunchtime and Mairéad was hungry. A delicious smell of garlic filled the air and Mairéad saw to her left a pizza restaurant in a small row of shops.

'Shall we have a pizza?'

'I don't know.'

'Have you had pizza before?'

'No.'

'It's nice, let's try it.'

It was only when Mairéad sat down at the table that she realised she still had her teddy under her arm. She set it down in its own chair and ordered the pizzas. She took her napkin off and put it on her lap.

'Put your napkin on your lap.'

'Why?'

There was a pause.

'Because it's what we do on this planet.'

A WhatsApp from Cass arrived as they were sitting at a table. 'Wyd,' it said.

Mairéad went outside to ring her with the news.

'She's here! This is great!' said Cass. 'I am so bored, waiting to hear about jobs. Let's all go to the zoo. Ah, kids freak out for the zoo. I used to do childcare, did I tell you? When I'd just arrived in London and was auditioning my head off. I basically lived in the zoo in summer. Tomorrow – I'll meet you there.'

'All right, but brace yourself. Sunny is bloody weird. She's the rudest person I've ever met.'

'Oh, wow. I'm going to enjoy this.'

TEN

The next morning Mairéad announced, at breakfast, 'We're going to the zoo today.'

Sunny ignored her, as usual, and carried on reading her book, the first in a series of thick novels about a fourteen-year-old girl who's recruited to be a spy. Mairéad was very nearly used to this, now. She was starting to see that Sunny was at all times lost in a sort of muffled zone and needed some prodding in order to surface for instructions and short commands, let alone any of the hated conversation.

'We're going to the zoo today. Sunny. Today, we're going to the zoo.'

Sunny finally looked up from her book but said nothing.

'We're going to the zoo,' Mairéad tried again.

'I heard you,' said Sunny.

'So why didn't you say anything?'

'What was I supposed to say?'

'I don't know. Great? Thanks?'

Sunny glared at Mairéad. 'Great!' she barked, unsmiling. 'Thanks!'

Mairéad found herself shaking her head in disbelief as she went to gather her things together for the trip. But Sunny did not object to going and even put her book down while she looked for her shoes, no longer so smelly after going through the washing machine, but now gently coming apart at the seams. It was 9.30 a.m. and already warm when they stepped out of the building, but Sunny insisted on wearing her hoodie. This was now at least mostly clean, although Sunny did have something of a habit of dropping food down herself and also of wiping her hands on her clothes. So while her hoodie and joggers no longer stank of pigs and woodsmoke, they often had smears of tomato sauce and chocolate on them.

They arrived at the zoo at around 10.15 a.m. to see Cass pacing around in front of the entrance, holding her phone flat and talking into one end of it. She was wearing a pair of grey joggers bunched up under her knees, white high-top trainers and a pink T-shirt that was full of artful holes. Her white-blonde hair was in a messy top-knot.

'Ah!' she called. 'You must be the famous Sunny!'

'Why does everyone say that?' said Sunny.

'Your auntie says you're very rude,' said Cass.

'I told a lady her dog looked like a rat.'

Cass let out a cackle.

'Auntie Mairéad was cross.'

Sunny pointed at Cass's left side. 'What happened to your hand?!'

'Oh!' Cass held up her left arm, which ended just above her wrist. Mairéad lurched to a stop. She had forgotten absolutely and entirely up until that moment that Cass did not have a left hand.

'Do you know, it was the weirdest thing,' said Cass. 'I woke up this morning and it was just gone. Wandered off. I'm hoping it'll come back later.'

Sunny let out a brief, uncertain huff of laughter. She put her head on one side and blinked at Cass like a small, curious bird. She held up a finger, as if this was a test she had come across before. 'That's not true,' she said.

'You're right. No flies on you. Okay, so really what happened is that I was here last week and a tiger escaped from his cage and bit it clean off.' Cass said this so sombrely that Sunny said, 'What, really?'

'No,' said Cass. 'I'm making up all this stuff because the truth is very boring.'

'I want to hear the whole story,' said Sunny, suddenly animated. 'I won't think it's boring.'

'All right, then, let's get into the zoo and I'll tell you the whole tragic tale. Now, with the zoo, you'll want to come back again so make sure you get a pass for the whole year. It's value, trust me. There's tons to see.'

The photograph that the very pale, red-haired lady in the kiosk took of Sunny for her membership card made her look like a hostage. Mairéad looked beaky and cross in hers. She reminded herself to always put on her pleasant face. Cass paid a token sum as the guest of members.

'So,' said Sunny, tapping Cass on the arm. 'What happened?'

'When I was younger than you are now, I was an absolutely class swimmer. I was like a little fish. There was a joke in my family that my ma found me under some seaweed at the Forty Foot – that's a stretch of sea near where I grew up. And what you do if you're a great swimmer is that you swim in competitions against other little swimmers, to see who's the best.'

'Were you the best?' said Sunny.

'Quite often I was the best. You should see all my medals. A whole wall of them. And these competitions, they were all over the place and we had to drive there in a coach – well not a coach, more a wee minibus. One day we were on our way back from a competition and it was raining and the driver skidded on a very wet road and we went flying.'

'You flew?'

'No, more like we turned over. Rolled right over and then slid down a slope at the side of the road. It was a terrible mess. I was holding the seat in front with my left hand and it was crushed, you see?'

'So what did they do with it?' Sunny stood, transfixed.

Cass bared her teeth and said, 'They had to cut it off!'

'Did it hurt?' said Sunny.

'Let's go in here,' said Cass. She pushed open the door to Gorilla Kingdom, made from large bamboo poles lashed together. It brushed against the green bamboo fronds that arched over the top of the bamboo fence.

'Oooh, wow, look at him,' said Mairéad. A large gorilla, silver fur greying his flanks, sat on the floor of a large room looped with thick ropes for the gorillas to amuse themselves with. He was behind a glass partition, with his back to the crowd. He turned his cone-shaped head with its low brow, dark nostrils and rubbery mouth over his shoulder every now and again, to give visitors a disgusted side-eye.

'I want to hear about the hand,' said Sunny, not interested in the gorilla. 'Did it hurt when they cut it off?'

'Shh,' said Mairéad. 'We can all hear you, no need to shout.'

'I don't remember,' said Cass. 'The truth of it is, I don't remember any of the accident. I took a whack on the head, too. And really, I think you forget these terrible things on purpose. Who needs to walk about remembering all that?'

'It must be awful, only having one hand,' said Sunny.

'I'm used to it,' said Cass.

'Maybe you could get a fake one. Made from metal.'

'I don't know about that. After the accident, my dad decided that he wasn't going to spoil me about it. He was crazy about my swimming, wanted me to be, you know, the world's greatest swimmer, and he was the one lashing me up and down the pool. So this was worse for him than it was for me. He lost his mind a bit, is the truth.

'I've these two brothers and they were instructed not to help me do anything – I had to work it all out for myself.

My ma was furious, she wanted to send me to bed forever and wait on me and fuss about. I was pretty annoyed about having to do it all myself, I'll admit that. But in the end it was for the best. There's not much I can't do. I mean, I'll have to work that little bit harder to be a concert pianist, I suppose. But,' she said dramatically, 'I'll tell you this.'

'What?' said Sunny. She was transfixed, her eyes huge.

'Most days I'm grateful. My friend Caitlin, she was in a wheelchair for years after the accident and then she died. The driver died, too. I could be dead. Or worse, I could have lost the other hand as well. Or my legs! Something could have happened to my *face*.' Cass put her right hand to her face. 'My gorgeous face! Where would I be then?'

Sunny stared at Cass in wonder for a bit, then stuck her thumb in her mouth, bowed her head and wandered off to digest all this.

'God, I didn't know all that,' said Mairéad.

'You never asked!' said Cass. 'You're one of those who thinks it's rude to ask.'

'Isn't it?'

'Not really.'

'Do you get sick of having to be so upbeat about it?'

'No way,' said Cass. 'Caitlin, Jesus, you should have seen her. I saw her around the place and I felt humility, just pure humility. And then there's another thing: I was spared the life of a child athlete, spared a life just marinating for years in a swimming pool. My dad would never have let me quit, not until I literally dissolved in chlorine. How much fun would that have been? I don't know. The accident meant I never had to make that choice to quit or not. There was never a suggestion that I would get back in the pool, and I was glad.'

Cass took a deep, cleansing breath in and then out.

'No. There's no need to feel pity for Cassandra Kelly. I am blessed. I'm blessed by God himself, I tell you. I feel it.'

They moved through the gorillas, then on to a cage full of noisy parrots, a flabby-necked pelican, two elegant giraffes, and a male lion, who looked uncannily like a domestic cat as he licked a paw. They walked through a plastic tunnel in the shape of a caterpillar into a hot, greenhouse-smelling place filled with butterflies and a lot of other visitors, cooing. Sunny disliked this space intensely, gave a bark of fright when a butterfly landed on her and hustled through the people in front of her towards the exit, shouldering them out of the way.

'Is she all right?' said a woman, nastily. Mairéad turned to see she was wearing too much make-up and a purple fluttery top. Her child, small and neat, was mesmerised by a butterfly feasting on a mangy-looking piece of mango.

'Ah, she's fine,' said Cass. 'She just doesn't like flying insects very much. It's only sensible, if you think about it.'

Mairéad hurried after Sunny. She rattled through the long strands of plastic links, designed to keep the butterflies inside the plastic tunnel, bashed through the scuffed plastic doors and caught up with her niece.

'What happened back there?'

'What do you mean?' said Sunny.

'With the butterfly and running out?'

'Oh – I didn't like it, it was flapping in my face.'

They pressed on through the zoo. Mairéad pointed at a kiosk and said, 'Ice cream?'

'Where?' said Sunny.

'There. There, where it says, "Ice Cream".'

Sunny looked at the kiosk where Mairéad was pointing and screwed up her eyes, lifting her top lip to under her nose, her cheeks rising up under her eyes. This reminded Mairéad of something but she couldn't put her finger on what. She chose an orange lolly for herself and, after spending a long time describing to Sunny what all the different ice creams would

Well, This Is Awkward

taste like, got her a Cornetto. Cass bought a Magnum and closed her eyes in ecstasy and went, 'Mmmmmm-num' when she took a bite.

Eating their ice creams, they strolled towards the camels, which were yanking hay from nets suspended from a very dead-looking tree. To the left of the camels was a sign towards 'The Farmyard'.

'Let's go down here,' said Mairéad. 'There are pigs.'

'Yeah, this place. This place is the *most* fun,' said Cass. 'You can actually interact a bit with the animals, it's not just staring and going, "Look, it's an okapi!" You used to be able to feed the giraffes! Now that was a gas. I think they stopped that, though. Sad times.'

Sunny walked directly towards the pigs. There were two, one in each sty, and they were gigantic, their enormous ears flapping down in front of their eyes, their moist snouts twitching in the air.

'Lots bigger than Dennis and Minnie,' said Sunny, finally.

'Oh look, you can feed the goats,' said Mairéad. 'Not quite a giraffe, but let's go and feed them. Goats are so sweet.'

They walked over to a large fenced-off area containing eight pygmy goats in various shades of white, black and ginger, each sporting a pair of jaunty little horns and pattering about on tiny hooves. In the middle of the pen was a manger filled with hay. The goats surrounded it. Small children of various sizes were pulling out handfuls of hay and offering it inexpertly to other goats, who nibbled and pulled at the strands.

They hung over the fence, finishing their ice creams. Then they went inside the pen. Sunny went silently to the manger and started carefully drawing out hay and feeding the goats. She patted and stroked them and pulled out more hay. She towered over the little toddlers and five-year-olds who were also feeding the goats, but she seemed quite unembarrassed about this. The other children were clumsy with the goats, who shied away from them. A pair of goats fell into an argument, put their heads down at each other and butted horns. One knocked down a toddler, who fell backwards onto its bottom, hard. A look of total surprise crossed the child's face and then, not knowing what else to do, it started wailing in shock. As its mother rushed over to pick up the child, the other pygmy goats scattered like naughty children and gathered around Sunny, hiding behind her legs, peeking out.

After about ten minutes, Mairéad looked around for somewhere to sit down while Sunny carried on feeding and petting the goats. She left the pen and she and Cass sat nearby on a bench. After twenty minutes, Mairéad went back into the pen and asked Sunny if she wanted to go and look at something else.

'No, I like it here,' replied Sunny.

She was so delighted that Sunny finally seemed pleased and occupied that she went back to sitting on her bench. After forty-five minutes she returned to Sunny.

'Really, it's time to go and look at something else now.'

'Why?' said Sunny.

'You can't stay with the goats all day long!'

'Why not?'

'Because...' Mairéad stared at Sunny. Sunny looked back at her, steadily, pulling some hay between her hands. 'Well, because it's nearly lunchtime.'

'I'm not hungry,' said Sunny.

'I thought you were always hungry.'

'I had that thing, that ice cream thing.'

'How weird is she on a scale of one to ten?' said Mairéad to Cass as she sat back down on the bench. 'In your professional opinion.'

'Absolutely no weirder than some of the kids that I've had to look after,' said Cass. 'She reminds me of my cousin's kid. With all the pacing around in circles, you know? It's all fine. Children are all weird.'

Cass thought for a bit and suddenly laughed out loud while remembering the weirdness of kids she had known. 'But she's not rude like you said. She just says what she sees. Don't try to fix her – I can see you looking at her all hungry like you're going to put her through your Instagram project machine and spit her out the other side looking like a little dolly.'

'The thought never crossed my mind,' Mairéad lied. 'But seriously, what am I going to do?' She put her head in her hands. 'I can't take her into work, I can't leave her with Mum… I don't even know how I'm going to be able to come to your party – I really can't bring her there.'

'Get a nanny,' said Cass.

'From where?'

'From an agency!' said Cass. 'My old agency, Skippy's. It's not cheap, mind.'

'Money, I've got.'

'Give them a ring – we had some good people on the books.'

In the end it was two hours before Sunny wanted to part with the goats and even then she made Mairéad promise that they would come back the next day.

'Tell you what,' said Cass, 'Auntie Mairéad will bring you back here tomorrow as long as you agree to go and get some new shoes. Those look like they've walked ten thousand miles on no sleep.'

Mairéad looked at Cass. 'You know what you're doing,' she said admiringly.

'Never,' said Cass, making a fist with her hand, 'miss an opportunity to negotiate.' Then Cass looked Sunny up and down. 'Actually, if I were you, I'd get her some nice Crocs. Just get them online. They can get as dirty as you like and you can put them through the dishwasher. They come up like new.'

'You're a genius.'

Cass clapped Mairéad on the shoulder in a boyish way. 'Try to enjoy all this,' she said. 'It'll be very good for you.'

'I've been waiting for someone to say that to me,' said Mairéad.

'Yes but it will be,' said Cass. 'It'll be good for your intimacy issues.'

'My what?'

'Your intimacy issues!'

'I haven't got intimacy issues!'

Cass laughed and laughed and then her phone rang. It was her agent and she had to run.

The agency booker at Skippy's laughed out loud when Mairéad rang looking for a nanny. 'It's the beginning of the summer holidays!' she said.

'Surely this is when people are most looking for childcare, though?'

'Yeah, but they booked their nannies back in January, February,' said the woman. 'You won't find anything now.'

Mairéad suddenly felt a savage burst of anger. 'Well fucking cheers for nothing,' she said, then hung up, wishing she was using a landline so that she could have slammed down the receiver.

She emailed Helen to tell her that in fact she only needed Sunny to stay with her for one night – the night of Cass's party. Then she started ringing other nanny agencies and discovered that, while rude, the woman at Skippy's was also correct. Trying to find a nanny in the last weeks of July was like trying to find tickets for Taylor Swift, perhaps, or Glastonbury.

An email from Helen: 'I'd love to babysit but I'm out at the theatre that night,' she said.

'Ha! You *liar*,' Mairéad snapped at her laptop.

The nanny agencies kept recommending Boop. It was an

app that offered daily childminding, rather than long-term nannies. It also had babysitters. Eventually, she gave up on the agencies and downloaded the app.

Sunny and Mairéad spent so much time at the zoo in the next three days that they got to know all three of the keepers by name. Sunny was even trusted to carry hay from the storeroom and fill up the manger. Mairéad started bringing a cushion with her, as the hard benches at the zoo gave her a sore bum.

ELEVEN

'Why are you dressed as a... wizard?' said Sunny.

It was 7 p.m. on Saturday and Mairéad was getting ready to go to Cass's costume party.

'I'm not a wizard, I'm Superwoman. I was supposed to be Harley Quinn but there was a mix-up at the costume shop and now I'm Superwoman.'

Mairéad looked at herself in the mirror and felt deeply disappointed. The costume was tacky and dumb and not what she had wanted at all. It also smelled and had stains on it. The tiny blue shorts covered in gold stars rode up her backside horribly and the cuffs were very itchy. The wig had arrived in a terrible state and had needed much washing and combing before it was wearable. She leaned closer to the mirror and gave the wig a settling squish on her head.

'I'm going to a party. Do you remember Cass?'

'Who?'

'The lady we went to the zoo with.'

'Uhhh,' said Sunny.

'With only one hand.'

Sunny lit up. 'Yes!'

'She's having a costume party, where you dress up. So you're having a babysitter.'

Well, This Is Awkward

'What's that?'

'Someone who comes and looks after you when your auntie goes out. Don't you have babysitters with Mum?'

'No. She just leaves me in the cabin. Sometimes I stay a night with Evan.'

'Where were you the night Mum had the accident?'

'I was with Evan.'

'And was he the one who told you that Mum was in hospital?'

'I can't remember.'

Beckii T lived locally and her photo on Boop was of a friendly-looking lady with pink hair. But what Mairéad opened the door to was a shrivelled woman with stringy brown hair and eyes that looked in different directions. She smelled strongly of an intense and ongoing cigarette addiction.

'Hello,' she said, in a breathy little-girl's voice. 'I'm Beckii.' She was barely taller than Sunny.

'Oh. Hello.'

'That's a smart outfit,' she said, looking Mairéad up and down.

'Sunny!' called Mairéad. Sunny appeared at her bedroom door.

'This is your babysitter, Beckii.'

'Okay,' said Sunny, clutching her blanket.

'Helloooo,' said Beckii, creepily. 'I hope it's all right,' she continued, turning back to Mairéad, 'but my boyfriend is going to pop by and drop something off? He won't be a minute.'

No, Mairéad wanted to say. *That is not okay.*

'Oh yes of course, fine,' she said warily, fixing her gaze firmly between Beckii's wandering eyes, hoping that this was the right place to look.

'Just to drop off some keys,' said Beckii.

'Yes, sure, sure. No problem. Sunny goes to bed at about 9 p.m. Make sure she brushes her teeth.'

'Okay,' said Beckii.

'Okay.' Mairéad stood uncertainly between Beckii and Sunny.

'I'll be back soon,' she said. Sunny was turning her blanket in her hands.

'When?' said Sunny.

'Soon. Just go to sleep and I'll be here in the morning.'

'All right.'

Mairéad hobbled off to Cass's party in her gold platform boots. The zips rubbed against her bare skin and she had to yank at the back of the shorts approximately once every four minutes.

While waiting for her Uber, she rang Helen's landline. Helen answered on the fourth ring.

'Hello?'

'So you're not at the theatre.'

'Oh, I... My friend stood me up,' said Helen.

'Ha! *Nonsense.* "Live for others", my arse. You are unbelievable.'

Cass's party was at a very modern warehouse apartment that belonged to one of her many friends. The front door to the apartment was wedged open with a fire extinguisher and Cass was standing just inside, dressed as Charlie Chaplin, talking to a man who was dressed as a policeman.

'You hosted an entire fancy-dress party just so you could come dressed as Charlie Chaplin?' said Mairéad.

Cass looked Mairéad up and down and let out peals of laughter. 'What the hell are you wearing?'

'I was supposed to be Harley Quinn but the bloody costume shop messed up my reservation. I need a drink.' Tetchily, she started shouldering her way through the crowd, feeling like she had never been in less of a party mood. She had wanted to ask Cass more about what she'd meant by her 'intimacy issues' but it wasn't the place for that sort of chat.

The loft looked like it had recently featured in an interiors magazine. The windows soared from floor to ceiling and there were sprawling units of seating areas, punctuated by open shelves, hanging plants and odd-shaped armchairs. To one side there was a set of DJ decks, and quiet music grooved away overhead. There were candles lit everywhere and a table set up as a bar. Mairéad relaxed a tiny bit. Yes. Yes, she wanted a very large glass of cold white wine. That would stop her freaking out that she had left Sunny with a complete stranger who was about to invite her random boyfriend round to 'drop off some keys'. But was it keys? It could be anything. Drugs? Stolen items? A sack to stuff Sunny in, in order to kidnap her and sell her into child prostitution?

Cass appeared at her elbow. 'Isn't this apartment crazy?'

'What does your friend *do* for a living? Drug dealer?'

'It's not hers – she's house-sitting for Friedrick Bluerghlerler.'

'Sorry, who?'

'Friedrick Bluerghlerler!'

'Who the hell is that?'

Cass pointed at a huge exhibition poster for MOMA on the wall. The main image was an enormous modern concrete sculpture with 'Friedrick Bugh-Luerler' written in 6-inch-high letters underneath.

'Friedrick Bluerghlerler!'

'Oh!' said Mairéad, not wanting to ask who on earth this person was. She took a deep sip of her wine.

'Kathleen!' said Cass. A woman with a mass of pneumatic wavy red hair, dressed in hospital scrubs splattered with fake blood, said 'Hiiiii!' and extended her arms.

Oh, *Kathleen*, thought Mairéad. Kathleen with all the *hair*.

'Have you just come from work? Is that blood fake or what?'

'The blood *is* fake, but I'm sorry, that's the extent of my costume. So I've come as a surgeon, but I am also actually a surgeon.'

'You remember Mairéad,' said Cass.

'Of course! Mairéad-who-isn't-Irish,' said Kathleen, pouring herself a dash of neat vodka and slugging it back.

Cass spotted someone, shouted 'Liam!', and took off into the crowd.

Mairéad smiled benignly at Kathleen, trying to think of something to say so that she wouldn't ask about Richard. She opened her mouth but ran dry.

'So, you went on a date with Richard?' said Kathleen.

'Yes!' Mairéad beamed. 'What a lovely guy.'

'Honestly,' said Kathleen, taking Mairéad's wrist, 'he's great. Surgeons are almost all complete psychos. You know, rude, weird, zero social skills. He's actually ten per cent human.'

'Totally,' said Mairéad, with a rictus grin.

Kathleen knocked back another neat vodka, which was also visibly at room temperature. She narrowed her eyes at Mairéad. 'Give him a chance. He's the best of a terrible bunch.' Then she poured yet another slug of vodka into her glass and plunged into the party crowd without even saying goodbye.

'. . . like with the vibrancy of all things and I was, like, is this me? Some split-dimension copy of me? You know?' The girl took a drag of her cigarette.

Mairéad nodded. 'Totally.'

'Uh-huh, uh-huh,' said the girl, chewing madly on some gum.

Mairéad tipped her drink towards her mouth but there was none left. She needed to get away from this girl, who was dressed as a cheerleader. She'd realised within about five minutes of arriving that she didn't know anyone at the party. She didn't know why she'd ever thought she would. She didn't know what the time was and her phone was wedged into her superhero belt. She was worried that if she tugged it out her hot pants would ride so far up that she wouldn't be able to get them out again.

'Hey, Instagram Lady!' said the man she'd been talking to before. She'd met him at the bar and he was very over-friendly in a way that made her think he was on drugs, but she couldn't think what sort of drugs they might be. He was wearing a Donald Trump mask pushed up on top of his head. Why was he calling her 'Instagram Lady'? Oh yeah, because she'd told him what she did for a living. He reached for a high five and she returned it, accidentally bumping into someone in the process. 'Whoops, sorry.' Across the jostling crowd of people she saw Cass waving her drink around and gesticulating at someone wearing a fluorescent green beanie and fiddling with some decks.

The cheerleader girl had her head on one side and now Mairéad was speaking, but she suddenly couldn't remember what she was saying, like when she was running up the stairs and briefly thought, How am I doing this? and then missed a step or stumbled.

'It's just important to modernise,' she heard herself saying. Something, something, blah, blah, '. . . my age at risk of being left behind by technology.'

'. . . back in 2014, but it was kind of bogus so I went back to Cambodia for a bit.' The Donald Trump mask guy was talking now, but by god he was boring.

'Oh great, Cambodia, wow,' said Mairéad. She tipped the glass back to her mouth and found that it was empty again. 'God, I've finished my drink – another?'

'Sure,' said Donald Trump mask guy. 'I'll come with you.'

'Okay,' she said, planning on losing him in the crowd.

And then she found herself staring at the back of Harley Quinn. Harley turned round.

'Jenna!'

'Oh hi!' said Jenna. Her mouth was smeared with red lipstick, just like Harley Quinn, and she looked absolutely outstanding in the costume.

'How do you know Cass?' she had to shout over the roar of the party.

'Ummm, gosh... I don't know! How do you know her?'

This was absolutely typical of Cass, to know two people from the same office and not even mention it.

'I can't remember either. Great costume! Is it from Bombardiers?'

'Yeah,' said Jenna, popping her hip. 'My friend Andy works there and got me an amazing discount on it. Great costume, too. Are you, like, Charlie's Angels or something? I think you need to go check your wig, though.'

Mairéad clutched her head – was her Superwoman wig wonky? On backwards?

'So I got the email about you having to take time off,' said Jenna. She put her head on one side. 'How is your niece, is she okay?'

'Yes, she's fine, fine. She just... children, you know. They're a bit more time-consuming than I thought and it was all such a surprise, so unexpected.'

'Yah, right,' said Jenna. 'My sister tried to go back to work with kids and it was just impossible. She quit after two weeks. And *she* had a husband and help and so it's...' Jenna stopped and turned her lips in on themselves before she pointed out that Mairéad had no such safety nets. 'I mean it's just a society-wide problem, right? Kids mess up your career? So how long do you think you'll be away?' She took a sip of her drink and looked at Mairéad with wide eyes.

'Oh, not long at all. It's just details, I'll work something out.'

'I mean good for *you*,' said Jenna, squeezing Mairéad's arm and making an aw-hun face. 'What an amazing auntie you are. You wouldn't catch me doing that for my sister's kids. They are a Night. Mare. But I want you to know that we're all here to support you. Take as long as you need, okay? I was saying to Gretchen—'

Well, This Is Awkward

'Gretchen! I was really kind of hoping to keep all this away from Gretchen.'

'Why? Gretchen was so nice about it,' said Jenna. 'Look, I know we all think of the New York office as these masters of pain but, when it comes to it, they're people, too.'

'Oh yeah,' said Mairéad, faintly. 'What did Gretchen say about it?'

Jenna shrugged. 'She said we should all do everything we can to support you.'

Mairéad felt a little sick.

'Oh hi!' said Jenna to a woman dressed as Elizabeth Taylor, dressed as Cleopatra. 'Rachel, hi!'

Elbowing her way through the crowd, reeling from both Jenna's unwitting theft of her costume and the frankly dastardly behaviour from Andy at Bombardiers, Mairéad stumbled in her stupid, death-trap boots. The wine and the noise of the party and the people had made her briefly forget about Sunny, but talking to Jenna had reminded her. Sunny! At home with the strange babysitter. She needed to leave, now. She stumbled and grabbed onto some blue serge, which turned out to be the policeman Cass had been talking to.

'You all right there?' he said.

'I need to get out of here,' she said.

'Well, let's get you out of here, then.' He turned and started wading through the thick, hot, crowd of Donald Trumps and Jessica Rabbits and Captain Jack Sparrows while Mairéad crouched in his wake.

'Coming through,' he said. 'Police emergency, thank you sir. Step aside please, ma'am.'

They reached the front door and she said, 'Thanks.'

'Happy to help, ma'am,' said the policeman and, tipping his hat, went back to the party.

Mairéad readjusted her wig, hoping that it was now

positioned properly. She didn't want to whip it off, as underneath was an ugly skullcap fashioned from some nude tights.

How could she have left Sunny with that weirdo? She clenched her bottom hard and then yanked her phone out of her belt, feeling two-large-glasses-of-wine wobbly. Two hours! Anything could have happened. She started clattering down the wrought-iron stairs in her stupid boots, clinging onto the railings. She sat down on a step and took off her boots, clutched them in one hand and continued her journey.

She bashed through the front door and scrabbled for the Uber app, then saw the saintly orange light of a taxi.

'Taxi!' she bellowed.

'Blimey,' said the cabbie as she climbed in.

'What do you need a cab for? I thought you could fly!' he cackled and set the meter going.

Mairéad gave him a weary thumbs-up to acknowledge his joke.

The taxi trundled the twenty-minute journey from Cass's party to home, with Mairéad perched on the edge of the bench seat, jiggling her foot with nerves. When the taxi drew up outside her building, she shoved her phone at the Zettle, then ran into the building and up the stairs, bootless. She fumbled her key in the lock and burst through the front door, panting.

'Hold on,' she heard Beckii saying. There was a smell of cigarette smoke in the air and Beckii guiltily appeared from the balcony, her mobile phone held to her chest.

'I was just having a cheeky one on the balcony!'

Mairéad turned to see Sunny standing in her bedroom doorway, looking frightened.

'No, it's fine,' she panted, relieved. 'Don't worry. Sorry. You can go. I came back early, not feeling well.'

'All right then,' said Beckii grumpily. She fetched her crumpled bag. 'Though I want paying until the time you said you'd be back on the app. And it's polite to give sitters notice when you're on your way home,' she added. 'I'll have to tell my boyfriend not to come round now,' she grumbled.

'Sure, sure. Whatever.' She ushered Beckii out of the flat and closed the door behind her, her shoulders slumping with relief.

A message pinged through from Dodie. It was a picture of a sunset over some water. 'Devon!' it read.

TWELVE

Mairéad raised her phone to take a snap of Sunny. She was sitting on a log with her thumb in her mouth and with the other hand she cuddled one of the smaller goats, who was black and white and went by the name Caesar. The goat leaned into the contact while Sunny scratched it between its little horns. Mairéad looked at the screen and then remembered yet again that Lenny didn't have a phone that could receive pictures.

It was Wednesday. Or was it Thursday? She couldn't be sure without checking on her phone. Yes, Wednesday. Sunny had been with her for ten days and on seven of those days they had visited the zoo. Every day, while Sunny pottered around with the goats, Mairéad used the time to check in with the three nanny agencies she was registered with to see if they miraculously suddenly had a chatty and presentable childminder with impeccable qualifications who was available immediately, but only for a week. Then she rang the hospital, to be told that Lenny was making a recovery more or less as they expected and ought to be out in seven days.

And every day she checked in with IGS, and every day was immediately shooed away by Jenna.

Well, This Is Awkward

'We've got this!' Jenna said. 'Relax. I'll send you a memo later with all the key info from today, okay? Enjoy!'

Whenever she called Andreas she received a text saying that he would call later, but he never did. An email to Biba got her the response: 'Don't worry about a thing, we're all here to support you and your family at this difficult time!!!'

She looked up from her phone to see Clara, the head keeper of the pygmy goats.

'We're expecting some babies soon,' she said. She wore khaki shorts, green wellingtons and a dark green fleece. She was always, at all times, carrying a bucket. The large set of keys attached to her shorts jingled constantly, noisily. Her wild hair was trussed up in a knot on top of her head. 'Little kids – they'll be seriously cute.'

'Which one is the mum?'

'Champ, that one. The all-over ginger,' said Clara.

'Oh right, I see,' said Mairéad, picking out the little goat staggering around under the weight of the unborn goat-babies. 'Don't know why I didn't notice before. Are goats good mothers?' she asked. She thought a lot about goats these days.

'Depends,' said Clara. 'Mostly they're pretty good, but you get the occasional one who acts like they'd rather be doing pretty much anything else. They're a bit like sheep – they'll adopt an orphaned kid, if they're in the right mood. But you get bad ones, too. I grew up on a sheep farm and around lambing time you'd sometimes get sheep trampling on their lambs or wandering off, not feeding them. Just not interested.'

'What did you do?'

'We sprayed a big red X on them,' said Clara, rinsing a bucket under a tap and sluicing it out down a drain. 'And they didn't get put in with the mums the next year.'

'One strike and you're out,' said Mairéad.

'Yep. We didn't muck about. I mean, I know I'm not supposed

to say this,' Clara stood up from where she had been bending over a large bag of hay, 'but sometimes I think it would do the world a lot of good if we did the same to humans.'

Mairéad and Sunny stayed at the zoo for another hour, then they had a sandwich at the café and went back to the flat.

Sunny's capacity to do nothing more than read her book and pace in circles was in some ways heroic. Her pattern was to read silently for up to half an hour at a time and then get up from her preferred reading place, which was the sofa in the living room, and pace the edges of the room, sucking her thumb, deep in thought.

She read shoeless and sockless and liked to pick at the dry skin on her feet while she read. She was a wide and voracious reader, willing to give anything she found a go, including recipe books and *The English Cottage*. While Sunny was in the bath – Mairéad insisted on nightly bathing – Mairéad vacuumed up the bits of dead, discarded skin from her parquet, grimacing. Sometimes Sunny slid the door to the balcony open a crack, slipped out and paced the perimeter of the balcony, then came back inside. She occasionally appeared in the kitchen with the alert, snack-hungry look on her face.

Mairéad was reminded of Lenny's words at the hospital, 'She's no trouble.' She understood what her sister had meant: Sunny was no trouble at all. She didn't fuss or whine or complain that she was bored, but she also didn't want to do anything other than read, pace about, or visit the goats or the bookshop. When they weren't at these activities, they were confined to the flat, and Mairéad quickly found that *she* was very bored, but also unable to completely relax. Nor could she leave the flat and find diverting things to do. It was a new feeling, and not very welcome. She laughed a brief and nasty laugh when she remembered how she had always thought that 'house arrest' didn't sound like much of a punishment.

She proposed to Sunny walks, trips to the cinema, to the shops, to the park or cafés, all of which were met with that same feverish head-shake. It was the goats or the bookshop and nothing else. Mairéad took Sunny to a large local playground, which she had walked past many times but never been inside. But Sunny sat silently and stubbornly on a bench and would not even go on a swing. Sunny did not want to chat about anything – not about what she'd learned at home with Lenny or what Evan the farmer was like or her travels with Dennis and Minnie or things she'd once got for her birthday. When Mairéad had asked Sunny what *Watership Down* was about, Sunny had replied, 'Why don't you read it yourself?' She was firmly, occasionally rudely, resistant to chit-chat. She didn't watch television, had never seen a movie and wasn't interested in either.

Mairéad started to feel a little stir-crazy and antsy. Not even another read of *The English Cottage* was soothing. She had taken out and reorganised all of her already meticulously organised drawers and cupboards. Her plants were fed, their leaves polished, the balcony swept of imaginary bits of soil and dried leaf. She went through her sparsely stocked food cupboards and moved things around a bit and then moved them back. She filled online baskets with thousands of pounds worth of clothes and then didn't check them out. At least, she thought she didn't check them out, yet every few days an item of clothing was delivered that she must have bought in a sort of zombie daze. Perhaps in a reflection of her state of mind, they were often shapeless, tent-like things in brown and khaki and black.

She spent hours on Instagram, removing the daily limit she had on her app, and revelled in how it atrophied her mind. She read Jenna's dull memos about the office, which she strongly suspected were leaving out pertinent information that Jenna didn't want her to have. She became addicted to one very strong gin and tonic at 6 p.m.

It was in this near-catatonic state of boredom that Mairéad excitedly answered a call from Ashley. Ashley, who had not replied to her for days and wanted to have a meeting before she 'disappeared' for the summer.

But this did not go down well with Sunny. She refused point-blank to go and see Ashley. Sunny said that *Mairéad* had *said* they were going to the zoo to see the goats and that's what she wanted to do. Perhaps today the kids would be born and she didn't want to miss it. She didn't want to go later; she wouldn't be bribed with a snack. She was even grumpier than usual and had a simmering look about her that said that, even if you threatened her with being tossed from the balcony into the street, she would not be attending this bullshit meeting with Ashley.

'Just leave me here,' snapped Sunny, pressing her knuckles into her closed eyes in a very adult expression of weariness. 'I told you, Mum leaves me on my own all the time.'

Mairéad stood, poised on the edge of indecision. She looked at her watch, then looked at Sunny.

'Fine,' she said. 'I won't be long.'

So she went to the meeting on her own. And, oh! The glorious feeling of being alone without Sunny was like being slowly pumped up with helium. She tripped along the pavement at practically a trot, listening to her own music, thinking her own thoughts. She felt that if she breathed in a little too hard she might lift and lift and her feet might gradually rise into the air and she might float away on the summer breeze, eyes closed, mouth in a gentle, Zen smile. She felt that light, that free.

Was this what Cass meant by her intimacy issues? That she was so relieved to be away from Sunny?

Whatever, she didn't care. She laughed gaily at literally everything Ashley said in the meeting, even though what

Ashley was mostly saying was how amazing Jenna was, how she just totally 'got' it. But Mairéad didn't even care.

'I know!' she shrieked. 'Jenna is amazing!'

Ashley shifted in her seat a little. Her lips were painted a putty colour and her eyelashes thickly coated in mascara. 'I was a bit worried when you said you were going to sell to Americans,' she said, 'but actually it's a breath of fresh air.'

Mairéad paused but then smiled. 'Great!' Then something occurred to her. 'Your boys,' she said.

'Yes?' said Ashley. She had two boys, eight and ten.

'I mean, how do you cope with them?'

Ashley looked confused.

'Sorry, I should explain – I'm looking after my niece for a bit, she's eleven.'

'Oh, I see,' said Ashley.

'It's just such hard work. Such a slog.'

'It can be,' said Ashley, her eyes looking uncertain. 'It's the juggle, isn't it?'

'I know, right.' Mairéad suddenly felt a great rush of relief to be able to talk to someone openly about this. 'There are so many hours in the day to fill. My days have never felt so long. It's like you literally can't get anything done when they're around, even if they're reading, or whatever, but I can't find any childcare for love nor money.'

'Mmm,' agreed Ashley. 'It's a challenge.'

'And she doesn't want to watch telly – that's my niece who doesn't – but even if she did just watch telly all day I feel like I'd feel guilty? Like I really ought to be taking her out and doing things and showing her stuff. But she doesn't seem to be interested in anything. Not anything!'

Ashley raised her eyebrows and smiled. 'Getting them off screens is difficult, yes. Most parents write down an agreement between them and their kids when they buy a new piece of tech. To agree that they're allowed this much or that much time on them.'

'That's a good idea,' mused Mairéad, only half-listening. 'Oh, and the constant catering! It's like being a really bad B & B.' She laughed at her own joke.

Ashley laughed politely. 'You definitely need a plan.' Then she looked at her watch. 'Anyway, look. It's been lovely to see you,' she said. 'I must be off.'

They wished each other a great summer and Ashley left.

The world was amazing. Mairéad's cool juice, sipped on the shaded terrace of a fashionable hotel, was amazing. All was well in the world. Mairéad had made contact with her superstar client and could relax. It was actually great to be able to connect with Ashley about children. In the past, she had always had to just do a sympathetic face and go 'Yeah, yeah, nightmare,' when parents unloaded about the hardships of parenthood. Now she felt she really understood what they meant.

After the meeting, she allowed herself ten minutes luxuriating in the low-slung rattan armchair on the terrace before setting off back to the flat. She would take Sunny straight to the goats and then they would go to the bookshop and then to buy peaches, to make up for her being left alone.

But she returned to find the flat empty. Sunny was gone. Her blanket was there, as were her new Crocs, but the current book she was reading was not. Mairéad raced out into the street.

'Sunny!' she called. 'SUNNY!' The street was empty, dusty and hot, and she felt nauseous and dizzy with panic. Her hands shook and her knees felt wobbly. Her heart was hammering out a disco beat and she had to clutch at a hedge just as she felt like she was going to faint.

Sunny was *gone*.

And it was Mairéad's fault. *All her fault.* Her stupid intimacy issues.

Well, This Is Awkward

Where, where, where, where the hell could she have gone, where, where, where, where? Sunny, Sunny, Sunny.

'SUNNY!' she screamed.

A man in a baseball cap asked if she was all right. 'No, no, lost my, lost my, lost my…' she gibbered. She didn't stop to talk, she just ran on and on but where to, she had no idea.

On and on, she circled the streets. She coughed with self-pitying tears. She did not want to call the police. Why had she left Sunny at home on her own in the first place? Because she was trying to save her career, because Sunny was no trouble but also an enormous pain in the arse, because she just wanted to be free for two hours, okay? God damn it, god DAMN it, was that too much to ask?

Feeling terribly unwell, as though she had slipped through some sort of no-return abyss of horror, she sank down onto a wall.

She did the only thing she could think to do and rang Cass.

'Okay,' Cass said. 'Talk me through it.'

Mairéad rattled through the meeting and the zoo and the baby goats and how she was selfish and insane and probably going to prison.

There was a pause; Cass was clearly thinking. Probably in this moment assessing and distilling all she knew about the latent insanity involved when it came to all children into a helpful suggestion. And then it came.

'She's gone to the zoo, that's what I reckon,' she said.

'The zoo, oh my god, of course!' shrieked Mairéad.

'I…' said Cass, but then there came the muted *moop, moop, moop* of a failed call.

Mairéad didn't pause to call Cass back; she swivelled round and about, searching for a taxi, but the streets were deserted. She started trotting and then cantering in the direction of the zoo while also fumbling with her Uber app. Her fingers were shaking and she said, 'No, no, no,' as Uber presented her with a car that was a full ten minutes away. She cancelled the request and stood on the side of the road clutching the front of her hair and cursing herself for not owning a bicycle. Then, in the distance, a black cab.

'Please,' said Mairéad, setting off towards it, 'please have your light on.'

She stuck out her arm and she did a thing she had never done before. She yelled, 'Taxi!' She had always envied other people who just confidently shouted, 'Taxi!' or, better yet, were able to whistle. She had lost out on many cabs due to shyness around this.

But now she didn't care. Her voice came out as embarrassingly high and hysterical as she had always feared it would, but the taxi flashed its lights and drew up beside her.

'Zoo, please,' she said, panting.

She scanned the streets as the taxi trundled along. Mairéad had both her and Sunny's membership cards in her wallet, so Sunny would not be able to get in. Where would she be? Ambling along? Sitting on the kerb?

Cass was calling again.

'Any sign?'

'Not yet.'

'Just a thought: how do you get to the zoo normally?'

'Normally bus,' said Mairéad, feeling so frightened and sick that she rolled down the taxi window in order to feel some fresh air on her face.

'Right, well, if you don't see her around the zoo, check the bus stop. Keep me on the line.'

Mairéad didn't wait, but redirected the taxi driver back to the bus stop.

'Sorry,' she said by way of explanation. 'I've lost my niece.'

'Bit careless,' said the cabbie.

The taxi turned two corners and Mairéad squinted at the bus stop. Was it? Was it? Please let it be.

Yes, there it was. A small figure on the bench next to the bus stop. Not sitting but lying on the bench, a book tented over its face.

'She's here, she's here,' said Mairéad to Cass. 'I think I'm going to throw up. You're some kind of… some kind of child… *whisperer*.'

'You give that girl a telling-off,' said Cass. 'I'd have had a smacked bottom for that.'

Mairéad paid the taxi driver and, still feeling unsteady on her legs, got out of the cab and shut the door. She sat down next to Sunny. There was a throbbing in her head, the feeling of an elastic band around the top of her skull squeezing in and out. She inhaled deeply and then exhaled.

'Hey there,' she said.

Sunny looked up, unsurprised. Then she sat up slowly, as if she was very old and stiff, and closed the book.

'I was going to the zoo,' she said, after a while. 'I wanted to see the goats.'

Mairéad breathed out, hard. 'Right. And how were you going to get into the zoo?'

Sunny shrugged. 'Is it difficult?'

'No, but you need a card. Did you bring the card?'

'No.'

'No, because I've got the cards. How were you going to pay for the bus?'

Sunny looked at her feet, shrugged again.

'Look, can you not do this again? Wander off like that? It was a bit worrying.'

'I wanted to see the goats,' Sunny repeated.

'Okay, well, I can see that. Anyway, I'm back now and I was going to actually ask you if you wanted to come and see the goats. How about it? And then an ice cream?'

'I don't know,' said Sunny. 'My head hurts. And I'm so cold.'

Mairéad frowned and touched Sunny's arm, which was

boiling hot. She held her palm against Sunny's forehead, which was even hotter. Sunny shrank from her touch.

'Woah. Can you walk? Can you stand up?'

Sunny got unsteadily to her feet. The distance back to the flat was too absurdly short to call another taxi, but it seemed rather far to walk if you had a fever. Especially if, like Sunny, you had no shoes on.

'We'll try to walk a *bit*. See how we get on.'

Sunny walked slowly with her arms folded and her head down, padding silently along on her bare feet. She staggered slightly. She let Mairéad put an arm around her. Her head flopped onto Mairéad's shoulder and Mairéad saw that Sunny's eyes were closed as she walked.

'Just one foot in front of the other,' said Mairéad, steering her around the occasional dog mess and fag butts. 'You're doing great,' she rambled. 'Nearly there.'

They arrived back at Mairéad's flat, Sunny's head drooping.

'Let's get you into bed.' But when she pushed open the door to Sunny's room, it just seemed cramped and hot and mad with its stupid, faux-rustic motifs. She directed her instead into her own room: large, airy and relatively cool – north-facing, away from the sun.

Sunny crawled onto the bed and lay down on her side. Mairéad switched on the ceiling fan. Then she fetched a glass of water.

'My eyes hurt, my head hurts,' said Sunny.

'I know. You must feel bad.' Mairéad put the water down on the side table, closed the shutters against the glare of the day and then half closed the curtains, casting the room in a balmy, dim light.

Sunny was very still, her eyes closed. Then they fluttered open and she pitched forward over the side of the bed and vomited onto the parquet, just a thin spurt of harmless gloop. Mairéad scurried to fetch a towel and laid it down on the mess. Sunny vomited again, neatly, onto the towel.

'Urgh,' said Sunny and wiped her mouth.

Mairéad perched on the edge of the bed. She felt Sunny's forehead again and encountered that alarming, unnatural heat. She felt, in the edges of her consciousness, a prickling of panic.

She had no medicine for children and didn't even know what it would be or look like. Then she remembered that Sunny thought medicine was poison anyway. Would she even take it, if she had some? She had no thermometer. She often prayed not to get ill herself so that she didn't have to contact her local GP surgery, which had proved over the years to be impervious to charm and only moderately helpful for non-urgent conditions.

She wanted Sunny to have a sip of cold water from the glass, which was now blurry with condensation, but knew that Sunny would not be able to sit up. She went back to the kitchen and rummaged in all the drawers for an abandoned straw but couldn't find one – she had clearly done too thorough a chucking-out job when she'd moved back into the flat. She rattled through all the cupboards until she found a sports-style water bottle. She filled it with cold water, brought it back to the bedroom and encouraged Sunny to take a tiny, sucking sip through the nozzle.

Then she cleared up the vomited-on towel and found the number for her local GP surgery, which, when she rang, turned out to be shut for the rest of the day. She paused for a moment and then opened her laptop.

The internet told her, variously, to: take Sunny directly to a hospital if she suspected she might have sepsis or meningitis; but not to take Sunny to a hospital if she suspected that Sunny might be infectious; not to take Sunny to a hospital because they were very understaffed; not to take Sunny to a hospital because she might contract MRSA when she was there; take Sunny to a hospital immediately if she was very hot or sleepy or unconscious; to attempt a homeopathic remedy; not to attempt a homeopathic remedy; to keep Sunny cool; to wrap Sunny up; to alternate doses of paracetamol and ibuprofen; to let the fever run its course, unmedicated; to pay £120 for this GP video call; to pay only £90 for *this* GP video call; £200 would get her an actual at-home visit from a real doctor!; not to use private doctors, therefore creating a two-tier system that was catastrophic to society.

She went back to the bedroom. Sunny was asleep, quiet, on top of the covers. Her eyelashes fluttered against her cheeks, which bloomed bright red. Mairéad fetched a light shawl from a cupboard and put it over Sunny's legs and feet.

She plumped up some pillows and sat down on the bed, listening to Sunny's breathing, which seemed normal: not fast or that mystifying medical term, 'shallow'. She went back to her phone and scrolled through a list of sepsis symptoms. Then she went into the living room and rang 111.

The first call was accidentally cut off.

The second time, she got through.

'Hello, 111?'

'Hi, I'm looking after my niece and she seems a bit unwell, I'm not sure what to do.'

'Is the patient awake and breathing?'

'Yes, she's fine. Well, she's not awake, but she's breathing. She's asleep, she's got a fever, I just don't know what to do.'

'Is the patient awake and breathing?'

'Well... no and yes.'

'Could you wake the patient up, please?'

'What? Why? But she's only asleep.'

'Are you not able to wake up the patient?'

'Well, I could, but she won't be happy about it. Look, all I want to know is when I ought to worry. On the internet I've seen things about sepsis and meningitis. How do you know when that's happening? Or when something is just a bad cold? Or flu or whatever?'

'Are you with the patient?'

'Yes, she's just in the room next door.'

'Are you able to wake up the patient?'

Mairéad hung up. She went back to the bedroom and stared at Sunny for a bit, feeling on edge and vigilant against an unknown, nameless threat. She reached out and put a hand on Sunny's shoulder and left it there for a while. Then she rang Dodie, who didn't answer. She left a strange, rambling voicemail.

The bright day mellowed to afternoon, then twilight, then darkness. The ensuing night undulated with Sunny's fever. She shivered uncontrollably as it went up, her teeth chattering. She squawked at the grinding pains in her joints and the burning sensitivity of her skin. Mairéad cajoled her to take sips of water and helped her to a dimly lit bathroom to pee. Her urine was dark, and smelled strongly. Mairéad held the bottle of water to Sunny's lips and kept saying, 'One more tiny sip, one more,' until Sunny weakly pushed the bottle away.

Sunny talked during her fevers, about things that Mairéad assumed were from the books she'd read. Her dreams seemed to be fraught with complex practical problems to do with some people not understanding where other people had left important keys. There was often a person called 'Bridget'. There was occasionally some pitiful whimpering. At times she was coherent, but at others said words that were only half recognisable. They slid around, out of reach. Sunny had not woken up fully or sat up now for more than twenty-four hours.

Mairéad dozed by Sunny while she slept. She didn't know if it was Sunny's periodic stirring that woke her up, or if she somehow had a sixth sense that Sunny was going to stir and she woke up in anticipation of it, but when Sunny woke, so did she. She found herself, gritty-eyed and headachy, standing by the living-room French doors as the summer dawn changed the light back from black to grey to blue to gold.

Sepsis, whispered a voice. *Sepsis, meningitis*. She kept wanting to ask the internet, but then stopped when she remembered that not only did the internet not know, it made things worse. She did not want to call Lenny, who would want Mairéad to treat Sunny with mad tinctures containing eye of newt and tongue of bat.

Dodie called, ticking her off for leaving a voicemail ('I never listen to those, you know that!'). She recommended Nurofen and Calpol and said she was sure all you had to do was make sure their hands and feet didn't go cold. 'And if her skin goes a funny colour, watch out for that. For god's sake don't bother calling 111.'

Mairéad sat silently on the end of the line. She was underslept and felt dizzy and confused.

'Do you think I have intimacy issues?' she said to Dodie.

'What? No, don't be absurd. You're a very intimate person. Who's been telling you that? They're insane, don't listen to them, you're doing a great job.'

'Call Richard,' insisted Cass.

'No,' said Mairéad. 'Not him.'

'Why not?' whined Cass. 'For god's sake. He really likes you, you know. He was pestering me to set him up with you after he saw a photo and it *wasn't even a good one*.'

'Sorry. I know this wasn't your plan.'

'Just tell me why, though. I mean why you won't call him.'

'I don't want to encourage him. He's kind of a simp. I've just had enough of all that; I don't need to owe anyone a favour right now.'

'A simp! God, where have we got to that just a nice man is called a simp. Okay, sure, but he's a simp who can give you free medical advice. And I bet it's good medical advice, too,' said Cass. 'I can't believe you're letting this get in the way of medical care for a *child*.' She was getting pompous now.

'It's not my pride, it's my gag reflex. I just can't,' said Mairéad. She paused. 'Is this what you mean by my intimacy issues?'

'It's exactly what I mean,' said Cass.

At 6.15 the next morning, after another textured and cyclical night, Mairéad sat at her laptop with a cup of tea and her head in her hands. She read and re-read and read again everything she could find about childhood fevers and the correct treatment thereof. Was it 'slapped cheek', was it scarlet fever? Could it be measles? She bet Sunny wasn't vaccinated against anything. She was about to risk leaving Sunny on her own in order to dash to the local pharmacy in order to track down the Nurofen and the Calpol that Dodie had mentioned, despite knowing full well that Sunny would refuse it on the basis of it being poison. But then she started reading a long piece online about how there was no need to use pain relief if there was a fever because the fever was 'doing a job' in fighting a virus.

There were 1,983 comments on the piece, all viciously arguing with each other about whether or not this was good advice. Mairéad found herself sucked into the drama of it. She read and read until her eyes burned.

She broke away from her laptop and went to check on Sunny; after the chaos of the comments, the thousands of ringing voices, which ultimately came to no clear conclusion about whether you should or should not treat fever in children with painkillers, she was convinced that she would find Sunny in great pain or distress. But Sunny was just there in the bed, breathing in and out quite peacefully, the fever blooming on her cheeks.

THIRTEEN

Mairéad's father was diagnosed with pancreatic cancer when Mairéad was thirty. Lenny was by that point living with honour and purpose in a range of German off-grid bases with Misha. She was, nevertheless, told about the diagnosis by email. She objected by return of email, about a week later, to the use of chemotherapy. But she was in Germany with patchy internet and so was easily ignored.

But then Lenny arrived back in London, having hitch-hiked, and started waving her arms around and lecturing everyone, ranting, about the chemo. She was then much less easy to ignore as she was always there, stamping about, filling the room with her obsessive monologues. She had wanted to take Gavin back to the True Earth community in Germany, where natural healers would see to him.

Mairéad was the one taking Gavin to his chemotherapy appointments, sitting in hospitals for hour after hour, watching Gavin submit to the infusion of drugs, the names of which she could never remember. And she was stressed out and upset by it. The idea that Lenny would drag Gavin to Bavaria to offer him up in sacrifice to those True Earth weirdos was unbearable even to contemplate.

And yes, she was sick to death of caring for Gavin. And of

playing along with Helen's repeated claims of very urgent things to do, which meant that she couldn't possibly take Gavin to his appointments. With hindsight, Mairéad saw that perhaps it had been Gavin's illness that had triggered Helen's reluctance to leave the house, but at the time it was just infuriating. She was also sick of the absolute zero thanks she was getting from anyone. Helen wasn't even totally aware that she *wasn't* taking Gavin to the hospital. She said she was going to, didn't she? It wasn't her fault that things kept getting in the way.

Mairéad had been legitimately angry with Lenny, but, at some point during the visit, Mairéad flipped. She went apeshit. She screamed at Lenny because there was no one else she could scream at. She couldn't scream at Helen, or the hospital staff or that one nurse who was a bit clumsy when getting the infusion going, or people at work, or anyone else. So she took it out on Lenny.

'Just stop with your stupid hippy bullshit!' she bellowed. 'Take Dad to Germany? He can barely walk up the stairs! You're off your bloody head, you mad, paranoid cow. Lecturing us with your crazy crap. *God you're boring!* You sound like a *nutter*, you know that? Fuck off back to wherever you've been with that idiot Misha. You're fuck-all use.'

Helen barged into the kitchen, where they were rowing. 'What the hell is all this noise! Your father is unwell, do I need to remind you? You're upsetting him. You're upsetting me, for god's sake!'

Lenny stormed out and left shortly after that. When Gavin died six months later, she didn't return for the funeral and only sent a long, angry letter to Mairéad. 'Chemo is *chemicals*,' the letter read. 'That's why it's called *chemo*. It killed him! How can you not see that?' After that, she had seen Lenny only once more – on her visit to fit grommets in Sunny's ears.

Mairéad got up from her living-room sofa, filled a bottle with tap water and took a sip. She looked at the calendar on her phone. According to the hospital, Lenny would be out in two days' time. She texted Lenny to ask how she was getting on and when she wanted Mairéad to arrive with Sunny. She spent the next hour looking up very expensive boutique hotels in the Mediterranean.

The next day, she was unpacking a grocery order when she heard the bedcovers rustling and the unmistakable sound of two small feet landing on the parquet floor. She turned and peeked down the hallway to see Sunny gingerly picking her way to the bathroom.

Afterwards, Sunny went back to bed but she didn't go back to sleep. After about an hour, she sat up. Later, Sunny took sips of chicken soup made from a packet. She was too drained and fuzzy to read, so Mairéad brought her laptop to the bed and cycled through some children's television shows. There was a series of short cartoons, silent except for music, featuring a little figure that seemed to be a cross between a monkey and a mouse. These raised a smile and Sunny actually laughed when a hooting owl was bothering the little monkey creature as he was trying to get to sleep in his tent. Sunny watched all of those animations. Then they discovered an irreverent show about history and Sunny watched all of those too, while occasionally drinking chicken soup and eating crackers.

Mairéad texted Lenny again and then rang the hospital, but neither Bethan nor Bronwyn could be located.

Mairéad offered Sunny Coca-Cola, both because she believed it to have magical salt-and-sugar replacement properties and also because she knew that Lenny would hit the roof if she knew. Coca-Cola was as much of a poison as, if not more so than, chemotherapy drugs. Sunny didn't much like the Coca-Cola, though, much preferring sparkling water, with ice. She couldn't get over the miracle of ice, and requested as many cubes as could be fitted in the glass.

Well, This Is Awkward

The day Lenny was supposed to leave hospital came and went. Mairéad moved on from TV series to movies. She signed up for an expensive streaming service she'd had no need for in her life up until this point. They watched movie after movie. Sunny wanted some paper and a pen so she could write down a rating for each film as they watched them. *Big Hero 6*: 5 stars. *Ron's Gone Wrong*: 5 stars. *Frozen*: 5 stars.

'I've heard so much about *Frozen* but never seen it,' said Mairéad.

'Olaf is so funny,' said Sunny.

'When he says he's got no bones. And he doesn't know that he's going to melt in the sun.'

'Yeah!' said Sunny, and collapsed into giggles, scrunching her blanket up to her face.

Frozen II, on the other hand, got no stars.

Moana brought about a whole new category: 5 stars *plus*.

Sunny migrated to the sofa and watched TV while Mairéad changed the bedlinen. She hummed 'Let It Go' as she punched the sheets into the washing machine. Then her phone rang. Castell Cerys Hospital! At last. They would be wanting to know when Mairéad could bring Sunny back.

But that was not why they'd called.

FOURTEEN

Bloxcombe dazzled white, blue and yellow in the sunshine. The taxi crested a hill and then made its slow and winding way down increasingly narrow lanes to the water. Fleabane flourished in any nook in the stone walls, the little daisy heads nodding in the sea breeze that billowed lazily off the glittering estuary.

'Are we here?' said Sunny blurrily as the taxi stopped by the side of a small playing field.

'I think so.'

'The quay's over there.' The taxi driver gestured across the playing field. 'I'll bet smart money that Quay Cottage is that-a-way.'

Mairéad paid the taxi driver and then started dragging the wheelie case across the parched playing field, following Sunny to the quay.

Following Dodie's instructions, she found the keys to the cottage perched on the door lintel.

The front door of the cottage opened directly onto a square sitting room, which had two blue and white striped sofas, a coffee table and a TV. Up a short flight of stairs was a kitchen. There were two bedrooms – one with a double bed and one with a bunk bed. There was a tiny shared bathroom.

A dog barked nearby and Mairéad turned to see a panting

Well, This Is Awkward

mongrel appear in the kitchen doorway, with the floppy ears of a border collie and a black patch of fur over one eye. Sunny was standing in the living room with her rucksack still on her shoulders and her arms folded.

Outside there came a further sound – of feet against the gritty surface of the quayside. Round the doorframe appeared a sandy-haired child. He wore blue shorts, a baseball cap, a faded yellow T-shirt with a cricket bat and ball embroidered in one corner and a pair of battered pool slides. He peered nosily into the cottage, saw Sunny and then adopted an air of exaggerated nonchalance.

'Hi,' he said, casually turning his baseball cap backwards. He thumbed at himself. 'Dibs,' he said. 'That's Digger,' he added, pointing to the dog, as if wanting to ensure that there was no mix-up.

'Oh right, Dibs,' said Mairéad, clicking her fingers. 'I know that name. Dodie mentioned you. Are you the welcoming committee?'

'Yeah,' said Dibs, staring at Sunny again.

Mairéad went to pat Digger, who was friendly and bright-eyed, with highly mobile and expressive ears.

'Dibs is a weird name,' said Sunny.

'It's a nickname. My real name is *Charles*,' he said in an affected, plummy accent. 'But no one ever calls me that. You must be Sunny, then,' he added.

'Yes,' said Sunny.

'That's a weird name, too.'

'S'pose,' said Sunny.

'Coming crabbing?'

'What's crabbing?'

'I'll show you.'

'No,' said Sunny, with her insistent head-shake.

'You don't kill the crabs,' said Mairéad. 'You just catch them and put them in a bucket.'

'Yeah,' said Dibs. 'There are big ones. You let them go afterwards. You know, back in the water.'

'So what's the point, then?'

'To catch them! To see them close up in the bucket. Sometimes they fight,' said Dibs, balling his hands into fists and rolling them about.

'Go on,' said Mairéad. 'Give it a go.'

'Well, okay,' said Sunny.

'Maybe leave your rucksack here. You can have a snack afterwards. Both of you.'

Once the magic s-word had been uttered, Sunny shrugged off the bag and warily followed Dibs away from the cottage and towards the pier, which was lined with bobbing rowing boats. The dog trotted after them.

Dodie answered a FaceTime. She was resting against white linen cushions, wearing a pale green frilled blouse and a sunhat embroidered with cherries.

'Oh, you're here!' she exclaimed. 'Oh, yay! Come and see us at once.'

'We met Dibs. He seems like a nice boy. He's adopted your dog, it looks like.'

'They keep each other company. Yes, he's very sweet. Very emotional. He'll show you where everything is. I've told him about Sunny. He can't believe she doesn't go to school. Nice for him to have a change of scene – he's been hanging out with me and Digger, and the dog's all right but I think I'm quite boring company. I just read and drink lemonade. I've made Sunny out to be quite glamorous.'

'Well. She sort of is.'

'So what happened with Lenny, then? God, tell me.'

Three days previously, back in London, Mairéad had stood next to her washing machine with the phone to her ear. As she'd listened, she'd seen, in her mind's eye, her bougie, expensive, child-free Mediterranean getaway exploding in flames. Her magnificent return to IGS melted and drooped and dribbled like the world's most boring surrealist painting.

The consultant, whose name Mairéad had instantly forgotten, explained that Lenny was in theory ready to leave hospital, but not to have sole care for a child. It was hard for her to get around, she said. And she was worried about Lenny's mental health.

'I am not a mental health *expert*,' said the doctor carefully. 'But she seems a little paranoid to me.'

'Oh, that's normal! She's always been like that.'

But still, said the consultant, she could not in good conscience see Lenny and Sunny on their own with Lenny in this state. Not if there was an alternative.

'Of course.' Mairéad looked at Sunny watching *Wreck-It Ralph*: Sunny blinked, then half smiled and slipped her thumb into her mouth. 'Of course, totally. Totally. I can keep her.'

'Lenny's mental health?!' screeched Dodie. 'What about your mental health?'

'Well quite. No, it's fine,' said Mairéad. 'But very glad to get down here, for a change of scene.'

'But what about work, can you take the time off?'

'I've had to take it as holiday. They gave me two weeks' compassionate leave and now it's my whole two weeks' annual leave going up in smoke. Or however long it takes Lenny to sort herself out.'

Jenna had sounded actively thrilled about Mairéad not coming back to the office. She imagined Jenna sitting at her desk, cluttering it up with her things, Margot shedding hair all over her coral pink sofa...

'This will be a holiday,' said Dodie. 'I promise. More fun than sitting by some dreary pool in Greece.'

There was a pause.

'Nice try.'

'Well, I had to say something.'

Bloxcombe was a small village of fewer than a hundred houses, built onto a hill and painted white, pink, yellow and blue. Six cottages lined the quay, along with the Jolly Roger pub. Halfway up the hill there was a post office and a general store. The Jolly Roger served pizza in the evenings, every day except Wednesday, and Mairéad agreed to meet Dodie outside with Sunny for a pizza dinner that evening at 6 p.m.

The village, which had been hot, silent and empty except for Dibs when Mairéad and Sunny had arrived at 3 p.m., bustled with activity by 5.30 p.m. A series of sailing boats appeared down the estuary and soaking-wet children scurried to and fro along the quay in full wetsuits and life jackets. Hearty-looking women and very brown men with windswept hair lugged oilskin bags about. A louche crowd of about thirty gathered outside the Jolly Roger, crunching through the shingle and cradling pints against linen-shirted chests. Sweating bottles of rosé perched precariously on uneven stone walls. Dogs dashed about through milling legs, their undersides spattered with sand. They leaped into the water after balls, sat and panted, barked at waved sticks. Rangy, sunburned teenagers with elaborate hair lounged around the edges of activity.

At 6 p.m., with Sunny set pacing on the pier, Mairéad picked her way through the crowd, looking for Dodie. She felt observed and out of place amongst all these haw-hawing people who knew each other.

'Mairéad!' called a voice. She turned. It was not Dodie but Dodie's husband, Miles. A handsome, sporty man of about forty-five, Miles did something unfathomable in tech, which involved flying about the world a lot and being charming. He earned a lot of money. Dodie had fallen gratefully into his arms aged twenty-six, and wailed to Mairéad that she was just so relieved her terribly hard life of just work, work, work every single damned day was over. Both Dodie and Mairéad

Well, This Is Awkward

had, at the time, been working as assistant buyers in a large department store. Dodie was in the children's section and Mairéad was in homeware. On her hen night Dodie had confessed to Mairéad that Miles was not a dream kisser. 'But some things are more important,' she said, blinking soulfully. 'Like money. And I feel like maybe he can be trained?'

'Hi, good to see you,' said Miles. He wore a white linen shirt that was wet in places and crumpled in others and a pair of baggy khaki shorts held up with string that made him look like one of the Famous Five.

'Dodie's had a turn, can't face the rabble. She says grab a pizza and then head to ours. It's River House, over there.'

Miles gestured to the other end of the quay, where a white archway led up to a large, square house with a stubby, Italianate roof.

'Ooh, that's a nice house,' said Mairéad. 'Dodie never said it was that grand.'

'Yuh,' said Miles, leading her to the Jolly Roger to order the pizza. 'Been in the family for ages. It was actually due to be sold by my great-aunt and it was a real fixer-upper. But in the end we thought, sod it, let's just have it. Didn't want some awful hedgie to get it.' Miles flashed his teeth, dazzling in his tanned face, in acknowledgement that he was *also* awful.

The crowd was four deep in the pub, but Miles felt the elbow of a man in a blue polo shirt that said 'Jolly Roger' all over it and commanded some pizzas and drinks.

'Gonna do sailing?' he said to Mairéad.

'What?'

'Sailing, there's a sailing school. That's really what people come to Bloxcombe for.' Miles batted his thick salt-and-pepper hair out of his eyes.

'Oh not for me, thanks. I'm not crazy about open water.'

'Fair enough,' said Miles. 'You should talk to Dodie about that. All mine do it. Maybe your nephew—'

'Niece.'

'Niece, would like it.'

'Ummm... I'll ask. I like your new dog.'

'Digger!' said Miles. He visibly brightened. 'What a champion. Total legend. Love him to absolute bits. Well, if your niece wants to have a go at the sailing, we've got all the kit. Plenty to spare.'

They stood outside the pub while they waited for their pizzas, and met a woman called Nina. She was dressed in white sailor pants and a navy cotton popover shirt with big white buttons. She had a dark bob and heavy-framed glasses and was about sixty.

'Which one is your niece?' said Nina, peering through the crowd.

Without turning round, Mairéad said, 'She'll be the one walking round and round by herself somewhere.'

'Oh yes! Over there, on the pier. Does she do that a lot?'

'All the time.'

'Like Darwin.'

'What?'

'Darwin,' said Nina. She took a sip of her half of beer and delicately wiped her top lip. 'Charles Darwin. He used to walk round and round his garden having a good old think. And he carried stones in his pockets and put one down every lap. Or he picked one up. Or something. Anyway, she looks utterly fascinating.'

'Is Douglas here this year?' said Miles.

'Yes, he is,' said Nina. 'Douglas is my youngest,' she said to Mairéad. 'He's a rower,' she added, as if that ought to mean something.

'Has Dodie told you about the regatta?' said Miles. 'It's at the end of next week, there are races and so on. The two-man rowing race is the really... it's the big deal of the event. There are these boys, the Callaghan brothers, who always win it. But

Well, This Is Awkward

with Douglas in a boat...' Miles trailed off and gestured at Nina, who beamed in a very unattractively smug way.

'I mean, it's what he does,' she said with a shrug.

Miles said that the pizzas would be ready in a moment and now would be a good time to get Sunny, who he had seen disappearing back into Quay Cottage. Mairéad made her way back, crunching along the noisy shingle beach and hopping up the wonky stone steps cut into the quay wall.

'Sunny!' she called, into the cottage. She looked around and then went up the stairs, to find Sunny lying on her bed, reading a book and picking her feet.

'Pizza time,' she said.

Sunny had enjoyed her first pizza very much and so made a happy face at this news. She tossed her book aside exuberantly and got up. They came out of the cottage and stopped: on the bench outside the cottage was Dibs.

He sat hunched forwards, his elbows on his knees and his hands over his face. Tears dripped through his fingers and onto the ground.

'Oh!' ventured Mairéad. She looked around. Surely a parent would be here any moment now to investigate.

Dibs said nothing, his shoulders just shook.

'You look a bit unhappy,' added Mairéad. Dibs remained silent.

She got up, went to find some tissues and a glass of water and came back. She set these things down on the bench.

Dibs sniffed loudly and said in a half-whispered, high-pitched voice, 'I just wanted to see what they were looking at.'

'What who was looking at?'

Dibs didn't reply, he just said, 'You don't have to sit with me.'

'I know. But I want to, if that's okay. I mean, do you mind if I sit here?'

Dibs shrugged. There was a pause. The laughter and chatter

from outside the pub floated over to them. Some rigging clanked against a mast and a seagull threw back its head and bellowed at the sky.

'I'm curious to know what it was you wanted to see.'

'It was… just my brother. I wanted to see something that he… and he's just… he's just so horrible…' Dibs dissolved into tears again.

'Siblings *are* horrible in my experience. Which one is your brother?'

Dibs flung his hand out to the side. 'Orange T-shirt,' he said.

She squinted into the distance and saw a teenage boy with an orange T-shirt in a crowd of other teenagers.

'They all look very similar, his friends.'

'They're my brothers.'

'All of them?'

'Four of them. Don't know who the others are.'

'Four brothers?! I mean, five including you. Five children.'

'Yes.'

'Oh well, that sounds like it might be fun.' Mairéad contemplated how alone Sunny was with no sibling. No witness.

'It's not fun, it's awful,' Dibs huffed, his voice breathy with emotion. 'It's terrible, they're the worst people in the world.'

Sunny appeared again silently, shoeless. Mairéad briefly wondered where her Crocs were and opened her mouth to ask Sunny to go and find them and put them on. Then she closed her mouth again. Who cared where the shoes were. Sunny had tried to walk to the zoo with no shoes on. No amount of nagging was going to make her remember to wear them.

'What's wrong with him?' said Sunny, her eyes round and curious.

'He's upset.'

'About what?'

'Something to do with his brothers.'

Well, This Is Awkward

Sunny paused, thinking.

'Are they dead?' said Sunny.

'Unfortunately not,' said Dibs.

Mairéad let out a bark of laughter.

'How old are you?' she said to Dibs.

'I'm ten.'

'You're very witty for ten,' she said.

'I watch a lot of YouTube,' said Dibs. 'It's where I get most of my material. YouTube Shorts,' he added. 'It's like TikTok but I don't use TikTok because it's how China spies on us.'

Dibs was showing signs of recovery. Mairéad offered him a tissue, which he took and blew his nose with. He smelled of biscuits and sun cream and wore a very tatty friendship bracelet on one wrist.

'Can we watch a movie?' said Sunny.

'Yeah!' said Dibs. 'Anything except *Jaws*.'

'Sure. Later. We're going to have pizza first.'

There was a call of '*Dii-ibs*,' by an unseen female voice from within the crowd outside the pub.

Dibs was suddenly alert, like a gun dog or a meerkat.

'That's Mum, gotta go,' said Dibs, and ran off without a backwards glance.

Mairéad looked up and saw Miles waving with one hand. In the other he was balancing about eight pizza boxes.

'Come on, then,' she said to Sunny. 'Dinner time.'

FIFTEEN

River House was a 1930s square house, painted white, with large picture windows facing out onto the estuary. The garden ran down to a sea wall, which was lapped at at high tide by the water. Inside had been decorated with stripes, checks, scalloped edges and colour – as if it was wearing one of Dodie's loud dresses.

'Oh... my *god*,' said Dodie, coming down the rather grand curving staircase, clinging to the bannister. She wore a dress that could possibly be a nightgown, with puffed sleeves and dotted with charming little sprigs of green foliage. Her feet were bare. She pressed her hands to her chest.

'I can't believe you're actually here,' she said.

'Pizza!' Miles bellowed up the stairs. There was some shuffling and thumping from above.

'You must be the famous Sunny,' said Dodie.

Sunny popped her thumb out of her mouth.

'Yes, that's me.'

'I literally love you,' said Dodie.

'Okay,' said Sunny, scrunching up her nose in distaste.

'You sound like a very funny person,' said Dodie.

'All right,' said Sunny.

Dodie's daughter, Matilda, appeared at Dodie's shoulder. She was a stone-faced girl of thirteen and had Dodie's black hair and brown eyes but was as stoic and flat as Dodie was frilly and fizzing.

'Can you please order more poo bags for Digger,' said Matilda. 'And we've nearly run out of laundry liquid.'

'Oh, I think Jane is going shopping tomorrow – I'll tell her,' said Dodie, vaguely. Then, 'Look, it's Mairéad. And this is Sunny. Sunny, this is Matilda. And that's Stella,' said Dodie, gesturing to another dark-haired girl of about ten, who waved back, cutely. Her arms were full of brightly coloured bracelets. She was wearing little stick-on earrings and pink hot pants, studded with diamante.

There was a blood-curdling yell from the top of the stairs.

'Oh my god and that's Olly,' said Dodie. 'Brace yourselves.'

Olly, who at seven was as uncontrollable as he had been aged three and also aged five, appeared at the top of the stairs waving a stick.

'Yaaarrgghhh!' he yodelled. 'Yaaarrgghhh!' He was wearing a billowing piece of black material tied around his neck like a cloak. He launched himself down the stairs, waving the stick. 'Avast!' he shouted at no one in particular.

Dodie flinched and made a face. Then she made shooing motions with her hands.

'Get away,' she said, as if she was talking to a beastly stray dog. 'Go away. Go and have pizza.'

'Pizza!' yelled Olly. 'Pizza! Yaaarrgghhh!'

Matilda, expressionless, said, 'As you can see, my brother clearly has advanced ADHD, but my parents are in denial.'

'Christ, you and your… your… *opinions*,' said Dodie.

Stella was quietly arranging figures inside a Sylvanian Families house while Miles flipped open the pizza boxes on the large dining table. Olly, charging about, barged into her, knocking the table and spilling the figures all over the place.

'OLI-VER!' screeched Stella. 'Bloody just bloody stop it, you annoying bastard!'

'Stella!' admonished Miles.

'Very restrained language, actually, seeing as she lives in this house,' muttered Dodie.

Dodie insisted on taking Mairéad and Sunny outside to eat, saying that it was too overwhelming to be inside with the others. Dodie declined pizza but sequestered an entire bottle of rosé and two glasses.

'Do you have fizzy water?' said Sunny.

'Loads,' said Dodie.

'Do you have *ice*?' she said.

'Not only do I have ice,' said Dodie, 'but – follow me – I have ice that never runs out.' She went to the second of the two fridges in the kitchen and opened a door. 'Look at that.' She gestured at a chilled box filled with ice cubes. The fridge made a *whirr-clunk* noise and fresh ice clattered into the box.

'Look, it's showing off. It's trying to impress you,' said Dodie.

'Wow,' said Sunny. 'So much ice.'

It was very pleasant, sitting in Dodie's garden. It had a delightful view of the pub and the sun was setting just behind them.

'God, this is, like, bliss,' said Mairéad.

'It's all right, isn't it?' said Dodie, leaning back in her teak garden armchair. 'I mean my children are bored to death, but that's summer for you.'

Sunny looked at her pizza carefully, inspecting each piece for anything new, unwanted or suspicious. She guzzled her iced sparkling water.

'Are you feeling better?' said Dodie to Sunny.

Sunny gazed off to the side and didn't reply.

Mairéad poked Sunny. 'Dodie asked you a question.'

'What? Yes. I feel all right now,' said Sunny. She looked off into the distance and emitted a fizzy-water belch.

'I thought she was going to die.'

'Who, me? Did you?' said Sunny.

'Yeah, I really did.'

'But I didn't. I am indestructible,' said Sunny. 'And famous.'

'That reminds me, I keep meaning to ask: who's Bridget? You said that name in your sleep a few times.'

'Bridget Mum's friend?' said Sunny.

'Does Mum have a friend called Bridget?'

'Yeah. I don't like her. She keeps trying to hug me,' said Sunny.

'Gross,' said Dodie. 'That sounds so annoying. Do you tell her to *get lost*?'

'I just, you know…' Sunny shrank away and made a flapping motion with her hands.

'Oh well I'm glad it's not just me, then,' said Mairéad. 'You don't want a hug from me, either.'

'No, it's not you. I hate being touched,' said Sunny.

'Do you see Bridget a lot?' said Mairéad.

Sunny shrugged. 'Sometimes,' she said.

'Anyway, Sunny was very brave about being ill,' said Mairéad. 'Didn't take any painkillers, just toughed it out.'

'By painkillers do you mean medicine?' said Sunny.

'Yes,' said Mairéad. 'Sunny will now tell you that medicine is poison,' she added to Dodie.

'Poison!' said Dodie. 'Not where I'm from.' She took a slug of rosé. 'I am the biggest, most awful coward with pain. Next time you're ill, Sunny, try it. No need to be a hero. Oh, Jane!' Dodie said to a woman who had appeared in the doorway. She was in her mid-twenties, with blonde hair set in a rather eighties haircut. 'Jane, love, this is Mairéad.'

'Hi,' said Jane. 'Matilda said we need more poo bags?' Jane was Australian.

'Yes, and laundry liquid. Thank you, I literally love you so much.'

Jane waved and retreated.

Dodie sighed and turned to Mairéad. 'She turned up one day and never left. She's a godsend.'

Dodie had a tremendous knack for acquiring helpful people. They were never formally hired, nor taken in as an au pair or other similar role. They just appeared from places, attracted (presumably) by Dodie's kindly air and limitless resources for anyone, anywhere, who would make her children's tea, do the shopping or the laundry. Anything so Dodie didn't have to do it herself. Mairéad didn't understand exactly how it worked, but she had never known Dodie, since she'd had children at least, not to have at least one or two young people around the place who simply wordlessly *did* stuff.

'Don't let anyone bully you into sailing,' said Dodie. 'It's the most ghastly thing. I make my children do it because otherwise they're hanging about fighting and driving me mad, but you and Sunny can find other things to do. You can go to the beach! There's a nice one, Winklesham. It's got a café. And hang out with Dibs, he's hilarious.'

Sunny had sunk low in her seat and was looking dazed.

'I think she's flagging,' said Mairéad.

Sunny had always been a low-energy child, but post-flu it was more pronounced. It was only 8.30 p.m. but she was more than ready to bathe, get into her pyjamas and watch a film. They said their goodbyes to Dodie and her family and walked back to Quay Cottage.

Mairéad set up her laptop on the double bed, then she made Sunny a hot chocolate and they watched *Zootropolis* side by side in the waning evening light. Sunny was so tired from the train journey and the hot day that she fell asleep twenty minutes into the film. Mairéad turned out the light and covered her with a single duvet from the bunk room. Since her illness, Sunny had silently migrated to Mairéad's bed. There was an unspoken agreement that this was where she wanted to be and Mairéad didn't mind. Sunny was a quiet and immobile sleeper.

She went downstairs and sat by an open window, watching the light changing over the estuary and the crowd outside the pub: smaller now, breaking up, drifting towards homes.

Bridget, she thought.

A) *Lenny's lover?*
B) *True Earth comrade?*
C) *Both?*

SIXTEEN

Mairéad was woken by the sound of a ping-pong ball bouncing on a bat somewhere outside the house, the sound round and mellow in the warm morning air.

Tok, tok, tok, tok, tok… tok, tok, tok, tok, tok…

Sunny was up and gone. Mairéad fished for her phone – 08:45. She came down the narrow wooden staircase and found Sunny at the kitchen table with one of her new books pinned open in front of her. It was the second-to-last book in a series of weird dystopian novels about floating cities, recommended by a bookshop assistant they had befriended. Mairéad had tried to read the first chapter of the first book in the series three times and found it completely impenetrable. Sunny had no such trouble.

Tok, tok, tok, tok, tok, tok, tok, tok… tok, tok, tok, tok, tok…

There was no point in asking Sunny about the noise as she would neither know nor care. Mairéad followed the sound out of the front door and onto the quay, where she found Dibs doing keepy-uppies with a ping-pong bat and a ball.

'Morning,' she said, shading her eyes against the sun.

'Hey,' said Dibs. 'Have you got a timer? Like on your phone?'

'Yeah, sure. Why?'

'I'm tryna break the world record for longest control of a table tennis ball with a table tennis bat.'

'What's the current record?'

'Six hours, fifteen minutes and thirty seconds,' said Dibs, his eyes fixed on the ball.

Tok, tok, tok, tok, tok, tok, tok, tok… tok, tok, tok, tok, tok…

'Where are you staying? I mean which house?' Mairéad was puzzled by the unabashed nature of this child.

'Up there.' Dibs gestured vaguely with his head. 'Near the shop.'

'Have you had breakfast?'

'Yeah,' said Dibs, still looking at the ball. He missed a bounce and the ball sailed gracefully to the ground. They both looked at the ball.

'So, the timer?'

'Sure.' She picked up Sunny's discarded cereal bowl from the bench outside the kitchen, then went inside and got her phone from the bedroom and gave it to Dibs.

'Cheers,' he said.

Mairéad suddenly realised that in her just-woken-up daze she had given her phone to a strange ten-year-old boy. So she said, 'In fact I might just keep it with me… You say, "Go," and I'll set the timer. And then you tell me when to stop it.'

'All right then,' said Dibs, reluctantly handing the phone back. 'Ready? Go.'

Tok, tok, tok, tok, tok, tok, tok… tok, tok, tok, tok, tok…

She went inside and made herself some toast and a cup of tea. She could barely think straight before her first cup. Any notion of a diet had gone out of the window some weeks earlier and she was richly enjoying having her morning toast at whatever the hell time of day she wanted to have it. Sunny had branched out from muesli to Weetabix but was now back on muesli.

Tok, tok, tok, tok, tok, tok, tok… tok, tok, tok, tok, tok, tok…

'Damn! Stop the timer,' called Dibs, officiously.

'Okay!'

There was a pause and Dibs appeared at the door.

'How long was that?'

'One minute and twenty-three.'

'Tch,' said Dibs. 'That smells nice,' he added.

'What, the toast? Do you want some?'

He shrugged and said, 'Well, you know, maybe yeah.'

She got up and cut a slice of bread. 'It's quite grown-up bread with seeds in it and stuff.'

'I'll try it,' said Dibs.

'So what do your brothers get up to here?'

'They all go sailing,' said Dibs. He had ventured into the kitchen and was now sitting at the table with one plump, tanned cheek resting on a palm. The fingers of the other hand were drumming on the kitchen table. He twitched his nose and then rubbed the underneath with a forefinger.

'What, all of them, all day?'

'Yeah,' said Dibs.

Sunny was reading her book, eating more muesli and ignoring everyone.

'But you don't go?'

'No.'

'Why not?'

'Sailing is shit – 'scuse my language. Hate it. Hate the water.' At this last declaration, Dibs gave Mairéad a side-eye.

'Oh, I hate the water too. Open water, like the sea or a big lake? Not my favourite.'

'Really?' piped up Sunny. 'Why?'

'Because you don't know what's at the bottom.'

'Exactly!' hollered Dibs. 'There could be anything down there. Man-eating fish, sharp stuff, just gross scary giant squids or something that might drag you to your death…'

Sunny barked with laughter. 'Scaredy-cats,' she said and returned to her book.

'That's what my brothers say,' said Dibs, looking weary.

'So what do you do all day?'

Dibs shrugged. 'Hang out with Auntie Dodie, go to the shop, play with Digger, practise for my world record. Run errands. There's lots to do,' he added, a little defensively.

Dibs's stray status suddenly became clear. Mairéad found herself feeling furious towards his parents, allowing him to roam about like an orphan while they indulged his cruel brothers in their pointless activity. She angrily buttered some toast, overloaded it with jam and then set it down in front of Dibs. 'I was going to make a hot chocolate,' she said, in a defiant gesture against Dibs's negligent parents. 'Would you like some?'

'Oh yeah, thanks. Yeah,' said the boy, hunched over his plate, talking through a jammy mouthful. The way he was attacking the toast made her wonder if he had, as he'd claimed, had breakfast.

'We never have hot chocolate in the morning,' said Sunny, frowning.

'Well there's a first time for everything,' said Mairéad, getting the milk out of the fridge.

After breakfast, Sunny went out to pace on the pier and Dibs trailed after her, talking and bouncing his ping-pong ball. Digger trotted about, wagging his tail and panting, then paused to rest in the shade of a boat hauled up on the shingle. Sunny stopped and turned and glared at Dibs from time to time, baffled by this chattering boy who was following her everywhere. But she didn't dismiss him, even though she would think nothing of doing just that. She was more than capable of one-handedly pushing him over if he was even slightly irritating her.

Mairéad cleared up breakfast, dressed in the same shorts she'd been wearing the night before and went to the kitchen to assess their meagre rations.

She joined Sunny and Dibs on the pier.

'Dibs, you said you were staying near a shop?' she said. 'Will you show me where it is?'

'This way,' said Dibs, walking ahead, holding his ping-pong bat and ball. They walked up a steep, rising lane, lined on either side with small houses fronted by tumbledown gardens and white fences. After a few minutes, Mairéad had to stop.

'You'd get fit living here,' she said.

'Not far now,' said Dibs, who wasn't even out of breath.

She didn't hold out much hope for the contents of the shop. On past experience of village stores, there would be digestive biscuits, scary bacon and Just Juice. Dibs pushed open the store door with his foot. Behind the counter was a very red-faced man with white hair and a bulbous nose. He wore an old green polo shirt that was slightly too big for him with stains on the front and sun-bleaching on the collar.

'All right, Nelson?' said Dibs, touching the peak of his baseball cap respectfully.

'Hello, young man,' said Nelson.

Mairéad lifted a hand in greeting and Nelson nodded. Sunny asked if she could stay outside.

'So,' said Dibs, clapping his hands together. He turned his cap backwards, which Mairéad now knew usually preceded some sort of performance. 'Let me show you round the old place. Over here you've got your wine. I know ladies are into their "wine".' Dibs incorrectly put finger-bunny-ears around the word 'wine', as if it were a euphemism for something dastardly. 'And there's your crisps, chocolate. Whatever that stuff is over there. All the handy junk. Everything you could possibly need…' He trailed off and then nodded and put his hands on his hips like a cricket outfielder during a lull in a match.

'It looks great,' she said. She reached for a Diet Coke and Dibs gave her a short lecture about the link between sweeteners and cancer, which Mairéad would come to understand was one of his favourite topics. This led on to other conspiracy theories such as who'd shot JFK (Dibs was extraordinarily knowledgeable about this), and then a damning indictment of false conspiracy theorists who spread lies on YouTube for likes and clicks. She stared at Dibs in wonder. Was *this* how much children were *supposed* to talk?

Contrary to her expectations, the shop was rather smart, with chillers holding bottles of white and rosé wine and posh-looking packages of burgers and sausages. There was a large rack of expensive crisps, Lindt chocolate and a rack of vegetables. There was no Just Juice but there were Belvoir cordials, little pots of tapenade, fresh pasta and rows and rows of rosé, ranging from raspberry pink to the palest blush. She wondered who it was that was doing the buying for the shop. Nelson did not look like a man who ate Tyrrells or drank Whispering Angel.

She picked up a basket and put in some potatoes, sausages and broccoli. Then a few burgers, buns and ketchup. Butter. More milk. A pot of yoghurt.

'Will you get me some Tic Tacs?' said Dibs, holding a small plastic box filled with orange and green ovals. Mairéad looked down at Dibs's round and hopeful face, his liquid hazel eyes completely free of malice or expectation.

'Of course. Do you think Sunny would like some?'

'Oh yeah, totally. And if she doesn't like them, I'll have them.'

'Perfect,' she said. Nelson rang up the purchases very slowly and she tapped her card on the reader.

'Right-o,' said Nelson, peering at the machine through spectacles.

Nelson had packed the groceries in a cardboard box that said 'Royal Gala' on the side of it and Mairéad held it in front of her as she walked back to the cottage.

Dibs fell back to talk to Sunny, both of them occasionally pushing Tic Tacs into their mouths. Sunny had frowned at the Tic Tacs when Dibs extended the box out to her.

'What are they?'

'Tic Tacs! How do you not know what Tic Tacs are?'

'I just don't.' Sunny was annoyed.

'They're sweets. These ones are orange, those are lime.'

Sunny had shaken her head, in that tiny insistent way. Dibs shrugged and put them in his pocket. But then a few minutes later, Sunny said, 'Okay, I'll try them.'

Dibs had his ping-pong bat tucked under his arm and the ball in his pocket.

'So you don't go to school, right?'

'That's right.'

'So what do you do?'

'Lessons with my mum.'

'What, just at home?'

'Yeah.'

'That's mad,' said Dibs. 'What's your best subject?'

'Uhh, English probably.'

'I hate maths. Like *hate* it. We've just started Latin, that's quite cool.'

'Latin,' repeated Sunny.

'Yeah, like *Grumio est in culina*,' said Dibs.

'Is that Latin?'

'It means Grumio – who's this bloke in the book – is in the kitchen.'

'Kitchen,' repeated Sunny. 'Say another thing.'

Dibs looked at the sky for a moment and then said, '*Mater est in horto*.'

'Let me guess. Mum is in the garden.'

'Do you do Latin too?'

'No, it was a guess.'

'But how did you guess that?'

Well, This Is Awkward

'Because it sounds like that's what it means.'

Dibs was quiet for a bit as they walked along.

'Do another one,' said Sunny.

'I can't remember anything else,' said Dibs huffily.

'*Per ardua ad astra*,' offered Mairéad, which was the only Latin she knew.

Sunny and Dibs were both quiet. Dibs's relief that Sunny was not some sort of Latin prodigy was visible.

SEVENTEEN

After some discussion with Dodie, Mairéad decided to take Sunny and Dibs to Winklesham Beach. But there was a problem, which was that Sunny had no appropriate clothes for the trip. She had arrived in London with two pairs of worn-out jogging bottoms, two T-shirts, three pairs of knickers, the hoodie and the gross trainers. That was still her entire wardrobe, supplemented by the pair of Mairéad's pyjamas and the Crocs. Now she was staying for longer – for who knew how much longer – she would need some clothes.

So they borrowed Dodie's car – a shiny navy Volvo – and drove to Dartmouth, which was the nearest place with clothes shops. Dibs heard 'clothes shopping' and declined to join them.

'Oh yes, stay with meeee,' said Dodie, clasping Dibs's head to her bosom. Dibs performed a cartoonish flailing struggle with his arms and shrieked, 'Help!' Dodie was wearing striped Victorian pantaloons and a flat straw boater, trimmed with black grosgrain ribbon.

'We can play cards and eat Nutella out of the jar because there are no grown-ups at home,' said Dodie. 'But also, please take Digger for a walk? I will literally love you so much forever if you do.'

In Dartmouth, Mairéad placated Sunny with a croissant

Well, This Is Awkward

from a bakery and then, as they arrived outside an outdoor clothing shop, declared they needed to buy a swimsuit.

'No way. I am not wearing a swimsuit.'

'But… but what do you wear to go swimming at home?'

'A wetsuit,' said Sunny.

'So what do you wear under the wetsuit?'

'A vest and my pants,' she said.

'But… how is that different from a swimsuit?'

Sunny said nothing, just angrily chewed her croissant. Mairéad looked at the poster in the window of the shop. It showed a happy toddler wearing a long-sleeved UV top and a pair of stout shorts.

'How about something like that?' she pointed. 'The shorts and the shirt.'

Sunny looked at the poster.

'Let's just look,' pressed Mairéad, sensing weakness. 'If you hate it, we don't have to get it.'

'All right,' said Sunny.

Sunny refused to try anything on.

'But won't it be fun?' said Mairéad. 'Like dressing up?'

Sunny looked at her as if she had suggested shutting her hand repeatedly in the door for a laugh.

'No. It will be annoying and scratchy.'

'I mean,' said Mairéad in despair, holding a pair of shorts in one hand and a shirt in the other, 'don't you care what you look like?'

'What for?'

'To… I don't know. To just be polite, I suppose, to other people who've got to look at you.'

'If people don't want to look at me,' said Sunny, 'then they can look away.'

Mairéad felt a teetering panic, as an entire belief system started to crumble about her.

In a dizzy scramble, with Sunny increasingly irate at being

imprisoned in the shop and hemmed in by rails of clothes, Mairéad guessed at sizes, haphazardly grabbing at shorts and T-shirts, socks and a sunhat. She felt like a parody of a parent, holding items up against Sunny to guess if anything was the right size. The total was £125. She was careful to keep the receipt.

'What's your refund policy?' she asked, sweatily.

'Twenty-eight days,' said the assistant, glancing briefly at Sunny. 'If something doesn't fit him, you can bring it back.'

Mairéad nearly said, 'Her,' but couldn't be bothered.

They made it back to Bloxcombe in time to eat a sandwich, made by Jane, and then go to the beach. Dodie had gathered a pile of sandy beach kit for them to borrow. 'Wish I could come with you,' she said, 'but I am totally incompatible with the beach. I've also got tons of work to do.'

'Work? What work?'

'Well, just emails, you know. About the start of term. New uniforms and all that. Oh, and, we're having our living room re-done. That's just endless to-ing and fro-ing. Exhausting.'

Dibs had at first been a little reluctant to go to Winklesham and leave behind his jar of Nutella, the cards and an unattended iPad.

'Question,' he said, holding a forefinger aloft.

'I'm listening,' said Mairéad.

'Will there be ice cream?'

'As much as you like.'

'I see,' he said, stroking his chin. 'In that case, okay. But I am not going in the sea. No way, José.'

'Don't worry, neither am I.'

'What?' said Sunny.

'I'm not going in the sea,' said Mairéad.

'That's crazy!' said Sunny. Then she did a thing that shocked Mairéad beyond measure. She cocked her hip sassily and said, '*On my planet*, everyone goes in the sea.'

Mairéad could only laugh. 'You got me.'

'Wow!' said Dibs, in a loud and credulous voice. 'You're from another planet?! That explains everything!'

The beach was lively when they arrived. Large family groups had set up near the entrance to the beach with what looked like enough supplies to live there permanently. They had striped windbreaks and folding chairs, changing tents, little Primus stoves and barbecues. Mairéad marvelled at a man retrieving a folding kettle from a bag. He un-popped it and then turned to a large plastic barrel of water in order to fill it up.

Mothers sat on towels with squirming toddlers between their legs and coated them in sunscreen. Older children lounged in the shade of the windbreaks, squinting at screens or playing cards. Mairéad watched a woman weigh down the four corners of a fitted sheet with rocks and then set up a folding tub of water to one side. She dipped her feet in it and then daintily stepped into her fitted sheet. A boy ran past with a bucket of sand, tripped and emptied the sand into the previously sand-free sheet. 'Dylan!' the woman bellowed.

Further down the beach were the hardier families, who only had a towel each and perhaps a changing tent. Older couples tended to gather by the rocks, where they baked like lizards in the sun, falling asleep with mouths open, listening to burbling wind-up radios.

Mairéad pointed to a spot towards the end of the beach where the sand met a rising grassy hill, at the foot of which were rocks and rockpools.

'Here,' she said, and stopped. She had with her a beach mat, three towels, a bottle of water and a large bag full of beach toys, which she tipped out onto the flat sand.

'Ooo!' said Dibs, reaching for a large spade with a wooden handle and a metal blade. 'I haven't dug a hole in the sand for ages.'

'Okay, but put sunscreen on the back of your neck. Hold

out your hand?' She squirted some SPF 50 on Dibs's hand and he smeared it on the back of his neck.

'You've missed a bit,' she said and rubbed it in with one finger.

'Sun's going in, though,' he grumbled.

'Yes but it will come out again and then burn you to ash.'

'Okay, *Mum*,' Dibs said, closing one eye and leaving his mouth to hang open to indicate what a mum-ish drag Mairéad was being. She stopped, with a double-blink.

'Where are you digging to?'

'To Australia!' hollered Dibs.

Mairéad looked about herself and saw that Sunny was already clambering on the rocks, picking her way with her tough little monkey feet over barnacles and sharp bits, her long spindly arms held out for balance.

Dibs was singing 'Joy to the World' by Three Dog Night, but didn't know the words properly and filled in the gaps with *ner ner ner*.

She taught him all the words that she knew and they sang it together.

'What does it mean, though?' said Dibs theatrically. 'Who is Jeremiah? Why is he drinking wine?'

'I think it's a religious, sort of happy-clappy song. About how everyone should have joy: you and me and all the fishes in the deep blue sea.'

Dibs sat back on his haunches and looked out to the sea. 'They're welcome to it. The sea, I mean.'

He dug a bit more and then said, 'Why does Sunny suck her thumb? It's a bit like something for babies, isn't it?'

'I don't know. She just likes it. And it's not very easy to tell Sunny what to do.'

'Oh, yeah,' said Dibs. 'I've noticed. Are you Sunny's mum?'

'No, I'm her aunt.'

'Oh, right,' said Dibs.

Sunny had picked her way back across the rocks and was now running towards them with a manic grin on her face that Mairéad had never seen before.

'You have to come in the sea with me,' she said.

'No way! Those waves are huge.'

'They're not, they're tiny.'

'Tiny! They've got white all along the tops. No.'

'I wouldn't get in there if you paid me,' said Dibs.

'Shut up!' said Sunny. 'Come on. It's fun.'

Mairéad looked at the waves crashing on the beach and then at Sunny, who was actually smiling and actually wanted to do something with actual Mairéad. How could she possibly say no?

'Well, all right. I will come in, just a little bit,' she said. 'I am not swimming out far and you mustn't either because I'm a terrible swimmer and I can't swim back with you if you start drowning.'

Sunny found this hilarious. 'Drowning! I'm not going to drown.'

There was then a fifteen-minute argument where Sunny would not get changed into her new beachwear. Eventually Mairéad huddled her by some rocks, held a large towel around her and squinched her eyes shut while Sunny rustled and hopped about, screeching, 'Keep the towel up!'

'Wow! Looks great,' she said, once Sunny had snapped and wriggled her way into a rash vest and striped shorts.

Sunny flapped her arms up and down.

'It's okay,' she said.

'Stay here, Dibs,' said Mairéad. 'Don't go anywhere. I'll be back in three minutes.'

'You're not going in the sea, are you? You're mad.'

'I know. But I don't want Sunny to go in on her own. Don't talk to any strangers while I'm gone, okay?'

'Okay,' said Dibs, warily. 'Wait, where's the lifeguard?'

'Over there – look.'

'If you're drowning, you do this,' said Dibs. He stood up and held his arms in a cross over his head. 'Don't wave. Make a cross like this. Then lie on your back and make a starfish shape.'

'How do you know all that?'

'I think about it a lot,' said Dibs.

Mairéad took off her dress to reveal her muddy-green one piece bathing suit, which had been very fashionable the previous year, and then tiptoed her way awkwardly down the beach to the shoreline. A wave crashed about 6 feet away, swarmed across the sand to their feet and then hissed backwards. Swimmers bobbed about in the shallows, laughing and calling to each other. Further down the beach, body boarders bobbed about in the shallows, waiting for waves. Further still, sleek, wetsuit-clad people with bleach-blonde hair surfed.

'Come on!' said Sunny, and waded in. 'The water isn't even very cold.'

Mairéad shuffled gingerly in, then turned back, anxious to keep Dibs in sight. Was this okay, leaving a boy in her care on the beach like this? His mother, she supposed, left him on his own for an entire summer – five minutes on a beach was surely nothing.

She hesitated as the water hit her knees.

Sunny marched back and took her wrist again. Her grip was hard and uncompromising.

'You're being pathetic,' she said, firmly.

Mairéad looked at the swimmers and the body boarders and reckoned that all those people couldn't be wrong.

'Okay, let's go,' she said, and waded in with purpose. Knees, thighs, stomach and then finally chest, as the shore fell suddenly away and her big toe left the sand. She treaded water and felt the motion of the sea and, yes, undeniably also felt the short breaths of panic. This, she finally understood, must be what 'shallow breathing' was. She spun round in the water to locate Dibs and felt a stab of anxiety at how far along the beach they had already drifted with the current.

Sunny was floating on her back, like a thing jettisoned from a sinking vessel, with a serene look on her face. Once out past the little waves, Mairéad realised it was really quite calm and she relaxed, allowing herself to luxuriate in the cool and silky water swishing about her legs and feeling quite small and insignificant – in a good way – in the vastness of the sea.

She turned to check on Dibs, who was happily digging his hole to Australia, and then back to Sunny. She put her head back and felt the seawater invade her hair up to her scalp and allowed herself a deep breath in and then out. This was probably what Gwyneth Paltrow did in the sea.

Then she righted her head. She sprang back in shock when she saw what looked like a wall of water approaching the shore. A wave. A very large wave.

'Suh – Sunny!'

Sunny righted herself in the water, too.

Mairéad pointed in horror.

'Swim! Swim away! Get out, out of the water!'

'No!' shouted Sunny. 'We have to swim towards it!'

'What?!'

'Towards it,' said Sunny, unafraid. 'If you swim away, it'll catch you and turn you over.'

Mairéad shook her head as the looming wave continued on its vast, inexorable journey towards them. 'I can't!'

'You can! Just swim! It's easy, it will pass over you. Swim! Swim!' Sunny was screaming now. Then she set off in her determined, splashy front crawl towards the towering wave.

Mairéad's eyes travelled up the wall of water. Everything in her body felt like it had turned to jelly. I am going to die, she thought. I am going to die and Sunny is going to die and Dibs is going to be on his own on this stupid bloody beach.

But she didn't know what else to do, so she swam with a hammering heart. She breathed short, deranged breaths, her vision staccato with terror as she swam to meet the towering, cresting wave of water. The last thing she saw was Sunny plunging, arrow-like, into the shining surface of the dark blue water. Mairéad closed her eyes and pursed her lips and mimicked the shape of Sunny's taut arms. She prayed.

Dibs stood up from his hole and looked around. What he needed was a bucket to fill with seawater and then pour into the hole. He rummaged in the plastic tangle of items from Mairéad's bag and selected a blue bucket printed all over with Goofy and Mickey Mouse. That would do. He brushed the sand off his hands and then walked down to the water.

A figure loomed, staggering through the surf towards him, rat-tail hair plastered over its face, a strand of seaweed on its shoulder. He briefly shrank back.

'Dibs!' panted Mairéad in joy and relief and wobbly-legged in post-terror.

'Yes?' said Dibs.

'Oh, it's just, I didn't think… I mean, did you see that massive wave just now?'

'Err, where?'

'It was… I mean it was *huge*.'

'Was it?'

'Wow!' called Sunny sarcastically, splash-hopping through the water. 'Wow, isn't it a miracle we're still alive?'

'Look, it's all very well for you. You're used to this. That wave was enormous.'

'It really wasn't,' said Sunny.

'It was, it was *huge*.'

Well, This Is Awkward

'It was about this high,' said Sunny, holding her hand out about 2 feet above the sand.

'Can we get ice cream now?' said Dibs.

'Yes,' said Mairéad. She breathed out heavily and looked from Sunny to Dibs and then back at Sunny. Then she leaned her hands on her knees and panted for a moment. Then she started laughing. She laughed and laughed and found that she couldn't stop until tears were dripping onto the sand and Sunny and Dibs were saying, 'What's so funny? What's so funny?'

EIGHTEEN

Mairéad only found out about the crows when they had been in Bloxcombe for nearly three days.

She came downstairs in the morning and, looking for Sunny, put her head round the open front door. Sunny was sitting at one end of the bench outside the cottage. At the other end, a large glossy crow was pecking something out of the bottom of Sunny's breakfast bowl.

'What's going on?'

'Shh,' said Sunny.

'Oh no, I don't want you to feed crows.'

'Why not?'

'Because he'll tell all his friends and tomorrow there'll be forty crows. And while one crow is cute, forty is not cute.'

The next morning, there were not forty crows, but there was one more.

'That'll be its mate,' said Dibs. 'I saw a thing on YouTube about this. Crows go around in pairs.'

'Don't feed them,' said Mairéad. But Sunny did not listen and instead trained the crows to take hazelnuts, picked by Sunny out of her muesli, from her fingers.

'A terrible lot of crows we've got, haven't we?' said Sunny. 'There must be at least forty of them.'

Well, This Is Awkward

'All right, smarty-pants. But don't say I didn't warn you when there are millions all clawing at the window, trying to pinch your breakfast out of your spoon.'

That evening, Mairéad found a piece of sea glass, a button and a drinks-can ring pull on the bench.

'Are these yours?' she said to Sunny and Dibs, who were on the sofa, watching *Moana*.

'No,' they said, peering at the items.

'Oh, okay.'

The next morning, there was a twisted piece of metal on the bench.

'Who's leaving out these random bits of rubbish?' said Mairéad.

Just then, Dibs arrived, bouncing his ping-pong ball on his bat as he walked along the quay, and Mairéad went inside to boil some eggs for breakfast.

Dibs and Sunny followed her in. 'Are you going to race in the regatta?' said Dibs.

'No,' said Mairéad, just as Sunny said, 'What's a regatta?'

'It's like this big, weird sort of party they have here every year,' said Dibs. 'There are races on the estuary and my brothers win them all, every year. Everyone's like, "Ugh it's the Callaghan brothers UH-GAIN." But there's also a party on the quay – a barbecue, games, raffles and stuff. Bash the Rat – that's fun.'

'Oh well, why would we bother entering the regatta if your brothers always win?' said Mairéad.

'They win the rowing race. But there's also a pedalo race,' said Dibs. 'That always looks good, though there's no way I'd do it, obviously.'

'Yeah, I'll do it. I'm good at racing,' said Sunny. 'What's a pedalo, though?'

'It's this sort of boat thing that you drive by pedalling with your feet,' said Mairéad. 'But no, I'd rather not. Knowing my luck I'd fall in and drown.' Or, worse, she thought, be rescued and hauled into a boat like a huge, dripping whale, shoulders hunched, flailing feet trying to get a purchase on the side of the boat.

Most nightmarish of all would be a rescue by one of the handsome teenagers who infested Bloxcombe. In the mornings and afternoons, before and after sailing school, they littered the village in groups, hauling sailing gear around, laughing, flirting and staring at their phones. The girls were lithe, with masses of hair and little snub noses. The boys were simply enormous – very tall and broad but completely flat when they turned to the side. Their hair was uniformly cut very close at the sides, but then billowed luxuriantly out at the top. Mairéad had met teenagers in her adult life, of course, but nothing like these. They were very unnerving.

It was almost impossible not to respond to these dazzling, young, fit, strong men in a similar way to how she had when she was an appropriate age: with trembling terror, towering admiration, undiluted interest. Occasionally they dragged their boats up onto the shore at low tide with their wetsuits peeled down to their waists and she had to go inside so as not to stare. She was no longer an appropriate age, and the compulsion to gaze greedily felt disgusting. She kept her distance, which was easy as she spent all her time with, or administering to, Sunny and Dibs. But the idea that she could fall off a pedalo and thus there could be even a five per cent chance that she would have to be rescued in an undignified way by these magnetic creatures was appalling, unthinkable.

Breakfast over, Dibs said, 'Will you time me?' He got out his bat and ball.

'Take my phone,' she told him. 'I've got to clear up here.'

She tidied the kitchen, slotting plates into the tiny dishwasher, wiping down surfaces and putting things away in the fridge, all the while listening to the *tok, tok, tok, tok* of the ping-pong ball.

'Do you need more books?' she said to Sunny.

'No, I'm all right,' she said.

'Is it still good, that series?'

'Yeah, it is,' she said. 'There are these prequels, too. But I've still got this one and then another massive one...'

There was a shriek from outside.

'My ball!'

Mairéad ran out of the cottage. Dibs's ping-pong ball had somehow fallen off the quay and bounced into the water – it was high tide and the ball bobbed merrily on the water, far out of reach.

'We need a stick or something! Quick!'

The only sticks available were an inch long and useless. She tried to retrieve the ball with a broom but it was already too far out.

Dibs was inconsolable; he wept and wept. He didn't have another ball; he couldn't even remember where he'd got this ball. There weren't any ball shops in this stupid, stinking place. He just wanted to go home and not be here in this awful dump – and so on.

'Look, I'll get you some more. On Amazon. They'll be here tomorrow, I'm sure. Look, look,' she said, getting out her phone and thrusting the screen under his nose. 'See?'

'Oh, you've got Amazon Prime,' said Dibs, looking at the phone. He sniffed and blinked a little. 'That's very fancy. Okay, will you really get me some more? Thank you. I'll pay you back. I've got a GoHenry card.'

Dibs then went back to his quayside vigil. He knelt, sitting back on his feet, his hands forlornly in his lap, staring at his ping-pong ball as it ebbed further away from the quay. He had the air of someone attending a funeral at sea.

'The crows liked the toast crusts,' said Sunny. She shaded

her eyes, looking into the tree that grew at the edge of the playing field, next to the cottage, searching for the crows, but they had flown elsewhere.

'I bet they did.' Mairéad picked up a shell and a bent nail off the bench, examined them and then took them inside to toss them in the bin.

That very same afternoon, Dibs's ping-pong ball appeared on the bench.

'Dibs! Dibs, look!' said Mairéad.

Dibs and Sunny emerged from the cottage. They all stared at the ball, agog. It had last been seen floating away on a rip tide, but here it was, back.

'Maybe it's someone else's ball?' said Mairéad.

Dibs picked it up and inspected it.

'No,' he said. 'It's definitely mine.'

They looked at each other for a bit. Mairéad looked into the tree and saw the crows perched there, shuffling their wings. Then Dibs looked at Mairéad and said, 'Will you time me?'

The day wore on. Mairéad heaved a basket of laundry to the back patio and flapped out the items, pinning them to the washing line in the baking sunshine. She had never had a washing line before and was now addicted to and intoxicated by the smell of sun-baked cotton.

'Are you still going?' she called to Dibs.

'Yeah!' he called in excitement. 'Still going! How long?'

'Fifteen minutes!'

'Wow!' said Dibs. 'Best ever.'

There was the sound of footsteps and Dibs said, 'Hi, Tig. Watch me!'

There was a pause and a bellow from Dibs.

'No!' he screamed. 'Why did you do that?'

Mairéad rushed to the door. One of the large teenagers stood in front of Dibs. Dibs, who filled her vision with his sandy hair and plump cheeks and filled the cottage with his constant

Well, This Is Awkward

chatter and rat-a-tat personality, looked puny in comparison with this hunk. The boy was wearing navy jersey shorts and a blue T-shirt, white sports socks and huge white trainers. He was holding Dibs's ball.

Dibs had collapsed onto his knees on the ground and was sobbing.

'What happened?' barked Mairéad. 'Who are you?'

'I'm his brother,' said Tig, throwing the ball up and then catching it.

'You didn't take that ball, did you?' She was white with anger.

'Yeah,' said Tig, defensive. 'Mum sent me to get Dibs back.'

'But it was his... record. And he was doing really well!'

'*Easy*,' said Tig, holding his hands up. She wanted so much to smack the boy smartly in the face that she felt sick at the effort of holding it in. From a distance, the teenagers all seemed like movie stars. Close up, Tig was not, in fact, terribly handsome.

Dibs was kneeling forlornly in the muddy dust of the quay, the bat limp in his hand, tears rolling down his cheeks.

'You've really upset him.'

'Oh god, don't get sucked in by that,' said Tig. 'The neverending psychodrama of Dibs. Seriously.'

'Give me that ball.' She held out her hand like a furious teacher. Tig narrowed his eyes but did not give up the ball.

'Your bloody family leaves Dibs to just wander about on his own all day and then you come here and just, you just *crap* all over him. It's not okay. You can't just say, "Oh, he's my brother," like it's somehow permission to be vile.'

A black plastic bag blew across the path and attached itself to Tig's face, which was strange because there was no breeze. But then, oh! It wasn't a black plastic bag, it was a crow. Tig started waving his arms and shouting to get away from the crow as another started a dive-bomb assault. Dibs and Mairéad crouched out of the way and shouted and shrieked and there was a great fuss and noise and a lot of flapping of large crow-wings. They were relentless. No matter how much Tig twisted about and waved his arms, the crows wouldn't leave him alone.

'Give him back the ball!' hollered Sunny from the doorway of the cottage. 'Give Dibs back his ball and they'll leave you alone!'

Tig dropped the ball and backed away, a furious expression on his face, his magnificent bouffy hair a little ruffled. Dibs picked up his ball and moved away from Tig, holding it out to the crows to show them that he had it. As quickly as they had appeared, the crows left. They hopped about sideways on the quay for a bit and then flew away.

'Are you some sort of witch?' said Tig accusingly. His hair looked pleasingly chaotic and ugly. 'Who can control crows? Are you going to *eat* my brother? What are you even doing here?' he said. 'Who are you?'

Dibs, wide-eyed, looked from Mairéad to Tig.

'Oh, that's nice,' said Mairéad, savagely. 'I'm sure your mother would be very proud that the first insult for a woman her son reaches for is "witch". Yeah, lovely. It's none of your *fucking* business what I'm doing here, you great lumbering twat.'

Tig coloured, his jaw working in rage. Eventually he turned and stalked off.

Dibs's eyes filled with tears as he looked from Mairéad to Tig's retreating form and back again.

'I think your mum wants you home,' she said to Dibs, her voice a little shaky. 'It's all right. Off you go, come and see us later maybe.'

Dibs's lip wobbled as he took off down the quay.

Mairéad heard him call, 'Tig, Tig…'

Tig turned and put his hand on Dibs's shoulder, and Dibs put his arms around Tig's waist. Tig said something inaudible and crouched down, thumbing at his back. Dibs leaped onto

Well, This Is Awkward

Tig's back and Tig started jogging away, Dibs cackling with laughter, lifting a hand from around Tig's neck to wipe his cheek.

Mairéad went back inside the cottage, yanked her suitcase out from under the bed and started to pack. A witch. A witch! So this is what it had come to, that she was a witch. A witch, living at the end of the quay, with children who were not her own, planning to put them in a pie.

'What's happening?' said Sunny. She stood at the doorway of the bedroom.

'We're leaving,' said Mairéad viciously. 'This bloody place. A witch! Fucking hell!' She was irate, red-faced, insulted and humiliated. She couldn't stay here one more moment. They would be better off in London where there weren't such stupid cliques, such revolting teenagers with their absurd hair and terrible manners. And what the hell had she been doing? Sliding like some fat, spoiled child into this slushy holiday zone, when she ought to be thinking and worrying about work. They would go back to London and she would try again with some sort of childcare, yes. Then spring a surprise attack on IGS. Ta-da! Ha, and catch Jenna in the act of doing something dreadful – like eating a salad at Mairéad's desk, while ordering Biba around.

'I don't want to go,' said Sunny. 'No.' She folded her arms and stood rigidly in the doorway, tapping one long forefinger.

'Yes, sorry. We're leaving. We don't belong here.'

'But my crows,' said Sunny, gesturing out of the window. 'My *crows*.' Her mouth smushed into an unhappy line.

Of all the things to miss about this place, the *crows*?

'Well, we can't leave immediately, I suppose,' said Mairéad. She suddenly felt completely exhausted by everything, particularly the thought of launching a surprise attack on Jenna, and sat down heavily on the bed. 'I'll sleep on it and we'll think again in the morning. Is that a deal?'

Sunny nodded.

Mairéad took a deep, cleansing breath and said, 'Right, dinner. Pasta?'

The kettle was boiling when she heard multiple crunching footsteps.

'Hello?' called a voice.

She ventured out from the kitchen and saw a woman she didn't recognise – and Tig. She shrank back.

'I'm Tess, Dibs's mother,' said the woman. She wasn't literally holding her son by the scruff of the neck, but she may as well have been.

Tess was very handsome, with high cheekbones, a glowing tan, startling pale blue eyes, strong shoulders and, rather unexpectedly, a diamond stud winking at her nose.

'Hello.'

'Jonathan has something he would like to say to you,' she said. She stepped to the side and folded her arms, glaring at Tig with a hard look on her face.

'Oh no, please. This is embarrassing,' Mairéad said. 'Don't worry.'

'No, it's fine,' said Tig, who had a perfectly pleasant look on his face. 'I was very rude and I apologise. I felt bad for taking Dibs's ball and I was acting out.'

Acting out?

'You can go now,' said Tess. Tig turned and sloped off down the quay.

'I owe you an apology, too,' said Tess. She wore a crumpled, striped linen shirt and battered blue culottes. 'I haven't said hello or thank you for minding Dibs even once. And then from what I heard, Tig behaved like an absolute c-word. What must you think of us?'

I think you're savages, thought Mairéad.

'Not at all. It's been great having Dibs about. My niece is… she's…' Mairéad searched for words.

'Your niece!' said Tess. 'I thought you had a son.'

'Oh, I see, no. Sunny is a girl. Sunshine. She's my niece.'

'Ahhhhh, okaaaaay,' said Tess.

'Yes, and she doesn't have any siblings and her mother isn't well and...' Horrified, Mairéad found herself welling up. 'Sorry, it's...'

'Oh, that sounds very difficult,' said Tess kindly.

She nodded, speechless, the back of her hand pressed under her nose.

'I think there were plans tomorrow lunchtime for a barbecue,' said Tess. 'At Dodie's. We'll all take the day off sailing. It would be great for everyone to meet properly. It can be a bit cliquey round here, we all forget that. I'll tell Dodie that we're definitely on for it. How does that sound?'

Mairéad swallowed and nodded. 'Sounds great. Who doesn't like a barbecue?'

Tess apologised for Tig once more and then wandered back along the path.

Mairéad turned and saw Sunny standing in the doorway.

'We're not leaving, then?' said Sunny hopefully.

'No. Not today.'

NINETEEN

The smoke from the barbecue at River House started billowing into the sky at about 11.30 a.m., Mairéad smelled it and then looked out to see it from her tiny bedroom window. She dressed in a pair of cropped khaki trousers and a white T-shirt, then peered at her reflection in the small bathroom mirror as if it were a person she had known from long ago. Her face was a little brown from all the hours spent watching Sunny playing with the goats and hanging out washing, but her hair was a nightmare.

Literally, she had nightmares about her naturally curly brown hair suddenly growing impossibly quickly, eradicating the careful blonde-and-straightening treatments. She brushed it into a centre parting and tied it into a tight bun at the nape of her neck, so as to flatten down the dark roots, which were threatening to start curling. She would have to wear her hair like this now until she could get to a hairdresser.

Mmm, the hairdresser. If she concentrated she could smell the luxurious shampoo they used, taste the free biscotti that came with her tea, feel the careful straightening, the application of the foils.

'Hi.' Sunny was standing in the doorway.

'Oh! You look great.'

Well, This Is Awkward

Sunny was wearing the new outfit that Mairéad had laid out on her bed: green, knee-length cargo shorts and a T-shirt with a picture of a surfboarding monkey on it. Sunny grinned. Or, rather, she bared a set of clenched teeth. But Mairéad could tell she was happy with her new outfit.

'Better than those old joggers.'

'What's for lunch?' said Sunny.

'We're going for a barbecue at Dodie's house! Yay!'

'Yay,' repeated Sunny. 'One of the crows talked to me today. I mean it didn't, but it felt like it. It looked at me like this...' Sunny turned her head to the side and eyeballed Mairéad. 'And it went "rark".'

'What would they say if they could talk?'

'Give me a snack!'

For want of anything else to do, they walked over to River House early. Mairéad clutched some packets of sausages and the box of ping-pong balls that had arrived for Dibs. They walked through the gates into the garden, which was hazy with billowing barbecue smoke, and were greeted by Digger, who barked and danced about. Sunny went to find a ball to throw for him.

Mairéad wandered through the front door, which was standing open, and went to the kitchen. She greeted Miles and Jane the Australian, who were busy in the kitchen, and offered them the sausages. Stella was industriously making something with bits of paper and colouring pens and Olly was watching *Paw Patrol*.

'Oh hi,' said Matilda, unsmilingly. 'Mum's in her bedroom. Obviously.'

Dodie was lying on her bed, wafting herself with a leaf-shaped seagrass fan. She wore a pair of bright green cotton pyjamas and a wide piece of embroidered silk was tied around her forehead, flapper-style.

'Oh my god, thank god you're here,' said Dodie. 'It's chaos.

I can't stand having people round. What happened with Tig? Tess wouldn't say. She was bloody cross though.'

'It was embarrassing. I lost my temper because Tig took Dibs's ball. I mean, it sounds so dumb and childish, now.'

'Right, right,' said Dodie. 'I mean with kids, the random petty stuff that you totally lose your mind over is astonishing. I once screamed at everyone because they rang the doorbell when they knew that Miles had a key.' Dodie held her hands out to the sides in disbelief. 'Talk about a loss of perspective.'

Dodie's bedroom was over the top but undeniably beautiful, decorated in white, eau-de-nil and pink. Her bed was a faux-four-poster thing, with linen draped artfully around the posts. The en-suite bathroom was lined with bold-patterned tiles and on the balcony, which had an awning, there was an Adirondack chair piled with linen cushions.

'Who else is coming to this lunch, then?'

'Literally everyone,' said Dodie, pressing the pads of her fingers to her eyes. 'Miles has invited *everyone*. He lives for this, I don't know why it doesn't stress him out. He had to get a huge, emergency delivery of food. I don't know who he thinks is going to do all the cooking and the washing-up. There's us and then the Callaghans – that's Dibs's family – and then Nina and her lot, she's got three grown-up kids but only one of them is actually here. Douglas. He's really, *really* hot. Sorry, that's a bit disgusting to say, isn't it? But he just is. Really hot.'

'Douglas the rower?'

'Yes!' Dodie sat up. 'Have you met him?'

'No, but I think I've met Nina. She was talking about a Douglas who's good at rowing.'

'They're all in a tizz because they think the Callaghans might lose the precious rowing race this year to Douglas and his cousin, Vinny.'

'His cousin is called Vinny?'

'No, he's called… what is it? Alex or something. But we

all call him Vinny because he's a cousin. As in *My Cousin Vinny*.'

'But aren't you all cousins?'

'Yes, yes. I know. I know! It makes no sense. Okay, that's them and then there's Gabby and Mike and their three, they're a bit younger. Gabby is nice but she's very, like... what's the word? She's one of those people who claims to be hopeless all the time. She says, "Oh no *you're* amazing, *you're* amazing." It's a bit annoying. Especially as she's a lawyer and she's got three children – she's not exactly incompetent. It's a bit disingenuous. And then who else? I don't even know. It will be a complete circus.'

'Will you come down?'

'Of course!' said Dodie, touching her fingertips to her head. 'If I'm not there, nothing will happen.'

Mairéad went back downstairs and started helping Miles and Jane. Miles was in a sort of trance, marinating meat and running out to the garden every three minutes to stare at the barbecue coals, then hustling back inside.

'Cheers, mate,' said Jane, when Mairéad took the kitchen bin out and tidied up some empty packets that were littering the surfaces.

'What's that?' Mairéad asked. Jane was mixing a salad in a bowl with the circumference of a lorry's steering wheel.

'It's a slaw – cabbage and carrot and fennel and mint and stuff.'

'It looks incredible. Are you a cook?'

'No, I just looked it up online.'

Guests had started to arrive and Mairéad helped hand out drinks. Small children migrated into the garden to play with Digger and with Dodie's children. Sunny was pacing up and down along the sea wall, sucking her thumb, deep in thought and completely oblivious to all the other children. Mairéad cleared the enormous dining table and poked through the kitchen, looking for ketchup, mayonnaise, mustard and so on. She opened more cupboards, looking for glasses.

'Who's that?' said Miles distractedly, looking up from finely chopping some herbs. 'Oh, Mairéad!' he said in astonishment.

'Hi.'

'Have you been here all this time?'

'About twenty minutes?'

'And you've got all this stuff out for lunch?'

'Well... yes. Was I not supposed to?'

'Yes you were! Wonderful! I just, I didn't...' Miles paused and looked at her. 'Never mind. Jane, did those paper plates and cups arrive?'

'Over there.' Jane was draining some pasta from a pot the size of a cement mixer's bucket. She gestured with her head to a blue grocery bag in the corner.

Mairéad set out a large stack of paper plates, napkins and paper cups. Dibs drifted through the front door, holding his ping-pong bat. He was followed by four boys, including Tig. Two were very obviously twins and the other was slightly older, wearing a rugby shirt with a popped collar and wrap-around sunglasses perched on his head. Following them was Tess, with her winking diamond stud, and then presumably Dibs's dad, who looked exactly like Dibs, only old.

'Hi, Dibs,' said Mairéad, waving stupidly.

'Hi,' he said.

'Your ping-pong balls arrived,' she told him, reaching for the white box that was on the side.

Dibs opened his eyes very wide and his mouth yawped like a howler monkey. He did a dramatic intake of breath as he opened the box. 'Waaaaoowwwww!' he said. 'Look, Mum, looooooook what I got, looooooook!'

'Wonderful!' said Tess. 'And they're orange! Snazzy.'

Mairéad suddenly felt embarrassed and stupid. 'I just...' She flapped her hand. 'He was upset when his ball went in the sea

Well, This Is Awkward

and he didn't have another one and… fix everything with money, you know. Probably wrong. Stupid idea. But I panicked.' She shrugged, uselessly.

Tess reached out and touched Mairéad's arm.

'It's a very thoughtful, very kind gift,' she said.

'I mean, you'd think I'd bought him a car,' said Mairéad, watching Dibs cooing over the box and showing it to anyone who would look.

Tess looked at Dibs and then back again.

'Dibs worked out a long time ago that if you're super, extra grateful, people are more likely to give stuff to you than to any of your brothers. When you're in a fight to the death for resources, that's a handy skill.'

'I mean, it works. I want to see what he does if I really do give him a car.'

'Seven years, then let's talk,' said Tess.

More guests arrived and Mairéad, not really knowing many people, fell back into the age-old party get-out of helping. She busied herself with Jane and Miles, did some washing-up, brought Dodie, who was chatting in her bedroom to Nina and Tess, a drink. Then she went outside to check on Sunny, and patted Digger, who was lying on his side in the shade, utterly exhausted and panting. Dibs had found a stomp rocket and was setting it up in the middle of the garden. 'No!' he was shouting at Olly, who was interfering. 'No, stop it!'

Miles and Jane leaned out of different windows and hollered, 'Lunch!' Mairéad hung back as she did not want to be elbowing enormous teens out of the way for burgers and sausages. Then she remembered that Sunny needed lunch, had a brief neurotic vision of the food running out, and joined the crowd. Reaching for the ketchup, she bumped hands with one of the teenagers. He turned and gave her a lazy smile that made her mouth fall open. He was tall and broad with dark brown hair cropped closely at the sides (obviously!) with snaky waves falling over his forehead. He had a rectangular face with strong eyebrows, a long nose and blue eyes, which vanished into his freckly face when he smiled. He had a *dimple*.

'Sorry,' he said, charmingly. 'After you.'

'Thanks.' Her voice was a little wobbly because all the breath had left her body and she was now made entirely of panna cotta. She took the mustard and splatted some out on her plate with a grotesque farting noise. She giggled and then looked up at the boy shyly, but he was talking to someone else.

'Are you teenagers taking all the food?' Nina arrived behind the very handsome boy and started stroking him all over his back and arms. 'Leave some for others, Douggie.'

Douglas. The famous Douglas. Of course!

'I'm not a teenager,' said Douglas.

'Aren't you?' said the woman, mock-stupidly, still fondling him. 'How old are you, then?'

Thirty-five, prayed Mairéad. *THIRTY-FIVE!*

'I am twenty-two,' he said.

Ach, damn it.

'Doesn't time fly,' said Nina wistfully. There was more fondling. Then she wandered along the table to get a plate.

'Oh, Mum,' called Douglas.

'Yes?'

'If you, umm…' he said, licking some sauce sexily off his thumb, making Mairéad want to throw her head back and laugh with deranged, nervous excitement, '… if you want me to go to Kingswear tomorrow, I can put petrol in the car then.'

'Oh yes, darling, will you still do that?'

'Yeah, yeah,' said Douglas and then went back to piling his plate with food.

Mairéad realised she had been staring nakedly at this exchange for too long. She blinked and shook her head a bit, picked up two napkins and went to find Sunny. They sat on the sea wall and Sunny ate her burger and ketchup in its white bun. Dibs was still running around the garden, hassling the stomp rocket, while also eating a hot dog and dripping ketchup onto his shoes. She pinched her knees together and tried to balance her paper plate on them. When this proved impossible, she picked up the plate and poked at the tangle of slaw and chicken with her compostable fork. When this still required both the food and the fork to defy the laws of physics, she put down the fork and started eating with one hand. Bravely, she chewed her chicken, which was a little burnt on the outside and a little pink on the inside.

'Hello!' said Miles. 'Can I join?'

'Yes! How lovely, what an honour to have the chef. Come and sit, sit with us. God, what a massive effort, what a spread!'

'Oh, it's fun,' said Miles. He put his cup of rosé down by the wall and perched on the edge with his overloaded plate. Then he wiped sweat off his forehead with the back of one hand and transferred it to his shorts. 'It's what summer is all about.'

'Can I have another one?' said Sunny, pointing at her empty plate.

'Yes, but you have to get it yourself. Just in there – look, the table's there, through the doors.'

'Uhhm...' said Sunny.

'No, come on. I'm not your maid. Off you go.'

'All right,' said Sunny.

Miles waited until Sunny had gone, then said, 'How's it been, then? Must be a crazy time for you.'

She paused and thought. 'It has been a steep learning curve,' she said.

'You look like you're absolutely nailing it,' he said.

Mairéad stopped chewing. 'Do I?' she said.

'Oh yeah,' said Miles. 'Look at her. Clean, calm.'

'That's a low bar. Alive, walking and talking.'

'You'd be amazed at how few parents can achieve even that. Especially the talking.' He gestured with his fork at a group of teenagers bent prawn-like over their phones.

'Does it, I mean...' said Miles.

'What?'

'This is a rude question.'

'All right, I'm ready for it.'

'Does it make you wish you had your own?'

Mairéad blew out a big breath.

'What you're asking is do I wish my life was fundamentally completely different?'

'Ummm,' said Miles, closing one eye and searching the sky for an answer.

'I live a version of a life that's very nice. And I can't possibly compare it with a different life that I *might* have had. You don't get to do that. So it's not a rude question, but I can't answer it.'

'Well, it suits you. You seem really different.'

'How?' She was very faintly offended.

'Just more solid. More really *all there*.'

She didn't know what Miles was talking about, so she just said, 'Thanks.'

Her life. Her *version* of a life. What had it been again? Where had she been going? Los Angeles, that was it. Her beautiful flat, her plant babies, her new life in LA. It was one version and it had been good. Hadn't it? It had all seemed so important, but she found she was losing her grip on it all; the rope of her life was slithering and sliding out of her hands.

When she went back into the house with her empty plate, there were three iced sheet cakes on the long dining table with score marks where they had been cut up with a knife. Jane was leaning against a kitchen unit, staring at them and looking tired. A child had hurt itself and was sniffling back tears while it sat on its mother's lap.

Well, This Is Awkward

'Cake!' said Sunny.

'Yup,' said Mairéad. 'Look at them.' She levered a piece of the chocolate cake out and handed it over, parcelled in a napkin.

'Caaaaake,' said Dibs, appearing at the table.

'One for you,' she said, and handed over a cube.

'Ooh, cake,' said Dibs's father.

'I think you can do your own.'

'I really ought to be able to by now,' he said. 'I'm Gus, by the way. You're Mairéad? Thanks for keeping an eye on Dibs.'

'It's no trouble. He's very charming.'

'Mairéad,' said Gus thoughtfully. 'That's an usual name.'

'It's Irish.'

'Oh, are you Irish?' said Gus.

'No,' said Mairéad. 'It's a long story. How on earth do you do five children, though?' she said, unable to stop herself from asking. And anyway, he had asked the Are-you-Irish question. 'Sorry. People must say that all the time.'

Gus shrugged and scrunched his face into a baffled look.

'Beats me,' he said.

'Yeah and we were all mistakes,' offered Dibs, spraying cake crumbs all over the floor.

'That's not true,' said Gus. Then he looked away into the distance. 'Or is it?'

'At least two of us were mistakes,' pressed Dibs. 'Or three, if you count that one mistake was twins.'

'Mistakes is the wrong word,' said Gus. 'Lapses in concentration.'

Dibs said, 'He means "mistakes",' in a stage whisper.

'How much longer are you here for?'

'Until Sunday,' said Gus. 'We all get to sail here for two weeks and then Tess and I are back to the grindstone and the boys have to occupy themselves somehow. Lucky old Dibs gets to go back to cricket camp, don't you, buddy?'

'Yup!' exclaimed Dibs, demonstrating his bowling action with his ping-pong ball. 'Why can't you just leave me at cricket camp rather than drag me out here?' he whined as he scampered off to fetch his ball.

'When they invent a boarding cricket camp we'll do just that,' said Gus. 'I don't know how we managed to get four sailors and this cricket outlier. I tell Tess all the time she must have had an affair with Shane Warne, but she swears not.'

As the afternoon waned, Miles insisted on a huge game of rounders on the playing field next to the quay so that Jane could clear up. Dodie waved them off from the balcony. 'I'd come with you but I haven't got a sports bra,' she said. 'I am totally incompatible with running.'

Sunny turned out to be rather good at rounders and extremely, shamelessly competitive. Mairéad didn't have the right bra on either, but joined in anyway, running with her hands clamped over her chest. She was beside herself with happiness when, against all odds and after many misses, she managed to connect her bat with the ball. Dibs and all his brothers, including Tig, shouted and whooped. She laughed in excitement and terror as she ran to second base. Then she saw Douglas, cleared her throat and smoothed her hair back into place.

Dibs and his brothers were gifted sportsmen; even Mairéad, who had no interest in any sport, could see that. They whacked the ball soundly and threw it with effortless accuracy. Mairéad watched as Dibs – small, fidgeting, chatterbox Dibs – levered back his arm and, with a look of savage intensity on his face, threw a ball 100 feet in order to stump Douglas in a nail-biting finish. Douglas fell to his knees and shook his fists at the sky. The Callaghan brothers went berserk, swarmed around Dibs and lifted him onto their shoulders.

'Those Callaghan boys need to be on separate teams,' said Miles to no one in particular, sounding a little annoyed.

TWENTY

Sunny seemed ambivalent about having Dibs around. It was now a given that Dibs would be at Quay Cottage in the morning and come in for toast and hot chocolate, or a boiled egg, or whatever else was on the menu for breakfast. Mairéad even attempted French toast, but everyone politely agreed – even Sunny, so as not to hurt Mairéad's feelings – that something had gone wrong with it because it wasn't very nice.

Sunny had stopped glaring at Dibs when he followed her around and Mairéad even dared to give him the occasional pat on the shoulder. She had been trained so fiercely by Sunny out of any physical touch that she was surprised not to be shaken off. One evening Dibs said casually, 'Bye, Auntie Mairéad,' and gave her a quick hug before he vanished into the twilight towards his real family.

Dibs and Sunny went crabbing and paced about, Dibs falling easily into Sunny's preferred hobby. They all trooped up to Dodie's house from time to time to eat Jane's sandwiches and loll about on the lawn.

When Sunny was exhausted and drained by company and retreated to the cottage to read her book, Dibs hung about, nattering away about the breath-taking cruelty of his brothers, his dumb school, cricket, and weird things he had seen on the internet, and asking many and varied questions about Donald Trump, Ebola, Brexit, American gun laws and so on, always prefaced with the phrase: 'So, Auntie Mairéad, what's the deal with…' He was not actually asking her, he was raising the subject so that he could chatter on at great length about it. This was, of course, mansplaining in its purest form, but Mairéad couldn't bear to pick him up on it.

Whenever Dibs fell silent, she knew that he had found her phone and was sitting on the sofa staring at it. She didn't mind. Her Safari history now contained random words and phrases such as 'worlds biggest boat', 'massive waves', 'scary snake', 'roblox', 'donald trump', 'boy with uke', 'backpack boy', 'floss', 'fortnite' and so on. Occasionally, in the heat of the afternoon, he fell asleep on the sofa and she saw shades of the baby he must once have been. Puffs of air escaped his pristine lips and his eyelashes fluttered to high, round cheeks. She tiptoed round him, tidying up, bringing in the endlessly discarded cereal bowls from the outside bench. The little items kept arriving on the bench, too. A button, a safety pin, a scrumple of aluminium foil.

Once, she found Dibs standing next to one of Sunny's dystopian books, his head craned sideways to read the cover.

'Read that if you want. Sunny enjoyed it, she won't mind.'

'Looks a bit complicated for me,' said Dibs bashfully, then asked Mairéad to time another ping-pong auto-rally.

'I'm sure Sunny will be down in a minute.'

'Oh, I don't mind. I get a bit much sometimes – people need a break.'

Mairéad frowned.

'Well, I don't know who told you that, but I don't need breaks from you. Do you want some of this orange?' She held out a dripping segment.

'No thanks,' said Dibs. He fumbled a hit, overreached and lost the ping-pong ball to the floor.

'Damn it,' he said.

Mairéad even nearly convinced Dibs that he should do the pedalo race with Sunny but, after being begged and subjected to attempted bribes for half an hour, Dibs refused finally and completely.

'I'm a man of principles,' he said.

The day of the regatta dawned bright, but the sky towards the sea was indigo with a gathering weight. Mairéad had been woken early by tremendous activity. The night before, great fronds of bunting had been unravelled and strung across the quay, and now there was a to-ing and fro-ing, calls and replies.

She looked out of the cottage door and saw Nelson on the quay path, dragging along a board to which a piece of drainpipe was attached, with the words 'Bash the Rat' painted on it. Folded trestle tables had been deposited here and there, among boxes stuffed with coiled wire, staple guns and masking tape.

'Do you need a hand?' she said to Nelson. He looked her up and down, squinting.

'Quite all right, thank you,' he said, a little snottily.

Sailing school was abandoned for the day and the quayside heaved with people setting up tables and putting out cakes and assorted junk for bric-a-brac stalls and a tombola. There was also a guess-the-sweets-in-the-jar competition and a contraption where competitors tried to get a loop of wire through an electrified linear obstacle course without making contact and therefore sounding a buzzer. Mairéad, Sunny and eventually Dibs observed from the bench outside the cottage.

The regatta opened with the famous two-man rowing race, unintelligibly commentated by Miles through a loudhailer, which kept squealing with feedback, sending spectators' hands to their ears, groaning. The bunting flapped in a sea breeze and the horizon heaved with bulging white clouds.

Mairéad both very much did and did not want to watch the luscious Douglas in this race. Her dignity was saved by the fact that the race passed near-ish to the cottage. Near enough to see that it was very close, but that ultimately Douglas and his cousin Vinny won. There were rather a lot of women watching with binoculars and Dodie sent her a WhatsApp from where she was watching from her balcony, saying, 'Swoon.'

'Tig and Jez will be really pissed off,' said Dibs, cackling with delight at the prospect of his vanquished brothers. Sunny and Dibs poked around the stalls. Sunny was infuriated by the impossibility of Bash the Rat; Dibs stood next to her, lecturing her on technique as he stuffed penny sweets into his mouth. Mairéad offered them cheese sandwiches for lunch but they both declined, having spent all their cash on cola bottles, Rice Krispies treats and bags of popcorn.

At 2 p.m. Sunny bowled up and said, 'It's the pedalo race! It's the pedalo race!'

'Oh my god,' said Mairéad, who had banked on Sunny entirely forgetting. 'Uh. Okay then.' She got up from the sofa, where she had been having a peaceful five minutes between domestic tasks, and followed Sunny along the quay and down the pontoon.

There were eight pedalos bobbing about in the water.

'You're on number 6,' said Miles, reading from a clipboard.

Mairéad looked at pedalo number 6 and then looked up to the finish line. The course was the same as the rowing race, and the finish line was along the estuary, near the sailing school.

'All right, Sunny,' she said. 'Let's hop on, then. Do we need life jackets?'

'On a pedalo?' said Miles. 'No, they're safe as houses.'

Miles hooked pedalo 6 with a long stick and dragged it to the quay. Mairéad hobbled onto it and sat down quickly. Sunny hopped on with her arms tightly folded, so that no one could help her, and sat down.

'Right, so do I steer with this thing?' said Mairéad, pointing to a lever in the middle of the two seats.

'That's right,' said Miles. 'Line up with the others near that buoy and we'll sound the klaxon for the start.'

They pedalled out towards the other contestants and she felt more hopeful. This was all right, pedalling was easy. Here they were, whizzing along. Sunny had got the hang of it.

'So when the klaxon goes "blah" we pedal like mad.'

Sunny nodded.

There was a lot of jostling and bumping against other pedalos near the buoy and, rather sooner than she would have liked, a klaxon sounded. With a furious churning of brown water, the pedalos set off.

'Pedal! Let's go!'

They made good headway for a few minutes. Visualise success, thought Mairéad. She closed her eyes and visualised standing on the far pontoon and being handed the pedalo trophy. But when she reopened her eyes, she felt a terrible listing to one side. She dismissed it as just the movement of the water, but then they stopped moving altogether, no matter how hard they pedalled. The rest of the competitors pulled away from them into the distance. Then with a terrible keening and sliding, the left side of the pedalo started rising out of the water.

'Oh my god! We're sinking!'

'Pedalo number 6!' said Miles through the loudhailer. 'You are sinking.'

'I know!'

'Help is coming. Please do not jump into the water.'

But the pedalo, once unstable, was impossible to stay on. They both slithered off the smooth plastic and tipped into the water.

This is it. This is the end, she thought.

The water was brown and extremely cold and, although

Mairéad had desperately tried to keep her head out of the water, she was fully submerged. She struggled back to the surface, coughing and blinking. She gasped for breath but her lungs seemed to be unable to inflate.

'Sunny!' she said weakly.

'Argh!' said Sunny hoarsely.

Mairéad fought for breath and felt her clothes fill with water and weigh her down. With a yawn and a creak, the pedalo turned upside down like a dying sea monster. She hung on to the wreckage with one hand and held on to Sunny with the other.

Sunny shook her hand free.

'No, no! Don't be an idiot! Hang on to something at least!'

She heard the buzzing sound of an outboard motor as it bounced over the water towards them. She pushed her wet hair out of her face. As the boat came closer, her face fell in utter horror when out of the blurriness loomed Douglas and Vinny. The breeze rippled their T-shirts and their glamorous hair whipped about. Oh, god and oh, *god*! They would pull alongside them and she would be heaved into the vessel like a vast, dripping whale.

Vinny cut the engine and they see-sawed close to the upturned pedalo.

'All right, don't worry, we'll get you out,' he said.

'Take Sunny first,' she said, her teeth chattering. 'They're going to pull you into the boat, Sunny – you have to let them, okay?'

'No,' she said. 'I'm all right now. I can swim. It's not far.'

'No! It's too far and too cold. You have to let them do this, all right? I'll give you, I'll get you... you can have whatever you want, yes? Snacks!' she cried. 'So many snacks!'

The boat pulled alongside the beleaguered pedalo and strong, tanned arms lifted a protesting Sunny out of the water and into the boat as if she was nothing more than a tangle of seaweed.

Well, This Is Awkward

Mairéad put a freezing cold hand to her face. Please, not *this*. How could it have come to *this*? Even though she could only breathe with what felt like the top three per cent of her lungs and she could no longer feel her feet, she desperately did not want to be hauled into the boat. She felt herself wanting to sob in despair, but she could also feel herself growing so, so tired. So dangerously tired that she could imagine herself just letting go of the slippery grip she had and allowing herself to be dragged under the brown water surface, down, down, down to the scuttling crabs and old bits of junk and the muddy estuary bed. What a way to go.

'Can't you tow me back?' she said.

There was a faint cheer from across the water as some lucky person in a seaworthy vessel won the pedalo race. And now the crowd on the quay turned and watched the rescue with fascination. She did not want her heaving, dripping body, hunched shoulders, graceless haunches and flailing feet to be visible through the curious binoculars that had earlier been trained on Douglas's biceps.

'Not sure that's safe,' said Douglas. 'Water's pretty cold.'

'Yeah,' said Vinny. 'And there are eels in there.' He made a grossed-out face.

'Eels! Fuck! Get me the fuck out of here!'

The boat was small, but from the water the sides looked vast, insurmountable.

'If I put my hands on the side, won't I just pull the boat over?' she said. She was panicking now. Panicking and cold and still very worried about being heaved into the boat like a huge, dripping whale. But more concerned, definitely, about the eels, which were no doubt even now contemplating slithering up to her feet.

'Yes, so don't pull down. Put both fingertips over the side of the boat, like this,' said Vinny, demonstrating. 'Just resting. Then we'll lift you in.'

'Oh god, but it'll be like...' She looked up into the handsome teenage faces, gazing at her expectantly, and imagined what they saw – a middle-aged woman, her hair in rat's tails, turning blue with cold. Then she saw in her mind's eye, with great clarity, an enormous grotesque eel, the size of an anaconda, zipping up through the water to eat her toes.

'Never mind. Okay, let's do it,' she said. She let go of the pedalo and swam the two strokes to the rescue boat, feeling herself even in that short time being pulled under by her wet clothes. She grabbed onto the side of the boat and her hands scraped the wood slightly. They were cold and wet and it was very painful.

Douglas and Vinny took hold of her shoulders and arms in a solid grip.

Try to enjoy it, she thought. The firm touch of these lovely young men. Imagine how envious everyone will be. Who cares what they think of you? You're old enough to be their—

'One, two, three. Up!' said Douglas. She heard the whooshing of water and felt herself fly through the air and land inside the boat. There was no rolling about and flailing at the bottom of the boat, no dripping or flapping or mooing as she'd so feared. She was surprised to see that she was shoeless.

'Right,' said Vinny. 'All right? Sit there, okay? Sorry, we forgot towels.'

'No, no, that's all right,' she said, covering her now completely see-through T-shirt with her arms and shivering. She plucked it away from where it was stuck to her stomach. Vinny was a stocky and cheerful boy, with floppy black hair. Dainty patches of acne across his cheeks and forehead didn't make him any less dazzling. His youthfulness burst out of his being like rays of light.

Sunny seemed very relaxed already, her ordeal behind her, leaning on one side of the boat, sucking her thumb and looking back towards the crowd on the quay.

Well, This Is Awkward

'Okay, Sunny?' said Mairéad, touching her on the knee. Sunny looked down at her knee and then up.

'Yeah,' she said.

Douglas yanked the engine pull cord once, twice.

Mairéad watched Douglas's back muscles ripple, visible through his T-shirt, as he went at the engine cord. She let out a strange noise, a cross between a short huff of laughter and the sort of cough of disbelief you might make after being grossly insulted.

Oblivious to this, Douglas pulled the cord for a third time. Nothing.

'Spark plug needs changing,' he said to Vinny.

'Yeah,' said Vinny. 'Give it a sec.'

They all sat in the boat, looking at the engine. The sun came out from behind a cloud and beamed warmth into Mairéad. She turned to face it fully.

'Well done on winning that race,' she said, through clattering teeth and blue lips. She felt like a teenager struggling to find something appropriate to say to the most handsome boy at school.

'Cheers,' said Douglas, smiling and showing his dimple. He gave her what was unmistakably a once-over. Mairéad worked hard to stop her eyes from rolling back in her head.

'I'm really hungry,' said Sunny.

'What?' She was transfixed by Douglas's triceps.

'Hungry. Hungry!' she said.

Mairéad picked a strand of something long and brown and muddy off her ankle and tossed it into the water. She stank. The estuary water stank. Her shirt was ruined. Had she mentioned that she stank?

'Okay,' she said, her teeth still chattering with the drama of the cold water and the once-over. The sunshine on her mottled, blueish goosebumped skin was making her itch. 'I promise we'll find something when we get back.'

'Fourth time's a charm,' said Douglas. He yanked the pull cord hard and it fired up, the engine grumbling and puttering loudly.

'Phew,' said Mairéad.

She wiped her fingers underneath one eye, certain that eyeliner was dribbling down her face in a way that was making her look like a freshly dug-up corpse.

'Can you remember to tell Miles about the spark plug?' said Douglas to Vinny.

'Aye, cap'n,' he said.

'So, have you really seen eels in here?' shouted Mairéad over the engine, looking into the water in disgust.

'Oh, yeah,' said Vinny.

'And giant squid,' said Douglas.

'Sharks.'

'Huge, man-eating, like, *crocodiles*...'

'Oh, I see. Okay. I get it. You got me.'

'Got you in the boat, didn't it?' said Vinny. He peered back into the water. 'But, like, there really are eels.'

TWENTY-ONE

When the bulging, dark clouds advanced over the horizon and crept up the estuary, heaving and foaming, heavy with rain, no one really knew what to do. It had been so many days – weeks, even – with unbroken sunshine, that even cloud cover, let alone the prospect of rain, was just weird. After hot showers, Mairéad and Sunny went back outside to the quay in search of more cake for Sunny. They ran into Dibs, who was looking at the sky anxiously.

'Are you okay?' Dibs said to Mairéad, slipping his hand into hers and then patting the top of it with his other hand. 'That must have been really scary.'

'Yeah, Vinny said there were eels in the water.'

Dibs looked at the estuary accusingly.

'Eels? Really? I knew it.'

The clouds were low and menacing, fat and monstrous. A little breeze had picked up, gusting skirts around and flipping paper plates off tables. When in the distance there was an audible rumble of thunder, Dibs covered his ears with his hands and ran down the quay to the cottage and slammed the door. Sunny looked about herself, blinking in surprise. Tiny spatters of rain started to appear and there was a rush of activity to get things inside before more rain arrived. Mairéad helped put away Bash the Rat, whipped away all the tablecloths that she could reach and headed towards the cottage, followed by Sunny. There was a flood of people towards the Jolly Roger.

'Dibs?' she called as she opened the door to the cottage.

'Here,' came a muffled voice.

'Where?'

'Where's Dibs?' said Sunny.

'I don't know – his voice is in here but I can't see him.'

One of the sofas heaved and Dibs emerged from between the cushions.

'I don't like thunder,' he said. There was another rumble in the distance.

'Aargh!' he shouted, and dived back under the cushions.

Sunny made a surprised face, then stuck her thumb in her mouth and went to pace around the kitchen table.

A flash of lightning lit up the living room and Sunny looked up. 'What was that? Was that *lightning*?' A deafening clap of thunder rolled around the quay, and the windows trembled. A high-pitched, terrified scream came from the sofa.

'Wow!' said Sunny, and rushed up the stairs to get a better look outside.

Mairéad knelt down by the sofa.

'It's all right, the storm can't get you,' she said.

'Two thousand people are killed by lightning EVERY YEAR,' said Dibs, only just audible through the cushions. 'And I'm not going to be one of them!'

'Shall I go and find your mum?'

'No! Mum's the worst. She finds it really annoying that I'm scared of thunder.'

There was another flash and another boom.

'Aaaaaaaarrgghghghgh,' screamed Dibs. 'Aaaaarrgghgh, make it stop!' The sofa cushions shook as he sobbed. Mairéad patted the cushions, unsure of what else she ought to do. She padded up the creaking wooden stairs to check on Sunny, who had thrown the double windows open and was vibing hard with the storm, as it swished her hair about and tossed droplets of rain onto her hot face.

'I saw forked lightning!' she shouted. 'Like, "crrch crrch crrch" from the sky to the water. It was incredible! Maybe one will hit a tree and it will explode!'

Mairéad didn't know whether or not to tell her to come away from the window. Sunny was enjoying herself so much that she didn't think she could get her away even if she wanted to. There came another heart-stopping, unholy flash of light outside and she covered her ears in anticipation of the thunder. It was so close that it arrived as the loudest 'bang!' that she had ever heard. Sunny threw her arms in the air and shrieked, 'Wooooooooooo!' Mairéad could hear Dibs's hysterical sobs from downstairs and she clattered back down to the sofa.

'It's all right, love. It's all right, it's all right.'

She patted the cushions for a while, then sank down to sit next to the sofa, with her back to it. The storm was short but had managed to do some damage. Gusting winds had knocked tables and chairs into the estuary, plates not taken inside had smashed onto the ground, and anything not tied down had been flung about. The electrical storm was followed by twenty minutes of lashing rain, which battered the windows in gusts, and then a further forty minutes of heavy rain. The estuary water churned and the sailing boats lurched crazily from side to side.

Dibs would not come out from the sofa until there had been no thunder for twenty minutes. He emerged red-faced and tear-stained and sat on the sofa clutching a cushion in front of him.

'What happens when there's a thunderstorm at school?'

'I go to Matron,' said Dibs. 'She knows me.'

I bet she does, thought Mairéad.

She fetched Dibs a biscuit and some water and they both

stared blankly at the pictures of boats on the opposite wall for a bit.

After two hours, the storm clouds slunk away, like a bully wandering away from a cruel prank, and people emerged from cottages and the pub to assess the damage. From the cottage window, Mairéad saw a man and a teenager get into a boat, holding a long pole. They puttered slowly out to the estuary to rescue various tablecloths and a white plastic picnic chair that bobbed about unhappily.

Dibs and Sunny came down from upstairs, where they had been watching a very long video on YouTube that boasted that it was 'the history of the entire world, I guess'. Mairéad had seen Dibs watching this before, and it was impossible to judge whether the narrator's voice was AI-generated or not; it spoke relentlessly, without taking a breath. Mairéad had felt faintly asthmatic just listening to it and had left, reckoning that they were safe watching this harmless drivel.

'Aha,' said Dibs as he spied his bat and ball and picked them up. He stuck his head outside the front door to squint at the sky and then called back inside, 'Can you time me?'

'Yep.' She flipped on her phone's timer. 'Go.'

She went to get the wash out of the machine and then untied the laundry rack from the kitchen wall and lowered it so that she could hang the washing up to dry.

Sunny appeared in the kitchen.

'Auntie Mairéad,' she said.

'Yes.'

'When I was outside, I saw a girl and she was wearing this thing on her…' Sunny gestured with a flat hand around her chest area. 'Sort of like a very small, tight T-shirt. Is that a bra?'

Mairéad screwed up her eyes and tried to think who Sunny might have seen.

'Oh yes, one of the lemonade stand girls. I know who you mean. She was wearing what's usually called a crop top.'

It had been an extraordinary thing, sporty and neon pink, worn with total unselfconscious confidence alongside a pair of tiny cycling shorts and a check shirt tied around her waist.

'Okay,' said Sunny, and began to disappear back upstairs. 'I want one of those. Not in pink!' she hollered as she got to the top of the stairs.

'Okay!' And she didn't know why, but this made Mairéad feel great. Sunny's utter refusal to change her status quo, even if it was in her best interests, was frustrating to Mairéad. Sunny had identified that this item of clothing would solve the problem of her peri-pubescent chest, which she rounded her shoulders and hunched over in order to hide, and the fact she was willing to even try something – anything! – was enormously fulfilling to Mairéad. She finished hanging up her washing and went to stand outside the cottage. The returning sunshine had dried out the quay and it was going to be a warm evening. She sighed a deep and satisfying sigh, right down into her spleen. She looked towards the pub. She would get herself a nice glass of rosé, why not? It was past 6 p.m. Tell you what, make it a bottle – she wouldn't drink the whole thing. Cork it, finish it another time.

'Back in a sec,' she called to Sunny and Dibs.

Everyone who had sat out the storm at the Jolly Roger was by now extremely drunk. Nelson was standing on a chair, playing sea shanties on a fiddle, and people were dancing about, holding their pints aloft.

'Farewell and adieu to you, fair Spanish ladies,' sang Nelson, 'farewell and adieu to you ladies of Spain...' There were yips and hollers and the air was thick and beery. People spilled out onto the estuary beach and unsteadily lit cigarettes and patted children on the head. The ubiquitous dogs charged about, gritty, wet and barking. Miles was demonstrating something with a pint, gesturing this way and that, causing beer to slop out over the sides.

She fought her way to the bar and asked for a bottle of rosé, paid for it and then said, 'I'll be back.' She had a sudden desperate need for the loo. She battled through the sweaty, drunk crowd and turned down an unlit passageway to the bathroom. She used the loo, washed her hands and then pushed back open the door.

In the dark passageway, a large figure emerged from the men's loo. It looked at her with unfocused, drunk eyes. Waves flopped over its forehead and when it smiled, the smile was wonky, only one eye disappearing into the crinkles.

'I know you. I pulled you out of the water,' said Douglas. He was wearing a grey T-shirt spattered with drips of something, a pair of dark green shorts and trainers without socks.

'Yes. That was me. Thank you again!' She turned sideways to squeeze past him in the gloomy, narrow space, but as she passed Douglas said, 'Wait, wait.'

He pushed her painlessly up against the wall.

'*You*,' he slurred, 'have got *amazing* tits.' Then he kissed her and he was so vast and incredibly hot and sloppy, and tasted so strongly of tomatoes, oregano and beer, that it was like being molested by a gigantic slice of pizza.

Later, Mairéad would be unable to recall what she did with her hands. She hoped very much that she'd had the wits about her to put them straight up his shirt. Alas, she may also have just held them up in a 'Don't shoot!' position, in total shock. She just couldn't be certain. After a little while, Douglas stopped kissing Mairéad and instead, holding her face in both hands, rested his cheek on top of her head. She froze. Her immediate thought was that this was some strange thing that young people now did that she didn't know about. Then he started to grow very heavy and she clutched onto his arms in fright, buckling under his weight. She managed to heave him

Well, This Is Awkward

away to the side and dragged him down the dark passageway and out into the hullaballoo of the pub.

'Tig!' she shrieked. 'Vinny!'

Tig and Vinny turned slowly and stupidly. They, too, were very drunk.

'Woah,' said Tig.

'Help,' she said, her knees bending as Douglas started to crumple sideways. The weight of him was staggering. She badly wanted to avoid being the one to break his fall. 'I think he needs some fresh air.'

'C'mere, mate,' said Tig. 'Fucking rowers,' he slurred. 'They can never handle their booze.'

He manhandled Douglas unsteadily away and he and Vinny staggered out of the pub with him slumped between them.

Mairéad stood still in the middle of the swirling, dancing, drunken, chaotic pub, watching the three boys lurch through the door. She put a shaking hand up to her cheek and then laid it flat on her chest, feeling as if she had been turned upside down, roughly shaken and then dumped back the right way up. She looked around, searching for judgemental eyes that might have seen her embarrassing clinch with, well, not *a child* but certainly someone far, far too young, but nothing came back to her except boozy leers, roaring faces. Nelson's eyes were closed; he plied his fiddle as if his life depended on it. Then he stopped and held his hands up. She wondered if he was about to keel over sideways, or vomit. But no, he started stamping one foot on the floor and then, after a good while of this, bawled the opening lines of 'Wellerman' and the crowd completely lost its mind.

She wondered if there was a back door she could escape through. There wasn't, so she peeked around the doorframe of the pub to see where Tig and Douglas had gone. Unable to spot them in the mingling mess of people, children and dogs, she snuck along the gravel path. Then she stopped and turned, and hustled back to the pub for her forgotten bottle of rosé, which was sweating gently on the bar. She jammed it into her armpit and scurried to the cottage.

After checking that Dibs and Sunny were all right watching *Minions: The Rise of Gru* (they were), she sat on the bench outside the cottage with a glass of iced rosé, which she sipped as she giggled at the absurdity of it all.

Before they left for the train station on their last day, Mairéad took Sunny to Dibs's house to say goodbye. It was a very short walk from Quay Cottage, just a few minutes.

'So here's where you've been all this time,' said Mairéad. He was standing outside the house with his ping-pong ball and bat. It was changeover day and the area in front of the house was a jumble of wetsuits, bags, paddles and snorkels. From inside there came the indistinct, grumbling sound of boys calling to their mother and the shrill responses.

'We're going in a minute. We've come to say goodbye,' Mairéad told him.

Sunny waved a skinny arm.

'Bye nerd,' she said.

'Bye freak,' said Dibs.

Sunny reached out and gave Dibs an awkward pat on the shoulder and he patted her back and then they had a brief slapping-hands squabble that ended, touchingly, in a hug.

Mairéad gave Dibs a squeeze, too, and then pinched the bridge of her nose very hard in order to stop herself from welling up.

'Thanks for the ping-pong balls,' said Dibs.

'Bye,' said Sunny again.

'See ya,' said Dibs.

As they walked away, Mairéad heard the ping-pong ball start up again.

Tok, tok, tok, tok, tok...

Well, This Is Awkward

Sunny walked ahead back to Quay Cottage and Mairéad strolled along behind her, taking in some final views of the water and the cottages. There was the sound of footsteps hustling down a flight of narrow steps and the large figure of Douglas emerged. He saw Mairéad and stopped short.

'Morning,' she said brightly.

'Hi,' he said, uncertainly. He looked underslept and queasy.

'It's Mairéad,' she said slowly and loudly. 'You rescued me from the estuary?'

'Oh, of course,' said Douglas, visibly greatly relieved. 'For a moment I thought I knew you from somewhere else.' He went bright red.

'Ha!' she said fruitily. 'I'm not that lucky. Have a great day,' and she walked confidently off. And she didn't know quite why, but she suddenly felt powerful as hell.

They gathered their bags together outside the cottage and Mairéad put the key back on the lintel. A large, bent nail sat on the bench.

'Just so weird,' said Mairéad. 'All this junk on the bench.'

'It's the crows,' said Sunny. She stood on the quay with her rucksack on both shoulders and her arms folded.

'The crows?'

'Yeah, they bring it.'

'How do you know?'

'I've seen them. I think they're paying for their breakfast.'

'Well, that's… I mean… That's completely crazy. Why didn't you tell me?'

Sunny screwed her face up and looked at the sky, then looked back.

'I don't know.'

TWENTY-TWO

The journey home was uneventful, but Mairéad did not fill with joy as the parched yellow fields gave way to ugly suburban housing and then the concrete fields of town. She felt like she had left part of herself behind in Bloxcombe. She kept checking her bag to make sure that she had all her things; she felt keenly that she had literally left something behind. As they got off the train in Paddington and she helped Sunny on with her rucksack, Sunny said lightly, 'That was fun. That place we just were.' She dibbled her fingers in the air behind her to indicate Bloxcombe. 'Can we go back soon? I want to see the crows again.'

As soon as Sunny woke up the next morning in London, she insisted on going to see the goats. Mairéad wanted to unpack and put a wash on, but whatever. She kicked their things into a corner and planned to deal with them later. They arrived at the zoo about an hour after it opened and went straight to the petting area. Sunny saw Clara and waved. Clara's face brightened in recognition as she saw Sunny and she waved back. She beckoned them over. Sunny sneaked through the kissing gate and ambled over to Clara, who handed her a bucket and ushered her through the 'Staff Only' gate to the food prep area.

'Why does she get to go in there?' a girl complained to her mother. 'She's going to see the baby goats. I want to see the baby goats.'

'I don't know, darling,' said the mother, sounding annoyed. 'She must just be special.'

The next day, Mairéad was tidying up the balcony and watering her plants while a wash trundled away in the washing machine. She was humming 'Joy to the World' and wondering what they ought to have for dinner. She thought about what Dibs was up to. He would be at cricket camp, most likely, chucking balls about and charming the pants off some instructor, bouncing about with his opinions and theories and saying, 'Question,' with his forefinger in the air. Sunny was inside, reading *The Catcher in the Rye* and picking her feet. A dry leaf skittered across the balcony and Mairéad felt, for the first time in a long while, a cool gust of wind.

Fish, they could have white fish for dinner: she'd made that once in Devon and Sunny had thought it was edible. Mairéad paused and remembered that she'd been going to check the local cinema for showings of a new children's film, set in space, that she thought Sunny might like. She had a feeling that Sunny would love the cinema. If there was a showing at 3.30 p.m. that would end just in time for an early supper. She patted her pockets and then looked around the balcony for her phone. As she went towards the doors to look inside for it, she met Sunny coming the other way, holding it out to her.

'Oh, I was just looking for that!'

'It's Mum,' said Sunny, holding out the phone. 'She says it's time for me to come home.' The look on Sunny's face, as usual, was inscrutable.

TWENTY-THREE

'You look terrific,' said Mairéad.

Sunny stood next to the car, which was parked on the dirt track leading up to Lenny's cabin, wearing her green cargo shorts and a T-shirt that said NASA on it.

She was standing up very straight and had a smattering of freckles across her nose. She had even submitted to a hair wash.

'Let's go,' she said.

As they got nearer to the cabin, Sunny started to run. She ran up the stairs and flung open the door, calling, 'Mum?!' Mairéad dawdled, wanting to give Sunny time alone with her mother for the first time in weeks.

She hesitated on the porch and set the bags down. Then she went back to the car to fetch the box of Sunny's books. During her time with Mairéad, Sunny had read twenty books. Mairéad had counted several times in disbelief. She, herself, had read zero books. The books were arranged neatly by series and in numerical order. As she came back to the cabin, she noted that the flowers in the pots on the porch were all dead. Round and about the cabin the grass was brown and desiccated.

She went inside, knocking meekly on the door as she entered. Lenny was sitting on the sofa with Sunny leaning into her, on her side. There was a vegetal smell in the cabin and it was untidy. Sunny sucked her thumb and Lenny had one arm around her. Lenny turned. One side of her face bore the pinkish shading of a healing wound and her hair was cut short. A pair of crutches rested on the floor.

'Hello,' said Lenny, and raised a hand.

'I'm going to see Dennis and Minnie,' said Sunny. She got up and vanished out of the back door.

'Hi! How are you doing?'

'Yeah, okay,' said Lenny. 'Sore.'

'Of course.'

There was the sound of an adult talking and Sunny came back through the back door with a woman Mairéad didn't recognise. She wore utility trousers, trekking sandals and a battered red T-shirt. Her mousy hair was cropped to her chin, topped off with a micro-fringe. She had about eleven piercings in one ear and none in the other. Sunny stood off to the side, arms folded.

'This is Bridget,' said Lenny.

Aha, thought Mairéad.

'Hi,' she said.

'Hey,' said Bridget. 'So good to meet you.' Bridget sounded Canadian. The horror violins, which had been silent for weeks, started up again.

'Bridget's been helping me out,' said Lenny.

Not very well, thought Mairéad, looking around the untidy cabin and recalling all the dead vegetation outside.

'So good to see this one again,' said Bridget, leaning into a side-hug with Sunny, who deftly spun out of reach.

'I'm going to the farm,' said Sunny.

'Is this to see Evan?'

Sunny shrugged. 'If he's there.'

'Do you mind?' Mairéad said, thumbing over her shoulder. 'I've heard so much about Evan and the farm.'

'Yeah, sure,' said Lenny, adjusting her leg in its medical boot.

Mairéad walked down the lane as Sunny stamped ahead of her, and breathed in great draughts of air, blown over the sea and into their faces. In the distance she could see the white tips of cresting waves and seagulls wheeling this way and that. The lane turned down between two fields of crops, golden and rustling, a shimmering golden wave, waiting to be harvested. Crickets scratched away in the long grass and the land had a dry, parched air. As they approached the farm there was the sound of barking and a brown Labrador bustled out of the yard and made it plain to Mairéad that she wasn't welcome to come any further.

'Bonnie,' called Sunny and the dog flattened her ears, wagged her tail and writhed around next to Sunny's legs.

'Yo!' called a voice. Round the corner came a burly man, perfectly good-looking in a rugged sort of a way, wearing shorts, wellingtons and a very dirty green singlet with the letters NFU written across the front. There was a Toyota pickup truck in the yard with a surfboard on it.

'Hello!' he said in surprise. 'Look who it is!'

'Come to get some eggs,' called Sunny.

'I'm Mairéad. Sunny's aunt.'

'Oh, right,' said Evan. Then he looked down at his singlet and boots and said, 'Will you 'scuse me just a sec? See you out by the hens.'

Evan must have emptied a bucket of water over himself as he returned shortly with wet hair, wearing a check shirt, the shorts and some sandals.

'Sorry about my appearance earlier. Farming, it's filthy work.'

'Oh no, that's fine.'

There were six chickens and a rooster, a handsome fellow who stalked about the place imperiously, scratching at the ground and cooing to his ladies. The rooster and Bonnie the dog glared at each other.

Well, This Is Awkward

'Mindy!' said Sunny, as a tortoiseshell cat slinked over a wall and sat, twitching her tail.

'Wow – it's a whole, literal, farmyard. No wonder Sunny's good with animals.'

'Oh yeah, she's got a gift with animals,' said Evan. Sunny was rummaging about in the nesting boxes and pulling out eggs.

'She trained some crows while we were in Devon.'

'Yep,' said Evan, unsurprised. 'That's Sunny.'

'That looks like fun – like an Easter egg hunt every day.'

'Yeah,' said Evan. 'I've never thought about it like that.'

Evan, it turned out, was a deeply soulful man and possibly in love with Lenny.

'She's fierce though, innit, your sister,' said Evan, starry-eyed. 'It's frustrating, really – I would have taken Sunny in, no problem. But not much compared to a fancy sister in London, I suppose.' He paused and looked sad.

Mairéad realised in that moment that Evan was actively offended that he hadn't been asked to take Sunny in.

'Not at all,' she said, hurriedly. 'You would have done a terrific job. I don't know what Lenny was thinking, sending her all the way to me. Maybe it was the bang on the head or all the sedatives. I mean, I'm glad she did, it was good having Sunny.'

'It broke my heart, really,' said Evan. 'I took the pigs in, of course. Sorry I couldn't get to the veg and the flowers and whatnot. It's been so dry and Lenny will only water using the butt, not from the mains. Sunny's the only one that Bonnie likes,' he added, pointing to the dog, who twitched her eyebrows to give Evan a grumpy look. 'But Lenny won't ask for help. Not that I want her to beg me or anything. Even if she just told me what was going on I would have offered. I had no idea she was even back from hospital. I don't know how she's managing.'

'She's got some friend. Bridget?'

'Oh yeah, Bridget,' said Evan. He scratched the back of his head.

'Is she bad news? I know about the… you know… activism. Is she one of them?'

'Look, I don't know anything about that,' said Evan, holding his hands up. 'And I don't wanna, if I'm honest. I know it gets all a bit, you know, dodgy. But that's her look-out.'

'Don't ask, don't tell?'

'She's my neighbour,' said Evan, dejectedly. 'I help out where I can. That's all.'

Mairéad returned to the cabin, following Sunny and her box of eggs. Bridget and Lenny were both looking at something on Lenny's laptop, and Lenny reached up and touched the lid protectively, but didn't close it completely. They both looked at Mairéad in an expectant but not exactly friendly way. Mairéad paused for a moment to give Lenny a chance to offer her a cup of tea, but nothing came.

'Well, I'd better be off, then,' said Mairéad.

'Okay,' said Lenny and Bridget in unison, with placid looks on their faces.

'Glad to see you've got help.'

'We're all set,' said Bridget.

Mairéad went to find Sunny, who was pacing outside the cabin.

'I've got to go now.'

'Are you coming back?' said Sunny.

'I will definitely come back and see you, if you'd like that.'

'Yeah, 'course,' said Sunny.

'I know you don't like hugs…'

Sunny pitched forward and hugged Mairéad round her stomach, far too tightly.

'That's okay, I know it's what you do on *your* planet,' she said.

TWENTY-FOUR

Mairéad left, barrelling the car back down the lane too fast, watching the dust blow up behind her. She was hungry and thirsty and started to need a wee but she didn't stop. She drove urgently and aggressively for a reason she couldn't quite pinpoint. After about forty minutes, she remembered that she had pulled over about here on the way to fetch Sunny, all those weeks ago. She pulled over into a layby and crossed the quiet road to a gate on the other side. She gave a nasty laugh as she recalled she had picked an outfit that she'd thought made her look 'not too London'. She was wearing, now, a hideous jumble of clothes. She had a stain on her top and only one earring in and she didn't care.

She leaned on the gate. The field beyond was empty, and her mind churned. She wanted to go back to the cabin and snatch Sunny away. Would Lenny look after her properly? Would she clean her clothes and launder the sheets and make sure she washed and replace her toothbrush regularly and not leave her in a corner to waste away? What the hell was the deal with Bridget? Mairéad felt like she had left a prized houseplant in the care of Worst Babysitter Ever Beckii T. She took a deep breath, opened her mouth and let out the longest and loudest scream that she could. Red-faced and shaking, wiping her mouth, she stood at the gate until she got her breath back. Then she climbed into the car and kept on driving.

She arrived back at her flat at 7 p.m., drained and aching. She regarded herself in her full-length mirror over the pile of detritus from Devon that was still there, undealt with. She looked crumpled and defeated, with seriously shit hair and a sagging jaw. On the mat was a letter. She picked it up and opened it: it was a speeding ticket from that first drive back from Wales. She tossed the letter aside with a dismissive puff of air through her lips. It sailed to the floor and landed with a splat.

She drank too much that night. Once she'd run out of tonic water she just drank neat vodka, topping it up occasionally with ice. She texted Lenny: 'Just got back, hope everything's okay there xx'.

Her feeling, since she'd left Bloxcombe, that something was missing, was compounded. It was strange and not very pleasant, like sitting at the bottom of a drained swimming pool, adjusting to getting off a boat, or taking off heavy walking boots. Ten times a day she had to remind herself: no, there's no Sunny.

She texted Biba – ridiculous *Biba* – to let her know that she would be at the IGS offices on Monday. She knew that she ought to sort herself out, sort out her hair, sort out that pile of crap, but she had absolutely no incentive to. What was the point? For two days she drifted about, living on junk and scrolling endlessly through all the photos on her phone of Sunny and Dibs, double-tapping her favourites.

On Monday, she was late for work, arriving in a unperturbed way at about 10.15 a.m., holding only her phone.

'Mairéad!' said Jenna. She was wearing beige chinos and a tight orange racerback vest, clompy black gladiator sandals and about a billion gold necklaces. 'God, are you okay?'

'Fine.'

Well, This Is Awkward

'Do you need...' Jenna was lost for words as she regarded Mairéad's dumpy clothes and wayward hair. Her roots were brown and starting to turn, unstoppably, true to their curly calling. Her chemically straightened blonde ends, untreated, were curdling to green. She hadn't bothered to put on make-up.

'Do I need what?'

'Do you need... a coffee?' said Jenna. Margot, tucked under Jenna's arm, put her head on one side.

'I don't drink coffee,' said Mairéad and pushed her way into her office.

Biba crept in later, wearing a terracotta-coloured drapey dress and gold sandals. 'Heyyyyyy,' she said. 'How are you doing?' She had a deep tan and her hair had been dip-dyed pink at the ends.

'I'm fine. You?'

'Super well,' said Biba.

'Wow, *super* well. That must be pretty great, then.'

'Um, yeah,' said Biba, swallowing a little. 'Anything I can get you?'

'I just need a catch-up meeting with Jenna. Can you ask her to prep herself and then come in when she's ready? Oh, and where is Andreas?'

'I'm pretty sure he's in Berlin. I'll get that message to Jenna. Uh, so cool. Okay.' Biba slunk out, closing the door carefully behind her.

Mairéad leaned back in her chair and looked out of the window. She was shocked to see that the man in the office opposite her was there, sitting at his desk, hunched over his laptop as if he had not moved, possibly not even gone home, in the weeks that she had been away. She stared at him and then stared through the glass wall of her office, at the IGS employees, at the Right Gabriel, at Biba and Jenna. They were all the same, everything was the same, nothing had changed. Nothing had changed, except her.

She took out her phone. Lenny had still not replied to her text, so she rang – but there was no answer. She found herself scrolling through her photos of Sunny and Dibs again to remind herself that she hadn't imagined it all, it had really happened.

Jenna pushed open the door.

'Hey,' said Mairéad, tossing her phone onto the desk. 'Sit.'

Jenna cleared her throat and started talking about the work that IGS had been doing since Mairéad had been away. She turned to the projector screen and poked at her tablet a bit until both screens showed the same images.

'So, um, this is @eaterboy – he specialises in freeze-dried cooking. Amazing numbers and visuals…' Jenna stole a look at Mairéad's stone-faced expression. 'We met with him, but… no – okay. And there's @hatthetat, she's just got, like, loads of tattoos… and then @greengirl, she's a gardener…'

'What happened to that mum? That woman we saw before, together. With the pottery.'

'Oh, Susie Twill?' said Jenna.

'Yeah, remind me of her stuff?'

Jenna fiddled about on her tablet and then beamed Susie's Instagram page up on the screen. The frazzled woman on the mug, with messy hair and a drained expression, with the caption 'Rock bottom', suddenly struck Mairéad as the best and most profound thing she had ever seen.

'We took her on, didn't we?'

'Oh, well. No, actually.'

'What? I thought that was the plan.'

'She just wasn't really on board with the culture. You might remember a while ago we had a round table with her about the importance of front-facing branding? Of having a unique personal image to sell? And she just wasn't really comfortable with that and preferred an off-camera role. So we thought she might be a better fit for another agency.'

Well, This Is Awkward

Mairéad shouted with laughter. 'Unique personal image!' She slapped the table and doubled up. 'An off-camera role! My god, we talk so much crap!'

'I mean she was just a little dowdy,' said Jenna, doubling down. 'But maybe...' she continued, giving Mairéad a bitchy up-and-down.

Mairéad's phone pinged and she glanced at the WhatsApp message from Dodie. It was of Dibs and Sunny on the pier, taken at a candid moment, Dibs reacting in pantomime horror to Sunny gleefully brandishing a huge crab.

She stood up and fixed Jenna with a glare. 'I'm getting a bit fed up with *your* front-facing attitude, Jenna, and your unique brand of being a total—' She stopped. '*I'm* in bloody charge round here. And I like Susie. Get her back. I'm going out.'

She barged out of her office, taking the stairs rather than the lift and slapping down each step in her dirty flip-flops, relishing the noisy reverberations through the echoing space. She strode through the reception area and smacked the door open with both hands. She charged out into the street, setting some pigeons clattering up into the sky, then breathed in, hard, through her nose and smoothed both hands back over her hair. The streets stank. They were hot and grimy and grey and loathsome. A pigeon limped towards a discarded carton of old chicken bones. A bin overflowed. A dog-waste bin overflowed further, a hideous waterfall of crap. She walked until she came to a hair salon, which was called 'Expressions'. She pushed open the door and asked to see whoever was available for a haircut.

'We've only got our trainee,' said a girl with an eyebrow ring and heavily lined lips.

'Fine! Don't care. Take it all off,' said Mairéad to the trainee. 'I want all the blonde gone. Crop it down to the curls. I've got curly brown hair.'

'You do,' said the trainee. 'It'll look great. Natural is often the best.'

It's me, thought Mairéad as she watched the trainee work, I'm the one at rock bottom. How could it be that nothing, plus something, minus that *same* something, equalled *less* than what you'd started with? She shook her head at herself, endangering an already rather rough haircut.

The trainee did an inexpert job but Mairéad didn't care.

'We all need a Britney Spears moment, don't we?' said the trainee and charged £30. As Mairéad paid using her phone, she noticed in the mirror that her shirt was buttoned up wrong and a little peek of her bra was visible.

She couldn't be bothered to re-button it. She didn't go back to the office, but walked through the park. It was still the school holidays and some children were playing, their exhausted, mute parents lying on blankets under trees with their arms flung across their foreheads. Well-worn Birkenstocks and picnic bags were spread about. A group of children filled up water-balloons at a tap on the side of a community centre. The little girls were pink-clad and fey. There was not one like Sunny anywhere. Now *Sunny* had a unique personal image.

The phone rang. Andreas.

'Hi.'

'What is this about you setting fire to the office?'

'What?'

'I hear that you marched into the office and told Jenna to go fuck herself?'

'I didn't do that.'

'Mairéad,' sighed Andreas. 'Young people are so incredibly sensitive.'

'Has she complained about me? Already?'

'Not a complaint, a concern.'

She paused under a tree and listened to the rushing of the

wind in the branches above. A *concern*. She'd heard that before, handled plenty of those. It wasn't a concern, it was a complaint.

'I've had a pretty intense month. It was a bit difficult adjusting back to Jenna's bullshit.'

'Oh yes, she has some bullshit,' said Andreas. 'I am with you. She can actually be kind of a total bitch, am I right?'

'Yes.' She could hear Andreas clanking about.

'Sorry,' he said. 'I am making my AG1. But you, of all people, know that being in charge is not about having a nice time and doing what you want. It's about managing people and trying to make sure they don't sue you.'

Mairéad closed her eyes. Of *course* that was what it was about. That was what she had been doing for the last five years.

'But what if I *do* want to have a nice time and do what I want?'

'Mairéad,' said Andreas. 'Are you having a nervous breakdown?'

'I don't know,' she said. 'Yes. No. I don't know.'

She walked about aimlessly for a long time. She rang Lenny again, who didn't answer. She thought about her relocation, about IGS, about Sunny, about life. At some point she turned for home and, by the time she got to her flat, she felt a little better. She closed the front door behind her and looked at the pile of post-holiday clutter heaped up against the wall. She felt, for the first time since arriving back from Bloxcombe, energised enough to tackle it. She put her phone onto charge, its battery nearly dead, then crouched down next to the pile of things and started to sift through it. A piece of material caught her eye.

No.

It couldn't be.

She tugged at it, then put her hand over her mouth. Sunny's blanket.

She collapsed backwards onto her bottom and held the material to her face. She rocked backwards and forwards, breathing in the musty, biscuity, sun cream and hot sunshine smell of the fabric. *Sunny.* Tears sprang instantly from her eyes. She reached for her phone to ring Lenny again but stopped. Why hadn't Lenny called her about this? Sunny must be losing her mind without her blanket. It was too weird. The horror violins slithered about. The right thing to do, the imperative course of action, crystallised in front of Mairéad like a many-sided gleaming thing, suspended in the air.

She slung the blanket round her neck like a swimmer's towel and slammed a half-unpacked suitcase down on its back. She eviscerated it, clawing dirty things out and throwing her remaining clean things into it, squashing them down, throwing in more items: trainers and sweatshirts and pyjamas. She would definitely need her swimsuit for this trip. She was going to move herself into Sunny's life this time, whether Lenny and vile Bridget wanted her to or not. Then, still with the blanket around her neck, she zipped up the case, jammed her wallet between her teeth, snatched up her phone and the car keys and marched out of the door, dragging her case behind her.

TWENTY-FIVE

The door of the cabin opened and Sunny peeped out.

'Auntie Mairéad?' she said after a pause. 'Blanket!' she screamed. She dashed out of the doorway, reaching out and making grabbing motions with her hands. She snatched up the blanket and rubbed it all over her face. 'Oh, thank you!' she said. 'Thank you. I never thought I'd see it again!'

'And your passport,' said Mairéad, reaching into her back pocket.

'Not nearly as important as blanket, though,' said Sunny. 'I can't believe I left it behind.'

'Hello again,' said Lenny, who was standing at the doorway. 'I've been calling.'

'Sorry,' said Lenny, not looking especially sorry. 'My battery keeps dying. Thanks for bringing that back. I thought her leaving it behind would be a good time for her to move on from blanket a bit. A sort of serendipitous moment, but she's been pretty upset about it.'

'I suppose I can see why you'd want to do that.' Mairéad looked at Sunny, who was walking in circles with her blanket slung over her head and around her neck, like a headscarf.

This was not true, though. Mairéad was horrified that Lenny hadn't tried to get the blanket back. *Sunny wants so few things in her life*, Mairéad nearly said. She wanted her books and her blanket. A few snacks. How could you take her blanket away?

'Stay for a few days,' said Lenny. Her manner suddenly and unexpectedly changed, her face and voice brighter as if something had only just occurred to her. 'I mean, if you've got time. The weather's still nice.'

The next day Lenny asked if she could run some errands while Mairéad watched Sunny.

'Of course. Can you drive?'

'Yeah, the car is an automatic, so I can, just about. I'm not sure I'm supposed to.'

'When has that ever stopped you?'

'We look just the same, now,' said Lenny, acknowledging the new haircut.

'Oh, yes,' said Mairéad, touching her hair. 'It was my Britney Spears moment.'

While Lenny was gone, Mairéad couldn't stop herself from tidying the cabin – she tracked down the vegetal smell to two apple cores sitting next to an armchair – and watering all the wilted plants with mains water. She went to the outdoor kitchen and spent a long time trying to make a cup of tea using the huge, old black kettle and failing. And anyway, there was only rooibos! Christ alive! Trust Lenny to enjoy living in such a basic place. Making everything so hard for herself out of sheer bloody-mindedness.

'Can we watch a movie?' said Sunny.

'Sure. I'll put my movie subscription password on Mum's laptop so you can have it when I'm gone.' They looked around but Lenny had taken her laptop with her. 'Never mind, I brought mine.' Then Mairéad looked at Sunny quizzically. 'Do you actually want to watch a movie, or do you want to watch YouTube?'

'Okay, I actually want to watch YouTube,' confessed Sunny with a sly smile.

'Go for it.'

Lenny spent the next two days running many errands. 'This is great, thanks,' she said stiffly. 'So much admin has piled up.'

'Where's Bridget?'

'She's at work.'

'What does she do?'

'She does legal work,' said Lenny, vaguely.

Mairéad and Sunny went to get eggs from the farm and tried to coax the garden and plants back to life. One evening, Lenny demonstrated how to use her kitchen and together they made Sunny's lentil dish.

'She will have really missed this,' said Mairéad.

'Sounds like you all had fun.'

'Not at first, really. But later, yes. I think she had an okay time.'

'I know that she's an unusual child,' said Lenny. 'She can be hard work. She's a bit limiting.'

'Limiting!' said Mairéad. She thought about Dodie's children and Dibs and Sunny. 'All children are limiting, it's not just her. You can't do anything when they're around. But that's life.'

'Listen to you,' said Lenny. 'The expert.' But it was not said aggressively, which was unusual for Lenny.

On the third night, Evan came round for a barbecue and brought Bonnie and his juggling balls. They ate chops and potatoes cooked over coals.

'You're really good at this,' said Mairéad, even though the chops were extremely chewy.

'Cheers,' said Evan. 'Don't get to flex my cooking skills much.'

'Can we get a machine that makes ice?' said Sunny to Lenny. 'For drinks. I like ice.'

'Argh!' said Lenny, throwing her hands up. 'What have you done to her?'

Lenny seemed a little restless and over-excited to Mairéad.

She was oddly un-ranty and pleasant. Mairéad put it down to her being released from hospital, having her child back, getting her life back. After the barbecue, Lenny asked if they could switch beds – Mairéad had been on the sofa and Lenny in the bedroom with Sunny.

'I feel a bit too awake,' she said. 'I don't want to keep Sunny up all night.'

'Sure. Maybe tomorrow we can go to the beach – it looks like it will be okay weather.' She failed, every day, to address when she might return to London. She fobbed Jenna off with excuse after excuse.

'Let's do that,' said Lenny.

But the next morning, Lenny was nowhere to be found. She wasn't with the pigs, or with Evan. She hadn't taken her car. She wasn't in the loo or in the wood store. Her phone was missing and it rang and rang but went unanswered and had no voicemail.

Mairéad stood in the middle of the living room in her pyjamas. Sunny appeared at the bedroom door.

'Hi,' she said.

'Hi.' Mairéad waited for her to say, 'Where's Mum?' But she only walked directly out of the side door and went to pace in circles. Mairéad stared unseeingly at the desk for a moment and then saw, plainly, that Lenny's computer had gone. With the charger. The desk was at a slight angle where she had disconnected the plug from the lead that ran down the side of the cabin from the solar panels. On the desk were three sets of keys, resting on bits of paper torn from an old exercise book.

'Car' was scribbled on one piece of paper in blue biro. 'Shed' on another. 'Trailer'. On a fourth scrap of paper was a recipe headed 'Sunny's Lentils'. The writing started out in blue biro, then faded and started again in black pen. On the side was

Well, This Is Awkward

another piece of paper with the Wi-Fi name and password.

Without thinking, Mairéad opened the desk drawer and swept all of these things into it. She glared at the space where Lenny's passport had once been. The balaclava was also gone. She slammed the drawer shut.

She went to look out of the window at the distant sea, the waves cresting white in the early-morning sunshine.

'Mother. Fucker,' she said.

TWENTY-SIX

Mairéad explained the situation to Sunny as matter-of-factly as she could. Sunny asked a few questions and then nodded and silently went to see the pigs. She then stopped speaking and stopped eating.

Nobody knew what the right thing to do might be. Cass was insistent that Lenny must be left alone and not dragged back to London. Dodie was uncharacteristically opinionated, insisting that she would call the police herself if Mairéad didn't. Evan burst into tears.

'I can't believe she's done this,' said Dodie. 'Why won't you call the police?'

'What crime has been committed?'

'Well, okay, I don't know actually. But she's a missing person.' said Dodie.

'But she's not missing, is she? She's gone, she's taken her passport and laptop.' She looked at Sunny, who was standing on the lane, still as a statue, looking out at the sea. 'If Lenny's going to change her mind and come back, I don't want to have called the police and got her into trouble. And I don't want social services interfering.' Mairéad had no experience of social services and simply assumed they would cart Sunny off immediately either to Misha or to foster care.

'She must be off her head, poor Sunny.'
'Yes, poor Sunny.'
'And poor you, what a nightmare of a situation.'
'It is.'
'Sunny's very lucky to have you.'
'Is she, though?'
'Yes, of course. Lenny's a monster. Sorry. Actually, I'm not sorry. It's true. It's always been true and now here is the evidence. It never made sense that she had a child and you didn't. I'm sure if she wasn't such a, if she wasn't so, *you know*, about medicine she might even have had… when… what I'm trying to say is that Sunny's better off with you. I'm sure there are loads of kids stuck with bad parents who would be better off with someone else, but there literally isn't anyone else. But Sunny's got someone else. It's fate.'
'Maybe.'

Sunny got thinner and thinner. She ate nothing at all except pieces of white bread. 'You're going to get awful constipation,' said Mairéad. At the start of the fourth day after Lenny had vanished, Sunny walked into the living room, stared at Mairéad and then started throwing herself against the walls of the cabin, howling and shaking. She doubled over and screamed, red-faced. She curled her bony fingers into fists and banged them against her forehead. Mairéad didn't know how to respond except hover nearby with her hands held out – in order to do what, she wasn't sure. She had in her mind, in that moment, that Sunny was going to pitch head first through the window or try to grab a knife – and that she, Mairéad, must prevent this.

Sunny started attacking her own face with her fingernails, forming her hands into claws, dragging the nails down her skin.

'No!' barked Mairéad, and wrestled her hands away, but not before Sunny had scratched three livid marks down her temple.

'It's all right, it's all right,' said Mairéad, holding Sunny as tightly as she could, even though she knew that this was Sunny's most detested thing. 'Mummy loves you,' she gibbered. 'Mummy loves you, Mummy loves you, Mummy loves you.'

She had no idea what she was saying – whether she was saying that Lenny loved her (a very moot point), or that she, Mairéad loved her, or what. But whatever the sense of the words truly was, they were what came out. Sunny fought her way out of the clutch and threw herself against a few more walls. Then she lay on her back on the hard floor for a long time but didn't scratch her face again. After about half an hour of an impenetrable mood, she turned onto her side, stuck her thumb in her mouth and fell asleep right there on the floor. Mairéad fetched a blanket and draped it over her.

She texted Dodie, who rang back.

'You need to phone my cousin,' she said. 'Dr G. She's a child mental health person. A whatsit, you know. Some sort of shrink. She's a bit unorthodox but she's a straight talker, no bullshit.'

Dr G was in the middle of eating something very crunchy when Mairéad rang.

'Sorry for the audio,' said Dr G. Her voice had an echoey quality and Mairéad understood that she was on speakerphone. 'It's been a hell of a morning.'

Mairéad explained the situation.

Dr G took her off speakerphone. She heard the clatter of cutlery and the noise of a tap running into a sink.

'So you're telling me that your sister has vanished, most likely left the country, without leaving a note, and you are now in sole charge of your niece?'

'Well, no note except the recipe for the lentils.'

'Sure. Well, I'd say this is an open and shut case. Your niece – Sunny, is it? – will start talking again. If you want to be really technical about it, it's called "selective mutism", though I'm not sure how helpful that is to you, to have that label.

Well, This Is Awkward

The main thing for you to know now is that it will go away on its own. The tantrum, the scratching, that's just her acting out.'

'I've never known what that phrase means,' said Mairéad, recalling the ease with which Tig had used it. '"Acting out". Shouldn't it be "acting up"?'

'Yes, it's annoying, isn't it? Dumb therapy-speak. Basically it means someone has a bad feeling inside – sadness, rejection, depression or whatever – and their actions are their way of getting the feeling *out*. In adults it tends to be things like screwing strangers or drinking or taking pills. Children have massive tantrums or break stuff, hit each other, chuck chairs around. Personally, I think this tantrum is pretty healthy behaviour, considering her mother is crazy. Have you got a dog? Get a dog if possible. Or a cat, whatever. Sea monkeys. Anything. Try, if possible, to act as if everything is completely normal.'

Mairéad thought about this for a moment.

'Do you think Lenny is crazy?'

'Is that your sister, Lenny? Well, look. I don't know. But I've been a psychiatrist for thirty years and I've seen some fucked-up shit and what I don't often see is totally *sane* women abandoning their children. Crazy women? Yes. Men? Sure. *Sane women*, no. In fact I would go as far as to say I have never in all my professional life heard of an emotionally stable woman calmly abandoning her children without a very pressing reason. Like a *gun* to her head.'

'That seems somehow unfair.'

'You're telling me. Dads just piss off and come back every now and again and it's all okay. They get to have their free-range life and their children. In some communities it's the norm. But when women do it, it's straightjacket time.'

'I don't get the feeling she really enjoyed being a mother.'

'Christ, who does? It's not about enjoying it. I've got three children and sometimes I look at them and want them to vanish, like, permanently. My youngest, especially, it's like she was sent here to destroy me. They bleed you dry financially, emotionally, physically. But the number of people who get hung up on the idea that you have to love your family, love every minute. It's not about love, it's about duty. Sorry, I know this is an unpopular opinion but when you're at the coalface it stops you from going mad. I blame laundry powder commercials for fostering this delusion that family life is lovely.'

They talked more about Lenny, about Sunny. About the living situation in the cabin, the pigs, Evan.

'What do you understand by "intimacy issues"?' said Mairéad.

'Oh, it covers all sorts,' said Dr G. 'Usually someone who doesn't want to be close to other people or to be vulnerable because they've been betrayed or let down. By a parent, partners or whatever. Or even siblings, actually. Who's the got the intimacy issues?'

'No one,' said Mairéad quickly. 'Just a phrase I've heard. Like "acting out", you know?'

'Yeah. The dreaded "therapy-speak".'

Mairéad was exhausted by the end of the hour.

'What do I owe you?' she said.

'Oh, on the house. Any friend of Dodie's.' Dr G started laughing. 'I swear one day I will get that woman out of bed. And anyway, I'm fascinated by this, I must admit.'

She heard Dr G start clattering about again. There was a sound like drawers being vigorously opened and shut.

'Your sister is a rare breed – like I said, women don't usually do abandonment. Dodie's right, though, you do have to call the police if you think she's not coming back.'

Mairéad paused. 'How long should I wait?'

Dr G let out a long breath. 'How long is a piece of string? You'll know when it's time.'

TWENTY-SEVEN

There was, as it happened, a vast number of practical and time-consuming matters to address. Relocating to the new IGS office in LA was out of the question for the foreseeable future. Even coming back to London was unlikely. Andreas was gripped by the drama.

'Interesting,' he said. 'Sometimes big decisions are made *for* us, yes?'

'Can Jenna step up?'

'Ah, I guess you didn't know. She bailed.'

'No!'

'I know, right? She went to ShowTime last week. Boom. Some asshole didn't write a notice period into her contract. And more bad news: she's taken Ashley with her, and signed Min Cohen.'

Mairéad gasped. 'What?' she bellowed. She reeled. She'd had neurotic daydreams about this very thing and now they had come true. It was as if the dark dressing gown hanging on the back of the bedroom door had suddenly jumped down in the middle of the night and revealed itself to be – yes! – a murderer.

'Gretchen is furious,' said Andreas.

Furious with envy, thought Mairéad, at what a steely badass Jenna is. She thought back to her last meeting with Ashley, when she had been so stressed out looking after Sunny and had rambled on about children. She pinched the bridge of her nose with her thumb and forefinger. She knew this was partly her fault.

'We'll hire our way out of it,' said Andreas.

'I suppose this is me resigning,' said Mairéad. She found, following the initial shock, the slight humiliation, that she couldn't give a damn about Ashley. Not really.

'No, don't do that,' said Andreas. 'Stay in the company as consultant advisor or some crap. It's better for us, for tax reasons, if you don't mind. Biba is moving up one to be a baby agent, and she will need you. Your mother lady, Susie Twill, she is doing well for us, you will want to be involved in this as she was your get. And also, maybe your sister will come back and we can repair this mess. Then you can come back and everything will be normal again.'

It took her a full seventeen days to ring Helen. She rang the landline, as she didn't want Helen to be wandering about with her mobile and not focusing when she delivered the news.

'Hyello,' said a voice.

'Oh. Sorry, I think maybe I've got the wrong number. Is it... who is that?'

'This is Roxana,' said Roxana.

'Oh I see! Hi, this is... I'm Mairéad, I'm—'

'Yes, Helen's daughter,' said Roxana. 'Nice to make your acquaintance. Your mother is taking a nap just at the moment, can I pass a message?'

'It's... I'm not sure how to explain it.'

'You sound a little stressed, is it all okay? I think you are with your niece. Is there an emergency?'

Mairéad blinked. This Roxana was no fool.

'My sister Lenny,' she began.

'Yes,' said Roxana.

'She's vanished.'

'Vanished?'

'She's left. She's taken her passport, wallet, phone, boots... everything. She's gone.'

There was a pause.

'This is very bad,' said Roxana.

'Yes.' Mairéad found herself slightly hyperventilating. Explaining the situation to Roxana had her feeling really panicked for the first time since she'd found Lenny missing.

'And you are on your own with your niece?'

'Yes. And we're in Wales.'

'Wales!'

Roxana ordered Mairéad to give her not only her telephone number but the location of the cabin. Then she read out her own mobile number and said, 'You will WhatsApp me.' Mairéad added Roxana's number and then WhatsApped her a panic-face emoji. Roxana replied with a pink flower.

An hour later Roxana called back.

'We are coming. Helen and I are coming to Wales.'

'What?'

'Yes, it is sorted. I am hiring a car. And there is a wonderful B & B I have found in this place near you, Castell Cerys.'

There was some shrieking in the background.

'Helen is not happy about this but I am telling her, "Helen, your daughter is very upset",' said Roxana, concerned and faintly scolding. 'Mairéad is very passionate about this matter. Family is very important, you must prioritise it. And also your grand-daughter. Tch.'

Helen said something in the background, and Mairéad could hear Roxana turn slightly away from the telephone to address her directly.

'A trip away, this is a good thing. Look, here is your daughter and grand-daughter who urgently needs you! This is a very exciting, fun thing! God bless me if I have such things at your age. My great-aunt, she was ninety-two when she dies and no one knew for weeks. She didn't see anyone for the last four years of her life because she was so crazy and stubborn. You don't want to be like this.'

'But the house…' Helen protested.

'Ha, "the house"!' said Roxana. 'Jethro and Maggie are here, knowing everything about the recycling, you know how Jethro is so crazy about waste disposal. They know all the important things, silly billy… you can call them any time. Now. I have a great suitcase you can borrow. Nice colour and many pockets for all kinds of things. I will not have any arguments about this, thank you.'

To Mairéad, she continued, 'You can expect us tomorrow, about noon. I must pick up the car 7 a.m. sharp and I am very fast driver so maybe more like 11 a.m.'

Mairéad felt her eyes boggling. No wonder her mother worshipped Roxana.

TWENTY-EIGHT

Helen hated the car journey, said Roxana when they arrived.

'She clings to the door like this,' she said, making a crouching motion. 'And her eyes is like this.' Roxana swivelled her eyes about. She giggled. 'I am sorry, I have made her very angry.'

'Good,' said Mairéad.

Roxana had changed her hair since her graduation photo and it was now a neat pixie crop, dyed a vibrant, glossy plum colour. Her glasses were rectangular and severe. Her hands and fingernails were beautiful. She was wearing sexy yet practical clothes – a pair of tight cargo pants, sturdy walking trainers and a khaki zip-up hoodie with a diamante butterfly on the front. The kind of thing Barbie would wear to undertake charity work in a hot country.

Helen was out of the car and leaning against it, as if she had just run a long distance. In her crumpled dress and with her messy hair, she resembled a full bin-bag bursting at the seams.

'What have you done to your hair?' said Helen.

'It was my Britney Spears moment.'

'You're the spitting image of Lenny.'

'Don't say *that*.'

'Okay, we are going to get organised,' said Roxana, clapping her hands together. She gestured to the cabin. 'Show me this place.'

They walked towards the steps leading up to the cabin and Sunny appeared in the doorway.

'You must be this famous Sunny,' said Roxana.

'Who are you?' said Sunny. She was gaunt and grey. Her voice was cracked and scratchy.

'I am Roxana. I am here to admire your pigs.'

'Okay,' said Sunny. It was the first time she had spoken in twenty days.

They walked out to the sty, refreshed Dennis and Minnie's water trough, filled up their scraps bin and supplemented it with pig feed. The pigs jostled each other at the trough and smacked their lips as they ate, grunting and making a compelling, terrible noise.

'Pigs,' stated Sunny. 'You're not supposed to feed pigs kitchen scraps,' she said. 'But as they aren't for eating, it doesn't matter.'

Mairéad stared at Sunny, talking as if the last twenty days hadn't happened.

'Can you imagine eating these lovely pigs?' said Roxana.

'No,' said Sunny. Then she looked at the sky for a bit and said, 'Actually, yes.'

'You and me, we are going to be good friends,' said Roxana.

Sunny gave her a sardonic but not unfriendly look, then settled herself to pacing about the terrace, while Mairéad introduced Roxana to Lenny's outdoor kitchen.

'I see,' said Roxana every now and again. She lifted things up and put them down. 'And you even have an oven,' she said.

'Where?'

'This.' Roxana pointed to a large clay bulb with a slot-shaped hole. Underneath was another hole, very blackened.

'Oh, that's what that is.'

'Yes, the logs goes in there,' she said, pointing to the black hole, 'and then the pot goes in there.'

'How do you know all this?'

Roxana was turning the tap above the stone sink on and off. 'My father is a hunter,' she said. 'For a hobby, you understand. And I have used this sort of outdoor kitchen many times.'

Helen appeared at the back door. 'The Wi-Fi's down,' she said grouchily.

'We will survive,' said Roxana. 'Perhaps you can look at the vegetable patch? Maybe something can be rescued.'

Helen flapped around, grumbling about being treated like a serf, and demanded to know how she was to cut the vegetables, or what she was to carry the vegetables in.

Roxana rummaged around for a minute and found Helen an old, serrated knife and a box.

'This is very good for the soul,' she said, firmly.

Helen stamped out to the vegetable patch and stood glaring at it for a bit. Then she put the box and the knife down and went to look at the pigs instead, where Mairéad found her later, still leaning over the sty wall, talking to Dennis and Minnie and smiling.

Roxana was delighted with the cabin and kept saying that everything was so clever and efficient and how it reminded her of all this hunting that she used to do with her father and uncles.

'This toilets is so good,' came her voice from the composting loo. 'So excellent for the environment and no smell. It's like a luxury experience. And look here. This pipe is taking heat to the boiler for a shower. It is not instant but this is real living. Someone has thought of everything. Except – tch – the hot water is only for the bathroom, not for the kitchen. Ah well. This beautiful day,' she continued. She looked at her neat wristwatch, which was studded with diamante. 'And only 2 p.m. Sunny, will you show me your beach? I have not seen the beach for a long time; I have just been looking at many spreadsheets. I must confess, I am very excited that you are here so that I could come to visit as I would so like to see a beach again. I am going to change and then we will go.'

Mairéad, Roxana and Sunny piled into Lenny's truck as Mairéad's BMW was not much good at navigating the rocky, unmarked tracks around the beach. They went to Harlech, a wide, unspoiled expanse of sand. Sunny had brought her wetsuit and now, on the beach, she put it on expertly, tugging the zip up independently, using the long tag. Seeing Sunny in her natural habitat was the difference between hearing someone express themselves in an adopted language and hearing them express themselves in their native language.

'You're coming in the water with me,' said Sunny to Mairéad.

'I think we all come in, no?' said Roxana, who had stripped down to a purple bikini, showing off a toned figure. Mairéad ogled her as discreetly as she could from the corner of her eye.

'Wooooo!' shouted Roxana, as she ran into the waves.

'Weeee!' shouted Sunny.

Roxana was irresistibly charming and helpful, yet also refreshingly strict.

'No, Sunny,' she said when they had returned to the cabin. 'Our towels belong on the rack, like this. See? Yes, folding up and pushing it through so it hangs so nicely for next time. It is a gift to yourself in the future. Excellent! Full marks.'

Mairéad was astonished. If she had done that to Sunny she would have received a clip round the ear. Or would she? Mairéad felt like she had spent most of the summer picking up Sunny's wet towels and cereal bowls.

In the afternoon, Roxana made everyone do housework – even Sunny. She wrote out a long list of groceries and cleaning equipment. She piled greasy, greying sheets into a duvet cover and left them by the door. Then she announced that they were due for dinner at the Red Lion in Castell Cerys at 5.30 p.m.

'You don't want to cook for us, even though this kitchen looks fun,' said Roxana. 'We will have a nice dinner altogether. We will take two cars because Helen and I are staying in this B & B in Castell Cerys.'

'What on earth is going on?' said Helen huffily, sitting next to Sunny in the backseat of Mairéad's car. 'I suppose you're just dragging me back to London now, without asking.'

'Do you fancy a nice cold drink?' said Mairéad.

'Well, I'll never say no to a nice gin and tonic,' mused Helen.

They arrived for dinner at the Red Lion in Castell Cerys twenty minutes later and were shown to a table in a corner by a waiter who was instantly dazzled by Roxana.

'Have they got a burger?' said Sunny, who was now familiar with children's menus in mid-priced restaurants.

'Almost without question,' said Mairéad. 'I'll get some drinks.'

As she stood at the bar, Sunny arrived at her elbow. 'Roxana told me to help you carry drinks,' she said grumpily.

'Very nice G and T,' said Helen later, squinting at the bottom of the glass with one eye and then staring out of the pub window. 'It's been years since I went to a pub.'

'I thought you went out all the time.'

'I do!' said Helen.

Mairéad looked at Roxana, who said, 'Helen leads a very full life,' and took a sip of her drink.

Later, Mairéad, who was sober, drove a very drunk Roxana and Helen the three minutes to their B & B and watched them sing and trip up the stairs to the door. She then drove a tired Sunny back to the cabin.

'Do I have to brush my teeth?' said Sunny.

'No, but you'll feel gross in the morning if you don't.'

Sunny brushed her teeth and then dived into her bed, made

with fresh sheets that morning. She draped her blanket over her face and fell asleep.

Roxana called at eight thirty the next morning.

'How's your head?' said Mairéad.

'My head is fine! I have just been for a short run, only 3k. It is a beautiful day. This Wales, wow. What scenery. We will be with you in one hours, we have to discuss practical things.'

She arrived with two bags of groceries and cleaning equipment. 'I found excellent laundry place in Castell Cerys, sheets will be ready tomorrow.' She told Helen firmly to first take Sunny to check on the pigs, then collect eggs at Evan's farm, then come back and talk to Sunny about 'educational things'.

Helen set off with Sunny without a grumble.

'How do you do that?' said Mairéad. 'She just argues with me.'

'And I am arguing with my mother, non-stop,' said Roxana. 'I argue with her so much I leave school and the house and run away at fifteen. My mother is an old bat, I cannot stand her. My father left her and I left her, too. But Helen is fine. Perhaps not to you, but she is to me.'

The fact that Lenny took her passport was a bad sign, said Roxana. But now, Roxana wanted to play a game, and the game was called, 'What if Lenny never comes back?' Where were Mairéad and Sunny going to live? Mairéad didn't want to go back to London with Sunny. On that, she wouldn't budge. She still had bad memories of those weeks after Sunny had arrived and it had felt like a crazy thing to do, to uproot Sunny from the few things she was still connected to and make her live in the strange rural fantasy room. It felt cruel to both of them. Like stuffing a wild turkey into a school locker and then having to be the person sitting outside the locker listening to it squawk and bash about. Fine, so in that case Mairéad's flat needed a caretaker and then at some point must be rented out, her post forwarded.

Well, This Is Awkward

'It is very inconvenient that Lenny did not leave us her intentions,' said Roxana, tapping her chin with the end of a pencil. 'You are living in a suspended moment, cannot make firm plans. This is very annoying for the tax situation. But leaving your child like this, it is a crime. I looked it up, it is called "child abandonment". Lenny will assume you have told the police, yes? And so she will be in big trouble if she comes back.'

Mairéad sat back in her chair. It hadn't even crossed her mind to research this, she was too busy being dizzy and stunned by it all.

'Anyway, just as we are playing this fun game,' said Roxana, 'suppose you are still here in winter. I think it is probably cold. Perhaps we need to send you clothes and warm boots from your flat.'

'I don't fancy the outdoor kitchen in the winter.'

'No,' said Roxana. 'Although,' she put her head on one side, 'it has been built in this position against the hill so it will not catch the wind. Yes, it will be cold but it is very sheltered. It might not be as bad as you think. You have so much logs, I am very impressed.'

The log store *was* impressive – it was about a fifth of the size of the cabin itself and tightly stacked with sweet-smelling wood. Attached to the outside wall was a large, sharp metal lever that Roxana pointed out was for slicing bits off larger logs to make kindling.

'The only thing is… do you know what would be nice one evening on that porch?' said Roxana. 'A rosé with ice. One cannot have a cold drink in this house. It is a simple pleasure. There is no need to live like a savage on the ground.'

Then Roxana had more questions. School, what about a school for Sunny?

'God, of course. School,' said Mairéad. 'Lenny was so against it.'

'But Lenny is not here,' said Roxana, coldly. 'An education is a human right.'

'Of course, of course it is.'

'So I am going to leave you to look at schools. There will be a nice one. Have you applied to be Sunny's legal guardian?' She blinked, expectantly.

'No.' Mairéad blushed.

'You must do this. It is important. Without this legal guardian, you cannot enrol her in school, signing forms, medical things and so on.'

'I thought they might come and take her away if they knew Lenny had left. And, I don't know…' Mairéad looked out of the window. 'I just thought she'd come back. I keep waiting for her to just come back.'

'They will not take Sunny away if there is a caring aunt here. If there is a caring aunt they will throw their hands in the air and say, "Hallelujah". The first thing is to call the police, I think. Don't look so scared. If they try to take her away,' Roxana's voice took on a nasty tone, 'you will call me and we will fix it together. There is nothing you can't fix with some research and correct attitude.'

Roxana had a tremendous item with her, a folder of sky-blue leather. When opened, it revealed a lush expanse of A4 lined paper, an internal calculator, a strokable opaque plastic zip-pouch filled with neat slips of paper and extra pockets. On the lined paper, Roxana wrote out lists and numbers and little points of fact in impeccable handwriting. She ripped it carefully off the stack and handed it over.

'You give me the key to your flat,' she said. 'I will make sure everything is perfect and send you nice cosy sweaters.'

Sunny and Helen eventually arrived back at the cabin, Helen ranting loudly at Sunny about Palestine. They came in through the door and Helen brushed back a sweaty strand of hair, planted her fists on her hips and looked at Sunny. She

Well, This Is Awkward

exhaled hard with the air of someone who has accomplished a mission.

Sunny looked at her. The cabin was quiet and expectant.

'Grandmother... Helen...' said Sunny, flapping her hand dismissively, 'wanted to tell me about this thing Palestine. But I don't know why.' She looked at everyone in turn in that flat, dispassionate way she had and then walked silently back out of the cabin.

Roxana insisted on a barbecue that evening and had, that morning, brought with her the ingredients.

'I love the English so much but you cannot cook outside for any of all the money. You must start the fire very early, like 5 p.m. Then you burn, burn, burn and cook when you have this just-breathing charcoal. I don't know how you say it.'

'Embers?'

'I don't know,' said Roxana. 'When it is grey, and breathing in and out with fire.'

Roxana deftly built a fire in Lenny's outdoor kitchen barbecue pit – which Mairéad had dismissed as a grubby old bit of blackened mess – waited until she had fiercely hot embers, and then cooked some steaks.

'So that's how you barbecue,' said Mairéad. The steaks were not chewy, or burnt.

'Yes. I will show this to every English person on this island, one by one,' said Roxana.

Helen sat back in her low wooden chair and watched as the sun set. Roxana was busily brushing around the fire pit and Sunny was inside, reading.

'You've got your work cut out here,' said Helen. 'Quite out of your comfort zone, as they say.'

'Yes, wouldn't it be great if I had someone to help me?' said Mairéad, drily.

'God doesn't give you more than you can handle,' said Helen.

'Since when did you believe in God?'

'I am actually a very spiritual person,' said Helen. 'You'd better just pray Lenny comes back.'

'How is it possible that you don't feel like any of this is your problem? How can you just airily dump it on me?'

Helen turned and looked at Mairéad evenly. 'I was a terrible mother,' she said after a pause. 'That's not an easy thing for me to say, but there it is. If you must know, if that's what you want me to confess, fine. I'm not suited to it. And I would be a terrible grandmother. The kindest thing I can do for all of you is get out of the way. You're more conventional – you always have been.'

'Don't you think the kindest thing is to just be a better mother? Or make up for it by being a better grandmother?'

Helen looked out to the horizon for a moment, wisps of hair dancing in the evening breeze. She made a dismissive noise. 'So like Gavin,' she said. 'This blind faith that people just need to try harder and they can be better. We are who we are. Some of us are not mothers, but we don't find that out until it's too late. That's our tragedy and we have to live with it.' Helen then nodded with a finality that suggested to Mairéad that the conversation was over.

The next day Roxana arrived with more groceries and more cleaning supplies and a huge checked laundry bag filled with fresh sheets. She then announced that they had to leave.

'I must go as I have to attend a big meeting tomorrow in the morning. I will drive Helen back to London now, if this is more convenient for you?'

'Yes,' said Mairéad. 'I think that would be more convenient for everyone.'

'There is one more thing,' said Roxana. Then she stood next to Mairéad while Mairéad called the police.

TWENTY-NINE

The days passed and the weather began to turn. The cabin became a different place. The first heavy rains turned the surrounding ground to treacherous mud. Heavy clouds hung about the hills at the back of the cabin and over the sea, which heaved and churned.

Two police officers visited: an overweight man with a messy beard, whose neck was splurging over his collar, and a female colleague, who was clearly the junior of the two but many times brighter.

The man was suspicious as to why it had taken Mairéad so long to ring them about Lenny's disappearance. Mairéad thought she detected a slight eye-roll from his colleague.

'I thought she would change her mind,' said Mairéad. 'I didn't want to get her into trouble if she was just, you know, taking a moment. But I just don't think she's going to. Come back, I mean.'

'Do you mind if we have a look around?' said the man.

Mairéad shrugged. 'Sure,' she said. She didn't like him.

'It's all right, love,' said the woman. 'Just got to make sure there's nothing dodgy. Just doing due diligence.'

And yet, Mairéad felt a little fearful and judged. 'Of course.'

She started to worry that a two-foot bong or a torture rack

or a bag of sex toys – items she had never owned or even considered owning – might suddenly materialise in a corner of the cabin.

The police spoke to Sunny, who delivered one-word answers, making Mairéad sweat with anxiety that this was some sort of red-flag indication to the police that Sunny was being abused and/or trafficked. Then the female police officer picked up the book Sunny was reading, which she had left tented on an armchair. The novel was a modern re-telling of the story of Achilles and the police officer exclaimed, 'Who's reading this? I loved this book.' She and Sunny nattered away for a few minutes about Greek gods.

The male police officer blinked and looked annoyed and tried to steer the conversation infuriatingly back to why exactly, precisely it had taken Mairéad so long to ring them. Mairéad had a sudden fantasy of an epic loss of temper with this fat copper. She saw herself red-faced, spittle flying, screaming, 'Stop asking me that! I've told you three times! Shut up, shut up!!'

But the female officer looked up and said firmly, 'I think she's explained that, Davey.' She added that someone from children's social services would call and Mairéad's stomach did an unpleasant swoop-plop.

'What do I do until then?' said Mairéad.

The fat policeman shrugged. 'Wait,' he said.

As she watched him lumbering away from the cabin with his colleague, she felt a powerful urge to stick up both her middle fingers at him. She resisted.

Mairéad updated Cass and Dodie with the news that there was no news. Sunny continued to pace about, but was now speaking and eating more. The cabin continued to stand upright and Mairéad appreciated for the first time how well built it was.

Well, This Is Awkward

Even when the wind howled and the rain lashed, it was peaceful inside. It was not cold, yet, but soon the two stoves, in the living room and the bedroom, would be the only thing keeping her and Sunny warm. As it was, if she wanted any hot water she had to build a fire in the living-room stove, light it and then wait hours for the water tank to heat up. She and Sunny had their showers twice a week. The rest of the time, Mairéad doused herself at the bathroom sink – a deep white enamel thing. She washed herself quickly, shivering. She thought of her own bathroom, back in London. Her pride and joy.

The evenings got darker and Sunny demonstrated how to fill the storm lanterns with lamp oil so that they could both read and find their way about. Lenny did not come back.

Mairéad lay in bed at night filled with worry, uncertainty and nameless dread. She thought over and over again about how this situation had come about. Had Lenny seen her arriving at the cabin and thought, now is my chance? Had she been planning to abandon Sunny all along and it was just sheer incredible luck that Mairéad had shown up? How could she? *How could she?*

Occasionally there was a faint scratching noise but she couldn't work out where it was coming from.

One night, in the darkness, Sunny said, 'When are *you* leaving?'

'Me? I'm not leaving. I'm not going anywhere. If Mum comes back and wants me to go, perhaps, but I'd never leave you on your own.'

'You might leave me with Evan,' said Sunny, fearfully.

'What would I do without you, though? Who would I watch movies with?'

The phone call from the social worker came one day as Mairéad was going through a box of textbooks that Lenny had been using as a sort of proto school for Sunny. She had been searching for any official documents that related to Sunny; the passport she had, but then she thought that must mean Sunny had a birth certificate. She started searching through cupboards and drawers, the sorts of places you might put important documents, and eventually found some boxes under Lenny's bed. From the first box Mairéad found, she pulled out workbooks aimed at different age groups for English and maths. She flicked through them and saw them filled in, Sunny's handwriting evolving from huge and wobbly to neat and precise.

And then the phone rang.

'Is it... Mer-ay-ad? Alexander?'

'Muh-raid,' said Mairéad.

The social worker – Lyn – had a timid voice and read her questions out uncertainly. Where was Lenny? Pass. Where was the father? Poland, maybe. Who else lived in the house? No one. Who else visited the house? *No one.*

'Is... is...' said Lyn. Then she went quiet. 'Sorry,' she practically whispered, 'it's actually my first day.'

'Oh,' said Mairéad, feeling a whoosh of relief. 'Well, I've never done this before, so maybe we can cut each other some slack.'

Lyn let out a little giggle and then stopped herself. 'Well, no, I must treat you the same as everyone else,' she said, quickly.

'Of course,' said Mairéad.

'Right, so, the next question is, oh yes. Is the father on Sunshine's birth certificate?'

'I don't know. Funny you should say that – I'm actually trying to find her birth certificate now.'

If Misha was listed on the birth certificate as Sunny's father, said Lyn, every effort must be taken to track him down. Mairéad stopped rummaging in a box and sat back down. No, she thought. Not bloody Misha.

'Oh no,' she let out.

Well, This Is Awkward

There was a pause. 'Oh no, what?' said Lyn.

'No, nothing,' replied Mairéad, cursing herself. She suddenly felt paranoid. Say nothing, to anyone. Just keep your mouth shut. 'I'll keep looking for the birth certificate, but what happens if I can't find it?'

'I'm *pretty* sure that we can get a copy of the birth certificate,' said Lyn. 'Umm, I'll have to ask. I'll need to visit where Sunshine is living, to do a welfare check,' she added.

They made an appointment for the following day and ended the call. But Lyn rang back later, sounding flustered, and said, 'On speaking to my supervisor I actually have to prioritise some other cases.' She named another date to visit, three weeks away.

A small van trundled down the lane one day with a box full of Mairéad's winter clothes, sent by Roxana. Roxana was passionately in love with the flat. 'If Lenny isn't coming back, you will rent this to me and I will care for it like it is a museum. This bathroom!' she shrieked, her voice echoing off the tiles. 'I have never seen something like this, oh my god. This is the most beautiful thing, you are like *artist*.' Finally, Mairéad felt like the refurbishment of her flat was being properly appreciated. She almost wanted Lenny to stay away so that Roxana could live her best life in Mairéad's flat. But she also suddenly felt a powerful tug, something like intense homesickness. She did want to go home. Her situation was unbelievable, so urgent that she'd never considered the possibility of going home, but when she allowed the thought in she was flooded with overwhelming grief for the perfect, handmade home she had temporarily lost. Yes, she had unexpectedly powerfully missed Sunny when she had dropped her back with Lenny, but if she'd known that rushing down to Wales with Sunny's blanket would have resulted in this, would she still have done it?

'If you wanted to move in for a bit, that would be okay,' said Mairéad. 'I don't want my plants to die.'

Mairéad continued to check in with IGS. She watched as, seemingly out of nowhere, Susie Twill's career expanded exponentially, like a sped-up video of a plant.

Mairéad called her.

'You're doing so well,' she said. 'When I started my company, this was the sort of work I wanted to support. I lost my way a bit, so it's great to have you with us.'

'I can't thank you enough,' said Susie. 'I've always resigned myself to being, you know, a bit niche. A bit cult. So for so many people to get it is pretty amazing.'

'Sometimes you just have to tell people, "This is cool," and eventually they get it,' said Mairéad. 'Like David Shrigley. He's super weird and yet most people understand. And if Pottery Mama can flog that really basic stuff just by telling people, "Buy this," we must surely be able to tell people to buy something with a bit of heart and soul.'

'I actually met Pottery Mama,' said Susie, her voice dropping. 'She's quite odd in real life.' Susie described to Mairéad how she and Pottery Mama had met at an event, with Pottery Mama flanked by hangers-on, looking like a mob boss. Pottery Mama had had a jittery air and looked hunted. 'It was so strange,' said Susie. 'She was so different in real life to how she is on camera. She was almost checking the exits.'

Mairéad was hit by another wave of homesickness. She had liked Ashley and her other clients, but Susie was a real person. A real, relatable person with a sense of humour, and she was an artist. It was sod's law that this client had come along just at the point when Mairéad was stuck on the side of a hill. Working from the cabin could only achieve so much, and taking care of the pigs, Sunny and the cabin was so time-consuming that she couldn't be as focused on Susie's career. She stared out of the window and remembered how she had literally held Ashley's hand in those early days. Sitting in the backs of cabs, holding her hand, saying, 'You were great, they loved you.'

One morning, Mairéad put on a long raincoat and boots and went to see the pigs. She squelched through the mud holding a bucket of pig feed and paused briefly as a side-swipe of wind threatened to knock her over. She continued trudging along and called to the pigs as she approached, then peered over the wall and aimed the bucket at the trough.

Dennis was out of the sty and waiting for his breakfast, but he was staggering to the right and kept shaking his head. Then he projectile-vomited everywhere. Mairéad seized up in horror. He did it again.

She called to Sunny.

'Come and look at this. Put your boots on!'

Sunny trotted out to the sty in her boots but no raincoat.

'Have you ever seen the pigs puke? You know, vomit?'

Sunny made a grossed-out face. 'No, never.'

Mairéad called the vet, who came the next morning. He was extremely young and slight. He didn't look like he could be much use around a heifer.

'How old are you?'

'I'm twenty-six,' said the vet.

'Must be hard work, all those cows.'

'Mainly sheep. I'm stronger than I look,' he said, huffily.

'What's wrong with him?' she said, after the vet had prodded Dennis about for a bit.

'It could be several things. He's mainly just very old.'

'Old!'

'Yeah he must be, I dunno, twenty-five?'

'How long do pigs usually live? As pets, I mean.'

The vet scratched his narrow head. 'Ten years? Fifteen? I've never seen a pig this old.'

'Okay,' said Mairéad. 'What can we do about it?'

'I'll give you something for the vomiting,' said the vet. 'It has to be delivered orally, in a syringe, three times a day.'

'Three times a *day*?' said Mairéad. It was starting to rain heavily now. The vet didn't even seem to notice, but it was beginning to run down Mairéad's nose and drip onto her bottom lip.

'Well, or I can…' said the vet. 'He's very old,' he repeated.

'No,' said Mairéad. 'He mustn't die. I'll give him the medicine.'

But giving Dennis the medicine was a task unlike any other. Dennis, being a pig, gobbled down the first dose with no trouble but it had clearly been an unpleasant experience as, from then on, he ran about the sty, squealing and dodging Mairéad whenever she approached – syringe or not. Sometimes, after a good half an hour of chasing him about, she managed to get him in a corner, between her knees, and get the syringe in, but at others she mis-timed and it went all over his face.

Sunny was no help whatsoever and stood about uselessly or laughed when Mairéad fell over in the muck and the wet. On day three of this, Mairéad had spent forty-five minutes at the midday dose trying to catch Dennis. It took so long that by the time she'd got the stuff down him it was almost time to start trying to catch him again. And often Dennis puked soon after she had administered the tonic, probably rendering it useless.

She eventually trapped him, got the syringe in the corner of his hairy maw and pushed the plunger. Dennis screamed and wriggled away, shaking his head and flapping his ears. Mairéad took a triumphant step back and then slipped and fell hard onto her side.

'Fuck's sake!' she bellowed. She sat in the filth for a moment and felt tears of surprise and pain flood her eyes. She got slowly and stiffly to her feet and hobbled back to the house, streaked with hideous, stinking muck, which, with no washing machine or easy access to a shower, was very bad news. She threw the syringe angrily into a corner of the kitchen and wrenched off her outer clothes by the back door. Then she stormed into the cabin and was so furious it took her three attempts to light a fire in the burner.

'Fucking ridiculous.' Mairéad was half laughing, half crying as she semi-gagged at the smell of pig faeces in her hair. She couldn't bear to wait until the water had heated up so she stripped off her clothes in the bathroom and washed in freezing water. She caught a glimpse of herself in the mirror; she looked pale and drawn, her lips blue with cold. She shook her head at herself, huffed in disbelief and swore a lot.

When later that day an email came from Biba to say that Susie Twill was going to have a meeting with a large department store about stocking her ceramics, Mairéad didn't think twice before replying to say, 'When? I want to be there.'

THIRTY

Evan was happy to take Sunny for two days. Sunny needed more persuading.

'You said you weren't going to leave!' she barked, her eyes huge and furious.

'I know,' said Mairéad. 'I know, I said that and I'm not *leaving* leaving, but it's not that easy just to stay here and never go anywhere.' She heard her voice taking on a whining pitch. 'I've left a whole life back in London and I had no chance to tie up any loose ends or do anything.'

'Well I can come with you,' said Sunny. 'I like the car journey.'

'No, I have to go out a lot, for meetings. And I would have to get you a babysitter.'

Sunny's face fell – clearly she was remembering Beckii T. 'I don't want a babysitter.'

'I'll be away two days. So I'll go, be away two days and then be back on the third day.'

'That's four days,' said Sunny.

'Two full days and two half-days. You can call me, on Evan's phone,' she said desperately. 'I'll bring you a present. What do you miss from London?'

Sunny thought for a bit. 'The goats,' she said. 'And that bath stuff you have, that stuff that I liked the smell of. Bring that.'

Well, This Is Awkward

Mairéad drove herself to the train station in Lenny's truck as she didn't like the look of the mud on the track up to the A road. She drove bumpily along as odds and ends rattled about in the boot. She felt guilty, but free, but then guilty for feeling so free. The train journey brought on a curious zombie-state. She was unable to do anything except stare out of the window. But she now knew this feeling. It was the feeling that she'd got when she'd been without Sunny, having been with her for a long time.

She'd had it when she had gone to Cass's party, when she had gone for the meeting with Ashley, and after she'd taken her back to Lenny. It had been exquisite and terrible. It was the same sort of feeling Mairéad remembered from when she'd been a child and had been taken ice-skating. When she'd sat down to take the ice-skates off and then got up to walk, it had been like being both weightless and also precarious, as if she might float off into the air. It was a sort of cousin of the nagging sense she got in the back of her mind when she wasn't quite sure where her phone was. It was the constant mild drone, the undercurrent of unignorable static, that something was amiss.

'Hope it all goes well,' she texted Evan. 'Let me know if you need anything.'

Hours later, all that came back was a thumbs-up.

Mairéad barely recognised Susie Twill. Her hair had been expertly cut and dyed a glossy chestnut. She was wearing heavy-rimmed glasses, wide jeans and a bomber jacket, and her fingernails were painted opaque white. But there was more to it than just new clothes; there was an aura of competence, satisfaction and solidity about her that had been entirely absent at their first meeting, when Susie had vibrated with trepidation and uncertainty. It was amazing, thought, Mairéad, what fifty thousand new Instagram followers and a deal with a department store could do for your aura.

Susie smiled when she saw Mairéad, which revealed that she had braces on her teeth.

'Susie!' exclaimed Mairéad, unable to conceal her surprise at the transformation.

'So weird,' said Susie, 'to have been talking to you all this time but not seeing you.'

'You look amazing,' said Mairéad.

Biba was also at the meeting and seemed to have solidified into a grown up during the months that Mairéad had been away. She was wearing sensible black trousers and a fashionable, oversized shirt, and said things like, 'Will you make sure to copy me into the deliverables on that?' Her previously long, oval fingernails had been snipped short and square and painted red.

'I've been onboarding the new me,' she said to Mairéad before the meeting started. 'I mean, like *so* young? She wants permission to go to the loo. It's crazy. But I think she's got potential.' My baby is all grown up, thought Mairéad, as she watched Biba bossily shuffling some contracts.

It was a done deal, this deal with the department store. They were just there to sign contracts and spend an hour preening and laughing too loudly at each other's jokes.

'You will fly off the shelves,' said one executive.

'Wooo!' hooted Susie. 'I've got so many great ideas, can't wait to share them with you!' Then she foamed on for a good five minutes about how she used to come to this exact store with her grandmother, who'd loved the haberdashery department. As Susie talked, she got a bit choked up. This upswell of emotion had clearly taken her completely by surprise and she sat back for a moment, the side of her forefinger braced against her upper lip.

'This is such a magical place,' said the executive in a hushed, respectful voice, while Susie pulled herself together. 'People have such beautiful and strong emotions about it.'

Mairéad bunched her lips together in order not to let out a giggle. They sold *underwear* and *chopping boards*.

Bidding farewell to Susie and Biba at the department store, Mairéad allowed herself to wander through town. Rather than kick Roxana out of her flat, she had booked herself into a smart hotel and left her suitcase there, but had arranged to visit Roxana later. She decided to walk there slowly and drifted aimlessly through the elegant streets that surrounded the department store, then moved outwards onto the more residential streets.

It was 4 p.m. and children were coming home from school. Mairéad could see them through the windows – either eating in kitchens or slumped in front of cartoons in living rooms, exhausted and overstimulated.

Mairéad watched a woman with a toddler in a buggy walk down the street, followed by a child who could not have been more than five, but was swathed in layers of stiff school uniform: patent buckled shoes, thick grey tights, a grey pinafore, a white shirt, a princess coat and a straw boater with a black band. The child trudged slowly behind the woman, one shoulder of the coat hanging off, looking completely defeated.

'Come on,' said the woman. 'Not much further.'

In her mind's eye Mairéad kicked off the child's shoes for her, tossed away the coat and the hat, and set her rummaging in Evan's chicken coop for eggs.

She arrived at her own flat at 5 p.m. and rang the bell, as she had given Roxana her key. She heard Roxana's footsteps. She opened the door and said nothing, just embraced Mairéad.

'I have kept it just as you left it,' said Roxana.

'It looks great,' said Mairéad. Roxana wasn't kidding. Nothing was out of place and everything was spotless.

'Are you even actually living here?' said Mairéad.

'Oh yes I am living here. It is a blessing for me, I tell you. I never thought that I would be somewhere so beautiful. Look at this plants, I want to show you what I have done.'

Roxana had re-potted a rubber plant and wanted to discuss with Mairéad a homemade recipe for plant food made from coffee grounds and crushed eggshells. Mairéad nodded, dazed. She had only meant for Roxana to water them, not train them for the Olympics.

'Where is all your stuff? Seriously,' said Mairéad. Roxana looked sheepish. 'Don't tell me you've hidden it all away in boxes or something.'

'I wanted for you to see the flat as you left it,' said Roxana.

'You're the most amazing person I have ever met in my life,' said Mairéad, and meant it.

Roxana shrugged and made dismissive gestures with her hands. 'This is sometimes said about me, yes. You are brave and I think right to stay with Sunny now in the cabin. But if you change your mind I am sure you can come back here and be happy.'

'I can't take her away from those pigs,' said Mairéad. 'Or from where she grew up. I really can't see her being okay in London. She needs so much space.'

'Well, all right. You're the boss. Maybe when she is a teenager.'

Mairéad looked at Roxana and nodded and blinked, but her casual declaration that Mairéad would still be taking care of Sunny when she was a teenager made the world suddenly rapidly expand away from Mairéad on all sides, and the floor underneath her slid away to the right. She staggered slightly left to compensate.

Roxana didn't seem to notice. She just tactfully said that she needed to go and post a letter and left Mairéad alone in the flat to collect some things she wanted: two bottles of the bath oil that Sunny had requested, her own passport, a few photographs, an address book filled with internet passwords.

When the door shut behind Roxana and Mairéad was alone

in the flat, she turned her head to see her bedroom winking at her through the door, which was ajar. She kicked off her shoes and went directly to the bed, dived under the duvet like a child, wrapped herself in it, spinning around and around and squeezing her eyes shut. She lay like that for a bit, wondering if she might cry. Then, when nothing happened, she got out of the bed and re-made it neatly.

She collected the things that she wanted and then looked around the flat. She couldn't believe how much stuff she had, how many clothes and books and pictures and knick-knacks. She had forgotten about almost all of it. At one and the same time she wanted to put the entire flat into a bag and take it back with her – and also turn her back on it and never see it again. She lovingly stroked one of the rubber plant's glossy green leaves.

It was a mercy that she had arranged to see Cass that night, in the bar of the hotel Mairéad was staying in. The bar was famous for its very low lighting and very low, squashy chairs, so Cass and Mairéad were sitting near each other for at least ten minutes before they realised that the other had arrived.

They chatted about this and that and then Cass asked, seriously, 'How are you?'

Mairéad thought for a moment and started to speak a few times. She eventually said, 'I don't think I can do this.'

'Do what?'

'Be someone's—' She stopped; she couldn't say the word 'mother'. 'To have so much responsibility. Live in Wales in a cabin with no bloody electricity? I mean,' she sank further back into her squashy armchair and took a sip of her chilled white wine, 'it's feral out there.'

'Bring her back here, then,' said Cass.

'I can't, I can't have her here, she'd go mad.'

'Well, then,' said Cass.

'When you say "well then" do you mean "stop whining"?'

'Sure,' said Cass. 'You're annoyed at your life being interrupted and inconvenienced.' She held up her abbreviated arm. 'Tell me about it.'

Mairéad blushed.

'This life you like so much, here? You made it, you know. It wasn't handed to you, it wasn't luck. You made the whole thing from scratch, didn't you?'

'Well, yes,' said Mairéad.

'Right, so you did it once, you can do it again. Ah, sure it's a pain in the hole to start again, but this isn't about finding your bliss or following your heart or whatever other crap spoiled rich people tell themselves when they're trying to make inconsequential decisions about their pointless lives. This is about a child. Children are a blessing.'

Mairéad let out an exhausted huff of air and then opened her mouth to speak, but Cass wasn't finished.

'There's a lot to be said for the English but you don't like kids like we do in Ireland. We love our kids, and they're just around and about the place. It's not strange to have them in your life. And look, I know I'm not supposed to say this, but a life with no children in it is no life at all.'

'That's an awful thing to say,' said Mairéad.

'The truth hurts.' Cass shrugged.

'The happiest women in the world are those that never had children,' said Mairéad.

Cass rolled her eyes. 'Oh, that old chestnut. I didn't say the children had to be yours, did I? And anyway, it's not about being happy, it's about having meaning. Those women with no children around them, as night follows day they get themselves a little dog or a million cats and put them in dresses and buggies and Christ knows what else.'

'What about you, then?' said Mairéad.

'I mourn the lack of children in my life every day,' said Cass, piously. 'I try to create meaning in my work but one day I will snap and just walk out of my life and back to Dublin and work in an orphanage.'

Mairéad let out a bark of laughter. 'What utter crap,' she said.

'I can dream, can't I?' said Cass.

'I've been thinking about you saying I've got intimacy issues,' said Mairéad.

'Go on,' said Cass.

'Maybe you're right.'

''Course I'm right. It's why you rejected a parade of perfectly all right men, culminating in Richard, who is a diamond. He's dating Kathleen now, by the way.'

'Oh!' Mairéad gave a laugh. She thought for a moment. 'They'll be perfect for each other. But I was thinking, I don't want Sunny to have intimacy issues. She's already a little odd.'

'You've got to step up, then,' said Cass. 'Her mother's run off. That's going to do some damage. Undo what you can.'

The bad feeling did not leave Mairéad. In the middle of the night she woke, anxious and sweaty, the terrible thought entering her mind that Evan was somehow a bad and evil person and that letting Sunny stay with him had been a horrible mistake. Lenny hadn't called on him to take Sunny before for a reason, right? She somehow got back to sleep, but when she woke in the morning she sent Evan a text, saying, 'All well?'

He replied half an hour later with a picture of Sunny standing on top of a wall, her arms behind her back, her head turned to the camera with that inscrutable look on her face. Then another photo appeared, with Sunny raising a sardonic thumbs-up. In the light of the morning, Mairéad knew full well there was nothing sinister about Evan.

But the feeling that something was missing just wouldn't budge. She thought about the absent birth certificate. If Misha's name was on it, would Sunny have to be sent to Poland or Hungary, or wherever he had washed up? A part of Mairéad knew well that it was only she who could care for Sunny properly. And if Sunny left forever, would Mairéad have to feel like this, forever?

The feeling of loss and incompleteness was unpleasant and unshakeable. As she lay in her four-poster bed in her fashionable hotel, listening to the terrible clatter of a bottle bank being emptied, she understood really for the first time that she could not go back or correct this. It would be like trying to get milk out of tea.

THIRTY-ONE

The weather welcomed Mairéad back to Wales with lashing, horizontal rain. She and Sunny stood next to the pigsty in boots and raincoats and looked at Minnie's immobile body, lying on its side.

Dennis had died first. Minnie had been aghast, whinnying and throwing herself about the place.

About a week later, she'd decided that a life without Dennis was no life at all.

'They were very old,' said Mairéad, putting a hand on Sunny's shoulder. Sunny left it there for a moment, but then slid slowly out of reach.

Evan dug a fresh grave, next to Dennis, as soon as there was a break in the rain, telling Sunny that it was a good time to go, as the ground was still nice and soft for digging. It took hours. Evan explained to Mairéad, who took up a shovel and helped for a while, that the holes had to be deep so that foxes wouldn't dig them up and eat them. As they dug, Evan shyly mentioned to Mairéad that he had installed Wi-Fi in the cabin for Lenny and Lenny paid him a small sum every month in return.

'I just thought you'd, you know, wanna know,' he said.

'I do want to know,' said Mairéad. 'I did wonder. Text me your bank details, tell me how much it is.'

Sunny arrived at the graveside, stone-faced.

'I don't want anyone to eat Dennis and Minnie,' she said, gnomically. She was pale and had only been semi-responsive since Minnie's death.

That night they ate their supper together at the small dining table, a robust fire in the burner and four storm lanterns lit.

'It's nice having all the lamps lit,' said Sunny. 'Mum only ever let us have two.'

'Well, I suppose the oil is expensive.'

'She said it was wasteful.'

Mairéad just nodded. That sounded like Lenny.

After dinner, Mairéad went to wash up in the outdoor sink. Away in the dark, beyond the kitchen, she knew the twin humps of the dead pigs' graves rose gently from the ground. She came back into the cabin, as usual feeling heroic for doing the washing-up in the clunky sink with no hot water, and looked at Sunny, who was staring at the fire.

Then she said, 'I think we need to get a dog.'

'Really,' said Sunny, with flat, deadening sarcasm. She sat on the sofa with her blanket draped over her head.

'Yeah, a nice dog.'

'I don't want a dog,' said Sunny.

Mairéad fetched her laptop, sat down on an armchair, opened it and typed in 'Dog rescue near me'.

'What are you doing?' snapped Sunny. 'I said I didn't want a dog! It will just *die* or run off. Stop it!' She slammed the lid of the laptop down and Mairéad only just snatched her fingers out of the way in time.

'Watch it!'

'I said stop it,' said Sunny, angrily.

'No, I don't think I will, actually. I want to look at some dogs. I'm not saying we have to get one, okay? I heard you. Go over there if you don't want to look.'

Sunny stropped over to the other old, brown armchair. She

pulled out a tatty cushion and clutched it angrily in front of her. She sat down and stuck her thumb in her mouth. But the allure of the glowing laptop screen was overwhelming and she eventually crept out of the chair and wandered about behind the sofa. Mairéad scrolled through the assorted border collies and terriers. She pretended not to know that Sunny was behind her.

Eventually Sunny gasped. 'That one,' she said. She pointed to the ugliest dog Mairéad had ever seen. It was some sort of terrier crossed with an array of other unsuitable breeds, which in an ideal world would not breed with even each other, let alone other dogs. It was a slurry of hideous colours, had mismatching eyes and an underbite.

'Hello, my name is Bogey,' read Mairéad. She turned to Sunny. 'You want this one.'

'I love him,' said Sunny.

'Her.'

Mairéad had never owned a dog before, and neither had Sunny. Mark, a flamboyant man in pink trousers and green wellingtons, from Snowdonia Animal Sanctuary, visited the cabin to make sure it was suitable for a dog. He wore a rainbow lanyard clattering with keys and badges bearing pronoun announcements. His pencil hovered doubtfully over the paper form when Mairéad confessed she had never owned a dog.

'Oh,' he said, cringing slightly. 'I mean there's the situation with no fence outside, and then if you've never had a dog before…'

Mairéad stared at Mark for a moment. 'That is my niece.' She jerked her head towards the porch, where Sunny was wearing two sweaters and pacing up and down. 'Her mother's run off god knows where without even leaving a note. She hasn't seen her father for years. Both her pet pigs, that she has known since birth, have just died. Winter is coming. We need this dog, okay?'

Mark blinked. 'As it happens, looking after someone else's dog does actually count?' he said. 'For the form, I mean – in the "Experience" box.'

'I see,' she said, taking the hint. 'I did in fact take care of a… of a sheepdog for six weeks this summer. You know, a border collie.' She warmed to her fabrication. 'Great dog, very active despite being disabled. Complex medication needs, too.' Then she tensed. Had she gone too far? What if he asked about this imaginary medication? But Mark merely executed a dramatic tick on the form. 'Lovely,' he said.

Luckily, Bogey had been owned before and knew what to do. She was a seriously ugly dog and so had been stuck at the shelter, which had a no-euthanasia policy, for a year. But she had an excellent personality. She trotted round the cabin in a full circle when she arrived, sniffing everything and looking about herself. Then she dragged the dog bed, purchased from the sanctuary shop for £18.99, into a corner and sat in it. The next morning, following a solid and silent night's sleep, Bogey ate heartily, stretched and then vanished.

'An underbite in a dog is called an "occlusion",' said Sunny, looking up from the laptop. 'Where has she gone?'

'Maybe to do a poo?' ventured Mairéad, unsure. She stood at the window in her pyjamas with a sweater over the top and her arms folded, peering out at the mist and drizzle.

Bogey returned fifteen minutes later with a dead rat in her mouth.

'Argh! Well, that explains what those scratching noises were.'

After three days, Bogey stopped being ugly and started being the most perfect being ever created. She smiled, she laughed. Fascinating thoughts were displayed clearly on her charming little face. She kept the cabin rodent-free. She even got along fine with grumpy old Bonnie. In a stroke, Mairéad stopped being scared of the cabin at night.

Well, This Is Awkward

Bogey's arrival seemed to knock something loose in Sunny. She poked Mairéad in the shoulder one morning.

'Wassup?'

'I think I should go to school.'

THIRTY-TWO

Lyn the social worker called from the top of the lane because she couldn't drive her car, a stylish little turquoise thing, through the mud. She had dark hair scraped back in a sensible low bun and was wearing a red raincoat, smart wellingtons and clutching a tartan umbrella.

'It's a bit wild round here,' she said when Mairéad arrived to collect her in Lenny's truck.

'Sure is,' said Mairéad.

They drove back down the bumpy, muddy track with Lyn bracing her hand against the dashboard.

'Beautiful spot, though,' she said, looking at the view.

They sat around the log burner, which by now was running more or less constantly.

'I'd make you a cup of tea but it takes about an hour,' said Mairéad.

'Yes,' said Lyn, looking around. 'Very unusual place.'

'So how are you getting on in the new job?' said Mairéad. 'You said before, you'd only just started.'

'Oh well it's quite… it's quite a lot to take in,' said Lyn. 'A lot of children in need.'

The most important thing, said Lyn, was to get Sunny into

Well, This Is Awkward

school. 'That's my number one priority,' she said, sounding like she was reading from a handbook.

'School, yes. That would be okay,' said Sunny. 'I didn't want to go. But now I think it might be fine.'

'What changed your mind?' said Lyn, her pen poised over a notebook.

'My pigs died,' said Sunny. 'And then we got a dog. And she made me think I should go to school.'

'Oh, well,' said Lyn, looking confused. 'I suppose that…' She clearly struggled to make sense of it.

'I think what Sunny means is that the dog has made her see that new things can be positive,' said Mairéad.

'Absolutely,' said Lyn, looking relieved.

'What are you writing?' said Sunny.

'I'm writing down what happens in our visit,' said Lyn.

'Why?'

'Well, it's… it's… So I can remember.'

'Can't you remember things?' said Sunny.

Lyn coloured and looked lost for words.

'When Mum left, everyone was quite interested,' said Mairéad to Sunny. 'It's a mystery, right? Lyn's just wondering what's happened and she wants to keep notes while she works it all out.'

'Yes. You can read the notes if you want, when I've typed them all up,' said Lyn. 'They're not a secret.'

'No, that's fine,' said Sunny, turning back to her book. '*I* can remember things,' she added pointedly.

The most suitable school for Sunny was Pantbach, a twenty-minute drive away. Lyn pulled a piece of paper from a folder.

'Is that…' said Mairéad, 'is that Sunny's birth certificate?'

'Yes,' said Lyn. 'Apparently lots of people lose their birth certificates. Getting hold of it was very easy.' She sounded surprised about this fact.

'My birth what?' said Sunny.

'Certificate,' said Lyn, offering it to Sunny, who took it slowly, as if she was witnessing herself coming into existence.

'Does everyone have one of these?'

'Oh, yes,' said Lyn. 'You need a birth certificate to prove you exist.'

Mairéad scrambled behind Sunny's shoulder and her eyes neurotically scanned the paper for Misha's name, but it was not there. She let out a sigh and put her hand on her chest. Lyn and Mairéad shared a significant look.

'I should...' said Lyn. 'No wait, actually. Sunny. Will you show me round your home? It's so unusual – I'm very interested to see how it all works.'

'I'll stay here,' said Mairéad, indicating that she understood Lyn wanted to talk to Sunny alone. Lyn gave Mairéad a thumbs-up. Bogey got out of her bed and followed Sunny and Lyn around the cabin and then outside and around the kitchen and the log store. Mairéad sat on the sofa and stared at the birth certificate. Sunny's birthday was 6 February and she had been born at Castell Cerys Hospital. The sections concerning 'Father' had thin black lines through them.

Sunny and Lyn were blown back through the front door ten minutes later by a gust of wind. Mairéad held up the birth certificate. 'Can I keep this?' she said.

'Yes, that's a copy for you – I've got one,' said Lyn. 'I don't suppose your sister left a piece of paper anywhere saying that she appoints you as legal guardian, did she?' Lyn laughed a little. 'That would make things a lot easier.'

'Unfortunately not,' said Mairéad. 'All I've got is scraps of paper and a recipe.'

'Can I see them?' said Lyn.

'Sure.' Mairéad went to the desk drawer and collected the scraps that Lenny had left.

Well, This Is Awkward

Lyn held them up and looked at them and Mairéad pointed. 'Oh my god, how did I miss that?'

Lyn turned over the paper with the lentil recipe on it. On the back it said, 'She is happy with you. L.'

Lyn and Mairéad looked at each other.

'I mean, will that do?' said Mairéad. Lyn put her head on one side and squinted at the paper. 'I don't know.' She took a photo of the note and giggled. 'This is all quite exciting, isn't it? It really is like a detective story.' She held the paper out to Mairéad, 'You'll need that for your dinner.'

Lyn then explained to Mairéad what would happen next, using phrases like 'private family arrangement', 'Section 20', 'kinship foster carer', 'special guardianship order' until Mairéad's head was swirling with acronyms and she felt like she was in the middle of a double maths lesson. 'But our priority is permanency,' said Lyn, in that way she had of sounding like she had swallowed an instruction manual.

Mairéad blinked a bit and then said, 'So what do I do now?'

'Oh, well. Nothing. We'll try to find your sister, but our resources aren't infinite. What we really want is her consent for you to be legal guardian. But I will do my best to make a good case for this note as tacit consent. Nothing goes quickly in the system, especially if a child is, you know,' she gestured at Sunny, who was sitting in Bogey's dog basket with Bogey, 'clearly fine.'

A fortnight later, Sunny started at Pantbach Secondary School, which was a large, red-brick building sitting in a few acres of scrappy lawn. Sunny was, in fact, very pleased with her uniform: a pair of grey trousers, black trainers and a dark green sweatshirt with a crest. She ran her fingers over the embroidered badge. She was completely uninterested in things like new bags or pencil cases, so Mairéad just chose the plainest ones in the uniform shop. 'I recommend these,' said the shop assistant, tapping a laminated card advertising sheets of little white stickers printed with 'Joe Bloggs'. 'If you don't use them already. Much easier than name-tapes.'

Mairéad felt sick with nerves as she walked Sunny into the school on the first day, through the chattering crowds of children and the loping, lounging teenagers. The corridors smelled the same as school corridors everywhere: like industrial cleaner, wax, hot breath and coffee. They reported to Mrs Pringle in the office, who was wearing a yellow pointelle sweater.

'This must be the famous Sunshine,' she said.

'It's usually just "Sunny",' said Mairéad.

'I'll make a note. Pick-up is three thirty,' said Mrs Pringle.

'Okay then,' said Mairéad.

Sunny looked completely frozen, her eyes huge and worried.

'You've got your water bottle,' said Mairéad. 'Don't forget to drink water.'

Sunny nodded slowly.

'She'll be fine,' said Mrs Pringle, firmly. 'We love a new student.'

Mairéad went and sat in the car in the car park for twenty minutes, blinking and staring at nothing. She felt that awful feeling again: that untethered and crazy feeling. Her movements were suddenly too loose, free and light. Sunny was not a noisy child but the silence she left behind was profound.

Bogey whined slightly.

'Yes, don't worry. We'll go for a walk.'

Over the next few weeks it turned out that there were many things Sunny didn't understand about school: that she would be teased for sucking her thumb, that she was going to have to wear the shoes all the time, that she would have to queue for her lunch and put up her hand in class if she wanted something. Things that Mairéad didn't even know she wouldn't know.

Sunny came home every day very tired and occasionally

irate at some petty rule. But she was also fascinated by this school business and determined to somehow defeat it, or otherwise triumph. She had a lust for tests, relishing every single one. At the end of the first week, there was an email to say that Sunny ought to have an eye test.

Mairéad looked up from her laptop and at Bogey, who was loudly picking her toenails with her teeth. Sensing she was being observed, Bogey looked up. 'Of course!' she said to Bogey. She recalled immediately all Sunny's squinting and the holding of books one inch away from her nose. That face that Sunny sometimes pulled, which looked familiar to Mairéad. Familiar because it was the face of someone who couldn't see. 'Of course she needs glasses.'

She sat back in the desk chair and it creaked. Mairéad thought for a long time about how she could not have noticed and worked it out before. She'd just been so busy looking absolutely anywhere except directly at Sunny.

That weekend, they drove to the nearest optician, and discovered that Sunny, who enjoyed the eye test enormously, totally needed glasses. She picked out a large, round, owlish pair. The following week they went back to collect them. She let out a coo of discovery when she first put them on. Then they went food shopping at a big supermarket. Mairéad saw the wine aisle and suddenly remembered: alcohol! She slipped a bottle into her trolley. Sunny went about the supermarket looking at everything, reading signs far away and taking her glasses on and off to compare and contrast.

'That's how you know where things are,' she said. 'There are signs.' She pointed urgently at one that said 'Home Baking'. 'Wow,' she said in wonder. 'There have been signs, all this time.'

THIRTY-THREE

The days settled down into a rhythm, as they always do, no matter the size or the shape of an upheaval. They woke up in the morning and got themselves off to school. Bogey came with them and, after drop-off, Mairéad took her for a walk along the beach. She brought with her a re-useable cup and filled it at the beach café, so as not to have to tackle the outdoor kitchen first thing in the morning. Then she returned to the cabin and got through her duties: fill the lamps with oil and the log baskets with logs, tidy up, put laundry into a laundry bag, assess food stores, add to lists, fetch eggs from Evan.

She checked in once or twice a week with IGS, occasionally laughing while on mute at the minor things that they considered to be important: the exact name of a campaign, cooling-off periods in contracts. She joined in on meetings, mentored Susie and earned her modest consultancy fee. She pushed the agency to take on more wild-living Instagram accounts. 'Woodcraft, off-grid living. Young people are into what happens after the apocalypse,' she said.

Lyn came to the cabin again, bringing a packet of the Welsh fruit cake bara brith. Her hair was in a messy plait and she was now driving a 4 x 4, which was covered in mud. She

Well, This Is Awkward

smelled of cigarettes and was chewing gum. Mairéad got the kettle on in good time for her arrival and managed to produce some tea.

'Ooh, it's nice to be here,' said Lyn, sitting down heavily, leaning back and closing her eyes for a moment. She was in only her socks, having jettisoned her dirty boots at the door.

'Tough week?' said Mairéad, cutting the cake on a board.

'I went to a house yesterday,' said Lyn, still with her eyes closed, 'that had fourteen dogs. I had to actually ask how many there were as I kept losing count. Fourteen dogs, four children. No one at school or eating properly. Rubbish piled up right over the window.'

'Woah,' said Mairéad, looking around the neat and cosy cabin. 'That puts things into perspective.' 'Oh yeah,' said Lyn. 'You guys are living in paradise. I've had to start smoking again.'

Lyn chatted to Sunny about school and looked at a graphic novel Sunny was reading, about a girl who turns out to have a brain tumour.

'I feel bad about having waited so long to call the police after Lenny left,' said Mairéad, smushing together some cake crumbs between her thumb and forefinger.

'Oh, no,' said Lyn. 'I don't blame you. You must have been in total shock. And who wants social services scrutinising your every move? Even we don't want to do it. We just want to close files and move on, trust me.'

Mairéad also attended daily to her online shopping. Cass was right. She, Mairéad, had made her life in London by herself and she could make a life for her and Sunny here, too. She was living in a rudimentary cabin on a remote hill with no flushing toilet, but she had a huge amount of disposable income. She was rich. Roxana had initially been paying a peppercorn rent but had recently got herself a job at Ernst & Young and insisted on upping her rent to market rates. She brought with her a similarly frictionless friend. Money poured into Mairéad's account every month. Her living expenses in the cabin, with only a few bills to pay, were tiny.

And so she made sure they had the best of everything. They had three sets of fine, high-thread-count sheets each – one on the bed, one in a blanket box, one at the laundrette – beautiful pyjamas, excellent wellington boots, artisan blankets, cosy dressing gowns to wrap themselves in after a stove-fired shower.

Books upon books upon books arrived for Sunny, smart raincoats, rain hats, an iPad, a special pen with which to draw on the iPad. A beautiful set of plates, new crockery, glasses, cushions and pillows, side tables for the sofa. Mairéad ordered more hurricane lamps and oil in gallon bottles. She burned through it with impunity; there was light in every corner of the cabin, all evening. She took Lenny's car to a garage for an MOT, then she had it cleaned inside and out and replaced the bald tyres with a heavy-tread set that looked like they belonged on a tractor. In the boot of the car she found more boxes and in one was Sunny's birth certificate, folded up casually, like it didn't matter one way or another. Mairéad smoothed it out and put it with the one that Lyn had brought round. She pushed threatening feelings of vulnerability away from them both with as many heavy-duty things as she could, and it helped.

Once a week they drove to Castell Cerys to do a laundry swap: clean sheets and clothes for dirty ones. They picked up groceries and sometimes parcels from Annie at the Co-op. They went for a rummage in the antiques shops. Sunny had a fondness for small things: miniature coffee cups, tiny spoons, books the size of a thumb, which they arranged on a shelf in the cabin. Mairéad stockpiled things because it made her feel better: dog food, luxury toilet paper, boxes and boxes of firelighters (the environmentally unfriendly kind, because fuck you, Lenny).

Well, This Is Awkward

She hated the outdoor kitchen with a passion. She hated the sheepskin-lined Crocs and fingerless gloves she had to keep by the door. Roxana was right, the kitchen was sheltered and covered so it was at least mostly dry and not blown about, even when a westerly wind came bellowing off the sea, but it was absolutely freezing. What she would give for a warm room to shuffle into when she wanted a cup of tea! *Tea*, the simple thing in her life that gave her hope and warmth and now it was this absurd performance. When she went to see Evan, she occasionally lingered in his flagstoned farmhouse kitchen, glaring at the strip light and fantasising about how lovely it could be. She ran through Farrow & Ball colours in her mind as she hovered. Vert de Terre, perhaps. Or Dorset Cream. She allowed herself the sheer, dangerous thought that one day she might again be able to walk into a kitchen in January in nothing more than pyjamas. She swooned at the humming fridge. She missed being able to hang up her own laundry.

She cleaned and organised the outdoor kitchen viciously, hoping that this would perhaps make it not an outdoor kitchen anymore. She swept again and again at the stone flags that gathered earth, dead leaves and small sticks. She gave grudging thanks when it turned so bitterly cold that she was able to store perishable things outside without the need of a fridge – meat, milk and cheese – in new locking tubs. With the arrival of Bogey, there were no more rats, but she didn't want to send out an olfactory invitation to any new ones.

Eating habits had to adjust to the technological limitations. Breakfast was overnight oats. Lunch while Sunny was at school was often just a tin of tuna and some crackers. Dinner was a rudimentary stew. She placed basic ingredients in a very expensive cast-iron pot and blasted it in the bulb-shaped oven for a few hours. Washing up with no hot water was the worst, so she used items sparingly and washed everything up quickly in one go. She slipped Marigolds on over the fingerless gloves, shivering and cursing Lenny's name all the while. She bought lavish hand creams and slathered them on three times a day.

Mulling over what to do with herself beyond housework, Mairéad spent an entire week planning a brand-new Instagram account that would document trying to live with the damned outdoor kitchen. She calculated reach and monetisation and planned out three months' worth of content. She filmed a video of her making a stew and edited it to calming music. She drew up a planning document and wrote out a list of potential new Instagram handles. So many ((@outdoorliving, @welshliving, @welshkitchen, @my_welsh_kitchen) were already taken. She was about to settle on @rustic_little_kitchen when Sunny arrived in the living room with a grey look on her face.

There was this craft project, she said. Her most hated thing. Nothing about schoolwork fazed Sunny, not English or history or even maths – it was all easy, as long as it wasn't a presentation to the class, or the dreaded craft. The project was to make a diorama inspired by *The Tempest*. Mairéad put down her phone and drove Sunny to Castell Cerys to see what they could scrounge in terms of boxes, tissue paper and glitter. She spent the next three days making the diorama. @rustic_little_kitchen left her mind so completely that, when she came across some notes for it in the desk drawer a fortnight later, it was as if they had been written by someone else. When she looked up @rustic_little_kitchen she saw that it was now in use by someone else. She decided to take it as a sign.

And in the evenings, she drank. Not a lot at first, never enough to give herself a hangover but yes, increasingly. Every week, one, two or three bottles of red wine went clanking into her trolley during the grocery shop, even though she didn't even really like red wine, it was just what could be drunk at room temperature. The following week the empties

Well, This Is Awkward

went clanking into the bottle bank. She resisted putting them into her recycling as she knew full well she was drinking too much and she didn't want Evan to see.

Her drinking didn't get in the way, though! She had become that modern phenomenon: the functioning drunk. Life was just so boring. So hard. During the day, she had enough work to occupy her: keeping the stoves in the living room and bedroom alight in cold weather was almost a full-time job. Everything had to be planned hours, even days, in advance. The fire under the cooking-plate had to be lit before she went to fetch Sunny from school, meals had to be planned meticulously as there was no running up the road for forgotten ingredients.

Yes, it was possible to relish slipping inside the machinery of a life lived close to the land, but it was relentless. It needed to be done every day, without fail. Mairéad occasionally felt something close to panic at the prospect of these daily, looming chores.

In the evening, there was some free time to think, and she did not want to think. She didn't want to think about Lenny, or where her life was going, or any of it. And two large glasses of red wine did the trick. But then after a few weeks it had to be three, then four.

Oh, that winter was cold! Cold and wet and very hard. The rain and winds blasted the cabin relentlessly. The daylight was weak and grey and some days the solar panels produced no electricity. She bought a huge battery pack, which Evan allowed her to charge up at the farmhouse, and she wondered what on earth Lenny had done in the winter.

She also bought a raincoat that went right down to her calves and a waterproof hat lined with fleece that tied under the chin. Some days she was grateful that simple things, like getting Sunny to school, taking Bogey for a walk and making dinner, came with such a sense of achievement. In this, Bogey was essential. The weather was so wild that, without Bogey to walk, she could see that she might take no exercise at all. Other days, she felt lunatic and hostile about the fact that every simple thing required a battle with something: the cold air, the rain, the lack of electricity, their remote location.

Then the snow came and settled on the ground. The school closed for two days. Mairéad celebrated by producing cashmere sweaters and socks she had bought in anticipation of this. She bathed in a smug feeling at how their rain boots, lined with neoprene, doubled as snow boots. There was much about life that was undeniably pleasant. In the evening, when all the lamps were lit, the curtains were drawn, dinner was made and Bogey was snoozing in her basket in front of the ticking log burner, Mairéad felt almost high on the cosiness. She sent pictures to Dodie, who sometimes rang, wanting to know how Sunny was. 'Will you come to Devon again in the summer?' said Dodie. 'I'll post that aunt to Kuala Lumpur or something. You can have the same cottage back.'

The summer. It seemed as far away, as much like a completely different world to Mairéad, as Mars.

Lamplight had a magical, burnishing quality and Mairéad always made a point of laying their modest dining table with her wildly expensive crockery and linens. These moments mattered to her and she learned that she had to inhabit them peacefully. At the start of winter, round about when she had thought of starting the Instagram account, she had felt an urgent need to post beautiful scenes publicly, but she had not because they would simply take too much explaining. Later, her urgent need to share certain idyllic scenes waned. It was enough to occasionally share them with Cass or Dodie on WhatsApp. Dodie passed on news from Dibs and a photograph of him playing the Artful Dodger in his school production of *Oliver!* 'You'll come back to Bloxcombe in the summer,' said Dodie. It wasn't a question.

Well, This Is Awkward

Sunny adjusted to the new luxuries. While sitting in front of the fire, cosy in a white waffle robe and slippers, after a hot shower using sweet-smelling, expensive non-eczema products, she took her thumb out of her mouth to say, 'This is my best thing.'

There was also an unexpected and new feeling of indestructibility. Mairéad had, once or twice in her life, experienced power cuts and broken boilers, and the sense of panic and helplessness was not nice. But here in the cabin, you didn't have to worry about a power cut, because there wasn't any; or the boiler breaking, because there wasn't one. They were at the mercy of the elements, sure, but they weren't at the mercy of the elements *and* of Pimlico Plumbers.

Evan spent Christmas in Pembrokeshire with his sister and offered up his kitchen so that Mairéad could cook a Christmas lunch. She lavished time and even more money buying gifts for Sunny and Bogey, gifts for her *from* Sunny and gifts for everyone from Bogey. It very much had to be an extremely magical Christmas. For her, if nothing else. She wrapped all the gifts herself and spent a further fortune on Christmas decorations for a small tree that Evan found and chopped and carried in for them. This was all new to Sunny, who had never had a Christmas before; Lenny believed that everything associated with Christmas was an environmental catastrophe (on this, she had a point, thought Mairéad).

On Christmas Day, which dawned with horizontal rain turning to sleet, Mairéad backed the car right up to the door of the cabin and they scurried in, holding a box of food. Then they trundled down the lane and unloaded it at the other end. She luxuriated in the farmhouse, despite its distinctly bachelor air. She had brought with her a tablecloth and napkins, that together had cost £180, and some candles. They ate a roast duck with roast potatoes, stuffing, gravy and sprouts.

Bogey bustled about wearing a bow tie and sniffing all the

places that Bonnie had been. After lunch Mairéad washed everything up, packed away their things and, with one last, lingering glance at the flushing toilet and the wall sockets, hustled Sunny and Bogey into the car. They trundled back up the lane to the cabin in the pitch black, the wind and the sleet, which was now turning to snow. The cabin was still warm from the heat logs that Mairéad had slotted into the stoves that morning, which burned hot and slow. Then they lit the lamps and watched a movie. Mairéad gratefully poured herself a drink and left the curtains open so that they could watch the snow as it fell in whirling eddies outside.

THIRTY-FOUR

By February, Mairéad was drinking so much that she did have hangovers in the morning. She dealt with this by stockpiling Alka-Seltzer. She never started drinking before 6 p.m., but she could polish off a bottle, a bottle and a half in an evening, no problem. And it *was* no problem! She never screamed at Sunny and they were never late for school. The cabin was clean, Bogey was fed and walked. It was fine!

Okay, the hangovers were sending her back to bed during the day and she looked terrible, slept like shit and sometimes in the middle of the night felt like she might be having a heart attack, but other than that? A-okay. On Sunny's twelfth birthday, in February, they went on a special trip to the big Waterstones and then for tea and cake at a nearby hotel. At the table next to them, two women were having a champagne brunch and as the flutes of cold, golden liquid went past Mairéad she felt her pupils dilate as if she were a shark. Or a vampire.

In late March, when Mairéad had been living at the cabin with Sunny for more than six months, the sun finally came out again. The ground was dry, birds were singing and it was a pleasant evening. Sunny was capering about in springtime high spirits, saying, 'Next year I'll be thirteen. I'll be a teenager,

I'll be thirteen!' Bogey was cantering about too, barking, soaking up Sunny's bouncy energy.

Mairéad was sitting on the porch with her feet up, about three quarters of her way through a bottle, when Sunny mis-timed a leap and came down, hard, on her side.

'Fuck,' said Mairéad, sitting up and spilling her wine.

Sunny was wordlessly cradling her wrist, her face twisted in pain. Then a cry, right from her guts, filled the air.

'Fuck!' Mairéad shouted. She ran over, unsteadily. Sunny's wrist was not right at all; it was already swelling and a strange colour. Sunny was white as a sheet and pitched forward and vomited. 'I can't see!' she screamed.

'Okay. Wait.'

She was far too drunk to drive, but knew for a fact Evan was not at home and an ambulance would not reach them for hours. She ran inside the cabin, doused her mouth with water, gargled, and then stuffed two pieces of chewing gum in her mouth. She glared at herself in the antique mirror near the front door and gave herself a smart slap in the face.

'Hi,' she practised. 'Hi, please help – I think she's broken her wrist.'

She fumbled for the car keys, put the rest of the pack of chewing gum in her pocket, snatched up her wallet.

'Let's go!' she cried to Sunny and helped her to the car.

She chewed her gum and focused on the road. Not too fast, not too slowly. A pheasant burst out from a hedge and Mairéad slammed on the brakes too hard, too urgently and skidded very slightly. Sunny was jerked forwards and screamed in pain as her wrist was jolted.

Mairéad's heart hammered and she felt herself partially sobering up with shock. She breathed heavily, her entire being vibrating with the manic thudding of her heart. She gave thanks for the remote roads, free from traffic. She felt herself starting to sweat as she entered the hospital car park. Not too fast, not too slowly. Check mirrors. Inside, she was careful to keep her distance from the A & E staff, aiming her red-wine breath away from their faces, chain-chewing her gum.

Sunny's wrist, which turned out to have a tiny, slim little crack in it, barely visible on the X-ray but perfectly painful, was strapped into a fuzzy grey wrist support and she was given a sling. They got back to the cabin at 11.30 p.m. Mairéad already had a hangover and drank an Alka-Seltzer. The bottle of wine was where she'd left it, on the porch. She took it and poured it down the sink. But she left the two unopened bottles of red wine as they were, resting on the side in the outdoor kitchen, as a reminder. In the gloom they looked like a pair of devil's horns.

They both crawled into bed and Mairéad lay in her £200 pyjamas, in her £1,500 sheets, and wanted to die. She often lay awake at night in this bed, wanting to die, knowing full well that the wanting-to-die feeling was the alcohol, but now it was something else, something darker. At 3 a.m. every single night for months she had promised to give up drinking, yet when 6 p.m. rolled around the next day it was as if there was a pair of invisible hands pushing her towards the bottle. It was her *friend*.

But after Sunny's accident, Mairéad stopped drinking. In some ways it was straightforward: she just didn't allow herself to buy any alcohol on their weekly shop and that was that. She never felt like drinking when they went shopping; in fact on their weekly weekend trips she was usually at her most regretful. It was only later, as the clock crept towards the evening, that she felt the irresistible pull. So if there was no alcohol in the cabin, no local pubs or parties or dinners in restaurants, there were no excuses, no cheeky Just-Ones.

But she kept the two original bottles of red wine, the devil's horns, sitting on the side as a warning. Her terrible heartburn vanished. She bought three books about sobriety and read them all, then re-read them. She followed sober Instagram accounts and watched *28 Days* four times. She drew the line at cold-water swimming. Every week at Castell Cerys she stocked up on tonic water and bought herself a bottle of angostura bitters. It wasn't quite the same without ice, but there were worse things.

Spring settled in and one day in early May they met Evan while walking on the beach. He was in his wetsuit with his surfboard under his arm, talking to a girl with blonde hair, dimples and a baseball cap.

'This is Brooke,' he said, blushing with his whole face.

Mairéad could see that Brooke was, in fact, not very pretty. But she had a wonderful tan and spectacular teeth.

Brooke was from Australia and Evan had only met her just now, twenty minutes earlier.

'I'm touring Europe,' she said. 'You know, taking it all in.'

'Most people don't make it to Wales.'

'Oh, they're missing out,' said Brooke. 'Ha ha! That's a cute dog,' she said, as Bogey cantered up with a sandy stick in her mouth. 'Look at its little underbite.'

'Underbites in dogs are called "occlusions",' said Sunny.

Evan and Brooke fell in love that day, on that beach, and Mairéad marvelled at the fact that she had been there for the moment. Brooke stayed in Wales for six weeks, living with Evan and working on the farm. Then her visa ran out and she had to go back to Australia. Evan, in a locomotive flush of infatuation, decided to follow her. Would Mairéad look after the farmhouse? He'd be gone for two months, maybe longer. Mairéad screamed in joy. Yes, yes she would! And Bonnie, too, and the chickens and Mindy the cat. Just leave it all to her. Sunny was not happy about this, but Mairéad wore her down. Just think – Sunny could have her own bedroom! They could have ice *whenever they wanted*.

Roxana was most interested in this development. She had moved out of the flat and into a house with her boyfriend, who, Mairéad saw from the pictures that Roxana sent, had very shiny, stiff hair and slim-cut suits. Roxana rented out the flat to carefully vetted tenants, and went in to check every month for scuffs and breakages. Mairéad laughed at what a terrifying landlord Roxana must make. She was impressed over and again at Roxana's apparently limitless capacity for pin-sharp detail. She received meticulous inventories of changed light-bulbs and repairs, along with, as requested, her copy of *The English Cottage*.

'You must rent out this cabin,' instructed Roxana. 'Then you will have double rents.' Mairéad argued that she was unlikely to be able to find someone who would want to live in the cabin, with its medieval kitchen and stove-fired shower.

'Ha!' said Roxana. 'This is not a challenge for me.'

Not long after this, two Swedish research scientists, a man and a woman with matching frazzled blond hair in matching frazzled buns, moved into the cabin. Lena had very pink cheeks and pale green eyes, and Matteo had huge, square teeth that seemed to barely fit in his mouth. They were a couple, not married, and were experts on algae. They planned to live in the cabin and study all the different permutations of algae along the Welsh coastline. Sunny and Mairéad referred to them only and always as 'The Scientists'.

'I love this kitchen,' said Lena, bending down to look inside the oven.

'You wait until January.'

Lena shrugged. 'I once lived on a glacier for nine months.'

Sunny was fascinated by Lena and Matteo and kept wandering up to the cabin to look at their samples under microscopes and pore over their meticulous sets of data. Mairéad kept checking with The Scientists that this was all right.

'Yes,' said Matteo. 'She is no trouble.' This was a relief, as, in all the time that Sunny had been at school, she hadn't mentioned a single other student, except the ones who annoyed her because they were so slow, disruptive and stupid.

Sunny herself was entirely unbothered about her non-existent social life and was happy, or at least content, to spend her weekends running errands in Castell Cerys, reading, watching complex documentaries on YouTube about space, and walking Bogey and Bonnie.

Mairéad consulted Dr G about this. 'She doesn't have any friends. But she doesn't seem to care.'

'This is just my personal opinion, but friends are very overrated,' said Dr G. 'Our culture is so obsessed with friends and sure, friends are fine, but what really matters is your close familial relationships. She's a quirky kid – were you a quirky kid?'

'No.'

'Well, I was. Mega quirky. And I didn't really have any friends until my first year at medical school and even then only one or two. She'll find her people eventually.'

'She's actually made friends with some scientists up the road, now I come to think of it. They like algae. But they're grown-ups.'

'That's all right. Maybe she just doesn't like twelve-year-olds. That's a valid point of view.'

Shortly after Matteo and Lena arrived, it came: the postcard. One morning Mairéad greeted Greg the postman at the top of the lane as she arrived home from walking Bogey and Bonnie. He held out a clutch of things for the cabin and for the farmhouse: a few letters for Evan and then the postcard – from Alberta, Canada. On the front was a picture of a moose. There was no salutation and no message, but the address was in Lenny's handwriting all right. Mairéad stared and stared at the postcard. She had always assumed that this was how it would be, this was how she would find out. But the fact that

Well, This Is Awkward

this was actually how it *was*, that it had happened just as she'd imagined it would, seemed totally unreal.

For a good two or three hours she resolved not to show it to Sunny, ever. She felt like tearing it up and stuffing it in her mouth. But then, what if Sunny one day found out that Mairéad knew where her mother was and hadn't told her? It would be world-ending. She took a photograph of the postcard, front and back, and sent the pictures to Lyn, with an explanation of their significance.

Sunny took the postcard between her thumb and the knuckle of her forefinger. Mairéad explained, as evenly and calmly as she could, what she believed the significance of it was.

Sunny nodded and was quiet for a long time.

'Can I keep this?' she said, eventually.

'Of course. Are you... all right?' Mairéad asked.

'Fine,' said Sunny shortly. She pushed her glasses up her nose. 'I hope she's happy.'

Her stone-faced glare into the middle distance made Mairéad understand what she meant.

After what she's done, it had better have been worth it.

THIRTY-FIVE

Mairéad's own lack of social life hit her hardest when something funny happened. Or when she was looking at something beautiful or interesting, like the blooming of snowdrops around the edge of the compost heap, or when she and Sunny saw a dolphin leap right out of the water on a visit to Cardigan Bay. It was such an extraordinary sight that they couldn't quite believe what they had seen. But it also reminded Mairéad of one of those soft-focus posters in Athena circa 1991; she was pleased with this observation but had no one to share it with. Sure, she could tell Sunny, but some things went over her head. And there was no one else except Bogey, Bonnie and Mindy the cat.

Silently, one morning, after spreading fresh straw in the hen-house, she re-downloaded Hinge. She sat on a crumbling wall, still in her dirty boots, as Mindy weaved around her legs and then sat down in a sunny spot and started washing her face. Mairéad was suddenly gripped by an urgent need to make something happen, here and now in this place. Nothing was going to happen by accident in the middle of a field on the shores of the Irish Sea.

On Hinge, even though she had entered her real date of birth, there were a lot of young men, who looked to Mairéad like children. But then there was Graham, a chartered surveyor living the other side of Harlech Beach. He spelled everything correctly and from his photo had a friendly smile and liked Guinness. They messaged back and forth, back and forth. He had a dry sense of humour and seemed normal, but she still felt exhausted by it all. She knew that if she hadn't had two years away from this crap she would never have the energy to engage with it all – the flirting, the sharing of stories, the dissembling.

Graham wanted to meet, but sounded weary about it. He sounded as weary as Mairéad felt. She pushed on. She arranged for Sunny to spend an evening with The Scientists, which they were all thrilled by. She did not say she was going on a date – the idea would have appalled Sunny – merely that she was going to see an old friend who was passing through the area.

No stranger to this process, Mairéad didn't meet Graham in Castell Cerys, but in a coastal village halfway between them, in a pub called the Red Dragon. Graham was already there when she arrived. He was looking out of the window and smoothing his hand repeatedly down the back of his head. A Guinness, one third drunk, rested on the table in front of him.

He had a kindly, fleshy face. If Mairéad was being generous, she would say that he looked like Gerard Butler. But it was quickly apparent that Graham was a miserable bastard and she had mistaken this for a dry sense of humour.

'This place,' he said gloomily. 'I don't know if I can die here, you know?'

'Well,' she said. 'You don't have to. There are other lovely places to live that aren't here.'

Graham looked moody at this suggestion, like living somewhere else nice might make him have to cheer up, which she now suspected he did not want to do.

'So how about you, then?' he said offhandedly. 'How can you stand it here?'

She wanted to dash her iced tonic water into his glum, potato face and run out of the pub.

'I think it's nice,' she said primly. 'The fresh air, the sea. Living close to nature. I lived in London for a long time and it can be very claustrophobic.'

'Dating scene good in London, though?' said Graham.

'Not really. Same old perverts and dog stranglers you find anywhere.'

Graham's Guinness glass paused on his lips.

The next morning, Graham received a standard Hinge kiss-off that Mairéad found, with a smile of familiar recognition, still on the Notes app of her phone. Then, with a kamikaze feeling, she tried again. This time it was Lawrence, a retired helicopter engineer and camping enthusiast who she arranged to meet in a charming seaside bistro bar with a panoramic view of Harlech Bay. He had spent most of his career in Malaysia but decided to retire to Wales 'for the climate'. He wore a Leatherman multi-tool on his belt and his hair was completely white, his beard contrasting with his weather-beaten face. He was delightful, with startlingly blue eyes, and declared that, if Mairéad wasn't drinking alcohol, then neither would he.

'Mairéad', he said, pronouncing it deftly and correctly, was one of the world's most underappreciated names.

'I sailed round Ireland once,' he said. 'I loved it but I still went to live in Malaysia. Strange the choices we make. It gets terribly muggy in the tropics,' he added. 'You get used to anything in the end, but one day I woke up and all I wanted was to feel cold, fresh air on my face that wasn't from an AC unit.'

'Well, you've certainly got that here.'

He liked to take off, he said, just him and his camping stuff, striding for miles around Wales, Dartmoor and up in the Lake District.

'The freedom, god it's amazing,' he said wistfully. 'You can spend a fortune on kit, though. You start off looking at a camping stove and it's twenty quid or whatever, then you start thinking about it and researching and end up spending three hundred on some space-age thing that can start a fire underwater. Because obviously that's what I'm going to do,' he added drily. 'I had this tent once that was a thousand pounds. It looked the business, like something a Bond villain might go camping in, all 45-degree angles. But it caught the bloody wind like a kite and nearly took me off the edge of a cliff.'

Lawrence listened to Mairéad as she explained what she was doing in Wales and didn't cut his eyes at the weirdness of the story. When she got to the part about Lenny vanishing, he puffed out his cheeks and exhaled heavily. 'That's quite the… that's quite. Honestly, I don't know what to say about that.'

As she talked more, he said, 'Oh wait, now. Don't say that's the cabin outside Castell Cerys? On that hillside.'

'Do you know it?'

'Well, I've only admired it from afar,' said Lawrence. 'I walk that way sometimes and someone the other day was telling me that it's a self-sufficient cabin, and I was really dying to have a look.'

'Come and have a look! If you're into that kind of thing, it'll knock your socks off.'

'I'd love that,' said Lawrence. 'Another?' He pointed at Mairéad's tonic water. 'Shall we get a snack? Some of this charcuterie maybe? When I get back I want to hear all about it.'

Later on, Lawrence sent a message on Hinge.

'It was so wonderful to meet you, but I ought to say now that I didn't feel there was that "spark". I know this is a ridiculous thing to say as you are plainly such a knockout, but I need to be honest. I hope I might still be able to come and see the cabin?'

'Of course, come any time,' Mairéad texted back. She was surprised to be rejected, but it was done with such openness, so pleasantly, that she found herself letting out a huff of laughter.

Cass came to stay for three nights. Sunny was touchingly excited about her visit – Mairéad could tell, because she asked her every twenty minutes what time Cass was arriving, which made Mairéad swear to herself never to give Sunny advance warning of anything ever again.

When Cass finally arrived, Sunny immediately dragged her up to the cabin to show The Scientists that Cass had no left hand and didn't even care. Matteo shared a story of how he'd had to have a toe amputated due to frostbite. 'Good luck it is not my big toe,' he said.

'I meant to tell you,' said Cass in the kitchen, after dinner. 'I made it to LA in the end.'

'How was it?' said Mairéad.

'You were right about the beaches in LA. You said that they're not as nice as you think they're going to be and they're not. The water's freezing. And the traffic? Three hours to get from here to there. I saw my life flash before my eyes.'

Cass paused.

'Things seem great, here. You're really leaning in.'

'I heard what you said, about building a life. You were right.'

'Of course, I'm always right. This might seem dramatic, but have you ever thought about believing in God?'

'What?' said Mairéad.

'Okay. Not God,' mused Cass, taking a sip of wine. 'But a higher power. Or, listen, what about this: determinism. It's a thing in philosophy about how we're all on a predetermined path. It's a very modern, Western sort of state to labour under the illusion that you've got any say in how your life turns out. It's a big problem.

'And there's nothing you can do about it except tend to

Well, This Is Awkward

your surroundings. The French have got a phrase for it: '*Il faut cultiver notre jardin*'. It means, like, be at peace with the world as it is, not how you want it to be. And also grow things and you'll be happy.'

'Since when have you been such a sage?'

'Always. You just weren't listening, or you didn't want to hear. I'm Irish, is the thing – we're a nation of sages. That's how you can tell you're not Irish, even with that name.' Cass tittered. 'You've no philosophy about you at all. You're very lucky to have me.'

When her visit was over, Cass promised to come again, sooner. She told Mairéad that she looked wonderful, that her hair was glorious. That it was a shame Bonnie was such a terribly grumpy dog but you can't have everything.

In the days and weeks after Cass left, Mairéad had never wanted to drink herself into a stupor more powerfully. One of the quit-drinking books she'd read had introduced her to the phrase 'Thoughts are not deeds', which meant that, just because you are thinking very clearly about how you would very much like to have a drink, it doesn't mean you have to follow through on this. She said it to herself about three times a day, as she visualised pouring the drink into a glass, raising it, closing her eyes, feeling the... she scowled at the devil's horns red wine bottles on the side. Beside the bottles she had laid the fuzzy grey wrist support Sunny had worn after her accident. The seascape stared back at her day after day, flat and bleak. A tyrannical view.

Sunny grew and solidified. She became less obsessed with her thumb. There was more and increasingly confident conversation, flashes of self-awareness, empathy and insight. At a parents' evening Mairéad laughed out loud when Sunny's form teacher praised Sunny for working so hard on 'her patience with less able students'. Sunny gave her a stern side-eye.

As Sunny expanded, like a new butterfly drying its fresh

wings in the sunshine, Mairéad felt herself desiccating and weakening. Her knees hurt for a good three to four minutes in the mornings. Some days, she felt like Sunny's portrait in the attic.

THIRTY-SIX

All right, she'd actually *cultiver* her real-life *jardin*, then. What with the constant work of looking after Sunny and herself, the farmhouse, the chickens, the dogs and Mindy (though Mindy was very independent), adding to her duties felt reckless. But she did understand what Cass was saying and perhaps tending to a garden would help. Perhaps some flowers would be enough? What about sweet peas? She remembered that her father used to call sweet peas 'pound-shop orchids'.

It was a bright, brisk day at the end of June and she decided that step one was to clean out the greenhouse. It was a mess, with more than one cracked pane of glass. It smelled strongly of old tomato plants and something a bit pooey – probably fertiliser – and there were old pots and plastic sacks littered about the place. Evan was a farmer, not a gardener. With a tidy it might be useful for growing things. Seedlings? She remembered the rows of seedlings Gavin had always had, basking on window ledges in sunbeams. Helen was always complaining about them. The greenhouse enjoyed a south-facing position and was fuzzily warm inside, sheltered from the sharp sea breeze.

She pulled on her new chore gloves – her first pair had fallen to bits from over-use – and tugged at the greenhouse door, which in theory slid across but was rusty and jammed. She got it open and started dragging out all the greenhouse junk and piling it up. She went at the seed bench first with a dustpan and brush, getting all the leaves, tiny sticks and spiders out of the corners and onto the floor. Then she went in with a stiff yard brush and swept and swept. A huge spider dropped on her arm and she screamed, batted at it and ran out of the greenhouse, swatting at her clothes. She needed a cup of tea after that. She had been living in the farmhouse for only six weeks but the relief to have a kettle that she could boil whenever she wanted was still there and she was peaking at about five cups a day. While the kettle boiled she remembered the ancient, greasy bottle of WD-40 under the sink and used it to oil the shrieking greenhouse door.

She was whizzing the door along its rails and feeling pleased with herself when she heard the crumple of tyres on gravel. Picking off her gloves, she went to meet whoever had arrived. Must be Greg the postman. But it wasn't. A very shiny grey SUV was coming to a stop, bouncing around on the uneven earth track. The door opened and out stepped Lawrence, in a pair of wrap-around sporty sunglasses.

'Hello!' he said. 'I am so sorry to do this.' He took off his sunglasses. 'I know I was supposed to come next week but I was in the area and popped by on the off-chance. I messaged you on the app, but there was no reply. Is this very bad? I can leave. It's intrusive. I'll go. I'm so sorry.'

Bogey and Bonnie had jogged out of the farmhouse, and greeted Lawrence with gruff woofs and sniffed his legs and shoes all over.

'An occlusion!' he said, pointing at Bogey. 'You don't see those often.' Bonnie growled at him a bit.

'Bonnie!' remonstrated Mairéad.

'No, she's got a point,' said Lawrence.

'Oh, ignore her, she's got a bad attitude. There's no need

Well, This Is Awkward

to go. I was just doing some gardening,' she said, and then felt fraudulent. 'I'd love to show you round the cabin now. I'm not busy.'

'Let's whizz back up the lane in the car, shall we?' said Lawrence with a dazzling smile. 'It's new, I'm very pleased with it. Terrific suspension.'

Lena was pottering about in the cabin kitchen when they arrived, and she and Mairéad both gave a tour of the cabin to Lawrence, who examined it with as much care and delight as if it were a rare Fabergé egg.

'Oh, look at this,' he said, pointing at a piece of pipework that meant nothing to Mairéad. 'And this, heavens! I've only read about this in books. Who installed this?'

'What?'

Lawrence was pointing to a box on a wall.

'This! It stops rainwater from getting Legionnaires' disease.'

'Wow! I don't know,' she confessed. 'I'm very glad someone did, though – I don't want Legionnaires' disease.'

'It's a very special piece of kit. May I take a photo?' he asked.

'Please do!' Mairéad and Lena stood about beaming, as if their home-grown squash had just won first prize at a fair.

Lawrence took his phone out of his pocket. The lock screen showed a photo of a frankly gorgeous man.

'Who is that?' said Lena.

'Where? Oh, him. That's my son,' said Lawrence. He turned the phone off and on again so that the lock screen photo reappeared. He turned it towards them.

The photo was of Lawrence standing next to a grizzled, lantern-jawed hunk with a snub nose and the bluest eyes Mairéad had ever seen. They were both wearing fishing waders and grinning. The man's face looked as if Lawrence had been put through some sort of Instagram 'younger' filter. Mairéad and Lena just stared.

'Your son is very, very handsome,' said Lena after a pause.
'Yes,' said Lawrence, ruefully.

After a full and thorough investigation of the cabin, Mairéad invited Lawrence back down to the farmhouse for some tea.

'Well!' he exclaimed. 'This is very cosy.'

'It's coming together,' said Mairéad. 'Evan, the farmer who lived here, wasn't really into interiors. I thought I'd start with the kitchen as that's where we always are, but the rest of it is pretty bleak. He did leave us the most enormous telly, though.'

'What is it with men and their tellies?' Lawrence put his fists on his hips and gave the corner of the room a faux-puzzled glare. 'Mine is pretty big, I must admit. Great for watching the rugby, though. Did you paint the cabinets this green? That's a very nice colour. Where did you get this?' Lawrence peered at an oil painting of some sheep under a tree.

'Oh, that's from the antiques place in Castell Cerys – there are some lovely things if you look hard enough.'

Lawrence picked up a platter decorated with blue flowers that was resting on the side, then put it down again. 'Wonderful,' he said.

Lawrence insisted on meeting the chickens and looking underneath some bits of farm machinery that Evan had left behind.

'I didn't tell you about James the other night,' he said. 'He came along when I was very young, only twenty. His mother and I never married,' he said and blushed.

'It's all right,' said Mairéad, touching his arm. 'I forgive you.'

'Well, she did a wonderful job, raising him,' said Lawrence. 'I've seen him, of course; looked after him, you know, financially. But we've only really reconnected properly recently. He's a wonderful lad.' Lawrence looked misty-eyed.

'Twenty!' said Mairéad. She had meant to say this to herself but accidentally said it out loud.

'One doesn't want to have regrets, but...' Lawrence heaved

a sigh in and out. 'Well. Best to appreciate all the time you've got left. I never got a chance to do all those dad things. At the time I ran a mile, of course, and counted myself lucky. But then, later... I see my grandchildren a bit, of course, but it's not like being there all the time. And they've got other grandparents, now.'

'How old are they? The grandchildren, I mean.'

'Lily is eight and Thomas is ten.'

'Ten. A lovely age,' said Mairéad, thinking of Dibs.

'Oh yes, he's a scamp, he makes me laugh. Always got his pockets full of string and odd bits he's found. James is coming to visit me here, actually. Quite soon.' Lawrence paused and then a thought seemed to occur to him. 'You should come for a drink with us,' he said. 'You're about the same age, I'm sure you'd get on famously. He's just been through a terrible divorce. We're going to go for long walks and set the world to rights.'

'Wonderful,' she said, nodding gravely. 'You sound like a great dad. Divorce,' she added, shaking her head. 'Terrible.'

She knew that Lawrence was sixty-five. So this James was forty-five, was he? Interesting. Lawrence squinted out of the kitchen window, which looked straight down to the sea. 'What a view,' he said, then, 'Does it get a bit lonely out here?' He took a sip of his tea. Mairéad shrugged. 'A bit, I suppose, at times. But it's not a terminal condition.' Then she took a deep and cleansing breath in and out. Something indefinable left her with that breath and she was glad to see it go.

Her phone started ringing. She took it out of her pocket and looked at the screen.

'Oh, it's the school,' she said. 'This is never good news. Hello?... Yes. Oh, hi, yes. We haven't met yet... Oh, poor *her*. Right in the face or... ? I see. Right. No, yes of course I'll be there. Okay, thanks, thanks.'

Lawrence looked concerned. 'Everything all right?'

'It's my niece, she's been hit in the face with a door. By accident, I hope.'

'Ouch,' said Lawrence, standing up. 'You'd best be off. Oh, just one thing, though. Your chicken coop out the back, that needs securing on the left side. I've got some wire and some two by fours in my shed that are looking for a new home. You need it really secure. Even if you've never seen one, there'll be a fox here, somewhere.' He narrowed his eyes. 'There always is.' Mairéad gave Lawrence her phone number so that he didn't have to message her on the dating app and set off for the school, feeling a warm glow from what a nice man Lawrence was.

She drove possibly a little too fast and was at the school in under twenty minutes. She parked, hurried up the stairs and skittered down the long, shiny corridors to the nurse's station. Sunny was sitting on a narrow camp bed in the nurse's room, which was very warm and smelled like TCP. She held something blue to her forehead and looked as desolate as a hen caught in the rain. Tears filled her eyes as soon as she saw Mairéad.

'Hit me right in the face,' she said in a wobbly sheep's voice. 'I was just nnnstanding there and looking at this thing on the wall annnn, annn... *kicked open so hard...*' She trailed off and wiped her nose on her sleeve.

'Oh, no.' Mairéad knew exactly how Sunny had been standing; she had seen it many times. Sunny would have been fascinated by scuffs on a wall that looked like a face, or a spider, or a strange poster, and she would have been immobile, watermelon-like, a complete sitting duck to a door in the face.

'You poor thing, what a horrible shock. Can I see?'

Sunny took the blue wad away. The injury to the side of her forehead was raised in a lump. The inner part was white, with a red mark in the centre; a pale blue-grey radius was already spreading outwards.

Well, This Is Awkward

'Does it hurt?'

'A bit. Don't touch it!'

'I won't.'

She knew already that Sunny would enjoy watching the rainbow progress of the bruise so much that she would end up declaring confidently that being smacked in the face with the door had been worth it.

'You can show your bruise to The Scientists,' she said.

'Oh yeah,' said Sunny. 'Yeah, I will. Can we go home now?'

There were footsteps and the school nurse walked in. She was short and round and wore yellow Crocs studded with Jibbitz, and a lavender cardigan. There was a sheaf of papers in her hand and a pair of glasses on her head.

'Hello, are you Mum?' she said.

Before Mairéad could answer, the nurse put on her glasses and looked at the pair of them. Then she said, 'Oh, of course. Who else could you possibly be?'

ACKNOWLEDGEMENTS

Felicity 'Boo' Cousins, Simon Conway, Alice Saunders, Katy Loftus.

To my editor at Bedford Square, Carolyn Mays. Thank you also to Jamie Hodder Williams, Laura Fletcher, Claudia Bullmore, Anastasia Boama-Aboagye and Polly Halsey. My copy editor was Amber Burlinson.

Charlotte Edwardes, Hannah Swerling, Salima Saxton, Melissa Katsoulis, Amanda Craig, Katharine and Samuel Coren.

Suzanne Cowie provided Cassandra Kelly's slang; Rosie Stewart from Stewarts Law advised on legal guardianship; Laura Valentine helped to bring Lyn the social worker to life; Henry Dimbleby explained how to get a person overboard back into a rowing boat.

Castell Ceri does not exist, neither does Pantbach, and David Bates, my cousin from the Welsh side of my family, had fun conjuring up these new names. David's brother, Ifan, is a book jacket designer and designed the cover of this book. Bloxcombe is loosely based on Dittisham in South Devon – well worth a visit, particularly during the regatta.

I am enormously grateful to my Substack subscribers who read an early draft of this book and offered invaluable notes.

It seems weird to be thanking my husband formally when

I can hear him downstairs making tea, but I suppose it would be weirder not to. So, I formally thank my husband, Giles. Once he understood I was serious about writing fiction and was unable to put me off by insisting that it is humiliating (true), exasperating (true), and there's no money in it (true), he was a total brick.

Photo credit © Jason Alden

Esther Walker is a lifestyle journalist whose work has appeared in *The Times* and *The Sunday Times*, the *Daily Mail*, the *Guardian*, the *Daily Telegraph*, the *i* and *Grazia*. She is the author of the cult cooking blog *Recipe Rifle* and now writes the Substack newsletter *The Spike*, which has over 6,000 subscribers. Her first two non-fiction books *The Bad Cook* and *The Bad Mother* are available as ebooks. Esther also co-hosts an award-nominated weekly topical podcast with her husband for *The Times*, called Giles Coren Has No Idea.

@onthespike
thespike.substack.com

Bedford Square Publishers

Bedford Square Publishers is an independent publisher of fiction and non-fiction, founded in 2022 in the historic streets of Bedford Square London and the sea mist shrouded green of Bedford Square Brighton.

Our goal is to discover irresistible stories and voices that illuminate our world.

We are passionate about connecting our authors to readers across the globe and our independence allows us to do this in original and nimble ways.

The team at Bedford Square Publishers has years of experience and we aim to use that knowledge and creative insight, alongside evolving technology, to reach the right readers for our books. From the ones who read a lot, to the ones who don't consider themselves readers, we aim to find those who will love our books and talk about them as much as we do.

We are hunting for vital new voices from all backgrounds – with books that take the reader to new places and transform perceptions of the world we live in.

Follow us on social media for the latest Bedford Square Publishers news.

@bedsqpublishers
facebook.com/bedfordsq.publishers/
@bedfordsq.publishers

https://bedfordsquarepublishers.co.uk/